Praise for Catherine Bybee

Wife by Wednesday

"A fun and sizzling romance, great characters that trade verbal spars like fist punches, and the dream of your own royal wedding!"
—Sizzling Hot Book Reviews, 5 Stars

"A good holiday, fireside or bedtime story."
—Manic Reviews, 4½ Stars

"A great story that I hope is the start of a new series."
—The Romance Studio, 4½ Hearts

Married by Monday

"If I hadn't already added Ms. Catherine Bybee to my list of favorite authors, after reading this book I would have been compelled to. This is a book *nobody* should miss, because the magic it contains is awesome."
—Booked Up Reviews, 5 Stars

"Ms. Bybee writes authentic situations and expresses the good and the bad in such an equal way . . . Keeps the reader on the edge of her seat."
—Reading Between the Wines, 5 Stars

"*Married by Monday* was a refreshing read and one I couldn't possibly put down."
—The Romance Studio, 4½ Hearts

Fiancé by Friday

"Bybee knows exactly how to keep readers happy . . . A thrilling pursuit and enough passion to stuff in your back pocket to last for the next few lifetimes . . . The hero and heroine come to life with each flip of the page and will linger long after readers cross the finish line."

—*RT Book Reviews*, 4½ Stars, Top Pick (Hot)

"A tale full of danger and sexual tension . . . the intriguing characters add emotional depth, ensuring readers will race to the perfectly fitting finish."

—*Publishers Weekly*

"Suspense, survival, and chemistry mix in this scintillating read."

—*Booklist*

"Hot romance, a mystery assassin, British royalty, and an alpha Marine . . . this story has it all!"

—Harlequin Junkie

Single by Saturday

"Captures readers' hearts and keeps them glued to the pages until the fascinating finish . . . romance lovers will feel the sparks fly . . . almost instantaneously."

—*RT Book Reviews*, 4½ Stars, Top Pick

"[A] wonderfully exciting plot, lots of desire, and some sassy attitude thrown in for good measure!"

—Harlequin Junkie

Taken by Tuesday

"[Bybee] knows exactly how to get bookworms sucked into the perfect storyline; then she casts her spell upon them so they don't escape until they reach the 'Holy Cow!' ending."

—*RT Book Reviews*, 4½ Stars, Top Pick

Seduced by Sunday

"You simply can't miss [this novel]. It contains everything a romance reader loves—clever dialogue, three-dimensional characters, and just the right amount of steam to go with that heartwarming love story."

—Brenda Novak, *New York Times* bestselling author

"Bybee hits the mark . . . providing readers with a smart, sophisticated romance between a spirited heroine and a prim hero . . . Passionate and intelligent characters [are] at the heart of this entertaining read."

—*Publishers Weekly*

Treasured by Thursday

"The Weekday Brides never disappoint and this final installment is by far Bybee's best work to date."

—*RT Book Reviews*, 4½ Stars, Top Pick

"An exquisitely written and complex story brimming with pride, passion, and pulse-pounding danger . . . Readers will gladly make time to savor this winning finale to a wonderful series."

—*Publishers Weekly*, Starred Review

"Bybee concludes her popular Weekday Brides series in a gratifying way with a passionate, troubled couple who may find a happy future if they can just survive and then learn to trust each other. A compelling and entertaining mix of sexy, complicated romance and menacing suspense."

—*Kirkus Reviews*

Not Quite Dating

"It's refreshing to read about a man who isn't afraid to fall in love . . . [Jack and Jessie] fit together as a couple and as a family."

—*RT Book Reviews*, 3 Stars (Hot)

"*Not Quite Dating* offers a sweet and satisfying Cinderella fantasy that will keep you smiling long after you've finished reading."

—Kathy Altman, *USA Today*, "Happy Ever After"

"The perfect rags to riches romance . . . The dialogue is inventive and witty, the characters are well drawn out. The storyline is superb and really shines . . . I highly recommend this stand out romance! Catherine Bybee is an automatic buy for me."

—Harlequin Junkie, 4½ Hearts

Not Quite Enough

"Bybee's gift for creating unforgettable romances cannot be ignored. The third book in the Not Quite series will sweep readers away to a paradise, and they will be intrigued by the thrilling story that accompanies their literary vacation."

—*RT Book Reviews*, 4½ Stars, Top Pick

Not Quite Forever

"Full of classic Bybee humor, steamy romance, and enough plot twists and turns to keep readers entertained all the way to the very last page."
—Tracy Brogan, bestselling author of the Bell Harbor series

"Magnetic . . . The love scenes are sizzling and the multi-dimensional characters make this a page-turner. Readers will look for earlier installments and eagerly anticipate new ones."
—*Publishers Weekly*

Not Quite Perfect

"This novel flows extremely well and readers will find themselves consuming the witty dialogue and strong imagery in one sitting."
—*RT Book Reviews*

"Don't let the title fool you. *Not Quite Perfect* was actually the perfect story to sweep you away and take you on a pleasant adventure. So sit back, relax, maybe pour a glass of wine, and let Catherine Bybee entertain you with Glen and Mary's playful East Coast–West Coast romance. You won't regret it for a moment."
—Harlequin Junkie, 4½ Stars

Not Quite Crazy

"This fast-paced story features credible characters whose appealing relationship is built upon friendship, mutual respect, and sizzling chemistry."
—*Publishers Weekly*

"The plot is filled with twists and turns, but instead of feeling like a never-ending roller coaster, the story maintains a quiet flow. The slow buildup of a romance allows readers to get to know the main characters as individuals and makes the romantic element more organic."

—*RT Book Reviews*

Doing It Over

"The romance between fiercely independent Melanie and charming Wyatt heats up even as outsiders threaten to derail their newfound happiness. This novel will hook readers with its warm, inviting characters and the promise for similar future installments."

—*Publishers Weekly*

"This brand-new trilogy, Most Likely To, based on yearbook superlatives, kicks off with a novel that will encourage you to root for the incredibly likable Melanie. Her friends are hilarious and readers will swoon over Wyatt, who is charming and strong. Even Melanie's daughter, Hope, is a hoot! This romance is jam-packed with animated characters, and Bybee displays her creative writing talent wonderfully."

—*RT Book Reviews*, 4 Stars

"With a dialogue full of energy and depth, and a twisting storyline that captured my attention, I would say that *Doing It Over* was a great way to start off a new series. (And look at that gorgeous book cover!) I can't wait to visit River Bend again and see who else gets to find their HEA."

—Harlequin Junkie, 4½ Stars

Staying For Good

"Bybee's skillfully crafted second Most Likely To contemporary (after *Doing It Over*) brings together former sweethearts who have not forgotten each other in the 11 years since high school. A cast of multidimensional characters brings the story to life and promises enticing future installments."

—*Publishers Weekly*

"Romance fans will be sure to cheer on former high school sweethearts Zoe and Luke right away in *Staying For Good*. Just wait until you see what passion, laughter, reconciliations, and mischief (can you say Vegas?) awaits readers this time around. Highly recommended."

—Harlequin Junkie, 4½ Stars

Making It Right

"Intense suspense heightens the scorching romance at the heart of Bybee's outstanding third Most Likely To contemporary (after *Staying For Good*). Sizzling sensual scenes are coupled with scary suspense in this winning novel."

—*Publishers Weekly*, Starred Review

Fool Me Once

"A marvelous portrait of friendship among women who have been bonded by fire."

—*Library Journal*, Best of the Year 2017

"Bybee still delivers a story that her die-hard readers will enjoy."

—*Publishers Weekly*

Half Empty

"Wade and Trina here in *Half Empty* just might be one of my favorite couples Catherine Bybee has gifted us fans with so far. Captivating, engaging, lively and dreamy, I simply could not get enough of this book."

—Harlequin Junkie, 5 stars

"Part rock star romance, part romantic thriller, I really enjoyed this book."

—Romance Reader

Faking Forever

"A charming contemporary with surprising depth . . . Bybee perfectly portrays a woman trying to hold out for Mr. Right despite the pressures of time. A pitch-perfect plot and a cast of sympathetic and lovable supporting characters make this book one to add to the keeper shelf."

—*Publishers Weekly*

"Catherine Bybee can do no wrong as far as I'm concerned . . . Passionate, sultry, and filled with genuine emotions that ran the gamut, *Faking Forever* was a journey of self-discovery and of a love that was truly meant to be. Highly recommended."

—Harlequin Junkie

SAY IT
Again

Also by Catherine Bybee
Contemporary Romance

Paranormal Romance

MacCoinnich Time Travels

Binding Vows
Silent Vows
Redeeming Vows
Highland Shifter
Highland Protector

The Ritter Werewolves Series

Before the Moon Rises
Embracing the Wolf

Novellas

Soul Mate
Possessive

Erotica

Kilt Worthy
Kilt-A-Licious

CATHERINE BYBEE

SAY IT
Again

BOOK FIVE IN THE FIRST WIVES SERIES

Published by Montlake Romance, Seattle

www.apub.com

Amazon, the Amazon logo, and Montlake Romance are trademarks of Amazon.com, Inc., or its affiliates.

ISBN-13: 9781503905351
ISBN-10: 1503905357

Cover design by Letitia Hasser

Cover photography by Regina Wamba of MaeIDesign.com

Printed in the United States of America

This one is for Jocey.
I still find it hard to believe you picked the
PTA over the CIA.

Chapter One

The ceiling fan slowly moving air around the room did a piss-poor job of cooling her warm, damp skin. She needed a shower . . . and sleep.

Neither of which was going to happen in her current location.

Sasha stretched one long leg down the muscled length of the man lying beside her. Her eyes traveled up his thigh to the round globe of his chiseled ass. A tattoo covered his chocolate skin at his hip and expanded the length of his back and shoulders.

Firm.

That was the best way to define him.

His teeth grazed her shoulder, pulling her back to reality.

"You're leaving," he said as if he were accusing her.

Her resigned sigh told him what he already knew.

Sasha swiveled her feet to meet the floor and stood.

He watched.

His eyes burned into her back when she bent down to retrieve her dress. She slipped it over her head and picked up the small clutch she claimed to be a purse. It wasn't. Not really. All it held was a single key and a tube of lipstick.

And a condom . . . but that was gone now.

"I'm not going to see you again, am I?"

She slipped into her four-inch-heeled boots and walked back to the bed.

His eyes watched the sway of her hips as she approached.

"Thanks for the workout," she said, her voice husky.

With a brief touch of lips, she stood, turned on her heels . . . and walked out of the man's life.

Graffiti covered the staircase taking her down to the ground floor, the smell of something she didn't want to name lofted from the corner of the final landing leading her outside.

Outside, the air moved.

Hot, unwelcoming air . . . but it moved.

The sun had set hours before, but the humidity of Rome was thicker than normal for late summer.

Sasha rolled her head from side to side and welcomed the feel of her lax muscles.

She was tired, she thought to herself.

And bored.

"Bella!" Someone called from a group of five men . . . boys, gathered under the streetlight next to a bar still in full swing.

Sasha kept walking.

Four blocks and she found her ride.

She slid the key from her bag and turned over the engine. After pushing her head into the helmet, she did a quick check around her and sped off down the street.

Heads turned as she drove by.

A woman in a short black dress, wearing come-screw-me boots, and driving a motorcycle had a way of making people look. If she were being honest with herself, she'd say she liked the attention.

Maybe that was why she did it. It wasn't like she couldn't have rented a car when in Italy. Or anywhere she traveled. Instead, she drove a bike. Only in winter did she switch up her transportation.

Bikes had more versatility. Much easier to follow or lose anyone who might be on her tail.

Only no one was.

Hence the part where she reminded herself that she was bored.

She split lanes in traffic, skirted through a yellow light, and dashed over a bridge leading to a much nicer area of Roma.

You would think a city as ancient as Rome would have a better grip on the blithe that filled every block.

But no.

Outside the ancient city, and the parts heavily monitored to keep vandals from tagging stones built thousands of years before, Rome was tattered with graffiti and evidence of misspent youth.

She skidded to a halt outside her hotel, parked her bike just past the valet, swung her leg off to one side, and removed her helmet.

The attendant eyed her as she walked to the glass doors.

"Excusa."

She caught the kid's eye, and he switched to English. "You can't leave your bike there." His eyes traveled her frame as he spoke.

Sasha tossed the single key in the air.

He caught it.

"Room 610," she told him.

He looked at the key, then back at her, and shook his head.

Inside, the hotel's air-conditioning did what the night air couldn't. It dried and cooled her skin.

Once in the elevator, she reached for a hidden pocket in her boot and removed the key card to her room.

Locking the door behind her, Sasha dropped her key on the foyer table, unzipped one boot at a time, and stepped out of them, leaving a path through the living room of her suite and into the bedroom. She discarded her dress on the bed and moved straight to the shower.

The water started out cold, blasting her with sensation up and down her spine to the very tips of her fingernails. Slowly it warmed, and she turned around and washed the memory of her temporary lover from her skin.

Once out of the shower, she toweled her hair dry and then spread out, naked, on her bed.

The blinds to her hotel room were open and the view of Rome, lit up in the night sky, was a feast for the eyes.

She'd flown to Italy on a whim . . . a restless impulse that had turned into two weeks and three different hotels. She should probably move on. The evening receptionist had smiled and waved at her when she had walked by earlier that night. It wasn't in Sasha's nature to let people recognize her.

She asked herself why . . . Why move on? It wasn't like anyone was looking for her. She wasn't searching for anyone. Wasn't protecting a single soul.

She closed her eyes and attempted to still her mind. She'd been tired an hour ago.

Her fingers tapped against the bed.

She concentrated on the noise of the fan blowing cool air around the room. White noise.

Sleep.

If only she had something to wake early for.

Knowing that she had nothing to occupy her time the following day, or week . . . or even year, kept her from being able to rest.

Nothing.

It was nearly four in the afternoon on the West Coast of the United States, dinnertime in Texas, where Trina and Wade resided with their infant daughter, Lilliana.

Sasha opened her eyes and stared at the ceiling.

The quiet was killing her.

She reached for her cell phone, charging on the nightstand, and dialed Reed.

"What did I do to deserve a call from you today?"

Reed never answered a call from her with *hello*.

Sasha tried not to smile. "Nothing, I'm certain."

"Yet here you are. Where are you?"

He always asked.

She never told.

"Nowhere close. Are you a father yet?" Reed's wife, Lori, was expecting twins sometime in the next month, and with his world preoccupied, perhaps the security firm he worked with could use an extra hand. She wouldn't ask if Reed needed help, she never did. She simply checked in with him on occasion, and he would volunteer a need if there were one. On rare occasions, he would search her out. She could count on three fingers the times that had happened.

"Not yet. I'm not afraid to say that just the thought of the next year scares the crap out of me."

Now Sasha did smile. Reed didn't scare easy, and he most certainly didn't admit to it. "Sounds like you have everything under control."

Reed paused. "How are you? You don't sound like yourself."

She dropped her smile, lifted her chin. "I'm making sure you haven't screwed something up since I saw you last."

"And when was that?" he asked. "I never can tell if you're watching me from behind a pair of binoculars."

"Binoculars . . . how very adolescent." Obviously, everything was fine.

No need for her.

"You know how to contact me," she said and pulled the phone away from her ear to disconnect the call.

"Wait!"

A spark of hope flared in her chest.

"Yes?"

"We want you to come after the babies are born. Visit. Trina and Wade will be here with Lilly. The holidays are just around the corner."

Sasha didn't do social visits. "Perhaps, if I'm available." She'd be available, but she wouldn't go.

Reed's voice told her he knew she wouldn't. "The invitation is always open."

Sasha hung up without saying goodbye.

She walked to the window of her room, uncaring if anyone could see her nudity through the glass.

Things needed to change.

Memories of her younger years surfaced. She was only a short distance away from where she spent all of her formative years. A place that had molded her into the restless woman she had become. Perhaps some time there would help her find focus.

Germany . . .

With her mind made up, she lay back on the bed and closed her eyes.

The invitation is always open.

On the outside, Richter appeared like any other boarding school dotting the landscapes of Europe. The name alone should have shed light on the kind of education one would expect inside the fortress-thick walls of the main buildings and twelve-foot-tall fence that surrounded the fifty-acre grounds. But instead of the German word for *judge* making people scratch their heads and ask questions, most believed that a judge had at one time sent their child to the school and offered a large donation for the right to the name.

Richter only took in troubled kids.

Troubled *rich* kids.

At least that's what the brochure implied.

Sasha drove her motorcycle up to the locked and guarded gates of Richter and stopped when the stern-faced uniformed "greeter" stepped out of his box.

She lifted the visor of her helmet and met his unsmiling eyes. "Headmistress Lodovica."

"And you are?"

"Sasha Budanov."

Placing her visor back over her eyes, she turned toward the gates, expecting them to open. When they did, she gunned her bike and sped through the familiar tree-lined drive to the main entrance of the school.

A splattering of children followed her path with turns of their heads, but they never stopped moving to stare.

Always in motion.

One of the many things Richter had taught her.

She left her helmet dangling off the handlebars and swung one long, leather-clad leg off the back. Her neck stretched as she looked up at the five stories of the main hall. It hadn't changed. Even the shrubs surrounding the stone building didn't appear to have grown.

Some people had told her that when they returned to their childhood homes after extended periods away, the houses looked smaller.

So why was it that Richter looked just as imposing now as it did then?

Cutting off her thoughts, Sasha climbed the vast steps to the ten-foot ornately carved wooden doors.

They opened before she could grasp the handle.

Her lips lifted into a rare grin. "Charlie. I can't believe you're still here." Her heart swelled with warm memories of the man standing in front of her.

"That's Checkpoint Charlie to you, Miss Budanov."

The irony always made her grin. The man in charge of assuring that anyone entering the doors of Richter belonged had been dubbed Checkpoint Charlie long before Sasha attended the school. The fact that he was German and not American, but spoke with a perfect American accent, had all the students wondering if he was an international spy. Truth was, none of them knew if Charlie was even his real name.

She approached with her hands at her sides. They didn't hug . . . it wasn't allowed.

"You look well, Sasha."

"As do you. Keeping everything protected here, I see."

"No one comes in, or out, without me knowing."

Sasha tilted her head to the side.

Charlie's playful smile slid. "Not since you rappelled off the north wall, crossed the grounds without hitting one sensor, and scaled the fence before calling Headmistress Lodovica from twenty miles away to tell her she needed to tighten her security."

Sasha forced down the pride she felt with the memory.

"I couldn't let that French twit . . . what was his name?"

"Mr. Dufort."

"Right . . . Pierre Dufort." Her male antagonist in her final year at Richter. "I couldn't let him challenge me and not deliver."

Charlie shook his head and lowered his voice. "The senior class has attempted every year since, and has yet to repeat your actions."

"That's too bad."

He scowled. "How so?"

"That either means your students are unworthy or your teachers are slipping." Sasha felt the smile in her eye as she turned.

"I'm glad you're back," he said.

She paused. Was she back?

Shaking the question from her head, Sasha walked down the overgrown hall to the administration offices.

The quiet space of the teachers' area at the school did seem as if it had shrunk. A receptionist she didn't recognize greeted her. "Miss Budanov?"

"Yes."

"The headmistress is ready for you."

She tried not to show surprise. The headmistress didn't drop everything for anyone. Since Sasha came unannounced, she expected to wait at least a short time.

Her eyes glanced toward the office of the woman in charge. "Thank you."

Sasha hesitated at the door. Should she knock?

The buzz of the door being unlocked by the receptionist answered her question.

Sasha lifted her chin and turned the knob.

An unfamiliar chill of the unexpected washed down her spine and brought gooseflesh to her arms. Usually those sensations would be met with Sasha watching her back and pulling a weapon from wherever it was hiding. Only that wasn't necessary here.

Passing through the threshold flooded her with memories.

The poised and elegant woman behind the desk was exactly how Sasha remembered.

"Sasha. What an unexpected pleasure." Headmistress Lodovica stood. In black dress pants and a long-sleeve button-up blouse, her clothing choices hadn't changed. Behind her desk was a coat stand; on it was a hanger where she draped her robe. Sasha had seen the woman without her robe, but it was a very rare occasion.

"Thank you for seeing me."

She rounded the desk. For one brief, frightening moment, Sasha thought the woman was going to hug her.

Instead the headmistress indicated a sofa on the far end of her office. "I'm anxious to hear what has brought you back to our halls."

They both sat, and the headmistress crossed her slim legs at her ankles and rested her hands in her lap. The woman had to be in her midforties, maybe even older, but she didn't look a day over thirty.

"I'm anxious to discover what has me here as well, Headmistress."

"I think we can do away with the formalities, Sasha. You are no longer a student, and I am no longer *your* headmistress. My name is Linette. Please feel free to use it." Those perfect lips and high cheekbones spread into a smile, something Sasha had seen less than five times.

Sasha took a deep breath.

"I've made you uncomfortable."

"Coming from the woman who handed down punishment for addressing her as anything but Headmistress . . ."

"You, of all my students, know that control is easily lost when respect is absent."

It was Sasha's turn to return a slight grin. "Yes, I remember well. I wasn't punished for escaping the grounds, but for addressing you simply as Lodovica when I called you from the pub."

"One of my proudest moments."

Sasha narrowed her eyes. "You put me in solitary for five days." Solitary sounded as bad as it was. Like any prison, the room was dark and soundproof. It was meant to intimidate and break a person. It often did.

"For your lack of respect, not for the act. Besides, I'm aware that Charlie offered some relief."

He had. For an hour every night she was able to breathe fresh air and eat a real meal.

"Is Charlie his real name?"

"Is that why you're here? To answer the questions of Richter that don't need to be asked?"

Sasha shook her head. "I learned who my benefactor was two years ago."

Linette raised her eyebrows. "I was sworn to secrecy."

"I know. My father is dead."

"I'm aware."

That surprised her. "You knew who he was the whole time?"

Linette nodded. "Of course. I am in charge of the safety of the students here. Not an easy task with a parent that would just as soon see you dead. Why do you think we pushed you so hard?"

"Because I was difficult."

"Willful, not difficult. I knew that the day would come when you'd learn the truth of your parentage and need to protect yourself."

Memories surfaced of the one and only time she addressed her father, on the day he attempted to kill her. He nearly succeeded.

Sasha's hand moved to her neck. The pain of her recovery from his hands attempting to snap her windpipe turned her cold.

Silence filled the room.

When she looked up, Linette's practiced stoic expression replaced whatever smile had been there before.

"Students return to Richter for one of three reasons. Answers, refuge, or direction. Which are you?"

An unfamiliar knot caught in the back of her throat.

"All three."

Chapter Two

Linette picked up her private phone once Sasha left her office. Her contact answered the call in German and quickly switched to English when she identified herself.

"To what do I owe the pleasure?" his smooth voice asked.

"You will not believe who just walked back through my door."

"You know I hate guessing games."

Linette grinned as she looked out her office window toward the public courtyard. "Budanov."

She heard him sigh. "The untouchable one who got away?"

"Yes, well, the ties that kept her back are no longer there."

"But is she still worthy? Eight years makes most soft."

"She appears harder, if that's possible. I, too, am anxious to find out what she has lost and what she's gained. I'll be in touch."

"I look forward to it."

Linette lifted her chin as she hung up the phone.

"Very anxious."

The duffel Sasha carried on her bike sat on the end of the bed in the room she'd been given. It was the same two hundred and twenty square feet as the university students shared. The difference was there was only one bed instead of two. That beat the high school dorms, which offered a lofty four hundred square feet but had double bunk beds crammed into the larger space. The headmistress had offered refuge for as long as she needed it. All the privacy rules of Richter were still in effect, and Sasha was expected to follow them. Basically, everything that went on inside the walls of the school, from the classes that had nothing to do with math, science, and literature to the disciplinary actions, was sworn to secrecy. Like the faculty, she could keep her cell phone and use the Internet. Although she wasn't sure either would be a hundred percent secure.

She'd been given a faculty bracelet that allowed her access to nearly every room on campus. Considering she'd been in most already, she wasn't sure if there was more to learn from the place she'd called home since she was nine. Some things change, but Richter didn't invite that concept.

She slipped out of the thick leather pants she wore when riding and into something easier to move around in.

In front of the mirror, she brushed her long hair back into a sleek ponytail. Her naturally olive complexion set off her dark eyes, made a little more striking with the eyeliner she liked to use. She applied a nude color over her full lips and tilted her head to the side.

This was as close to her personal choice in appearance as she came. Well, when she was relaxing, in any event.

She left the small bathroom, shuffled past her bedroom space, and out the door.

Sasha told herself she wasn't being nostalgic, yet she couldn't stop her feet from moving the rest of her down memory lane.

How many of her instructors would still be there? It had only been eight years. In fact, there might even be students who would recognize her, although she doubted she'd remember any of them. She'd hardly known her own class, let alone one eight years her junior.

13

The academic building held no interest. She moved deeper into the campus and over to the dining complex. Long rows of tables like something out of Harry Potter, minus the floating candles, lined the room. Meals were a choreographed and orderly deal. The front of the room was for the youngest students. As the tables moved back to the doors of the hall, the age progressed. Faculty sat in front of everyone. Food was fuel, nothing more, nothing less. There were few indulgences at Richter when it came to meals. Birthdays were celebrated with a pat on the back or a practical joke from one student to another, not with cake.

She'd hated that when she was young. As an adult, she applauded the fact that she never struggled with food cravings. It helped that she was naturally thin. If not for her dedication to pushing her body past its comfort zone in her workouts to keep her muscles conditioned, she'd probably appear anorexic. The figure gods didn't hand her any significant curves, and she wasn't interested in buying them. The men she slept with didn't complain. Then again, they'd probably concluded that a complaint would be met with a broken bone. Or a broken ego, at the very least.

Through the empty dining hall, Sasha walked past the entry to the kitchens, where she could smell the staff working on the next meal, and to the locked double doors leading to the lower levels.

She had to scan her bracelet to unlock the doors and ignored the heavy click as they secured behind her. The stairway was wide enough to funnel three students across going up and down.

One level below, she went through another set of locked doors and into the sparring gym.

Here, class was in session.

The instructors—one woman, who had her back to Sasha, and one man—were dressed in white. The students were completely in black.

She slid in quietly and tucked behind the students to observe. From the ages of the students around her, she assumed it was a college level class. Their attention was on the woman speaking. Ms. Denenberg had joined Richter in Sasha's sophomore college year. The woman could kick any man's ass in at least three different forms of martial arts. She used all the disciplines she had studied, along with some good old-fashioned street fighting, with a splash of krav maga, and developed her own training. She was on the mat with the male instructor, demonstrating takedowns.

The students at Richter were never taught self-defense, they were instructed in offense only. If someone was after you, you met them head-on and made them regret they challenged you.

"The neck guides the head and forces the body to go with it." Ms. Denenberg motioned for her male counterpart to approach while she demonstrated to her students how to gain control of her opponent's neck and used her legs to take him down to the mat. She demonstrated the same takedown three times and then switched to a similar hold from a different angle. Sasha could think of at least six different neck takedowns that she'd been taught during this very class.

"You will break up in pairs. First, ones with ones, twos with twos. Then I will pair you with new partners."

One of the male students, a good six foot three whose neck size alone suggested he spent more hours in the gym than Richter demanded, said something under his breath to his friend standing beside him.

Sasha shook her head and the other student laughed.

"Would you like to share what you find so funny, Mr. Braum?"

Mr. Braum, or Thick Neck, as Sasha saw him, lost his smile. "No, Ms. Denenberg."

"Please, I insist."

It was never a good thing to be singled out in Ms. Denenberg's presence unless you were being asked to repeat a skill you'd mastered for the class.

"I-I was ah . . . wondering how some of the girls in here could even reach my neck."

That had the defensive backs of the girls standing taller.

"That didn't seem like a funny comment. Are you sure that's what you said?"

Sasha laughed and the students parted to reveal her presence.

The instructor narrowed her eyes briefly, and then smiled.

Sasha stepped forward. "What he said was, most of the girls here couldn't reach his dick, let alone his neck."

A murmur went up.

Ms. Denenberg lifted a hand in the air, pointed a finger toward the ceiling. "Now *that* sounds like something you would say, Mr. Braum. Thank you so much for clarifying, Miss Budanov."

The murmur grew.

Ms. Denenberg took two steps toward them.

Mr. Braum stiffened. He was in his early twenties, maybe even just nineteen. Sasha almost felt sorry for him.

Almost.

"Miss Budanov, will you be so kind as to show Mr. Braum just how quickly a woman can get to both his dick and his neck, so he's assured I'm not wasting his time?"

Now Sasha did feel sorry for him.

The class took a collective step back.

Mr. Braum lost his smile when Sasha found hers.

One second she was tossing her ponytail over her shoulder as she pretended to walk past the unsuspecting student, the next her heel purposely missed a direct hit to the kid's groin, but struck close enough to send shockwaves down his legs, and her arm caught the back of his neck. Before he could figure out where she even was, let alone how to counter, Sasha had flipped him onto his shoulder and the ball of her booted foot sat on his windpipe.

Ms. Denenberg moved to stand beside her, both of them looking down at the cocky kid. "Any questions, Mr. Braum?"

He pulled in a deep breath. "No, ma'am."

Sasha released her boot and reached down to give him assistance to his feet. He hesitated, as if he wasn't going to accept her help, and Ms. Denenberg narrowed her eyes.

His cold hand met Sasha's wrist. He squeezed it a little too hard.

In that moment, she hoped there was at least one female student in the class that would kick the cocky out of him before graduation.

Chapter Three

"We're drinking beer in a pub, you have to call me Brigitte."

Sasha sat across from Ms. Denenberg . . . Brigitte, with what the Germans considered a small portion of a local brew. Like wine in Italy, the Germans explored flavors of beer with fervor.

"It pushes against everything Richter taught me."

Brigitte tilted her glass to her lips. "Titles, class, and rank of the person are necessary in a school and your employment. Nowhere else. One of the many problems with societies everywhere is when a CEO thinks he's better than the waiter."

Sasha saw the wisdom in that.

The bar they occupied was only a few miles from the school. Sasha had passed by it on occasion when leaving the school in her senior year. Most of her rebellious drinking had taken place on campus. Being spotted in the bar would have been much more likely. And having determined that many of the staff at Richter were known in the local place, Sasha was right to have stayed away.

"I wonder how long it will take before I no longer feel as if I'm sneaking into the faculty's lounge."

Brigitte smiled. "It took me about a month."

Sasha paused. "You were a student at Richter?"

"I was."

"How come I didn't know that?"

"It's our policy that students have no knowledge of the instructor's life outside of Richter. Our past, or families . . . nothing. It's safer that way."

The word *safe* had Sasha hesitating. "I'm safe now?"

"You came back. Very few students ever return to Richter."

Sasha sipped her beer. "You mean students don't want to return to a school that is half education, half prison, and half military training? I'm shocked." Her condescending tone made it clear she wasn't.

"There is one too many halves in there."

"The military and education I understood. The prison aspect escapes me."

Brigitte pushed a strand of her dishwater blonde hair behind her ear. "Even a whisper of a military boarding school as diverse as Richter, inside the borders of Germany after the Cold War, would be a lot for the general public to swallow. Having our students spending their evenings in places like this, talking and carrying on, would not be received well. You know the demographics of our students. It's for everyone's safety that the doors are locked at night."

"I suppose."

"Although I wouldn't mind a little easing up on some of the rules."

"Maybe things will with time."

Brigitte tilted her head to the side. "Why *did* you come back?"

Sasha felt the eyes of someone on her and glanced around the pub with the slightest of movements. "Because Richter was something more for me than most. It was my home. I know I wasn't the only orphan in attendance, I'm sure others have come back in the past."

Only Brigitte didn't confirm Sasha's thoughts.

Heat moved up the back of her neck.

She didn't turn around. Instead, Sasha leaned forward and lowered her voice. "Someone behind me is watching."

Brigitte picked up her beer and used the movement to distract where her eyes went.

Instead of being alarmed, she grinned. "A very fine specimen."

"Excuse me?"

Brigitte laughed. "Not everyone looking wants to hurt you. It appears he might want to do naughty things to you, but I doubt harm is his goal."

Her shoulders relaxed and Sasha felt a genuine smile on her lips. "I'm sitting in a bar, drinking . . . and apparently picking up men, with Ms. Denenberg."

"You pick up the men. Testosterone is not my flavor."

Sasha knew her expression matched her surprise. "I had no idea."

"Few ever do. I like to keep it that way."

She tilted her head to the side. "Understood."

Brigitte pushed her chair back. "I'll be back."

The moment she left, Sasha felt those standing hairs on her neck dance.

The secret man who was staring revealed himself as he slid into the chair Brigitte had vacated.

The casual smile Sasha had found the moment she stepped into the bar became one cloaked in caution. It didn't say hello, it didn't say go away . . . it was simply there.

"Hallo," he greeted her with an attempt to sound like he was German.

Sasha said nothing and stared. Broad in the shoulders, taller than most men . . . the stubble on his chin was either a poor attempt at looking European or TSA confiscated his razor before he boarded the plane.

He licked his full lips, and not in a lecherous kind of way, but one filled with nerves.

She liked her men nervous.

"Please tell me you speak English," he said after a moment of silence.

Sasha narrowed her eyes.

"French?"

Oh, please.

"You're American."

Those nerves she saw dangling off his skin now turned to confidence. "Thank God. Yes, I'm American."

"And I speak English. Can I help you with something, Mr. American?" She let her Russian accent hold *r*'s a little longer.

He opened his mouth to speak, closed it . . . opened it again. Those nerves returned. "Everything running through my head right now sounds like a glossed-over pickup line. So, I'll just ask if I can buy you a drink."

Sasha looked at the beer she'd hardly touched, back to him. "What's your name?" she asked.

"AJ. What's yours?" His smile trickled up to his eyes and put an unfamiliar flutter deep in her gut.

She leaned forward. "I'm here with a friend, AJ. Which you obviously know, since you've been watching us since we walked in the door."

"You're hard to miss." It should have sounded like a line. It didn't. AJ turned his eyes to something behind her. "Your friend is coming back."

"Then you should move along."

"One drink."

He was tempting . . . she'd give him that.

"I'm away less than five minutes and my seat is taken."

AJ stood from Brigitte's chair and pulled it out. "Sorry, I, ah . . ."

Brigitte cut him off with a grin. "Yes, I'm sure you were, *ah* . . ."

Sasha swallowed back her smile.

He looked between the two of them, his eyes narrowed. "Maybe next time?" he asked her.

She took a breath. "Perhaps."

That's all he needed, his head bobbing with a nod as he walked away.

"He looks thick in all the right places," Brigitte said, her eyes lingering on the man's back. "If you're into that sort of thing."

"I never play where I eat," Sasha told her.

"Probably a smart move. Unless he's here on holiday . . ."

Sasha laughed, glanced over her shoulder, and admired AJ's backside from across the room.

Perhaps . . .

❧

AJ positioned himself at a table by the only window facing the parking lot and waited. He'd seen the blonde in the bar before.

Sex on a Stick . . . not so much.

He went through his mental database of accents and had a hard time placing hers. A mixture of German, American . . . Russian. Maybe those were the three languages she spoke. It never ceased to amaze him how many people in Europe spoke more languages than he had socks in a drawer.

He was damn sure she'd caught the attention of every heterosexual man in the bar the second she walked through the door. She wore confidence like a cloak with her purposeful strides and pulled back shoulders. The woman was stunning and she knew it, and not in a teenage cheerleader *look at me* kind of way. But one born of comfort in her own skin.

AJ observed a few other qualities the woman had quietly displayed. She'd scanned the room when she walked in before making her way to a table with her friend. Both women positioned their chairs so neither of them had her back to the front door. She didn't carry a purse or a cell phone. The purse, he got . . . the cell phone? Yeah, that's what stumped him. He didn't know an able-bodied adult that didn't have access to the whole world in their back pocket.

Or maybe she didn't want the outside world to have access to her?

The most important thing he noticed about the woman, who conveniently didn't reveal her name, was her companion. A woman he had no chance of getting to know socially without a heterosexual woman by her side.

It appeared that after a week in Germany, his luck was starting to change.

AJ waited until the women were done with their single drink before watching them leave.

Denenberg left in her compact car while the sex kitten jumped on the back of a motorcycle and kicked it over with a purr that befitted her.

AJ didn't wait. He dropped several euros on the table and followed.

Following someone on a motorcycle had proved difficult in the past, but with so few roads to travel out where they were and a pretty good idea of where she was going, AJ gave her a head start and slowly made his way behind her. A small amount of traffic offered him some disguise. The fact that the sun had set aided him in his effort to go unnoticed.

Denenberg took a predictable turn down the road he knew led to her flat.

A lift in his chest filled him with a ray of hope when Sex Kitten stayed on the road leading to Richter.

Maybe he should bug off now and follow her again on another night from a different starting point.

Memories of his sister's smile kept him moving forward.

AJ peered out at the nearly deserted road and eased off the gas.

Sex Kitten didn't bother with a directional when she turned on one of the last twists in the road that would take her to the school.

He should just drive past.

Only as the turn drew closer, he knew he couldn't.

He rounded the corner and his heart skipped several beats.

No taillights. None. Not hers. Not anyone else's.

There was at least a mile between this point and the turnoff to the school.

"Where the hell did you go?" he asked himself as he sped up.

He made it four hundred yards before his windshield was flooded by a single spotlight in the middle of the road.

AJ slammed on the brakes and swerved. His tiny rental car pitched to the opposite side of the road to avoid whoever was in his lane.

Once his car stopped, he jumped from his seat and outside the vehicle. "Jesus!"

She stood there, legs spread two feet apart, her high-heeled boots lifting her three more inches toward the sky. Her helmet dangled from her fingertips.

"I could have killed you!"

"Why are you following me?" A *don't fuck with me* voice replaced the smoky purr from the pub.

AJ shuffled his feet.

He was fucked.

His palms itched.

"You're from Richter."

Crickets filled the air in the dark space between them.

His statement was met with deadly silence. A weapon to intimidate.

It worked.

Instead of saying anything, she lifted the helmet above her head.

He sprang forward, hands in the air. "Wait!"

Her helmet took a defensive position in front of her, one of her hands lifted in the air. "I wouldn't, if I were you."

AJ jolted to a stop. "Please, I just need to talk to you."

She shifted and lifted her helmet again.

He took another step.

Her eyes shot toward his.

"It's about my sister. She used to be a student at Richter. Last month she was found facedown on the banks of a river. Execution-style murder." AJ wasn't sure if he was getting anywhere, but the woman facing him wasn't walking away.

"No one at the school will answer my questions. Amelia was an analyst for the UN. Dead from three bullets is not how she should have left this world." Just reciting how his sister was found made his heart ache and his fists clench.

Something passed over the woman's eyes. Hesitation, concern . . . AJ wasn't sure which.

"Go to your embassy." She lifted her helmet again.

"It didn't happen here." He lifted a hand down the deserted street. "She was murdered in Washington, DC. The authorities have nothing. Not one lead. Three weeks ago I found a connection to Richter."

Sex Kitten narrowed her eyes. "What kind of connection?"

"One of her classmates died when someone shot holes in her tires while going around a curved road on the side of a cliff six weeks ago."

"Sounds like a coincidence, not a connection. People make enemies."

"Not my sister. Everyone liked her. Are you faculty at Richter?" She didn't answer.

"A visitor?" Richter didn't entertain visitors. They didn't let him past the gates without an escort to and from the headmistress's office.

She kept silent.

"Alumni?"

No emotion, not one speck of light, shifted on her face, but he was fairly certain he'd hit her association to the school.

"Two young women a half a world apart murdered within the same month. Both went to this school. A place I know damn well doesn't *just* teach reading and writing. Amelia knew better than to mess with anyone that would kill. Like anyone from Richter." He ran a hand through his hair before dropping his palm to the stubble on his chin.

"I'm sorry for your loss, but I can't—"

"No," AJ almost yelled, emotion choking in the back of his throat. "You can help. Maybe you don't want to. But don't tell me you can't." He took a couple of steps closer.

She stiffened.

With slow movements, AJ reached for his wallet. "I'm just getting a card," he told her as he carefully did just that.

The woman in front of him held her ground, like a cat watching a circling dog.

AJ approached with his card dangling from his fingertips. "Lodovica wouldn't talk to me outside of offering her condolences. The police have zero leads. Her name was Amelia Hofmann." He waved the card. "Take it."

She hesitated.

"Do you have siblings?"

She didn't answer, but something flashed on her face.

His heart sped in his chest. "If they suddenly ended up dead, wouldn't you want to know why? I didn't protect her."

Catwoman lifted her gloved hand and took the card.

For the first time in weeks, his voice grew husky with emotion. "I'll be back at the pub tomorrow night."

"I make no promises," she told him before tucking her head into her helmet and swinging one leg over the bike.

Two seconds later the night air roared with her engine and all the sounds of wildlife stopped.

Chapter Four

Hofmann, Amelia Hofmann.

Not only did Sasha know the name, she could picture the girl. Pixie short hair with lips many women paid for. Stocky. Amelia Hofmann wasn't a thin girl, and it showed in her efforts in the obstacle courses Richter put them through every week. Amelia was only a year younger than Sasha, and the memory of her stuck out because Sasha would often push her to move faster and train harder. She wouldn't say they had been friends, but they hadn't been enemies.

Then again, Sasha hadn't fostered friendships at Richter, nothing lasting.

She didn't foster friendships anywhere. She wasn't sure if she could classify Reed in the friendship pool. Colleague, confidant . . . someone she could count on.

She shivered.

Sasha lay on her bed. The open window allowed the cool night air to filter into the room. The card AJ had placed in her hand had just a phone number. No name.

She recited the number several times, committing it to memory, and then reached into her bag and removed a lighter.

In her private bathroom, she flicked the lighter to life. Flames licked up the single card until it was too hot to hold. Once it was all but ashes, Sasha turned on the water and removed the black soot from the white porcelain sink.

AJ's words echoed in her head. *"Do you have siblings? If they suddenly ended up dead, wouldn't you want to know why?"*

She thought of the brother she never had a chance to know. When Fedor had ended up dead, she'd stopped at nothing to find out why. Their biological father had killed him. Nearly killed her, too.

She was robbed of the only blood relative she had.

Sasha didn't want to care. Shuffled around from foster home to foster home, she didn't root in anywhere nor with anyone before her years at Richter. Her entire life had been a series of disappointments, especially when she thought she could depend on someone other than herself. Her life had taught her to depend on no one.

Ever.

She had three phone numbers memorized. Reed, Trina, and now AJ.

Sasha looked at her reflection in the mirror. Hands poised on the edges of the counter while water ran down the drain. Long sheets of black hair framed her face in a sight very few ever saw.

Dark eyes stared back at her.

She considered sending a message to Reed. *AJ Hofmann.* That was all she'd need to give him, and she knew, instinctively, that Reed would look up the name.

Was that depending on another human being?

Probably.

How secure was Richter? Would her message even meet its mark?

Keep your actions close and your thoughts even closer. Sasha knew she wouldn't reach out to Reed or Trina while at Richter. As firewalls went, the school had one with a pretty deep vault.

She finished in the bathroom and returned to bed. Familiar noises, or more to the point, familiar silence offered a sense of peace in the base of her skull. She closed her eyes and attempted to push the stranger at the bar from her head.

Her breathing slowed and the steady beat of her heart followed.

It was time to unplug and recharge.

A brief sense of panic had her reaching under her pillow.

Her fingers grazed the hard edge of the knife she kept within reach. She sighed and forced her heart to slow once again.

The library housed a smattering of students, mainly those at the college level who still attended Richter. The high school kids were in class, or so it would seem. And the primary school kids almost never spent time in the library during the day.

Sasha greeted the librarian by name when she entered the stately room. "Hello, Ms. Arnold."

The sixtysomething-year-old woman was the poster version of every librarian out there. Reading glasses perched on the end of her nose, salt-and-pepper hair pulled back in a bun, the extent of makeup was a nude gloss on her lips. Or maybe it was some kind of balm to ease the dryness.

"Ahh, Miss Budanov. I heard you were here. How are you?"

"Did the headmistress send out a memo?" The question was a joke. The silence it was met with confirmed that Lodovica had done just that.

"I don't recall you visiting me many times while you were a student. What brings you to my domain now?"

"I find myself at a crossroads, as I'm sure the headmistress has implied. I'm not sure what direction to take and thought it might help to see where some of my classmates ended up seeking employment. I wanted to start by looking over the old yearbooks."

"You didn't keep yours?"

Sasha shook her head. "I didn't see the need. Until now."

Ms. Arnold walked around the desk and led Sasha through the library. They zigzagged through the stacks until they reached the location of Richter alumni.

"You'll find what you're looking for here."

"Thank you."

"Let me know if you need anything else."

"How about an Internet password?"

Ms. Arnold blinked several times, smiled, and finally said, "Of course."

She walked away and returned a few minutes later with a card that had a written password on it. "The service here hasn't improved much over the years. All access to social media is restricted, much like when you were a student."

"I remember."

"Brilliant. Well, I'll leave you to your search."

Sasha pulled two familiar yearbooks out of the stacks, and another for the year following her last one at Richter.

The massive oak tables in the center of the library had a generous number of notepads, pens, and pencils. Sasha set her supplies aside and opened the book that marked her last year.

Pictures of familiar faces in various forms of activities stretched out before her. Cameras weren't allowed in any of the basement activities. And cell phones simply weren't allowed on campus. Recording the sins of your youth was not tolerated at the school. During her time at Richter, it seemed unjust, but in reality, it probably saved many students from lost job opportunities in their futures.

Sasha moved through the pages quickly and slowed down when she found the pictures of students on the obstacle course. She recognized her own image as she scaled the wall, one leg in the air, her arms wet with perspiration. Her face was hidden from the camera, but that didn't keep anyone from knowing who it was at the time.

She'd nailed the best time for any female student in her junior year of high school and then kept beating it, if only by a few seconds, for the next four years. How would her time be now? Sasha rolled her shoulders and turned the page.

The class pages started with the college students. There were only a couple dozen of them at that age. Most of the kids left after high school to go on to universities all over the world. The ones that stayed were often like Sasha. Their absent, dysfunctional families paid to keep them enrolled at Richter for their own good. Some students were hardened by military families and didn't do well without strict rules.

Sasha's gaze found the image of one of the male students she'd gotten to know in her last two years at the school. They'd been lovers, if you could call it that at that age. Russell Visser. He'd been kicked out of two boarding schools before he reached Richter in tenth grade. He'd tried to get kicked out of Richter, too. Only that wasn't an option. The headmistress never expelled students. She put them in solitary instead. It was the most effective way to keep students from crossing the line. In society if you can't follow the rules, and get caught, you're put in prison. Richter had its own version. And instead of hardening the students, it made them focus. When they broke the rules, they did it on purpose, and often it was immaculately calculated to avoid getting caught. A standard goal of any student, Sasha remembered, but at Richter, those who broke rules on epic levels became school legends. It wasn't until graduation that the offenders, or heroes of these legends, let themselves be known.

Sasha remembered listening to Russell speak in the ten minutes he had onstage during their graduation. Russell had been caught many times in his early years, but by the time he left Richter, he hadn't spent one night in solitary for two years.

She smiled when she thought of the scroll he'd unraveled to read from.

"The missing lion paperweight from the headmistress's office that was later found duct taped to the hood of her car; junior year.

"The entire supply of gym towels taped to the ceiling of the girls' locker room; senior year." Sasha had been a part of that stunt.

Russell was the physical joker, where Sasha took pride in a different type of prank.

She'd hacked into the mainframe security at the school and spent hours recording film of uneventful days and nights. Once a month, for her last year in school, she'd uplink her footage and cut the live feeds in order to break into various classrooms. She picked locks, hacked computers to display naked pictures of strangers on home screens. Those pranks aged quickly, and she moved on to placing hidden cameras and recording conversations she'd later pipe into the PA system at the school.

When Sasha had left Richter, she'd owned up to about half of her self-entertainment. All the talents she'd managed in those final years helped with her escape and trip to the bar her senior year.

She'd called the headmistress on purpose.

Why? To show off? To prove she could? A little of both, she supposed.

Sasha flipped through pages.

She wrote down the names of several students. Classmates that she remembered going on to criminal justice careers. Whispers of government agencies recruiting on campus were a constant buzz in those final months. Only the elite were offered interviews, and those students were not always vocal about where they went.

Sasha found Amelia Hofmann's photograph. Instead of writing down her name, Sasha searched for other photos of the girl to see who she spent time with outside of class. When her search came up empty, she opened Amelia's senior yearbook. She found a picture of Amelia in her room with two roommates.

She wrote their names down.

The hair on Sasha's forearms stood up seconds before a girl pulled out a chair opposite her and sat.

Sasha closed the book and looked up.

"You're *the* Sasha Budanov."

"I didn't realize I had a title."

The girl reminded Sasha of herself at eighteen . . . maybe seventeen. Stern expression, eyes without emotion, set jaw. It was hard to read the girl's thoughts with her guard so clearly raised like a wall around her.

"You do here."

"What is your name?"

"Claire."

"You're American."

Claire shrugged her shoulders. "I saw you yesterday in Ms. Denenberg's class. Impressive."

"I was taught by the best."

Claire leaned forward on her elbows. "Do you use it? Outside these walls?"

"You're asking if I fight?"

She gave a single nod.

"Why do you want to know?"

Claire scooted her chair back and stood. "Fine, don't tell me."

Sasha stopped her with one word. "Yes."

Claire made eye contact and held it.

"How long have you been at Richter?"

"Two years."

"You're what? Seventeen?"

"Eighteen. I graduate in May."

"Are your parents keeping you here, or are you going elsewhere for college?"

Claire looked away. "My parents are gone."

The words *I'm sorry* hovered over her lips but didn't come out. "So the decision to be here is yours."

"Sometimes."

"Only sometimes?"

Claire pointed at the faculty bracelet that scanned every door to open it. "I don't have one of those, so yeah . . . sometimes."

"You agree to the rules and conditions when you step on campus."

"Yeah, I know." She paused. "Did you choose to stay here for college, or did someone force you?"

"I had a benefactor who would pay for this school so long as I was here. I didn't see the need to finish my education outside these walls."

Claire narrowed her eyes. "You're not like the other people here."

"I'm not?"

"No. You didn't ask about my parents. Didn't offer sympathy."

Sasha placed both hands to the sides of the book she had been looking at. "I'm not very nurturing. Besides, if you wanted me to have details of your parents, you'd have told me. The loss of a parent isn't always something to be sorry about."

"How so?"

"When my father died, I cheered. My mother was gone before I had a chance to know her. Wasting emotion on someone's *assumed* life is rather pointless, don't you think?"

"Richter taught you that."

"Richter taught me many useful things."

Claire turned her head away. "I guess." She sighed.

Sasha gathered the yearbooks and stood. "It was nice meeting you, Claire."

The girl didn't offer the same. "Are you staying for a while? Joining the staff?"

"I'm not sure how long I'll be here."

"That's fair, I guess."

"What about you? Are you going to stay for college?"

Claire lifted her chin. "I haven't decided."

Sasha smiled. "You have a few more months to figure it out."

The girl shrugged her shoulders. "I'll see you around, then."

As she walked away, Sasha categorized the conversation with the girl as a completely new experience. Young women never sought her out and they certainly didn't ask about her education or school years.

After returning the books to the stacks, she checked out a laptop from Ms. Arnold and returned to her room.

Chapter Five

"Have you found any answers?" Linette interrupted Sasha's thoughts as she approached with her question.

She stood in one of the many archways of the outside halls surrounding the school's courtyard. Students were leaving their classes and going back to their rooms to get ready for dinner. The schedule of the school hadn't changed in twenty years.

"Good afternoon, Headmistress . . ." Sasha's address to the woman faded. "Linette."

"I was told you were in the library today."

Nothing happened at this school without the woman's knowledge, and oftentimes, permission.

"Examining old yearbooks. Trying to remember where my fellow classmates ended up."

"And did you turn up anything promising?"

"I found very little, actually. Seems many of the students left Richter and disappeared. I tried looking them up online and only found a few people working in the private sector."

Linette tilted her head down the corridor. "Follow me."

Sasha fell into step beside the woman and waited for her to speak.

"What would I find if I were to look up your name?" she asked.

"In a general search? Probably nothing."

"What about a detailed one? Like the kind we taught you in your final years here?"

"I've used an alias many times since I left Richter."

"To escape your father's attention, I can assume."

"Yes."

"I doubt you're the only student to pretend to be someone they're not. We taught you to go unnoticed when you want to, to stand out when you need to. Did you ask yourself why we did that?"

"You said it was to protect us. Considering Richter has educated senators' sons, dictators' daughters, and I'm sure many equally high-profile families in between, your explanation was sufficient."

Linette guided her to the dining hall and toward the back elevators.

"Would it surprise you to learn that the names of some of the students here at Richter were aliases from the beginning?"

She hadn't considered that possibility.

"Take yourself. Sasha Petrov."

"I never had my father's name."

Linette stopped at the elevator, waved her armband over the lock, and called the lift.

"Have you ever seen your birth certificate?"

"Of course."

"You mean the one your benefactor meant for you to have when you left Germany. The one Alice Petrov knew you needed in order to escape your father's notice."

The certainty Sasha felt a moment before about her birth name faded. "She lied to me."

"She protected you. Your mother, on the other hand, wanted to outsmart your father and stupidly gave you his name." They exited the elevator and took the stairs to the last subterranean floor.

"Then why was I not sent to him when my mother died?"

They passed the soundproof doors leading through the firing range, and around a corner.

Linette unlocked the administration room and then proceeded into yet another space, hidden behind a false wall. There was no way to see the room from the outside.

"I would appreciate that you keep this room to yourself. Very few members of the staff even know it's here."

"Why show me?"

Linette hesitated before crossing the threshold. "Perhaps because I feel I owe you an explanation so you can better understand why we do things the way we do here at Richter."

Sasha followed her inside.

"These are the archives of students such as yourself. I took the liberty of pulling your dossier when you showed up yesterday. For many reasons, I cannot show you any other files than your own." She crossed to a table and handed Sasha a folder. "The files never leave this room. There are no cameras in this room where, say, a *crafty student* could hack into the system and learn the secrets hidden here."

She smiled at the *crafty student* reference. She opened her file. A childhood image of her on her first day at Richter stared back. "I was only nine years old."

"Actually, you were eight."

"But I—"

"By the time Alice Petrov enrolled you here, your birth certificate had been doctored twice. Both copies are in the file, along with the original."

Alice Petrov had been Sasha's benefactor at Richter and in life. Sadly, Sasha hadn't made the connection when Alice was alive. Cancer had robbed Alice of her life, and Sasha of one of the only people on the planet who cared if she was alive or dead.

Sasha flipped through the first few pages and found them.

The first birth certificate had her name as Sasha Budanov Petrov. Mother's name Natasha Budanov, the father's name was left blank. Her birthday was a year off. "I'm only twenty-eight?"

"Surprise."

The second birth certificate had her name as simply Sasha Budanov. Father's name was marked as unknown. The third and final certificate had changed her birthday by a year.

"Alice went through a lot of work to keep Petrov from learning about me."

"He knew about you. He just assumed you ended up as a gutter rat somewhere. Alice went through great pains to keep you out of the government system and used a series of handpicked foster homes for you before finding Richter."

"And all those years I thought I was sent to Richter because I ran away from those homes."

Linette sat in one of the half dozen chairs in the center of the room. "You were, in part. Only Alice needed to keep you out of the public eye and, more importantly, away from your father. I knew she was going to employ you once you left here. It was her way of keeping an eye on you."

"She hired me to protect her son and his new wife. I failed."

"She hired you because she could no longer keep you locked up here at Richter. She made sure you were enrolled in every possible self-defense, firearms, agility, and investigative curriculum we offered. And when she felt you'd mastered what we had, she insisted that we find new instructors and new classes. We teach computer programing, but only a few students were in the advanced class that gave you the path to the back doors of computers."

"You taught me to hack."

Linette ticked her tongue. "You educated yourself on that skill. We simply showed you where the door was. You chose to open it. Not that we didn't know exactly what you were doing with your new skills."

"My pranks."

"Your fine-tuned skills used for mischief . . . yes."

Sasha rested her hands on her file. "I wasn't the only one in those advanced classes."

Linette tapped a finger on the table. "Some of our students went on to agencies that needed those types of skills."

"You mean the government?" Sasha thought of Amelia Hofmann.

"There are government agencies all over the world."

Sasha voiced what she'd always assumed. "Spies."

Linette held all emotion in. No denial. No validation.

"I suppose that would explain why my search for some of my old classmates has come up empty."

Linette placed a hand over Sasha's file. "Names change. People get married."

"People lie."

"Something we're all guilty of, I'm sure."

Sasha flipped through her file and read through a list of accomplishments she'd achieved in the underground education at Richter. "I was an orphan, skilled, without any family. I would think my profile would have been one sought after."

She looked up to see Linette smiling. "You were promised to return to Alice."

"And therefore not recruited."

"No job would have earned you what Alice set aside on your behalf. Financially, you're much better off than most of your classmates."

An understatement if there ever was one. Alice had set aside millions for Sasha. A bankroll she wasn't even aware of until after the woman died.

"Money isn't your motivator," Linette said.

"Which is why I returned searching for something."

Linette leaned forward. "And are you finding it?"

Sasha nodded, glancing around the locked room full of secrets. "I feel closer than I did yesterday."

An hour later Sasha sent an encrypted text message to Reed, spelling out AJ Hofmann.

The bar was much busier than it had been the night before. AJ sat at the far end, nervously watching the door. He'd gotten a text from a number he didn't recognize. He assumed it was her.

Hoped it was her.

The text had simply said I'm thirsty.

So there he sat, waiting for a woman who never gave him her name, while the beer in front of him grew warm.

He ran his fingers along the condensation on the glass, his nerves nothing but raw tentacles, exposed and jumping around in a state of madness. He'd been at a dead end going on two weeks, completely out of his element, sitting in a pub in Germany with very little of the language inside his brain. The police had rummaged through Amelia's condo in their half-assed attempt at finding her killer. They questioned him and his parents about a trip that his sister had apparently planned to fly to London. Since Amelia flew for work all the time, he hadn't thought much about it. When he took the time to look through his sister's home, he found a calendar with the dates circled and the words *Keri's funeral* in the center of the trip. That's when he followed his gut and flew to Europe. He spent less than forty-eight hours in Wales, realized the common bond his sister had with Keri, and flew to Germany. He really should have gone to Richter with Amelia. Then he'd have a better chance at getting on the inside.

Only he hadn't taken that opportunity.

The chair on his right scraped against the floor, drawing him out of his thoughts, and Sex on a Stick turned it around and straddled it like a man.

His mouth went dry.

Her hair was pulled back in a single ponytail. Eyes framed with eyeliner she didn't need and full lips painted red.

He ignored the stirring in his jeans and cleared his throat. "Where did you come from?"

"There's more than one entrance."

He glanced behind the bar. "You came in through the kitchen?"

"You must be new."

AJ scooted his chair closer and tried to keep their conversation to just the two of them. "What's your name?"

She lifted her chin, waited a beat. "You can call me Sasha."

"Is that your name?"

"Sometimes."

Damn, she was a piece of work. "I wasn't sure you'd call."

She looked at his glass, took her time moving those dark eyes to him. "What are you drinking?"

He pushed the warm beer aside. "Whatever you want."

Sasha flagged down a waitress and ordered in German. AJ had no idea what.

Much as he liked to watch her, AJ wasn't there on a social visit. "Did you find out—"

Sasha leaned forward and stopped his question by placing one long finger on his lips. Her eyes followed her fingertip as it slid off his lips and rested under his chin. She drew him close until their lips were a breath apart.

His entire frame tightened.

"First things first." Her eyes looked at his lips. The tip of her tongue licked a tiny portion of her upper lip.

His cock stood at full attention and all the energy inside his brain traveled south. He'd seen this before. Smoky woman in a bar enticing a man . . . right before she slips his car keys or wallet into her purse. AJ was pretty sure he'd taught that move to a couple of his friends in Florida.

Only his car keys were in his front pocket, and his wallet was outside of Sasha's reach.

She leaned back when the waitress set a bottle of vodka on the table with two glasses.

"You're serious?" AJ asked, looking at the liquor and then her.

"I told you I was thirsty." She opened the bottle and poured a generous portion into each glass. "Cheers."

"I didn't come here to get drunk."

Sasha picked up the glass. "Then don't." She finished her drink with one swallow.

He picked up the drink and followed her lead. The liquid burned the back of his throat like a trail of fire.

For the first time, she smiled. "What I need to know, Alex, is if you simply got better at breaking the rules or if you stopped breaking them altogether."

AJ cleared his throat. "You looked me up."

"A stranger goes out of his way to follow me home under the guise of concern for his family and I'm supposed to take his word as gospel? Of course I looked you up."

He supposed when she put it like that . . . "Both. I got better, and then stopped."

She poured another shot for each of them, took her time sipping her second round. "Why don't I believe you?"

"Which part . . . better or stopped?"

She kept silent.

"I got caught. And since my goal had been to gain the attention of my father, and that was never going to happen unless I followed his political path, I decided to follow the rules."

"Your dedication to your version of the truth is admirable." Her accent hit every *r* a little harder. She was calling him a liar in the best possible way.

AJ sat back in his chair, lifted the vodka to his lips. He knew damn well his day job hadn't followed him to Europe, or anywhere, for that matter.

Sasha was speculating.

"Your father, Alex Senior. US ambassador to Germany back when Amelia was at Richter."

"You did look into her."

"I looked into you. I knew Amelia. Remembered why she was at Richter to begin with."

Now they were getting somewhere. "She was killed as an adult. There shouldn't have been any threat for her safety, especially after my father left Germany and took a position on the Democratic campaign trail."

"Political affiliations are always targets."

"For my father, maybe, but not his adult daughter working with the UN . . ."

Noise from a nearby party grew louder.

"Executions of political families receive plenty of police attention. What do you think you can do or find out that they can't?"

"They aren't looking here. One death in Europe six weeks ago and Amelia's one month ago. They said they aren't related."

Sasha put back another shot of vodka, looked at his glass.

He wasn't sure of the test she was giving, but holding his liquor came easy. They finished their second round and poured a third.

She leaned forward, wiped her bottom lip with her thumb. "You were caught stealing your neighbor's car. Maybe someone was angry at you for taking something that didn't belong to you."

So they were back to him. "I was a minor."

"You're not a minor now."

He expected the same questions from the police, only they never happened. *That* was how good he was at what he did.

The fact Sasha knew about his record proved she was good at what she did.

"This isn't about me." He'd run through that idea so many times his nose bled.

Sasha skirted her eyes toward the group of people, sat taller, and then looked back to him. "I'm hot." Without another word, Sasha stood and dropped several euros on the table.

AJ jumped to his feet and grabbed her hand to keep her from running as they headed for the door. Surprisingly, she didn't pull away.

The cold night air snapped against him as they walked away from the light of the bar. AJ stopped in front of his rental car and Sasha positioned herself against the door, her gaze flickering to the bar behind him. With a move he wasn't expecting, she pulled him close enough to feel the heat of her body against his. Sasha reached up and placed a hand on the side of his face.

"Who else have you spoken to here about Amelia?" she asked in a voice just above a whisper.

What the hell was she doing? The warmth of her hand on his cheek distracted him. "Just Lodovica. I've hung out in the bar, waiting until I recognized someone from the school."

"How did you know to talk to me?"

One of her hands reached for his hip.

"The woman you were with. I've seen her leave the school, noticed her in the bar, but didn't think she'd let me buy her a drink." AJ stopped her hand with his as her palm started to move over his ass. "What are you doing?"

"You've caught the attention of several people in the pub, AJ. And either you're an exceptional liar, or you're being followed."

"No one knows I'm here."

"So you have a fake passport?"

He blinked a few times. "Why would I need . . . ?"

"You really are an amateur." She placed her body flush with his from knees to chest and lifted her lips. "You're going to kiss me and look at the man by the door."

Without any time for thought, Sasha pulled his lips to hers and moved her hands up his back.

Her breasts pressed against his chest. Pliant, soft lips blew warm air against his. His brain fried.

"Kiss me back," she demanded, her lips flat against his.

AJ looked into the depths of her gaze and grasped the sides of her face. He might not have realized someone was watching them, but he knew how to kiss. He tilted her head and opened his lips against hers. Her tongue darted in and he followed.

Her kiss was both fire and ice.

Dangerous.

AJ turned her around and kissed her harder while his eyes searched for a man at the door.

No one was there.

He closed his eyes, shifted positions, and kissed her again. Her hands moved over him like smoke, barely there but would leave a scent when she was gone. She lifted her leg alongside his.

She was good.

"I don't see anyone," he said between kisses. Purposely lingering over her frame and taking full advantage of the position she'd offered him. "Wait." He captured her head in his hand, bit at her lip, and pretended to scope out the bar a second time.

He drew away slightly.

Her lips opened enough for him to know she wanted more. Even if this was nothing but a game to her. He ran a free hand down the length of her, his thumb tracing the outer edges of her breast.

Her eyes darkened and it took all he had not to smile. No, he tasted her again, looked behind her shoulder. "No one," he finally said.

Sasha looked over his shoulder, and broke their kiss. "He was there a minute ago."

Right, sure he was.

AJ kept his body pinned to hers, her back resting against the car. He ran his thumb over her swollen lips.

She watched him.

"Anything you want to know about me, you can just ask. You don't have to steal my wallet to find out."

Slowly, she started to smile. Sasha stepped out of his arms, reached inside her boot, and handed him back his possession. "Not as clueless as you first appear."

"There was no one in the bar, was there?"

Her grin faded. "And you're not wearing a wire."

"You're testing me?" He gritted out the question.

"Trust no one. Richter taught me and your sister that."

He closed the distance between them, flattened his body against hers once again. Any amusement he may have had on his face a moment ago was now gone. He felt the anger pulling at his gut. "My sister obviously forgot that lesson and now she's dead. I don't have time for games, Sasha. Every day that passes makes the trail to her killer colder. I don't have to be a cop or a graduate of whatever kind of military school Richter is to figure that out."

"Get. Off. Me."

He narrowed his eyes. "Quite a change of tune from a moment ago."

She shifted her weight, clueing him in at the last second to what was coming. Her knee came up, and AJ doubled over and grabbed his junk. Absolutely the worst way to kill an erection.

Sasha pushed away. "Good luck in your search, Mr. Hofmann."

AJ leaned against his car, caught his breath as her footsteps faded. *Son of a bitch.*

He yanked open his car door and slid behind the wheel. Halfway back to his hotel, he removed Sasha's cell phone from his back pocket.

He knew he'd see her again.

Chapter Six

The difference between someone who attempts to be badass and one who is, is the education and skills behind them.

Sasha had the upper hand.

She stayed up until three in the morning obtaining any and all possible information about AJ, or Alex Hofmann Junior, from his phone.

She was pretty sure AJ hadn't even managed to get past her phone's security to make a call.

He'd taken a few precautions with the small computer that everyone trusted but few understood. The kind that turned off his tracking and didn't automatically offer access to his microphone. By midnight she was deep in his e-mail.

AJ lived in Florida, and from what she could tell, he'd had a series of go-nowhere jobs that he kept for a little over a year before moving on to something new. The address she found for him, or at least the address his Amazon orders were shipped to, was to a condo on the beach that his piss-ass jobs couldn't possibly afford. Smoke and mirrors. All of it.

There was no way he was exactly who he said he was. Only she wasn't going to find out much more without a juicer computer that wasn't recording her every move.

Sasha found flight information from Virginia, where his parents now lived, to London and then Berlin. He'd been in Germany for almost two weeks.

A quick track search of what he looked up online had plenty of Richter hits. The basic website of the school, the few faculty images they provided, most of those who actually lived on campus and didn't leave very often.

Right before she closed the phone for the night, she found where AJ had performed two extensive searches, looking for the names of Amelia's ex-roommates at Richter. Not that his quest for information had gotten him anywhere.

Apparently AJ was doing exactly what he said he was doing while in Europe. That didn't mean he wasn't keeping his personal truths to himself.

Then again, who didn't?

She'd trust him as much as he trusted her.

Probably less.

She slid into bed, a smile on her swollen lips.

And the man kissed like a demon.

⌒৩

A phone ringing by her bed woke her four hours later.

"Good morning, Sasha."

So he had managed to hack into her phone. "AJ."

"Seems we managed to pick up the wrong phones last night."

She swung her legs off the small bed, rubbed the sleep from her eyes. "Did we? I hadn't noticed."

He released a short laugh. "I can bring yours by . . ."

"I have business in the city. I'll meet you at the Brandenburg Gate at noon."

"Noon it is." He hung up.

Sasha smiled. Things were about to get interesting.

⁓੭

"Miss Budanov?"

Sasha turned with the sound of her name. Wearing black leather pants suitable for riding her bike and her hair pulled back into a bun, she was prepared for her hour-long drive into the city.

Linette stood outside the administration offices, holding the door open. "Do you have a minute?"

She couldn't help but feel a bit of déjà vu with the headmistress asking her to come into her office.

"Of course."

Sasha detoured out of her chosen path and through the admin doors.

"I have someone I'd like you to meet," Linette said as she walked beside her toward her private office.

"Oh?"

"An old friend."

Sasha followed Linette into her office, where she closed the door behind them. Standing by the window overlooking the courtyard was a man in a three-piece suit, short salt-and-pepper hair, and glasses. He turned their way when they walked in and instantly smiled.

"Sasha Budanov. You're as lovely as ever."

Sasha planted her feet and waited for him to approach. "Have we met?"

"Not officially," Linette interjected. "Geoff has witnessed many of Richter's graduation ceremonies, including yours."

Sasha's gaze moved from the headmistress to the man she addressed as Geoff. "You have me at a disadvantage, then."

He walked closer, the scent of his cologne moving with him. Geoff reached out a hand. "Geoff Pohl, Miss Budanov. We finally have an official meeting."

Sasha shook his hand, found his grip a little too familiar. Not a double squeeze from someone flirting, not a passing grip of a first meeting . . . but a knowing grip that put her on edge.

Linette indicated a chair. "What Geoff is trying to say is he wanted a chance to speak with you back when you were a student, Sasha. For reasons you and I have discussed, that wasn't possible. I thought perhaps you'd like an opportunity now that the reasons he couldn't offer you employment then are gone."

Sasha noticed that Geoff didn't sit, but leaned against Linette's desk with his hands gripping the wood.

"What kind of employment are we talking about?" *CIA, FBI . . . British intelligence in all their forms?* Many agencies came to mind. Much as she'd like to dismiss them immediately, she thought it might be best to find out what was out there.

"First things first, m'dear."

The hair on her neck went up.

"I need to determine if you still maintain the skills you obtained while you were here at Richter."

"Which skills are you referring to?"

Geoff paused, lost his smile. "All of them."

AJ was being stood up.

It was half past noon and Sasha wasn't there.

The Brandenburg Gate was one of the busiest tourist attractions in Berlin. The square was filled with families and walking tours led by someone holding a colored flag on a stick and talking into a microphone while a line of dazed, zombie-like visitors followed behind. Aside from those in the square learning about the history of the place, there were a dozen police officers and security guards moving around. Considering the American, British, and French embassies were all within a stone's throw of each other, AJ was surprised there wasn't a stronger military presence.

AJ kept scanning the crowd in search of Sex on a Stick in black leather pants and a bad attitude.

Nothing.

Left without options, AJ dialed his phone number on her phone and waited. It rang twice.

Behind him, the riff of "Bad to the Bone," his ringtone, shot through him. He dropped his hand from his ear and saw a blonde standing three feet away, her back to him.

Slowly she turned.

"Whoa."

Sasha stared back at him, wearing white capri pants and a bright floral top. The blonde wig overdid it but completely camouflaged her in broad daylight. She took a step closer, reached out her hand holding his cell. "Hello, AJ."

They switched phones. "How long have you been standing there?"

"Half an hour, give or take."

He looked her up and down. She looked like a typical American housewife, minus the kid in the stroller. "Impressive."

"I wanted to make sure you were alone."

AJ glanced around at the passing tourists. "Is there a reason behind the cloak-and-dagger?"

She moved closer, lowered her voice. "You've come here to look for your sister's killer. You think there is some connection to Richter. Went so far as to go there asking questions. You're stalking the local pub and hitting on, not to mention stealing from, the patrons . . ." Sasha waved her phone in the air before tucking it into her back pocket.

"I'm calling pot to kettle on that last accusation." Although all the rest she pointed out was spot-on.

"I like to go unnoticed. If someone followed me here, they lost me the second I made the city limits and went clothes shopping."

"What if someone followed me?"

"Then I would have seen them watching in the thirty minutes you've been standing around looking like a lost child without a parent." She turned and started walking toward the gate.

AJ had no choice but to follow.

"What makes you think anyone is following either of us?"

She smiled, didn't answer his question. "I used to help your sister on her agility training," she told him.

The mention of his sister brought his attention back to what he should be focused on. "She wasn't the most athletic woman." Amelia took after their mother, who didn't grow more than five feet five inches tall and had a sweet tooth that always kept her rounder than she'd liked. At least that's what she'd blame when she went on one of her many diets.

"No. But she held her own most of the time. Everyone at Richter was pushed to do at least that."

"Her coworkers said she had recently started taking morning walks before work," AJ said.

"Which explains the police report about her being murdered in the park and tossed in the river."

AJ stopped walking. "You looked her up."

"Only because I knew her."

He jumped in front of her, stopped her from moving. "Then you'll help me."

"There is nothing to suggest that Amelia's death is at all linked to Richter."

He shook his head. "I can't find any trace of Amelia's roommates. And the one friend she mentioned several times to me, Keri Shrum, was the roommate who died in the car *accident*."

"How did you find that out?"

"When I went into her condo after the police had done their investigation, I went through a few of her drawers. Found her calendar with Keri's funeral written on it. I made a couple of phone calls and flew to Europe to dig a little more."

"And what did your amateur investigative skills find?"

He didn't want to tell her this, but any research on her part would reveal it. "Her car was shot at and the police thought her boyfriend did it."

Sasha narrowed her eyes. "The reason they thought her boyfriend did it?"

"She broke up with him. He was popular with the local police."

"Well, there you go."

He sidestepped in front of her. "No. No, I'm not going, because this is Europe we're talking about. The UK. The average person on every corner can't buy guns there, and while her boyfriend is no choirboy, he didn't seem to have any history with weapons. The shots to her tires were painfully accurate."

Sasha gave him a hard stare. "What has your father said about all this?"

AJ stared back. "My father said that the kind of students that graduated from Richter and ended up dead were not like my sister or her friend. That maybe Keri had something to hide."

"What did you take that to mean?"

"I'm not oblivious, Sasha. I know that graduates from your alma mater end up in jobs all over government agencies, from those who carry weapons to those who go deep undercover. I know that wasn't my sister. If Keri Shrum was that woman, then picking a boyfriend who liked to test her fighting skills and go in and out of jail for his efforts wasn't covert by anyone's definition."

"A man who beats on a woman is capable of shooting out her tires."

Everything inside of him screamed no. *No!* AJ shook his head.

"Two women isn't a pattern, AJ."

"Which is why I need more names. More people Amelia associated with at Richter that I can look up and talk to."

Sasha kept silent.

"Listen, all I want is a few more names. Some of the other students she graduated with."

"Didn't Amelia keep her yearbooks?"

It was his turn to offer a knowing smile. "You would think so, wouldn't you? Only guess what I didn't find when I went to her condo after her funeral."

"Your parents' house, then."

He shook his head. "The only childhood possessions they kept of hers were those ceramic gizmos and handmade Mother's Day cards we all gave to our parents."

Sasha paused.

"Was her place broken into?"

"No."

"Then maybe she just threw them away."

"Why would she do that?" AJ looked over Sasha's shoulder and noticed a man eating an ice cream cone and staring at Sasha. The middle-aged guy turned his attention away and took a few steps in the opposite direction.

"Maybe she . . ."

AJ felt eyes, turned to his left.

No one.

"What is it?" Sasha asked.

"The guy with the ice cream, over your left shoulder."

She grinned, cocked her head to the side. "We did this last night."

"Yeah, only I'm not asking you to lay a lip lock on me. Tempting as that might be." Truth was, he'd thought about that kiss more times than he wanted to admit. "If how you're dressed is any indication, you're the expert on all things undercover. You tell me if you feel the weight of someone's stare."

Sasha paused, then looked over her shoulder. "That him?" she asked, thumbing toward the guy with the ice cream.

"Yeah."

She grabbed AJ's hand and walked directly toward the guy he thought for sure was watching them.

"What are you doing?"

She didn't answer. "Excuse me?" Her voice rose a full octave, her smile was sickeningly sweet. Any accent he'd detected from her voice was gone . . . or changed.

The man with the cone turned toward them. "Yes?"

"Are you American? You look American."

"I'm, ah . . . yeah." The guy looked directly at AJ.

Sasha kept going. "Good. Would you mind taking our picture? I can't get the gate behind us with a selfie."

Again the guy offered AJ unblinking eyes. "Ah, sure." He reached for the phone Sasha was handing him.

Next thing AJ realized, he was standing beside Sasha, her arm slipped around his waist, and he was smiling like all of the other tourists surrounding them while the man he thought was spying on them took their picture.

The stranger holding Sasha's phone, while trying to balance his ice cream cone, looked completely out of place.

"Take a second one, just in case." Sasha giggled.

The sound of her voice didn't suit her. The hand on his waist, however, suited him just fine. The feel of her there, the warmth, the softness he knew she would hate if he pointed it out, felt a little too right.

"Thank you so much."

The stranger handed her phone back with a nod. "Have fun."

She waved. "We will . . . thanks."

And he was gone.

AJ watched the man slip away as Sasha removed herself from AJ's side. He missed her warmth, instantly.

"Any self-preserving spy wouldn't have made contact," Sasha told him.

The two of them walked toward the center of the square. "Okay," AJ started. "Maybe I'm a little paranoid."

"You're a *lot* paranoid."

AJ paused in the middle of the plaza and stared at the massive horses that sat atop the gate. The image of his sister at Christmas the previous year surfaced. It was the last time he'd seen her alive. "I know Amelia's death wasn't random, Sasha. I feel it with every breath I take."

She sighed. "I know you do."

He looked at her. "You don't believe me."

"I believe you believe."

He lowered his head, studied the salt-and-pepper colored stones beneath his feet. "You're not going to help." Damn it . . . he was back to ground zero.

Another heavy sigh from the woman at his side. "I will help you."

AJ snapped his head up. "What?"

She placed a hand in the air as in warning. "Not because I think you have anything other than grief inside you. The not knowing, or never accepting the facts, can eat you alive."

Not ground zero. He wanted to kiss her. Not that she would be receptive to that kind of thing. "Why are you doing this?" There wasn't anything in it for her.

Sasha turned away from him and focused her attention on the Brandenburg Gate. "Because I'm not bored."

"Am I supposed to know what that means?" he asked.

"No."

She shook her head as if dismissing a thought and started to walk. AJ followed.

"I have a couple of names you can look into while I try and figure out if there was any connection between your sister and Miss Shrum."

Walking felt easier and the sky was a tad bit brighter. "I can do that."

"You need to do that from here. In Berlin."

He hesitated. "Why?"

"How long have you been hanging around the outskirts of Richter asking questions?"

"Do you always answer a question with one of your own?"

She didn't answer. "How long, two weeks?"

"About."

"Long enough for people to recognize you and warn anyone who might be able to offer some information. It's time you backed off and took your search away from Richter."

AJ stopped walking altogether. A serious cloud of doubt started to hover over him. "You're trying to stop me."

Sasha pivoted; the wind blew fake blonde hair in her eyes. "I'm approaching this as if there is a shadow of truth in your theory. Let's pretend that your sister is somehow connected to this other woman, if only by the person that removed them from this world—"

"There's a connection." AJ felt it.

Sasha continued. "*If* that person has ties to Richter, or has lumped them together because of Richter, then it's safe to say they will have their ear to the grounds around the school."

"My sister's death was in DC, Keri's was in Wales. I doubt the killer is in Germany."

Sasha looked around them, lowered her voice and her head. "What makes you think this person works alone?" She paused. "You're not."

She had a point.

"You stay in Berlin."

"But—"

"I make the rules, or I don't help. This is not negotiable."

Sasha's eyes met his and held.

His chest tightened. "Fine."

A satisfied smile crossed her lips. "I'm going to give you a phone number, someone I trust in the States. If you come across anything in your research, I want you to call Reed, not me. You and I will not have direct contact for the next three days. If Reed feels the need, he will get ahold of me on your behalf."

"A middleman." He hated middlemen.

She turned and started walking again. "I hope you're taking notes."

"I have a decent memory."

"Good. Now why don't you go find a hotel? Play tourist." She started to cross the street.

He stopped, called after her. "What about that number?"

"It's in your phone."

Of course it was.

The woman was cunning. "Hey, Sasha?" he yelled.

She stopped, peeked over her shoulder.

AJ grinned. "The blonde doesn't work for you."

He was pretty sure his comment made her smile. Not that she stuck around for him to see it. Within a minute, Sasha was swallowed into the crowd.

As much as AJ cautioned himself not to trust her, he knew that he did.

Chapter Seven

"Twice in one week, are you okay?"

Sasha had ditched the wig and the housewife clothes, and sat in a café drinking coffee before heading back to Richter. With her phone to her ear, she watched Berlin's rush hour traffic from a curbside table.

"Are you a dad yet?"

Reed released a sigh. "Obviously you're fine."

"I need you to do something for me."

"W-what? You need *me* to do something for *you*?"

"Was I unclear?" She knew he was being facetious.

"Name it. Although we already have baby names picked out."

That made her smile. Imagine if someone cared enough about her to name their child after her? *Yeah, not in this lifetime.*

"AJ Hofmann might contact you in the next few days and ask a question or need help."

"I'm here."

No questions asked. One of the many things she liked about Reed.

"Anything else?"

A tickle on her neck had her on edge. "Geoff Pohl. I need to know who this man works for and if there are any red flags."

"You got it."

Again, no questions.

"I'm in Germany. Spending time with the people who . . ." *raised me.* "The Internet isn't secure there or I wouldn't ask."

"I'm glad I can do something for you for once."

"Take care of your wife," she told him before hanging up.

⁓♋⁓

"You ready for this?" Brigitte asked on the sidelines of the obstacle course. Her hair was pulled back in a tight ponytail, as was Sasha's. They were both dressed for the race that they would do as a team. The skies decided to open up enough to make everything soggy and that much more difficult. The two of them would need to work together in order to tackle some of the steeper terrain. Only the last two obstacles would be taken on solo, making the last eight hundred meters a true race.

"I'm ready, the question is, Are you?" Sasha lifted her chin in good humor.

"You always were cocky."

Brigitte directed her attention to her students. In the mix, Sasha noticed the kid she'd delivered a fair amount of humiliation to the first day she'd been back, and Claire, who bounced on the tips of her toes with untapped energy. "Listen up." Brigitte demanded everyone's attention. "You've been paired with the student who came in closest to you on our last run. The only way to be paired with someone faster and stronger is if you overtake a teammate on the last eight hundred meters. The rules have not changed. You will not sabotage anyone's efforts. The goal here is for your best time, not you're better because the front-runner was tripped. You will wait for your partner through the slippery wall and the vertical rope climb. Officials are watching."

"And if our partner taps out?" one of her male students asked.

"Then you better hope someone is held up by their partner and lends you a hand, Mr. Norton."

Brigitte stepped closer, spoke louder. "I want you tired, wet, muddy, scraped, and even a little bloody, but I want none of you broken. You are no good to anyone broken. Am I clear?"

A chorus of "Yes, Ms. Denenberg" came from the students.

"Are you really running with us?" one of the girls asked.

Brigitte glanced at Sasha. "Miss Budanov holds the record at Richter, and none of you have come close to it. She wants to see how her skills have held up in the years she's been away."

"It's not her you should be worried about." The comment came from Claire.

The other students made surprised sounds and took a step away from the girl.

Brigitte let the comment roll off her shoulders. "We shall see."

Sasha and Brigitte took their places on the starting line. Timers pinned to their waistbands would keep track of their time at each point along the way. Much like those running a marathon, knowing your time between the miles always gave you a sense of your weaknesses and strengths.

A familiar buzz of excitement ran up Sasha's spine. Not that she needed to prove herself to the students, or even her previous instructor . . . but to herself. She'd had many opportunities to run races like these since she left Richter. Each time she ran under an alias and never collected the participation medals. She competed for herself, not to win recognition, so when she found herself up on the competition, she purposely hung back. The last thing she needed to do was win one of the damn things and end up on a stage somewhere.

Here she could push herself, see if she truly did continue to hold the record.

Around her, partners bumped fists while others tossed barbs at their classmates.

Sasha leaned in close. "You know if we lag behind, you'll never live it down."

Brigitte narrowed her eyes. "You just move that skinny ass. I'll take care of mine."

A genuine laugh escaped Sasha's throat.

With one of Brigitte's instructors starting the race, a blank was fired in the air, and everyone took off running.

If there was a strategy to these kinds of things, it was to haul ass on the places you excelled to give yourself a little more time on the obstacles you struggled with. It was the team aspect of the race that held Sasha back. Speed and balance were her superpowers, with agility and strength as decent runners-up. Working a teammate up a wall, or more importantly, waiting for them to come around the bend, was a struggle.

Sasha hit the course hard and fast. Brigitte was with her, along with three other teams, each posturing for the first set of ropes.

She jumped high, tangled one leg around the thick rope, and pulled herself up the slippery length.

Making a point of not looking around, Sasha only took in the sounds of the others in the race. Someone slid down, cussing as he went, while the heavy breathing of others told her she wasn't alone.

Once at the top of the rope, she heaved one hand onto the mesh of ropes she needed to master and climb on top of in order to get back onto the ground.

While her body was taking the ropes with ease, already Sasha felt the burn on her palms. The calluses she'd developed while in school had faded. Gloves were never an option at Richter. But she could sure use them right now.

Once her feet were on the ground, thoughts of her hands disappeared as she sprinted toward the next hurdle, a series of three-and-a-half-foot walls with pits of water on the other side. The goal was to launch herself off the wall and to the other side of the water pit or risk the wetness slowing her down. She'd nearly made all five of them, but the wet ground tripped up her landing and one leg went into the water.

Sasha cussed her slip but didn't slow down.

Footsteps pounded around her, whose she didn't know. She hoped one was Brigitte, because the slippery wall was up next.

The wall sat at a steep angle with a mud pit at the bottom. There was no way to avoid it. Sasha sprinted toward the wall.

Brigitte yelled from only a few feet behind her. "I'm right behind you."

Sasha launched into the mud pit, each foot sledged through twice. She caught the first hand pull, found a solid spot to place her feet, and heaved up one more arm's length before reaching down for Brigitte.

The older woman slapped her hand up Sasha's forearm, and all her energy was spent pulling her up. It took both of them to get up the wall.

Two teams were right there with them, keeping pace.

At the top, the same mud that made it hard to get up the wall aided them in sliding down the other side.

And it was race time again. They crawled under barbwire and ate mud as they moved.

A long series of monkey bars strained every muscle and reminded Sasha she needed to spend more time on the face of a mountain. The rock climb, where if your partner was anywhere close, you gave them a hand.

Running in water, mud as it stood, since the rain was coming down in soft sheets.

Her muscles were screaming, heart pounding, and adrenaline washing through her with abandon. God, it felt good. The last obstacle was a vertical wall where a partner needed to give you a foothold and then grab you at the top. Then it was home free.

Sasha called behind her. "Brigitte?"

She heard footsteps but not a voice.

Sasha stopped at the wall, placed her back to it, and cupped her hands. If her partner was there, she'd jump right into them and climb up. Only Brigitte was several yards behind. Right on her heels was Claire. No sign of her partner.

Covered in mud, Brigitte stepped into Sasha's hands and hurled herself up. The woman had more upper body strength than Sasha and took little time giving her the lift she needed to get on top of the wall.

Claire was on them, turning in search of her partner.

Brigitte looked at the crowd of kids coming. "I don't see him."

"Damn it!" Claire yelled.

Sasha and Brigitte looked at each other, and both reached down at the same time. "C'mon."

Claire took a step back and jumped. They caught her arms and pulled her over.

Now the race really began.

Run the logs with a small guide rope for balance. A wall of tires, up one side and down the other, and if your arms hadn't given out on you, the last section was a vertical rope draped over water that you needed to hang on, hand over hand, foot over foot, to reach the other side.

Then the final sprint.

She hit the ground and rolled after the final challenge and came up on her feet. Covered in mud and drenched in excitement, Sasha took off.

There were others close by. She was pretty sure Claire and Brigitte were in the mix but wasn't about to look and find out. Not that she'd recognize anyone with just a glance at this point. With the finish line in view, Sasha pumped her arms harder, moved her legs faster. The second she crossed the line, the electronic scoreboard listed the names and times.

Sasha ran straight through the line, giving her body several yards to slow down.

Her breath came in pants, her chest sucked in every breath with serious effort. If she wasn't covered in mud, she'd be able to feel the sweat rolling off her, but the dirt kept that from happening. Around her, students were stopping, hands on knees, pats on backs.

She looked up, saw the finishing times.

She was nearly a minute and a half behind her best personal record. Not bad.

The name that beat her was Claire, by less than a second. She stood in the crowd, accepting the praise of her classmates.

Brigitte came in third.

Times pinged on the board as the last of the kids crossed the line.

Breathing hard, Brigitte walked up to Claire and patted the girl on the back. "You PR'd by twenty seconds."

She grinned ear to ear. "I'm stoked."

Brigitte then turned to Sasha. "And I'm a little pissed you beat me."

The class laughed.

Someone started clapping, a slow, steady noise.

Everyone turned toward the spectator.

A familiar tingle ran down Sasha's back.

Mr. Pohl stood under an umbrella, a long coat covering what Sasha assumed was a suit. His dress shoes took on a fair share of mud.

"Well done, Miss Budanov."

Her smile faded. "Thank you."

"You've obviously not lost your touch."

Brigitte walked past Sasha and stood in front of the man. "Mr. Pohl, how unexpected to see you out here."

"I thought it was in everyone's best interest that I stop in from time to time." The man looked past Brigitte and focused on Claire. "And who is this rising star?"

"A high school senior," Brigitte told him, not giving him an introduction. "She has a lot to learn."

Geoff Pohl smiled and returned his focus to Sasha. "I'll be in touch."

He walked away.

Claire moved in behind them. "Who was that?"

Brigitte turned around, her smile a little too bright, her eyes too wide. "No one you need to know. Now go hit the gym showers. No need to track this mud into the dorms." She lifted her voice. "Anyone with cuts, scrapes, or anything else, report to the nurse after you're clean. Well done, guys."

The kids slowly peeled away, leaving only Brigitte and Sasha.

"That was more fun than I remembered."

"You're a sadist, Sasha," Brigitte said with a laugh.

Sasha started to walk away.

"Hold up."

She paused.

"Geoff is here for you, isn't he?"

"Linette said he might have employment for me. Something to challenge me."

Brigitte's lips went in a straight line.

"You don't approve," Sasha said after several seconds of silence.

"It isn't for me to approve or disapprove." Their eyes finally met. "His *challenges* come with a stiff price, Sasha. Know exactly what you're saying yes to before you do." Without anything else, Brigitte left her standing in the drizzle.

Chapter Eight

AJ spent most of his first day researching the two names Sasha had given him online, Jocey Schuster and Olivia Naught. Both were women who had roomed with his sister at one time or another at Richter. The names rang distant bells in his head. Amelia must have mentioned them at some point, but when she was away in boarding school, he was channeling his best bad boy attitude and not paying a lot of attention to what she said on the rare occasions they saw each other.

It took some time, but he was able to follow Jocey all the way to Arizona, where he found mention of her getting married and acquiring a new last name. Now Jocey Miller, it appeared she was living a typical suburban life complete with at least one kid that put her name on a PTA president list in an upscale school district.

Olivia Naught, on the other hand, wasn't so easy to find. No Instagram, Facebook, Twitter . . . social media had plenty of matching names, but none that fit the right age. Olivia's family was just as elusive. He tried searches all over Scotland on the off chance the origin of her name meant she'd have ties there.

Nothing.

Like she didn't exist.

He checked everything from obituaries to marriage announcements. Nothing, nada . . . zilch.

AJ looked at the time, calculated the difference between Berlin and Los Angeles. Between him and the man Sasha called Reed.

AJ knew the minute she walked away that he would use her contact in the States. If for no other reason than to find out whom this Reed guy was. Was he a friend, colleague . . . family member? A benefited friend? AJ didn't see Sasha sleeping alone very often. Sex appeal dripped off her like water from a tornado-drenched roofline. She pulled off the blonde thing with the American accent like a West Coast girl, but the dark-haired mysterious European thing . . . yeah, that did so much more for his libido.

Not that she'd noticed.

AJ tapped his fingers against his phone a couple of times and then gave in to temptation.

A male voice answered on the second ring. "This is Reed."

"Ah, yeah. Hi. This is AJ. Sasha said I could call you."

"She did. Can you hold on just a second?"

"Sure."

Noise in the background lowered and the connection clicked a couple of times.

"I'm back."

"Is this a bad time?" AJ asked.

"No. I just needed to move so I could hear you better. So, you're AJ?"

"I am. I'm sure Sasha told you why I would call."

Reed laughed. "You don't know her very well, do you?"

"I'm sorry?" AJ wasn't sure he understood.

"Sasha told me nothing, just that she gave you my number and to help you out if you called."

"Seriously?"

"Yeah, Sasha doesn't elaborate. Ever. But if you wanna fill in the blanks, I'm listening."

AJ considered retelling the story about his sister but decided to keep things simple. "I'm not sure if you can help with this or not. Sasha gave me two names to research, Jocey Schuster and Olivia Naught. I found Jocey in Arizona using her degree from Richter playing PTA president at her kid's school. Olivia Naught, on the other hand, didn't seem to exist after she graduated."

"How old is this woman?" Reed asked.

"I'm not positive, but it's a safe bet to say she is between twenty-seven and twenty-nine. She graduated with my sister."

"From this school . . . Richter?"

"Yeah. Sasha's alma mater."

Reed was silent for a second.

"Where Sasha is staying right now. Did she tell you that?"

"She went back to school?" Reed asked.

"Visiting, I think. It's a boarding school. Safe to assume some of the teachers are like family after living there."

AJ heard Reed sigh. "Ahh, that makes perfect sense."

"I'm sorry?"

"Nothing. So, Sasha gave you two names to research, one is present and accounted for, this Olivia lady disappeared, and you wanna know if I can find anything on her?"

"Yeah. If you can do that kind of thing. I've been online for hours and nothing . . ."

"My computers are a little better than average. And what am I looking for, exactly?"

"Anything, everything." It was then that AJ realized that he had to add a little information to the why behind the names. "These women were roommates with my sister back at Richter. Along with Keri Shrum. Now Keri and my sister are dead, and I'm convinced there's a connection."

Reed blew out a breath. "I'm sorry about your sister."

"Thanks. I want answers, which is why I flew all the way here. Only the mouths at Richter are closed. Much like Sasha's, but she agreed to help me."

Another pause. "Why is that? Why did Sasha agree to help you?"

AJ shook his head. "I'm not sure. She said because she wasn't bored. As if I knew what that was supposed to mean."

Reed started to laugh.

"I take it you understand the woman."

He laughed harder. "Oh, God, no. I don't think anyone understands Sasha. But the not being bored part . . . I get that."

"Has Sasha told you about Richter?" AJ asked.

Before Reed opened his mouth, he realized his question was going to be met with a negative answer.

"No. Only what I read on a brochure."

"Why would you read a brochure on the school?" AJ asked.

"To learn more about Sasha."

It was AJ's turn to laugh. "Let me fill in a couple of blanks. Consider what a military boarding school would look like in post–Cold War Germany."

"They have them?"

"No. Not in the truest sense. But Richter filled a void when the wall came down and high-profile political families wanted safe places for their children to go to school. Add in a few troubled teens with rich parents, put in some basic survival skills and maybe some arms training, and you have Richter. Some kids leave after high school, some stay on for an accelerated college degree. They finish in three years what takes everyone else four."

"How does the word *military* fall into what you just described? Outside of weapons training."

AJ remembered how his sister would talk about her years at Richter, about the things she observed. "The doors are locked for all ages, from the youngest students to the oldest. Punishments that would land any American principal in jail for quite a long time."

"They're abusive?" Reed asked.

"Think of putting a kid on restriction like an inmate being put in solitary. If the rules the students broke were severe enough, a couple of days in the hole slapped them into shape."

"Jesus."

"Yeah, but according to what my sister told me, it worked. According to my parents, every parent knew what they were getting their kids into."

"Why would anyone . . . ?"

"To make their kids street-smart. To keep them alive when the world might want them otherwise," AJ said.

"So locks and security kept the kids in and the bad guys out. And now that you want answers on Richter, no one there will talk to you."

"You got it."

"Give me twenty-four hours."

The tension in AJ's neck started to ease. "Can I ask a question?"

"Of course."

AJ had a hard time wording what he wanted to ask, so instead he started to ramble. "Sasha is very cloak-and-dagger, and a little badass."

"She defines *badass*," Reed chuckled.

"Yeah. Okay. I can see how she might know her way around finding people and such. What makes you qualified?"

"I'm in security. I still dabble in private investigating. And I was a detective with the police force."

AJ blinked a few times. *I'm talking to a cop.* "Overqualified."

"Be sure and tell my wife that if you ever meet her."

AJ's smile beamed. "Your wife?"

"Yeah, do you have one of those?"

"A wife?"

"Yes."

"No."

Another pause on the line.

"Are you still there?"

"Yup. Just taking down a few notes. I'll get in touch with you tomorrow at this time."

"Thanks, Reed."

"You can thank Sasha. I'm doing this for her."

AJ ended the call feeling a lot more accomplished than before he'd picked up the phone.

Reed knew what he was doing, was going to help . . . and he was a married man.

And a cop.

Ex-cop. AJ glanced at his cell phone, happy he made a habit out of never bringing one along when he got his adrenaline rush. The last thing he wanted was to find Amelia's killer and end up in jail for his own crimes.

Although if it could bring his sister back, he'd walk into the police station without a lawyer.

But that wasn't going to happen.

AJ decided the night needed to end with a beer.

∾

"For a woman in such great shape, you sure spend a lot of time in the library." Claire sat across from Sasha, much like she had the day they'd met.

And like the day they met, Sasha had her nose in a yearbook.

"Don't you have class?"

Claire grinned. "It's Saturday, and since Checkpoint Charlie won't give me a pass, I'm stuck here."

Sasha remembered those days well. "Let me guess, no family to come and get you."

"I'm gifted a week in the summer and Christmas with a host family. Just like you did when you were here." Claire looked her directly in the eye.

"You've been doing some research."

"I asked Charlie."

"He's a good source of information. You're right. I was stuck here, too. I made the most of it, as I'm sure you do."

"It gets old. There isn't a day I don't think about living on the outside. I already have all the credits I need to graduate. I could leave." Claire looked around the room.

"Why don't you?"

The girl shivered and lost her smile. "You'll think I'm weak if I tell you."

"You beat me on the obstacle course. I will never label you as weak."

Claire kept silent, as if contemplating whether or not to answer Sasha's question. "I know no one outside this school. Host families don't count. They do it because they're paid. If I leave with only my high school degree, what's that going to do for me? I can't go out and explore life and then come back after a year to finish college."

"Richter doesn't work that way."

"I know. And my benefactor made it clear that I had to stay all the way through to keep their support. But now that I'm eighteen, it's up to me."

Sasha's and Claire's situations at that age were nearly identical.

"Do you know who your benefactor is?"

Claire shook her head.

"Mine was a woman who was once married to my biological father. He was a disgusting human who murdered my mother. My benefactor kept me here to keep me safe."

Claire looked at her again. "Then you have family . . . kinda."

Sasha shook her head. "They're both dead."

"Oh."

"So that's why you're back. You don't have anyone." Claire released a sad breath. "Jesus, I'm looking at my future. I'm never going to have a life outside these walls."

Sasha clicked her tongue. "There's a lot of life away from here. You never know who you'll meet or what job you'll take."

Claire leaned forward, her jaw tight. "But do you still spend Christmas alone? Do you end up with some generic sweater that you'll never wear because you haven't worn a sweater since you were ten? Do you have a name to put on your emergency contact list or do you just leave it blank since no one cares if you're alive or dead?"

"Someone cares that you're alive or you'd be on the street with all the other orphans." Everything else the girl said was painfully accurate.

"Lotta good that does me if I don't know who they are. It's probably guilt money, anyway. Seems to be what everyone else around here is all about." Claire pushed away from the table and stood. "Whatever. Thanks for the look in the crystal ball. At least I know I'll have good taste in clothes."

Sasha watched her walk away.

Chapter Nine

The phone rang.

It was early . . . way too early after one too many beers the night before.

AJ flopped his hand to the bedside table and found his phone. "Yeah," he said.

"Alex Hofmann Junior."

It was too early for a quiz. "Who's asking?"

"Not asking. It's Reed."

That's all it took to wake AJ and bring his head off the pillow. "Did . . . did you find something?"

"I always find something. Are you still in bed? Isn't it nine there?"

AJ glanced at the clock by the bed. "Eight fifty. What did you find?"

"Olivia *Mc*Naught. And guess what?"

"Too early for games."

Was the connection bad, or did Reed chuckle? "She's in Berlin."

Rubbing the sleep from his eyes with a full palm, AJ said, "You're kidding."

"Nope. I have an address. Do you have a pen?"

"Yeah . . . hold on." He jumped from the bed, the cool air in the room hitting every bare part of him as he searched the hotel room for a pen and a piece of paper. "Go," he said after getting back on the phone.

AJ scribbled the address Reed rattled off.

"I only found an address. Nothing about work, a family. From what I can tell, she bought the apartment right after she graduated."

"Are you sure it's the same person? McNaught isn't the name my sister mentioned."

"Maybe Naught was an alias at Richter or McNaught is now."

AJ rubbed the stubble on his jaw. "Only one way to find out."

"I'll keep digging around, see if I can find anything else."

"I appreciate it."

"Oh, and, AJ?"

"Yeah?"

"Try not to steal anything."

AJ swallowed, fully awake now. "Excuse me?"

"Juvenile record. Sealed but not forgotten. PI, detective . . . remember?"

The air left AJ's lungs.

"Ah-huh. You know what I've found to be an absolute truth in my line of work?" Reed asked.

"No, but I have a feeling you're going to tell me."

"That people who let's say . . . take cars that don't belong to them when they're a teenager and get away with it, go on to do the same thing as an adult."

"I didn't get away with it. I was caught."

"But not punished. Which is the same thing. I did a little poking around. I can't help but wonder if maybe someone, somewhere, might think you took something from them. And perhaps, and I'm just tossing stuff out there, perhaps this all links back to you. Hypothetically speaking."

AJ sat taller, stiffened his jaw. "I can see how you might come to that conclusion, if there were someone out there who is missing something in their life and is blaming me. However, and I think a man with your background and expertise has already concluded this, killing my sister fits in your little hypothetical situation, but a school-age friend makes no sense at all. Which is why I have an address in my hands and a house call to make."

Silence.

"Yeah, that's kinda what I was thinking. But, AJ?"

"What?"

"Any new information that might change my thoughts comes up, you have my number. Sasha is family to me. We help out the good guys."

"Robin Hood was celebrated."

"Ha! I'll be sure and keep looking for the charities you support," Reed laughed.

"My halo may be a little rusty, but it's still there. I'll keep you better informed."

"I'm glad we had this talk," Reed said before hanging up.

Thirty minutes later AJ was following the map on his phone to a high-rise condominium complex that was situated far outside the city center. There were plenty of places in Berlin where graffiti littered every wall, but here, Turkish immigrants had taken up several corners on the streets, begging for handouts. AJ wouldn't say the neighborhood Miss McNaught chose was one he would have picked.

AJ pulled the collar up on his coat and rubbed his gloved hands together. Fall was definitely starting to add a bite to the air. He sized up the outside of the building from the sidewalk across the street. Industrial in its function, contemporary in its architecture. This was once East Berlin, and it showed in the lack of character and homogenized look.

The front door to the complex had a massive iron gate, as did most of the windows on the first two floors.

Dodging traffic, AJ jogged across the street and looked at the address he'd written down.

#625.

He looked at the long list of names.

#625 didn't have Olivia's name, or anyone else's, next to the number. AJ pressed the buzzer and waited. People walked by on the street.

No answer.

He pressed it again, gave it a longer ring . . .

Still nothing.

"Fuck it." He pressed several numbers all at once. The door buzzed open at the same time the PA crackled random voices saying hello.

AJ pushed the door open and said, "Sorry, mate. Pressed the wrong flat."

He took the stairs and started to climb. Once on the sixth floor, he exited the stairwell and made his way down the long, narrow hall.

The inside of the building was nicer than the exterior. Here the halls were clean, the walls freshly painted. Still not a place he would call home.

He knocked when he reached her door.

Nothing.

The back of his neck itched, like something just didn't seem right. Why would a new grad buy a flat on this side of town, change her name . . . or change it back, and have no trackable job or source of income? Oh, and no name on her flat number on the ground floor? Yeah, that felt off.

AJ took a quick look around, didn't see any security cameras in the hallway or any neighbors peeking out.

Still he ducked his head into his coat a little deeper and removed two long, needle-like prongs from his back pocket. He glanced at his gloves and smiled. He hadn't intended to need to hide his fingerprints from anyone when he'd left the hotel . . . yet here he was.

He briefly wondered what getting caught breaking and entering would get an American citizen in Germany.

When the lock clicked and the handle easily turned, he realized he was already guilty.

He moved slowly into the quiet apartment and closed the door behind him.

The place was practically empty. White walls and only the basics of furniture. A gray sofa, a glass coffee table, two white iron stools at a kitchen counter. There wasn't a single dish on the counter or seasonings by the stove.

Impeccably clean.

Not a speck of dust.

AJ wanted to probe more, but he first wanted to make sure he wasn't going to surprise a sleeping woman.

He tiptoed down the hall, pushed open the door to the bathroom, and then moved to the next door. He sighed. The bed was made and empty. "What the hell?" He opened the closet door, sure he would find it bare.

It wasn't.

Women's clothes hung on hangers, neatly spaced. Three pairs of shoes lined the floor of the closet. He bent down and picked one up, looked at the bottom. A dusting of scuff marks said they'd been worn.

He put it back and started opening drawers.

He found women's lingerie, but not an abundance of it. One neatly folded up pair of blue jeans and two T-shirts that looked like they could have been purchased at the corner from a street vendor. Everything was too perfect and too sparse. AJ searched for a hamper, dirty clothes . . . didn't find either.

The bathroom had a few cosmetics and shampoo in the shower, but the towels didn't look like they'd been used. There wasn't one TV or cord hanging from an outlet to charge a phone. No pictures.

Olivia McNaught might own the place, but she didn't live there.

AJ backed out of the flat and locked the door before he closed it behind him. A quick search of the hall and he made his way back to the stairs. His years of not playing by all the rules kicked in and he took the stairs to the roof, not the sidewalk.

The buildings were like brownstones, all pushed together. Using the rooftops as his own walkway, AJ jumped over several buildings until he found a door to the stairs open. Five minutes later he was walking away with his phone to his ear, adrenaline coursing through his veins.

Reed didn't answer his phone, so AJ left a message.

"The address you gave me might be owned by the woman we spoke of, but she doesn't spend any time there. Maybe her old roommate in Arizona will have some insight. I'd be grateful if you could find a phone number for me. Thanks."

⟶

"I don't think I can do it, Jax." Claire stared up at the ceiling, counting the same hundred and sixty dots in the tile she'd counted a zillion times.

"It isn't that bad." Her best friend sat on the edge of her bed, her Richter uniform rumpled from being tossed in a pile and swept under the bed before inspections.

"Easy for you to say, you get out once in a while. This place is like a prison, and now that I'm eighteen, I have the key and I'm not using it."

"What about college? How are you going to afford that on the outside? It's only three more years."

Claire stuck out her tongue and made gagging noises.

"If you go, I go."

"You're not eighteen until next August."

"But I graduate in June. I can convince my parents to send me somewhere else. I'll get on the outside, take my tuition money, and you and I can get a flat somewhere. Experience life."

"If they say no?" Claire asked.

"Then you'll just have to find a place for us. We can keep in touch, Loki."

Claire leaned her head on her friend's shoulder. "Okay, Yoda."

"We're going to be fine. Language tutor . . . something."

She gave her friend a fist bump and then flopped back on her bed.

⟨❀⟩

Sasha caught up with Linette walking through the administration hall. "Do you have a minute?"

Linette turned, her serious expression softened slightly. "For you? Of course."

Sasha took the space beside her and they continued down the hall. "Thank you again for letting me stay here."

"I hope it's been helpful," Linette said.

"It has been. I saw Mr. Pohl down in the shooting range, watching me."

Linette lifted her chin. "It's his way of interviewing you."

"For what, exactly?"

The headmistress was silent as they walked. "I couldn't tell you. He works in highly classified areas of the government."

"Which government?"

"Many."

"Doing what? Security? Surveillance?" Sasha asked.

They walked through the administration office doors and went straight to her office. Once there, Linette removed her robe and placed it on a hanger, hung it on a coat rack, and moved behind her desk. "I would assume that those skills are part of what he needs."

"You would know the people he has hired from Richter in the past. People I might talk to in order to determine if I want to take any job he might offer . . ."

"I do." She folded her hands together and rested them on her desk.

"You're not going to tell me."

"Classified, Sasha. If you choose to take a job with Geoff, then your name will also be one I don't tell others. It's for everyone's safety."

"That's fair." Cryptic, but fair.

"You seem more settled since you first came back," Linette told her.

"I feel more centered. Returning has helped me more than I expected."

"I'm glad. And if Geoff feels you don't fit, or you don't want the job . . . I wouldn't be opposed to a situation where you work here with us."

Sasha knew her jaw dropped. "Oh, I never considered . . ."

"I can't imagine you would have. Think about it."

A knock on the door interrupted them.

"Sorry to disturb you," Linette's assistant said with a shy smile. "There's a call for Miss Budanov."

Sasha's stomach twisted. The only people who knew she was there were those at the school . . . and AJ.

"It's a Mr. Reed, he said it was important?"

Sasha attempted to keep any emotion from showing on her face. "Thank you." She started to walk out of the room.

"I hope everything is okay," Linette said from her desk.

"I'm sure it's fine. His wife is expecting twins."

"How lovely," Linette uttered.

Sasha picked up the phone at an unoccupied desk. "Hello?"

"Sorry to bother you, darling." Reed's voice was elevated.

Darling?

"Are you a father yet?"

"No, no . . . but I wanted your opinion on names."

"And it couldn't wait . . ."

"Babies come whenever they want. So, we were thinking, Olivia and Jocey, if they're both girls. Or Alex and Blake if they're boys."

The familiar names kept Sasha's expression natural. Obviously, there was something Reed needed to tell her and didn't want anyone who might be listening to understand. "All solid names. Why do you need my advice?" Sasha noticed Linette's secretary smiling.

"You know my friend Neil? He tells me every Olivia he ever knew disappeared after the first date, no call, no forwarding number. But we really like the name. And Jocey . . . Lori loves it, but my sister's best friend in school was a Jocey, and she was pretty messed up, eventually killed herself. It was awful."

The air in Sasha's chest caught. Jocey was dead?

AJ was onto something.

"I think you skip both names. Too much baggage." She glanced at the clock on the wall. Almost five. She needed to touch base with Alex and get him to stop poking around until she could regroup and devise a plan.

"What about Alex?" Reed asked, keeping with the baby name ploy.

"Everyone I ever knew by that name was overly inquisitive. Always getting in trouble."

"Now that you mention it. We should scratch that. We both like Blake. It's a safe name. No baggage. I knew a Blake once . . . ended up in finance, made a shit ton of money. Had houses all over the world last time I heard."

As close as London, if Sasha remembered correctly. Blake Harrison could provide safe harbor for Alex until they could figure out what the hell was going on.

"It sounds like you need to go back to the baby books."

"I'll do that."

Sasha noticed Linette's office door open. "Next time, call my cell."

"I tried. It told me you were out of a service area."

"I'll look into it. Take care of your wife."

"Take care of you. Thanks for the advice."

She hung up.

"Is your friend a father?"

Sasha grinned. "No, he's a nervous mess. He thinks because I've been all over the world that I have more access to names."

"I suppose you do."

Sasha hesitated. "My phone isn't picking up calls. Is there a dead zone here?" They weren't allowed to have cell phones when she was a student. But her phone had worked fine when she first arrived.

Linette released a sigh and offered an apologetic smile. "Rolling blackouts. In case the students have managed to sneak something in. Social media will be the death of every student's opportunity to obtain a decent job after graduation. The system catches new IP addresses sending signals and blocks them unless we have them on file. I should have said something when you arrived. You can give your phone to tech and they will free it up for you."

Not in this lifetime. "I'll do that."

Chapter Ten

Reed tapped his foot against the side of his desk with the phone against his ear. The phone line did a double ring, indicating the call was going overseas. The top of his desk was covered in papers, printouts of newspaper articles covering the limited details of Amelia Hofmann's death. A female jogger simply killed by three precision shots from a considerable distance. Two to the chest, one to the head. Her earbuds were still connected with the aux cable when they found her body.

Amelia had been an analyst for the UN. Working on clean water rights nationally and internationally. From the description of her job title, she worked with a team in South Africa. From what he could tell, the woman sat at a desk analyzing data on pollutants, rainfall averages, population, and evaporation. It sounded boring as hell. And nothing worth being killed over.

Except now there were three dead women.

Jocey Schuster-Miller, the PTA mother of two, parked in a remote area and ate a bullet. Only there was no suicide note and no history of buying the gun found in her car. There was some evidence of a struggle, so the investigation was open.

Keri Shrum's boyfriend was accused of shooting out the tires of her car on a wet road in Wales, which resulted in her car going off a cliff. His slippery alibi and the lack of any physical evidence kept him from trial. While the case was still open, it appeared the police were trying to find more on the boyfriend and weren't looking anywhere else.

All of these women went to the same school, only a year apart from each other.

If there was one rule Reed lived by, it was that there were no coincidences in life.

Since these women all died a world apart from each other, no one connected the dots.

Until AJ.

But then again, for AJ, it was personal.

Reed was about to hang up the phone when AJ finally picked up.

"Hello."

"AJ. It's Reed."

"You got my message."

"I did. We have a change of plans. There's an estate just outside of London I need you to go to."

"London? Why? Did you find Olivia?"

Reed clicked on the surveillance cameras at Blake's estate. The only activity was the staff mulling about, doing what they did. Blake, his wife, Samantha, and their children were in their Malibu home.

"No. I haven't located Olivia, yet. You'll be safe in the UK."

AJ was silent. "As opposed to my safety now?"

Reed didn't answer. "Sasha will meet you there in a couple of days, tops."

"You found something. What is it?"

"Another dead woman. The one in Arizona."

"Jesus . . . I knew I wasn't crazy."

Reed told AJ the address and offered to make travel arrangements.

"What am I supposed to do in London? Sit around and wait?"

"Sasha works better alone. You'd just get in her way."

AJ laughed. "Yeah, but Amelia wasn't her sister. I'm not leaving without Sasha. I don't know what kind of crap we're uncovering here, but if there is a theme, it's that Richter alumni are turning up dead like fish in bad water. Last I looked, Sasha is a possible target."

"She is highly skilled to take care of herself." Something Reed had seen firsthand on more than one occasion.

"News flash . . . so were the other three dead women. Yet their hearts aren't beating any longer, are they?"

AJ had a point.

Reed's foot bounced, making his knee move with it. Lori was two and a half weeks from her delivery date; there was no way he was leaving her side.

"Where are you staying?" Reed asked.

"Hilton, smack in downtown."

"Okay. Sasha will probably contact you before she can talk to me without raising suspicion. When you talk to her, let her know the other name she asked me to look up came up clean. Perhaps a little too clean."

"Who is it?"

"I'll let Sasha tell you if you need to know."

"A suspect?"

"I don't know. She just asked me to look him up."

"Did she suggest they are related?"

"No, in fact it sounded the opposite when we talked."

"I don't like any of this, Reed."

Neither did he. "You text me, every six hours. Set your alarm if you have to." Reed wrote down the time he should hear from AJ next. "We need more names."

∽୨

Sasha stepped into Brigitte's home and was knocked back by all the vibrant colors. Floral motifs on sideboards, potted plants . . . even the print on the sofa was a soft white with a light green pattern. When Brigitte had suggested they have dinner away from Richter, Sasha jumped at the excuse to leave the grounds and make a couple of calls without any chance of eavesdropping.

"This is not what I expected to see," Sasha said out loud.

Brigitte dropped her car key on the foyer table and shed her coat as she made her way to the kitchen. "Make yourself at home."

Sasha looked around. "I'm not sure I can," she whispered to herself. *Floral* and *feminine* were not words that described her personality.

"I heard that."

Sasha followed her into the kitchen.

"How about a glass of wine?"

Not her thing, but she'd drink it. "Thank you." She sat at the counter and watched Brigitte walk around the small space. "What prompted the dinner invite?"

The woman didn't meet her gaze. "I thought it would be nice."

Sasha narrowed her eyes.

"And Linette suggested it. The woman isn't social, but she likes to have information that one can obtain by a simple conversation over dinner."

Sasha leaned back. "You have me here to ask questions?"

"That's what Linette thinks." Brigitte removed a bottle from a wine rack and proceeded to work at the cork.

"She can ask me anything," Sasha said.

"But as your former headmistress, will you be truthful in your answers? Old habits die hard."

Brigitte tilted the bottle and wine rushed into a glass. She handed one to Sasha and poured one for herself.

She took a taste, didn't exactly hate it, and drank a little more. "So, what does Linette want to know?"

Brigitte removed chicken from her fridge and an armload of vegetables. "She asked about your friend who called today. Wanted to know if you had fostered any deep friendships since you left Richter."

"Why would she want to know that?"

Brigitte floated around her kitchen, removed the chicken from its wrapper, and proceeded to season it while she talked.

"She assumed you hadn't. At least that's my theory. Then the call today made her think again. You don't have to tell me anything. And I don't have to tell Linette, if you prefer I don't."

Sasha sipped her wine again, thought about Reed and his wife. The men Reed worked with, and on occasion she did, too.

She thought of Trina, the sister-in-law through her lost brother. Trina was now married to a country singer and living her life in Texas.

"These are the kinds of things Mr. Pohl is going to ask you when you meet with him again."

"Why would he care?"

Brigitte stopped her busy hands. "Because spies don't have families. If they did, it would be a weakness."

"And that's what Pohl is recruiting? Spies?"

Her hostess turned on the oven and placed the chicken inside. "Every year I see our graduates line up, and I can pick out the students Pohl will approach. On a rare occasion, we'd have a graduating class that didn't have the profile of students he wanted. I would imagine that some of the kids didn't want the job."

"You make it sound like he's recruiting several every year."

She moved on to the vegetables and started to make a salad. "Linette has those numbers. Not me. I do know that the last ten years, you're the only student in that profile who has returned to Richter."

"I was never offered a position."

"That's going to change. Pohl has asked every instructor at the school to report to him after you've left the room." Brigitte leaned a hip against the counter, took her wineglass in her hand. "You're conditioned to do the kind of job he will offer, Sasha, but you might ask yourself if it's how you want to spend your entire life."

"You're warning me away from the idea."

Brigitte shrugged, returned to her task of salad making. "Yeah. I am. I despise that the man comes into the school and handpicks the most emotionally vulnerable students we have."

Sasha felt her hair rise. "I am not *emotionally vulnerable*."

"Ha. You're an orphan. No family at all. You returned to Richter because of those facts. I'm going to guess that your personal relationships consist of a good fuck and off you go." Brigitte looked her in the eye. "Am I missing anything?"

Sasha didn't deny her.

"That's what I thought. All fine and well, but what about when you want to let someone in? A good friend, or a lover that wants more? Living alone your whole life is overrated." She spread her arms wide. "Take it from me. Work and vacationing alone is no way to live."

"Richter doesn't stop you from having a family."

"No. My lifestyle has made that harder than it could be. But unlike what the religious conservatives out there think, being a lesbian isn't a choice."

Sasha considered the people she did have in her life, as distant as she kept them, and realized that she wouldn't want to cut them out for a job she didn't financially need. What if Reed needed her help, or Trina found trouble with one of her famous husband's fans?

"So I tell Pohl I'm not interested."

Brigitte bit off a piece of a baby carrot. "He isn't used to rejection."

"He can't make me take a job."

Brigitte's smile met with Sasha's. She served up the salad in two bowls and handed one to her. "Be sure and tell him that."

Sasha took her salad and wine and moved to the table Brigitte had in the dining room. It was her turn to ask a few questions. "I've been trying to find a few of my classmates and haven't been having a lot of luck. Linette had alluded to the fact that some of our alumni went on to highly secretive jobs, which would account for some."

"Those that were like you. Apt in all the physical challenges Richter put you through as well as those computer skills you so effectively used while attending the school." Brigitte was grinning.

Sasha played with her salad. "What if I told you I found an unusual amount of students who have died?"

Brigitte lost her smile. "If they worked for people like Pohl, I wouldn't be surprised."

Double agents, spies in general . . . that made sense.

"And if they didn't?"

Brigitte set her fork down. "How many are we talking?"

"Three that I've found so far."

Brigitte shook her head. "Linette has a great way of closing off if she feels her security is threatened. Anything that happens outside the walls of Richter is not something she's interested in. An investigation would lead to all kinds of trouble."

"If people are dying—"

"I'm not saying it's right. Just that it is. This is why you're poring over the yearbooks."

Sasha pressed her fork into her salad, brought it up to her mouth. "It started out searching for memories. Trying to recapture some of the fire you have when you're young and stupid enough to believe anything is possible."

"And you stumbled upon something else entirely."

"I did. I'm not a big believer in coincidence. Although these deaths may be unrelated."

"Your gut says otherwise."

Sasha nodded. "It does."

"I don't know anyone more qualified to find a connection than you."

Sasha took a bite, swallowed it down with the wine. "Wouldn't Linette be telling you to stop me from looking?"

"Maybe. I'm not her."

Which was a big reason why Sasha trusted Brigitte with the basic facts she'd found out.

⁓

An hour later she was astride her motorcycle and buzzing back to Richter. A few miles away, she stopped at a fuel station and called AJ.

"About damn time you called."

It wasn't often she was cussed at over the phone. "How do you like the Harrison estate?"

"I wouldn't know. I'm in the Hilton in Berlin."

Sasha topped off the gas and returned the nozzle to its holding space. "Didn't Reed contact you?"

"I don't take orders, Sasha."

She glanced around the deserted gas station. "I'm working on intel. I need you to keep low. London is perfect—"

"When you leave, I'll go with you to London. Otherwise I'm here."

"Why are you being difficult?" He wasn't safe in Germany. She didn't know what bugged the shit out of her more . . . the fact he wasn't taking orders or the fact that she cared for his safety.

"I'm not leaving now that I know I'm right. I'm not walking away." His defiance wasn't expected.

"We don't know you're—"

"Listen, sweetheart—"

Sweetheart? "I bust noses for that comment."

"Do you like *Sex on a Stick* better?"

She glanced down at her black pants, her leather jacket. A slight smile helped ease the tension in her neck.

Yeah, she did.

"Fine. Stay in Berlin, but don't go around asking questions. Use secure networks. I have names for you. Do you have a pen?"

"Go for it."

She told him half a dozen more names she'd found in the yearbooks and encouraged him to notify Reed.

"I don't like the idea of you being at that school, poking around," he told her.

"There isn't a safer school in a first world country."

"Richter alumni are turning up dead," he said, as if he cared for her well-being.

"Do I give you the impression I can't take care of myself?"

"You give me the impression that you trust too easily behind those walls. When I confronted Lodovica, I had the distinct feeling she was hiding something."

"She's protecting the school," Sasha defended the woman, half-heartedly.

"A little too passionately, if you ask me. What's in it for her? Wouldn't a normal dean of a school want to know if their students were being targeted even after they left?" His logic pissed her off.

"Richter is different. You know that. Now spend your energy looking up those names. Let me handle the school." Sasha straddled her bike.

"Fine. Wait. Reed wanted me to tell you that the other name you gave him came up unremarkable. Businessman."

Great, now what?

"You there?"

"Yeah. I gotta go."

"Who was Reed talking about?"

"No one."

"You're lying."

"You're smart, *sweetheart*." The last thing she was going to do was tell AJ Geoff's name. "It's unrelated to your sister."

AJ sighed, his voice softened. "Watch your back."

She hesitated. "I always do."

She hung up and kicked over the bike.

Chapter Eleven

Instead of using her all-access bracelet to wander around the school after everyone else had gone to bed, Sasha went about it the old-fashioned way.

The security system had been given a few more cameras since she graduated, but working around it proved just as easy for her now as it had then.

The college dorms would be the first place the faculty would have looked when it came to finding contraband.

Which was why the high school seniors and college age students preferred to use the primary students' building. The younger kids could sleep through anything and most often went to bed much earlier than anyone else on campus.

Sasha stood the risk of running into students, but the need was worth the gamble.

Each graduating class made a point of providing new tech to the incoming senior class, ensuring that the technology was current and wouldn't be outdone by whatever Linette and her security team could come up with.

All Sasha needed to do was find the room the seniors were using and tap into their computer.

The basement was a bust. The attic equally deserted.

A storage room over the laundry facilities had been converted into a series of closets.

Where the hell was it?

Sasha passed from building to building in search of some clue. She stared up at the college dorms. "Least expected it."

She glanced at the administration building, the adjacent onsite housing.

The sound of a stick breaking behind her made her freeze.

"Are you lost?"

Sasha's sigh was pure relief. "Claire."

"You're out late."

They looked at each other through the light of the moon. They were both dressed in black, their hair tied back. "The same can be said for you."

"Nothing good happens after midnight."

Sasha kept her voice low. "I'm not sure about that. Some of my best memories of this place happened when everyone else went to bed."

Claire regarded her for a moment. "It's the only time we have complete privacy."

"Is that why you're out now? Privacy?"

She shook her head. "No. I've been following you."

Sasha had her doubts about that. She was better at noticing someone lingering nearby.

"They stopped using the kiddie building three years ago. That's what you're looking for, isn't it? The computer room?"

Sasha stayed silent.

Claire turned on her heel and led her to the back of the administration building. They pressed against the building and out of the line of sight of the motion detector lights that would pop on if they were spotted.

Using some kind of electronic key fob, Claire opened a back door without setting off any alarms.

They moved quietly to a stairway that led to the basement. A place Sasha couldn't say she'd ever been in. After passing through two doors and securing both of them, Claire finally spoke. "This was a boiler room before they retrofitted the building with central heating and air. I'm surprised your class never found it."

"We never needed to."

Claire grinned. "We have two decoy rooms with old computers on campus. We know the staff is always looking."

Sasha smiled. "Good thing I'm not staff."

They passed through a third door and Claire turned on the lights. Two massive monitors filled one wall. The newest version of an Apple computer sat center stage.

Sasha rubbed her hands together and sat behind the desk.

"Why do you need this one anyway? You have access to the outside world," Claire said as she leaned against a table.

Sasha turned on the mainframe and typed a file name into the computer search. "Because what I want doesn't exist outside. I'm just hoping all the previous data wasn't lost through the years."

And from what was popping up on the screen . . . the senior class hadn't failed her.

Claire pulled a chair beside her and looked at the monitors. "What is all that?"

"Code."

"Yeah, I guessed that, but for what?"

The adult in Sasha battled with the former student. "Audio recording."

"Like a bug?"

Sasha clicked into the feed into Linette's office. "Kinda. Only it's not through anything placed in the office but rather . . ." She typed in a password and turned up the volume for the computer speakers.

Nothing.

"Do you have the new administration Wi-Fi passwords?" she asked Claire.

"Are you asking if I have obtained the off-limits codes that could land me in solitary if I'm caught with them?"

Sasha leveled her eyes, lifted one manicured eyebrow.

"Uppercase *x*, three, eight, lowercase *z*, hashtag, zero, uppercase *o*, the *at* sign, five."

Sasha typed in the password.

"But rather what?" Claire asked.

A slight hum in the line . . . and the sound of a clock ticking. Sasha looked around the boiler room to make sure there wasn't a clock there that was picking up the sound. "The office itself . . ."

She pulled up another window, one that would record.

"I don't understand."

"Every computer has the ability to hear you, even if you don't turn on the microphone. The technology is there. I devised a system to record once voices are heard. As long as the computer is turned on, I can hear what's going on in the office."

"That sounds a lot more sophisticated than you make it out to be."

"It is. The firewalls keep me from gathering this information remotely. It only works while on campus." Which was something she wanted to work on. Her days at Richter were coming to an end, but the information she needed access to was more than a simple conversation. What she needed was alumni names. And not just the ones found in the yearbooks.

Those could be changed.

Along with their birthdays and biological parents . . . apparently.

Sasha never used her . . . *less than legal* hacking skills at Richter for anything other than adolescent pranks.

Changing grades and obtaining tests before they were given was never a goal.

Embarrass the staff, make a name for herself . . . those had been her objectives.

What Sasha needed was a couple of hours.

"That's how you recorded Professor Neumann doing Nurse Palmer in the science lab," Claire said with sly laugh.

"I cannot confirm or deny that claim," Sasha offered. Even though the memory of the day she'd replayed that audio during the equivalent of a fire drill, for the entire campus to hear, made her glow on the inside. Linette had no choice but to cut the entire PA system off and end the drill. When they managed to trace the recording, they found it on Neumann's computer. Placing it on Nurse Palmer's would have been a gamble. The woman didn't always leave her computer on. Neumann, on the other hand, didn't turn his off.

He did after that day.

In fact, Linette had changed policy and mandated that all office computers be turned off during fire drill days to avoid a repeat.

Sasha had never been caught.

"Are you going to tell me why you want to hear what's going on in the headmistress's office?" Claire asked.

Sasha settled in and started to hack at Linette's firewalls. "What do you think about Mr. Pohl?"

"The creepazoid that follows you around?"

Good definition. "Yeah, him."

"He makes me itch."

Sasha sat back while the computer ran through a few million numbers. "I break out when I see him, too. I'm not sure Linette knows the man she invited to recruit here."

"So why hack into her office?"

"Because that is the only place I can. And since I'm meeting with him tomorrow, in her office, I wanted to hear any conversation that might be said before, or after, I'm there."

"You don't trust her."

Sasha shook her head. "I don't trust him."

"I heard he's here to decide if he wants to hire you for some kinda spy job."

She paused. "Who said that?"

"Students. Last year he offered one of the high school seniors on my floor a job. Denenberg was pissed."

"Really?"

"Yeah. Rumor has it that he only is allowed to recruit college grads. Since Denenberg got in his face after our race the other day, I'm guessing that rumor holds some truth."

Sasha typed in another command, sat back. "Recruiting an eighteen-year-old for that kind of a job should be illegal. Denenberg was right to be angry."

"I don't think twenty-one- or twenty-two year-olds are a whole lot different. Especially when they've spent most of their life behind these walls."

"Yet the lure is there, isn't it?" Sasha asked. "Especially for the long-term students of Richter . . ."

"Like you and I," Claire said.

Brigitte's conversation earlier that night rolled around in Sasha's head. Pohl hired the emotionally vulnerable, yet talented in all the *crime-worthy* skills.

"Yeah. Like us."

⁓

Instead of showing up early and sitting outside Linette's office like a student preparing for a lecture, Sasha waited until the last second to walk through the administration doors and up to Linette's assistant.

The assistant smiled the second she noticed her and pushed to her feet. "They're expecting you."

Sasha walked into Linette's office, shoulders back, chin up . . . confident.

Mr. Pohl sat across from Linette and stood when Sasha entered the room.

"Good morning, Sasha," Linette greeted her with a smile. That alone was a little off-putting.

"Miss Budanov." Pohl reached out a hand, which she accepted . . . then he leaned in for the *way*-too-familiar double kiss to the sides of her cheeks.

Claire's description of the man, *creepazoid*, surfaced.

All the pleasantries that Sasha was desperately bad at mulled around in her head. *Thank you for having me. I appreciate your time* . . . none rang true. She settled for "Good morning."

She watched for any sign that the two of them knew they were being recorded. From this angle, she couldn't tell if Linette's computer was on.

"Linette tells me that you've been enjoying your sabbatical here."

"Richter was my home for many years."

"Longer than the average student," Pohl said.

Obviously he knew her history with the school. Sasha wasn't about to waste time with a meaningless amount of chitchat. "Tell me, Mr. Pohl . . . have I maintained my level of expertise, in all areas, enough to know what kind of job you have to offer?"

Linette let out a single huff that passed as laughter. "I told you she wouldn't waste your time with small talk," she told Pohl.

He wove his fingers together and rested them in his lap. "As a matter of fact, you have." He then looked at Linette and nodded toward the door.

"This is where I leave." She pushed her chair back, reached for her robe. "I'll see you both later."

Sasha didn't question her leaving, just followed her with her gaze as she did.

When the door closed behind her, Pohl stood, smoothed his dress coat, and tugged it down. "You were one of the most remarkable graduates from this school."

"And now?"

"Even more so. Your sophistication and poise offers its own set of assets."

"Who do you work for, Mr. Pohl?"

"Before we go there, I need you to understand that this conversation is strictly confidential. I asked that Linette leave so that we can keep this between us."

"Fine."

He smiled. "I'm a recruiter."

"I understand that. For whom?"

"More than one organization."

"I'm listening."

Pohl took a couple of strides before turning and repeating the movement. "I hire agents, Sasha. When let's say . . . a government, needs a high level of expertise and low visibility, they come to me."

Spies. "Which government?"

"There are many— "

"Who would be signing my check?" she interrupted.

"You move straight to the point, don't you?"

"I don't see the point in wasting time. I'm sure you're a busy man."

His pacing began again. "The secure nature of the jobs I recruit for means they are not advertised on a job listing page. The individuals hiring would insist that you never tell anyone who you work for or what you do. Your checks come through me."

Sasha paused long enough to cross her legs and shift her body just enough to look at him directly. "You hire spies."

He paused, looked at her. "Intelligence is part of the job."

"I thought that was going to be your answer. What I find strange is how you go about it. Government agencies around the world start by further educating employees with criminal justice degrees, employees of the state department, FBI, CIA, BND here in Germany, British intelligence. The military recruits from their elite. Police officers move up to detectives. Yet you come to a school like Richter and offer positions to students who haven't even lost their baby fat . . . why?"

"Are you questioning my tactics?"

All politeness left her tone. "Yes. I am. I've been away from Richter, and I've seen this world . . . governments . . . all areas of official departments, recruit at colleges. Spies? No. Not the kind that have an official job in a reputable agency. Unless there is something you're not telling me."

Pohl's smile faded. "There are people in this world that government-like agencies would love to remove. But often their own bureaucratic red tape stops them from even finding these people. When you work for me and the people I recruit for, your job will be anything from obtaining information, analyzing, *spying*, engaging . . ."

"Removing."

Pohl hired assassins.

"I didn't say that," he told her.

Sasha kept a straight face. "You didn't *not* say that either."

No words of denial told her she was right.

He moved to the desk, leaned against it. "You could be part of a team responsible for making this world safer. Imagine being on the inside of stopping terrorists before they attack."

This guy was a piece of work. "And you recruit children for this job?"

Pohl snapped his mouth shut. Their eyes locked.

"Am I speaking to a child?"

"No. And I'm not *emotionally vulnerable* enough to be blinded by the kind of life you'd have me lead." Sasha uncrossed her legs and stood. "I've lived the first third of my life on the outside looking in. Watching but not truly participating. The last thing I'd want to do is have that lifestyle indefinitely."

A placating laugh escaped Pohl's lips. "It sounds like someone has an overactive, almost childish, imagination."

Her expression hardened. "Don't insult me."

Pohl met her granite stare with one of his own. "I want you on my team, Sasha. And will do just about anything to obtain your service."

His words smacked entirely too close to a threat. Brigitte's comment about Pohl not taking rejection well was showing.

"You can't afford me."

Pohl crossed his arms over his chest, a slow smile reached his lips. "That's unfortunate."

Sasha turned to leave.

At the door, he stopped her.

"If you change your mind, or if, perhaps, your circumstances change . . . my offer stands."

Sasha walked from the office, not bothering to close the door.

Chapter Twelve

Sasha walked to the center of the courtyard. Surrounding her were all the educational buildings, the kitchen, and dining hall, with all the lower levels there to hide what Richter was all about from the outside eye.

Students walked past her, rushing to class . . . talking among themselves.

How many students had Pohl recruited in the past?

How many young, innocent, yet talented kids took a job and found themselves stuck? She'd bet the bank that at least one of the women on AJ's list was someone Pohl knew personally.

She needed to leave. Analyze the data she'd managed to download the night before and find the links.

Her phone, the one that hadn't rung on campus in two days, buzzed in her back pocket.

Not recognizing the number, she brought it to her ear. "Hello."

"Holy shit, Sasha, Creepazoid is a total douchebag."

Sasha lowered her voice. "Claire?"

"He wanted to hire you to be a killer. You caught that, right?"

Sasha looked around. Students rushed by. "You heard the conversation?"

"All of it. That's why I'm calling. The minute you left the room, he made a call. I only heard his side."

"Could you tell who he was talking to?" *Linette, maybe?*

"No. But he said they needed to move on to plan B."

Plan B?

"No details?"

"Sorry. Like I said, I only heard one side of the conversation. Do you think he meant plan B to make you work for them?"

Sasha noticed a clustering of gray clouds blowing over her. "You can't make someone work for you . . ." *Unless . . .*

"I'm glad you told him what to do with his job."

"Are you still in the boiler room?"

"How do you think I called you? I don't have a cell phone."

Sasha headed toward the kitchens. "Can you copy the conversation onto a drive and meet me outside the library in twenty minutes?"

"Yeah."

"Perfect." Sasha hung up and made her way to Brigitte's classroom.

 ⌒⑨

"How did it go?" Linette asked Pohl once she returned to her office. The question was a formality. She could tell from his expression Sasha had turned him down.

"Seems your alum has no need of the income I can offer."

Linette took her robe off, hung it up. "I warned you that might be the case."

"I wasted my time, Linette. You know how much I hate doing that." She met his gaze, unfazed. "At least you haven't wasted your money."

Pohl tugged at the sleeves of his jacket, first the left, then the right. "And you have not earned a finder's fee."

"It appears so."

He glared, and she did her best to not let him see her discomfort.

"I'll be in touch."

Linette shook his hand and stayed on her feet until after he'd left her office.

Once gone, she sank into her chair and opened the bottom drawer. In the back, behind several files, she removed a flask and twisted off the top. She poured herself a drink into the empty coffee cup on her desk.

∽

Sasha stood in the doorway of Brigitte's studio and waited until she noticed her before motioning toward the locker room.

It didn't take long for the woman to find her.

"How did your meeting go?" Brigitte asked once she was at her side.

Sasha shook her head. "I didn't take his job."

The other woman smiled. "Good. Being a spy is dangerous work."

"You really think that's what he recruits?"

"Isn't that the job he offered?"

"No. More like a hired gun."

Brigitte stopped smiling. "What?"

"Those weren't his words, but I knew what he was suggesting. If I wanted to shoot at people, or be a part of a team that did that kind of thing, I'd have joined a military."

"I always thought his recruiting was more legitimate than that." Brigitte regarded her with remorse. "You're leaving, aren't you?"

"I am. I came here to find some kind of direction in my life and I now realize that answers aren't here. Time for me to move on."

Brigitte shifted on her feet. "I'm going to miss you. You've been a bright light in the last week." She moved in for a hug.

Sasha stiffened. "I'm not a hugger."

"Too bad." Brigitte wrapped her arms around her anyway. In her ear, she whispered, "Watch your back with Pohl."

Sasha stood back. "I will," she paused. "Miss you, too."

Brigitte's eyes glistened and Sasha felt an unfamiliar knot in her throat. "You have my number," she said.

"Be well."

∽

Claire was exactly where Sasha asked her to be nineteen minutes after her call. In her school uniform, minus the jacket they were required to wear during the fall, the young woman leaned against the brick building as if bored. In her hand she held a package of gum.

Students moved around them, some watched if only because Sasha wasn't dressed like staff and had burned her uniform the day she left Richter.

"Hey." Claire greeted her, pulled a stick of gum from the package. She lifted it toward Sasha. "Want some gum?"

Sasha shook her head.

Claire wiggled the package. "You sure? It's fruit flavored."

She glanced at the package, noticed a zip drive.

Clever girl.

"Maybe for later." She took the drive, placed it in her front pocket. "Thank you."

"No problem." Claire picked up the bag at her feet.

"Listen. I'm leaving."

The girl stopped smiling. "I knew that was coming . . . when?"

"I need to pack my bag, say goodbye to the headmistress."

Claire looked away. "So . . . when I'm outta here, maybe we can . . . I don't know, hang out?"

"I'm not good at—"

"I'll need a job. Maybe you know someone?" Claire interrupted, making that lump in Sasha's throat constrict. She liked the kid, reminded her of herself. "I guess if Creepazoid is still hiring . . ."

Sasha stopped her with a stare. "You have my number."

That was all the girl needed to hear. She winked and pointed one finger toward her. "See you on the outside, then."

Once Sasha turned around, she let her grin show.

Thirty minutes later a knock sounded on Sasha's open bedroom door.

Linette stood in the doorway, a smile on her face. "I heard you were leaving."

Sasha zipped her duffel and grabbed her leather jacket. "I am."

"Without saying goodbye?"

"Of course not."

They took each other in. "Just because you didn't take Pohl's offer doesn't mean you need to leave."

"Yes, it does, actually. If I stayed, I'd spend all my energy trying to figure out why you work beside that man."

Linette stepped inside the room. "He's found many jobs for our students over the years."

"Employment that can get a person killed."

"Joining the military can end the same way. Law enforcement. You can't be a humanitarian in a third world country without the risk of being kidnapped and used for—"

"That isn't what I meant."

Linette moved to the window and stared beyond the pane. "Do you know there are military departments that recruit through video games? Stealth drones fly over countries and drop bombs from half a world away. Richter trains many skills, as you know, but it takes a certain personality that can take on the challenge of that kind of job and still be a whole person."

"How do you know if the students that left to do those jobs are whole, Linette?"

"I don't. Any more than any other dean or principal or headmistress in any other school. What I do know is Richter has a ninety-six percent graduation rate for high school. Eighty-nine percent for college, and of that, seventy-seven percent are employed before they walk on my stage to grab their diploma."

Sasha shook her head. "So that's why you break bread with Pohl? To keep Richter in high standing?"

"Pohl is given very limited access to the graduates to even interview. I thought since you came back searching for a future, you'd appreciate the opportunity. I was wrong."

"Defending myself by any means necessary isn't something I'm opposed to doing. Using those skills to earn a living . . . or worse, keep from being bored . . . not me."

Linette lifted her chin. "Your stay with us wasn't in vain, then. At least you know what you *don't* want to do. I'm sorry I miscalculated your need and invited Pohl to talk to you."

Was she? Was that sincerity on her face, or a woman trying to hide behind a mask? "I can't fault you for that."

"I hope you won't find fault at all. But I can see from your eyes I'm asking too much."

Sasha tried to smile. "No, Linette. You're doing your job. The students here are safe and much more likely to take care of themselves out there. No one knows that better than me."

Linette looked around the room. "Well, I won't keep you. I'll let the staff know you've left and won't be returning. For what it's worth, I'm glad you survived your father, and that your benefactor made you financially independent enough to say no to Pohl's offer. I'm sure you'll do great things in your life."

"Thank you."

Sasha couldn't stop the disappointment in her chest as she watched a woman she'd considered her protector for years walk away.

Chapter Thirteen

AJ's phone rang, singing "Bad to the Bone" at an ear-piercing volume in the silence of the library.

Several people turned to him, giving the stink eye and muttering under their breath.

AJ couldn't get his phone out of his back pocket fast enough.

He didn't have a picture of Sasha in his phone, just her phone number next to the name he called her in his head. Sex on a Stick.

"Miss me?" she asked once he said hello.

"'Bout damn time." His curt words were said in a harsh whisper. He held the phone to his ear with his shoulder and gathered up the papers he'd been writing on. "Where the hell did you go?"

The phone sounded like it was cutting out, then he heard her.

"Are you laughing at me?"

"Get over yourself, Junior. I'm on my way. Check out of the hotel and return your rental car."

He closed the windows he had open on the library computer and filled his arms with paperwork.

Heads turned and watched him as he walked by. "I feel sorry for whoever marries you. You're more demanding than any woman I've ever met."

"Ha. That will never happen."

Yeah, AJ didn't see her married either. Outside the library, the cool autumn wind blew through him. "Where am I meeting you this time?"

"The subway. Alexanderplatz Station. You have an hour."

AJ turned on his heel, headed back toward the hotel. "That doesn't give me much time."

"Make it work."

She hung up.

Thirty-eight hours of no contact, and when she called, nothing but demands.

This pace is getting old.

But damn it was good to hear her voice.

❧

Sasha looked at the road behind her.

Richter was a mile away, but if you peered above the line of the trees, you could see the rooftop of the clock tower. Something told her she'd be back. Only the next time might not be on such friendly terms.

Sasha placed her phone in the inside pocket of her jacket and kicked over the bike. She made it half a mile before she sped past a lone person walking down the side of the empty road.

One look in her rearview mirror and she slammed on the brakes. A turn of the wheel and she skidded next to the pedestrian, cut the engine.

Sasha ripped off her helmet and yelled, "What the hell are you doing?"

"You can say I'm going AWOL, but I prefer *early leave*." Claire jostled a backpack higher on her shoulder and grinned.

"Does the headmistress know you've left?"

"Probably not yet."

Sasha shook her head. "Get on. You're going back."

"No, I'm not. You see, recording private conversations between men who hire killers and, well, anyone . . . might be grounds for punishment at the school, but it also happens to be illegal in Germany. I can't imagine Mr. Pohl would like to hear that a student on campus knows his agenda. So I think, for my safety, I'd be better off out here."

"He will never know."

"Can you guarantee that?" Claire asked.

Sasha knew she couldn't. Her gut twisted.

"That's what I thought." Claire approached the bike, tugged her other arm through her backpack, and secured it with a clip. She took the helmet from Sasha's hands and placed it over her head.

Sasha's mind raced for an argument.

"Since you got me into this mess, you can make sure I'm safe before trotting off to wherever you're going."

"The only mess is you running away."

"I didn't run. I hopped over the fence after leaving a little note for Linette. Walking past Checkpoint Charlie would have resulted in an inquisition. One, quite frankly, I wanted nothing to do with. Especially since Pohl was still poking around."

"I thought he left."

"Nope. He was down in the range. Just seeing him there made me puke a little in my mouth. So I left." Claire turned her head. "Now if you don't mind . . . I'd like to put some distance between me and the school before anyone knows I'm gone. I don't really trust my roommates to keep their mouths closed about the boiler room. All they ever did there was watch YouTube videos."

Sasha ran a hand down her thigh, fingers clenched. She cussed in three languages before giving up and kicking over the bike.

"Hang on."

Arms clung to her waist, and Sasha put some distance between the runaway and a recruiter of killers.

∽♱∼

AJ stood on the sidewalk above Alexanderplatz Station and searched the people walking. His gaze caught every dark-haired woman. He thought of the blonde wig and switched his search for that.

Too many women.

He glanced at his watch. An hour . . . on the nose.

He searched the crowd again.

He saw her. Her head popped above the others because of her height. Her dark hair was pulled back in a ponytail, dark sunglasses covered her eyes.

But it was her.

His gut stirred.

She leaned over and started talking to someone.

AJ's gaze narrowed on a teenage girl. Dark brown hair, wide eyes.

Sasha stopped in front of him.

"Who the hell is this?" he asked.

"Baggage," Sasha said without humor.

"Hey!" The girl elbowed Sasha and turned to him. "I'm Claire," she said, pleased with herself.

"Sasha?"

She pushed past him and headed downstairs to the trains. "I'll explain later."

AJ had no choice but to follow.

Claire fell into step behind Sasha.

A train pulled in as they reached the bottom steps. They pushed into the crowded car and held on to steel poles to keep from falling into the people standing next to them. He had a hundred questions but held each one in.

Claire, on the other hand, didn't. "So, are you the boyfriend?"

AJ laughed, looked up to see if Sasha heard Claire's question. Her blank expression said she'd missed it.

"No."

Claire glanced at their mutual companion. "Huh."

They rode in silence; the noise of the crowd around them filled the air. On the third stop, Sasha motioned for them to follow.

She immediately dragged them toward the bathrooms and stopped him at the door. "Wait for us."

"Again with the orders."

Only he did.

When they stepped back out, Claire was wearing Sasha's jacket and a baseball cap. Sasha had tucked her hair into a red pixie cut wig, and a long light gray sweater went all the way to her knees.

He took one look at her and grinned. "I like the red better than the blonde."

She muttered something in a language he didn't speak.

Claire laughed.

"Should I change?" he asked.

Sasha looked him up and down. "No one is looking for you."

Claire shrugged, and once again they followed Sasha out of the station.

"Now where?" AJ asked.

Sasha marched as if on a mission. Her long strides ate up the sidewalk; her head was buried in her phone. AJ looked over to see her on some kind of airline app.

"Sasha?"

She lifted the phone to her ear and hushed him with a finger in the air. "It's me."

AJ listened to one side of the conversation while Sasha took care of whatever agenda she was on.

"Is Blake's still an option? Great. I'll need a passport . . . no. I'll send you a picture. American. I'll make it easy, Amsterdam, Victoria Station." She stopped and looked between both him and Claire. "I wouldn't ask if I didn't have so much extra *help*."

Claire leaned in. "At least I'm no longer *baggage*."

Sasha turned and started walking again. "Precautionary. I'll fill you in when we get there."

She disconnected the call and stopped in front of them. She directed her phone at Claire and pointed toward the side of a white building. After making the girl remove her baseball cap, she snapped two pictures and sent them into cyberspace.

"I take it the papers are for her," AJ said.

Sasha stared at Claire. "Even if she had hers on her, we couldn't use it."

"Linette keeps all of them."

"I remember."

She started walking again, this time close to the side of the busy road. At an intersection, she waited. As a bus pulled around a corner, AJ watched as she dropped her cell phone into the road.

"What the?" Claire said.

A double stomp later, and Sasha bent down to pick up what remained.

Someone on the street said something AJ assumed was a gesture of sympathy for the loss of an expensive phone.

Sasha shrugged, turned the device over in the palm of her hand, and removed a SIM card.

On the move again, she tossed the phone in a nearby trash can, the SIM card made it into a city drain.

They worked their way to the Hauptbahnhof station and Sasha told him to purchase three tickets.

"Let me guess . . . Amsterdam."

"You pay attention, Junior. I like that in a man."

Claire's amused laugh reminded him of his sister when they were kids and he'd been busted by their parents for some offense or another.

"How long before we have what we need for our baggage?"

"Hey . . . I'm the help."

AJ ignored the girl.

"Before the last train leaves."

"You're kidding." He knew illegal passports could be bought, but that quickly?

Sasha stepped closer, tapped a finger to her chest. "Professional."

That same finger tapped his sternum. "Amateur."

The purr in her voice shouldn't be a turn-on.

He stepped farther into her personal space. "I'm going to find something I'm better at than you and turn the tables."

"I look forward to it." She slid past him, her shoulder grazing his as she marched into a convenience store.

Claire laughed and followed her.

AJ was reduced to jockeying tickets on the next train to Amsterdam.

Chapter Fourteen

So many things could go wrong.

By now, Linette would realize Claire was gone and probably started a search. How far would she reach? How long would it take before the girl's roommates sang and the boiler room was found? Would they reveal the information? Or was that smoke blown by Claire to make her cooperate?

Sasha watched Claire from across the aisle in the coach car on a westbound train. She took in the world around her like someone who'd been cooped up in boarding school for most of her life, with wide eyes and open ears.

AJ sat next to the window and was doing a pretty good job of taking orders even when she hadn't given him very much information.

"Is she linked to my sister?" AJ asked.

"No."

"Then why is she here?"

Sasha looked around, didn't notice anyone with eyes on them. "She stumbled upon a conversation that might result in a less than favorable way of life."

"What the hell is that supposed to mean?"

"Later, AJ. Believe me, I don't want the extra responsibility any more than you. But I couldn't leave her there."

He leaned into her as if he had the right. "You don't seem the maternal type."

Sasha shoved him off. "Younger sister at best."

She knew the minute she said *sister*, she'd picked the wrong choice of words. AJ's smile fell.

"At least you understand the need to protect someone." He turned to stare out the window.

"What is that supposed to mean?"

He looked deep in her eyes. "You're a lone wolf. From your own admission, you don't play well with others. In my experience, people like you aren't loyal to a cause that isn't their own."

"If that were so, why am I helping you?"

"Because that school is the link, and therefore personal."

She opened her mouth to respond.

He cut her off before she could utter one word.

"And you love the chase."

"Excuse me?" She glared at him.

He looked at her wig, touched the edge of her sweater. "All of this. You shine when you're snapping orders and taking charge. There's a light in your eyes that isn't dimmed by the sunglasses covering your face."

"It's called concentration."

"It's called excitement. Almost the same as the charge you get when you see someone across a crowded bar and the air snaps."

His words brought her to the moment she noticed him watching her at Brigitte's choice of pubs.

AJ's gaze fell to her lips.

That snapping charge he spoke of zapped attention straight to her breasts.

Sasha wanted to slap them as if they were disobedient children.

She looked away.

AJ shifted in his seat and stood. "I'm going to use the little boys' room."

She scooted her legs and let him pass, happy to have him out of her air so she could calm down.

No sooner did he leave than Claire jumped from her seat to the vacant one beside Sasha.

"So, what's his story?" Claire asked.

"That's not your concern."

Claire watched him as he disappeared down the car and pushed past the doors leading to the bathrooms. "He's into you."

Instead of pushing the girl's observations aside, Sasha met them head-on. "Of course he is . . . look at me."

Claire started to laugh until Sasha felt her gut laughing with her.

"I wish I had an ounce of your confidence."

"You have plenty. Don't worry."

Their laughter faded and Claire's lips pressed together. "Do you think they know I'm gone by now?"

"I'd be disappointed if they didn't."

"She's going to look for me."

"Probably."

"She'll want to drag me back."

Sasha placed a hand on Claire's arm. Even for her, the gesture felt awkward. "You're eighteen. She can't make you."

"I know what the rules are. I just have this feeling in here"—Claire pointed to her stomach—"that they aren't going to let me go quietly."

"What makes you think that?"

"I just do. I'm paranoid, I guess."

Sasha released a long breath, leaned close, and lowered her voice. "Get past that. Border agents everywhere clue in to nervous travelers. It makes them look twice. You're just another teenager backpacking through Europe. Make up a pretend itinerary and keep your story consistent. Leave Berlin out of the mix."

"I can do that."

"Good. Now go back to your seat and work on your story."

Claire stood.

"Keep it simple."

꩜

Amsterdam was a whole lot like Vegas, minus the casinos and flashy lights. The boardwalks were littered with people, even after the sun set and the temperatures started to drop. The number of sex shops on every corner corresponded with the number of pot shops . . . or coffee shops, as they called them. Although coffee wasn't on the menu. Well, it was, but that's not what these places were known for selling.

AJ assumed the lax attitude and acceptance of this alternative lifestyle lent itself to being a place where Sasha could obtain a phony passport in record time.

Sure enough, after grabbing a bite to eat deeper in town, they returned to the train station, where Sasha asked them to hold back in the off chance the passport exchange was being watched. Even in Amsterdam, obtaining fake passports was illegal.

Several yards away, AJ watched and attempted to calm his nerves when the handoff happened. A completely chauvinistic male part of him said he should be the one making the exchange. He didn't like Sasha putting herself out there. AJ would ask himself why later . . . right now he felt his heart squeeze in his chest with anxiety. He kept his eyes peeled to see if anyone else noticed a thing. But between the bicycles rushing by and the noise of the party crowd settling in for a long night, no one cared to even glance at Sasha and the twentysomething who handed her the papers.

She walked away after shaking the guy's hand.

"That looked way too easy," AJ said once she was back by their side.

"Money talks."

Sasha handed Claire the passport. "Your name is Crystal Smith. Your birthday was September ninth. You're nineteen. Just remember nine, nine, nine."

"Got it."

They'd already bought tickets separately for the same train headed to London.

"The train will stop in Brussels, and that is where we will need to get off the train and pass through immigration. From there, we spread out in line, meet up in the third coach car," Sasha instructed. "Keep your cool, *Crystal*. If something goes wrong, I won't get on that train. You'll have to trust me to have your back."

Claire shrugged with attitude. "I got this."

Sasha grinned.

"And me?"

"You get your ass to London, call Reed."

"All this and I don't even know why she is here and why we're hiding like we're the ones doing something wrong."

Claire looked at the two of them. "He doesn't know about Creepazoid?"

AJ shook his head. "I don't. Who's Creepazoid?"

Sasha sucked in a breath.

Claire kept talking. "Just a man who offered Sasha a job to kill people."

"What?" AJ asked.

"This isn't the place for this conversation."

AJ grabbed her arm. "We're talking about this now."

It took every ounce of concentration to keep her arm still and not attract attention to them.

She stepped into his personal space. "Do you like that hand?"

His grip tightened. "You don't scare me."

Claire backed up.

"I should."

Their breaths mixed, eyes locked.

"Ah, boys and girls. We have a train to catch." Claire brought their attention to the present.

⁌

Who knew that palms sweating was an actual thing?

Breaking up the pending fight between Katniss and Peeta had been cute and all, but the first leg of their train ride, and disembarking from the train only to be shuffled through security checks and immigration, was nail-biting worthy.

They had spread out per Sasha's instructions, and Claire was two people away from having her fake passport checked.

And yeah, her palms sweat.

Border agents sniff out fear.

She tried to look bored.

One more person.

I'm going to throw up.

The agent waved her over.

She hiked her backpack over her shoulder and stepped up. She handed her passport and train ticket. "Hi," she said.

"Hello." He looked at her picture and then her face. "Where are you going in the UK?"

"London, then maybe Ireland. I haven't decided yet."

He looked at her picture again, paused.

Breathing became an effort.

She was fairly certain the man could hear her heart beating.

"Stay away from warm beer. Don't let anyone tell you that's the way to drink it," he said with a wink.

His hand reached for his stamp. Down it went on the passport, and he handed it back.

"Thanks. I'll remember that."

Oxygen left her head as she walked away, leaving her a little dizzy. She took a second to tuck her passport into her backpack and catch her breath . . . then headed to the platform in front of the third coach car.

Sasha showed up next, kept her distance.

AJ stood a few feet away, rocking back on his heels.

She'd done it.

Her smile grew until she was certain everyone on the platform could see it.

Chapter Fifteen

A car was waiting for them when they arrived in London.

By *car*, he meant *limousine*.

AJ wasn't a stranger to luxury travel, but the accommodations they were taken to were something else. Even in the pitch-black of night, long past midnight, the silhouette of the estate Sasha had taken them to was impressive.

"Who lives here?" Claire asked.

"A friend."

AJ grabbed Sasha's bag and started up the steps. "Some kind of friend."

The massive front door opened before they reached it.

The man who opened the door filled it with broad shoulders and a thick neck.

"Neil?"

"Reed would have come, but—"

"I didn't request backup." Sasha moved past AJ and Claire.

"The fact you requested anything at all gives me a reason to be here."

Neil gave Sasha a stare that would intimidate the most hardened man.

Not Sex on a Stick. She stared back, her chest rising and falling with short breaths.

Claire brushed past AJ and straight up to the brick shithouse of a man. "I'm Claire." She put her hand out.

Neil stared at it.

When he hesitated a moment too long, Claire reached out with her left hand, grabbed Neil's right, and pushed his palm into hers. She shook it twice before letting go. "Nice to meet you, Neil," she said.

AJ bit his tongue to keep from laughing.

Sasha shook her head and walked around Neil and into the house. "I'll give you a briefing in twenty minutes."

"I'm AJ Hofmann."

"I know who you are," Neil told him. Unlike with Claire, Neil put his hand out to shake.

His grip proved what AJ had already determined. Neil was a whole lot of muscle behind his girth.

"Thank you for having us."

Neil closed the door behind them.

Sasha and Claire were following a woman in a maid's uniform up the stairs.

"Coffee or whiskey?" Neil asked.

"Is that even a question? I've been traveling with the two of them all day."

AJ couldn't say for sure if Neil smiled. But there was something in his eyes that passed as humor before he turned and led him into a den.

Sasha joined them nineteen minutes later. She was prompt, AJ would give her that.

She'd changed out of the wig and housewife sweater and slipped on a tank top that hugged her chest and abdomen like a good friend on a Saturday night. Upon entering the room, she crossed to the whiskey in the decanter and poured herself a drink.

"Where's Claire?"

"Facedown in a bed."

AJ envied her.

"What did Reed tell you?" Sasha asked Neil.

"The basics. Hofmann is searching for his sister's murderer, thinks it's linked to your old school. The names you gave Reed have met with unfortunate dates with the grim reaper."

"You've seen the data?" she asked.

"Everything Reed found."

"Your first impression?" Sasha sipped her drink.

"There's a link. I'm just not sure what yet."

Sasha moved to what looked like a small secretary desk and pulled out a drawer. From there she removed a Bluetooth keyboard and made a few keystrokes.

What appeared to be a solid wall with paintings of family members peeled back to reveal a series of monitors from floor to ceiling.

"Holy crap," AJ muttered.

Sasha slid a zip drive into the computer port after the wall revealed a second desk.

A few more keystrokes and a series of pictures were brought up on the screen.

"I took several pictures of the yearbooks from when Amelia Hofmann attended Richter. The group photos to help establish personal relationships. Senior photos with names." She pressed another button and two pictures popped up. "Top left. This is the headmistress, Linette. She's been in charge of Richter for as long as I remember."

"This is a current picture?" Neil asked.

Sasha nodded. "I took all of these this week."

"Who is the guy in the suit?" AJ asked.

"Geoff Pohl. Or Creepazoid, as Claire likes to call him."

"The businessman?" Neil asked.

"Yes, but maybe with this picture, we can find something."

"I'll get the team on it."

AJ sat forward. "Are you going to explain what Claire meant when she said this man offered you a job to kill?"

Neil narrowed his eyes.

Sasha slid a second drive into the computer. "It appears that Linette has some sort of arrangement with Pohl for him to interview students graduating from Richter for classified positions that require high marks in agility, self-defense, marksmanship, foreign languages, and computer skills."

"Covert operations . . . spies?" Neil asked.

"That's what I thought." Sasha pressed play, and a male voice sounded through the speakers. "That's Pohl."

They sat and listened to the conversation between Sasha and Pohl.

AJ could hear the tension in Sasha's voice when the man became condescending. Then when he said that his employer would do just about anything to obtain her services, Neil lifted a hand.

"Back that up."

Sasha paused the recording, replayed it.

"He's threatening you," Neil said.

Sasha stopped the playback. "That's what I got."

"Did I miss something?" AJ asked. "Sounded like he would offer her whatever she wanted."

Neil shook his head. "No, he said he would *do* anything to get her." He looked at Sasha. "He alluded to others, but do we know who he works for?"

"No idea."

Neil made little circular motions with his fingers.

Right before Sasha's voice left the recording, Neil had her stop the tape again.

"What circumstances would need to change for you to take that job?" Neil asked.

Sasha sat in a chair, pushed her feet out in front of her. "How do you get people to do something they don't want to do?"

"Pay them," AJ suggested.

"Sasha doesn't need the money," Neil said.

"Blackmail." Sasha sipped her drink.

Neil sat in silence. AJ could see the wheels in the man's head turning. "Does he have anything?"

Sasha shook her head.

"Then we'll have to wait and see what he creates."

She reached for the computer again. "Point taken. And this is where Claire comes in. Richter does not allow unsupervised computer access without firewalls to the outside. Cell phones are prohibited for the students. But when you teach intelligence to your elite students, they find a way. Claire helped me find the hidden upper-class computers that held the data from alumni . . . including me. Which was how I was able to record this conversation and the next one."

Once again, she pressed play.

Pohl's voice sounded once again.

"She didn't take the job."

A pause.

"Did you really think she would? We move on to plan B. I already have things in motion."

Neil brushed the back of his hand to the side of his face.

"That doesn't sound good," AJ stated the obvious.

"Is there any more?" Neil asked.

"I don't know. This is the first time I heard the recording. Claire called me from the computer room to tell me my plan worked. I asked her to put it on a drive. I shouldn't have involved her."

"Could you have obtained that without her help?" Neil asked.

"Not without a few toys I didn't bring with me."

"Then let it go."

"You just took Claire and left?" AJ asked. "That doesn't sound like the school my sister went to."

Sasha rubbed her forehead. "She jumped the fence and found me. She indicated that she wanted to leave when I first met her. Illegally recording a message from a man employing hired guns gave her the excuse she needed."

"Smart," Neil said. "How old is she?"

"Eighteen. Richter has their senior class taking their first year in college, so that when and if they leave after they're eighteen, they have a head start. The second Claire became of age, she could opt out and leave."

"So why run away?"

"It wouldn't be without an exit interview and a conversation with her benefactor," Sasha explained.

"You mean her parents?" Neil asked.

"She's an orphan. Like me."

AJ stop with his drink halfway to his lips. The way Sasha had revealed the personal information was so flippant it made his chest ache.

Processing the information didn't have a chance before the speakers crackled and voices filled the room.

"How did it go?"

"That's Linette," Sasha told them.

"Seems your alum has no need of the income I can offer."

"I warned you that might be the case."

"I wasted my time, Linette. You know how much I hate doing that."

"At least you haven't wasted your money."

"And you have not earned a finder's fee."

"It appears so."

"I'll be in touch."

Sasha tilted her head back and muttered in a language AJ didn't understand. "A finder's fee?"

Neil stood and crossed to the computer, turned off the audio. "She didn't sound upset about the loss of money."

"Doesn't change the fact she's taken it in the past."

AJ finished his drink, set the glass aside. "Or will in the future."

Sasha pushed up in her chair and reached for the keyboard. "I'm going to need coffee."

Neil placed a hand on hers. "This will all be here in the morning. The guys in LA are bored stiff. This will give them something to work on while you recharge."

"This is my—"

"You're right. And morning is in less than four hours."

Sasha looked like she was going to argue. Giving up . . . or maybe giving in to the fatigue that was hovering above them like smog, she removed another zip drive from her pocket and pressed it into Neil's palm.

"What's this?"

"Raw data from Linette's computer. Along with a list of students. Past and present. I haven't spent any time looking this over."

"We'll get on it." Neil reached for the drive.

Sasha kept it slightly out of his reach. "I'm not used to asking for help."

Neil took the drive from her fingertips. "You didn't ask."

She released a long-suffering sigh and turned toward AJ. "C'mon. I'll show you to your room."

AJ turned toward Neil. "Thanks again."

Neil nodded once and moved to the seat Sasha had just vacated.

AJ fell into step beside Sasha, grabbing his duffel bag on the way out of the room. They moved back to the foyer and main staircase. His feet felt like lead bricks now that he knew sleep was only a few feet away. "I could sleep on a sidewalk."

"Save that for another night."

They rounded the corner to a hallway with a half a dozen doors separated by a wide corridor.

She stopped long enough to open a door. "This one is yours."

The room held a queen-size bed with muted colors of tan and beige. It was a little more formal than you'd see in a guest room in the States, but perfectly acceptable for a manor house in the English countryside.

"Where's Claire?" he asked.

"Across the hall . . . why?"

He dropped his bag, sat on the edge of his bed. "I don't know. I didn't realize she was an orphan. There's no one outside of Richter for her to contact or depend on. The girl has a lot of attitude, but under all that has to be some vulnerability, maybe even a little fear of what's coming."

Sasha looked over her shoulder to the empty hall. "I'll put my money on her being just fine."

"Didn't say she wouldn't be fine, just that she might be scared." Had Sasha been scared . . . when she left Richter for the first time and had to join the world without a family? Where did she go? Who helped her out? How had she met Neil . . , and what did he mean when he said Sasha didn't need Pohl's money?

A hundred questions were there to be asked, and growing every hour.

AJ yawned.

She moved out of the room. "Get some sleep."

"Where's your room?" he asked, coming to his feet.

Is that a tired smile on her face?

Yeah . . . it is.

"You don't have to worry about me being afraid," she told him, and that tired smile grew.

AJ shook off her comment. "Oh, no, no . . . that's for me."

She narrowed her eyes.

"It's a big place, I need to know where to go for protection."

That had her laugh enough to know his charm wasn't completely lost on her. She took a few steps down the hall and opened the door next to Claire's. "Satisfied?"

"No. But I'm getting there."

She lifted a hand, showed him her palm. "Good night, Junior."

Only after she was securely inside her room did he move back into his room. He started to close the door and decided to leave it open a crack.

Chapter Sixteen

"I don't like this. Any of it."

"You have to trust me."

Linette reached out and placed the palm of her hand on the side of Brigitte's face. She wanted to smooth away the worry with the pad of her thumb, but the lines of stress were still there when she moved her hand away.

"I hope you know what you're doing. If Puhl has his way . . ."

"He won't. I've been waiting for this opportunity for seven years. Now that it's here, I won't fail."

"I hate this." The muscles on Brigitte's arms tensed with unused energy.

"Go, beat up your assistant. You'll feel better." It was a joke, one they used often.

"Come over tonight," Brigitte said in a softer voice.

Linette shook her head. "I can't, love. Too many people focused on me today. When things calm down . . ."

There was no way around the disappointment in her eyes.

Sasha sat across from AJ, a cup of coffee filling her hands. The man looked like he could use a week's worth of sleep, but he'd gotten up before she had. She gave him points for that.

The morning fog had yet to lift, and the view outside the windows gave a sense of security, as if the moisture in the air kept out anything bad and kept all the good inside.

"Your friend Neil has quite the spread."

"It's not his," she told him. "This house belongs to his brother-in-law."

AJ glanced around the dining room. "Be sure and thank him for me."

"I will."

The Harrison estate had a full staff, even when there wasn't anyone around to use it. One of the women who worked there brought out a try of scones and an assortment of jams. AJ looked up at the girl and mumbled a thank-you.

She smiled with a blush. "Mr. Neil likes a full breakfast when he visits. Would you like the cook to make one for you as well?"

"I don't want to be a bother."

"No bother at all. It's what we do."

AJ glanced at Sasha, his eyes requesting help.

"I'm sure if the cook prepares it, someone will eat it," Sasha told her.

The girl curtseyed. "Very well, mum." And she was gone.

AJ glanced over his shoulder as the girl left the room. "I'm used to pouring my own bowl of Froot Loops in the morning."

"Froot Loops is not on the English breakfast menu."

The coffee started a slow burn in her stomach. Sasha decided a scone was as good a source as any to keep that burn from becoming a hole.

"How did you and Neil meet?"

Not used to personal questions, Sasha answered as simply as possible. "Through Reed."

While she nibbled on her breakfast bread, AJ slathered cream on his and took a big bite. "So how did you meet Reed?"

"Why are you asking?"

He paused, looked at her over the knife in his hand. "I don't have a hidden agenda, Sasha. It's called getting to know someone. I ask a question, you answer. You ask a question . . . I answer." He took another bite, talked around it. "Conversation."

She took her time swallowing. "I'm not good at that."

A slight gleam hit AJ's eyes. "Conversation?"

"Answering questions."

"So, we're just supposed to sit here and watch each other eat?"

She washed her bite down with her coffee. "You can go in the other room."

His grin had the corners of her lips pulling up. There was light in his eyes that seemed to sparkle even brighter off the damp edges of his hair. His casual charm and patient questions might not have been her method of interrogation, but they seemed to be working on her.

He placed both his elbows on the table and stared at her as he took another bite. His mouth was overly animated as he chewed. He repeated the action in complete silence, eyes glued to hers.

Sasha gave up. "I met Reed while he was spying on my sister-in-law and her friends."

AJ stopped midchew. He quickly swallowed and wiped the cream from his lips. "I thought you said you were an orphan, that you didn't have any family."

"I am and I don't."

"Both your parents are gone?"

"Yes."

"But you have a brother?"

She took a bite. "He's dead."

Her short answers were killing him . . . she could see the frustration in his face. "I'll give you the condensed version, and then we're talking about something else."

AJ put his food down and rested his hands on the sides of his plate, offering his full attention.

"My mother whored herself out to my father. After she had me, she attempted to blackmail him for money, so he murdered her."

AJ's smile faded.

"I grew up in a series of foster homes until I was old enough to be enrolled in Richter. I didn't know it at the time, but my father's wife, Alice . . . my half brother's mother, knew about me the whole time. She kept me hidden at Richter, and Richter taught me how to defend and protect myself once I graduated. Once out, Alice was there, offering me employment to watch over her son, Fedor, and eventually his wife. Keep them safe from Alice's then ex-husband, whom she didn't trust. I had no idea Fedor was my half brother. But like all secrets, eventually things came to light. Alice died of cancer the same week my father murdered his own son."

AJ's jaw had dropped open. "Jesus."

"No, I don't think Jesus was there. I failed at keeping my brother alive, but I took Alice's request to the grave and kept watch over Trina. Where I met Reed . . . and eventually Neil."

"And your father?"

"He went after Trina through her second husband. I intervened. Now he's dead."

AJ's jaw dropped. "You killed him."

"I didn't have the pleasure." She rubbed her neck as if she still felt the man's hands squeezing the life out of her. "Reed saved my life and the authorities took my father's."

AJ blew out a breath. "Damn, I'm sorry."

"The night you and I met, you asked me what I would do if my sibling ended up dead."

"I remember that."

"I stopped at nothing to find the truth behind my brother's death and didn't even learn he was my brother until halfway through my investigation."

"That's why you're helping me."

Sasha sat back, willed her pulse to slow down. "That is why I started to help you. Now it's personal."

He dropped his hands to the table. "I don't know what to say."

He appeared genuinely concerned for her. Not that she knew what to do with that emotion. "Your turn."

"What?"

"I told you my story. What's yours?"

A puff of breath came from his mouth. "Nothing like yours."

"Few are."

He sat back in his chair, picked up his coffee. "My father is guilty of many things, but murder isn't one of them. He loves his career more than his family. He chased his political life all the way to Germany, as you know. Bounced around every time the White House changed hands. He expected all of us to bounce right along with him. My mother has stuck with him, for the most part. I head butted authority, as you found out. Guilty of theft because I could, not because I needed what I stole."

"Breaking and entering? Grand theft?" she asked, knowing that's what she had read about him.

"Yeah. All to gain attention from Daddy. Which I did. He was six months from taking the position in Germany and he gave me an ultimatum. Richter, with my sister . . . or the military."

"You didn't do either."

"No. I told him to screw off. Finished high school and went to community college for a couple of years." He finished his coffee and pushed away from the table. He grabbed the pot warming on the sideboard and refreshed his cup and then hers as he talked. "I straightened up my shit."

"You wanna start over with that comment?" Sasha asked, her question a warning.

"I got better at what I did," he confessed. "Had a close call a couple years ago."

"Why do you do it?"

AJ met her stare. "Same reason you put on wigs and flee the country with fake passports. Adrenaline. It's never boring."

"Stealing cars is nothing more than an adrenaline rush?"

He didn't even attempt to look embarrassed about his choice of extracurricular activities.

"I've considered giving it up."

She shook her head. "No, you haven't."

"I have. I just need something else to take its place and a good reason to find something else to do with my time."

"Like searching for your sister's murderer?"

Some of AJ's smirk left his lips. "I haven't stolen one car since her death."

"How do you stay under the radar?" she asked. Because while they assumed AJ still had sticky fingers, she and Reed weren't finding any concrete proof he was actively stealing anything.

He paused, his lips pressed together.

"It's called getting to know you, AJ." She used his words against him.

He smiled. "I work alone."

"You have to have some contacts when off-loading . . ."

He shook his head. "Where is the fun if I tell you all my secrets?"

He had a point.

Sasha leaned back. "So Amelia went to Germany and studied at Richter, and you moved to Florida."

"Yeah."

"Why did Amelia go to Richter?"

AJ sat back down. "Dad said it was to keep her safe. As if the US ambassador to Germany was some great target," he said with doubt. "He wanted Amelia contained in a boarding school so he didn't feel guilty about being an absentee dad. When he moved on from his job in Germany, Amelia stayed her final year."

"Did she ever tell you why she stayed?"

"No. We didn't spend a lot of time together after she graduated. Holidays, that kind of thing. I should have gone to Richter with her." He sighed when he said the last part of his thought. Guilt hovered in his eyes.

"It wouldn't change the facts now."

AJ locked eyes with her. "If you could go back and spend time with your brother, would you?"

A strange knot in her throat made her swallow. "You can't go back."

"Doesn't make me stop wishing I could."

"Waste of energy."

"You're right. So I do the next best thing. Make sure whoever is responsible for her death pays."

Footsteps in the hall outside of the dining room interrupted them.

Neil appeared in the doorway, a laptop in his hands. "We have a new development."

That's never good.

He placed the computer on the table and brought up a news channel.

"The missing student from Richter, a private boarding school known for its program to help troubled teens."

A picture of Claire in her school uniform flashed on the screen.

"The girl was ordered by the court to attend Richter until she came of age or face possible criminal charges, which leads authorities to believe she didn't leave on her own will. A person of interest in the case is Sasha Budanov-Petrov. Daughter of Ruslan Petrov, a man who escaped the criminal justice system many times before his death two years ago. It is said his daughter was responsible for his death."

"Lies." Sasha watched the fabrication on the screen and dug her fingernails into her palms to keep from slamming a fist on the table.

"Miss Petrov is no stranger to disappearing and never being seen again. The German authorities would like to bring this woman in for questioning before she can disappear with the missing teenage girl."

The cameras moved to the walls outside Richter, and in front of a half a dozen microphones, Geoff Pohl stood in his perfectly pressed suit and fake concern. "I'm the longtime benefactor for young Claire and students like her. Kids that have taken a detour and simply need the discipline to find the right path here at Richter. We're unsure why Miss Petrov would abduct poor Claire, but we want her back."

"Abduct?" AJ asked the screen.

"Once again, here are the most recent pictures of the missing seventeen-year-old and the woman of interest in her disappearance."

AJ reached out and placed a hand over Sasha's.

"Slimy media calling you Petrov," Neil muttered.

She would just as soon die than use her biological father's last name.

"Because a minor is involved, authorities have been notified throughout Europe to be on the alert."

Neil turned off the computer and closed the lid. "We need to get you out of Europe."

"Creepazoid was my benefactor?"

Claire stood in the doorway, her face a sheet of white.

All eyes turned to her.

"He was the one waiting for me to graduate to give me a job?"

Sasha could imagine what kind of job that would be.

"You don't have to worry about that now," Sasha told her.

Neil crossed his arms over his chest. "How old are you?" he asked.

"Eighteen."

"Pohl said you were seventeen," AJ said.

"He's lying. Ask my roommates. We celebrated my eighteenth birthday with liquor we stole from Checkpoint Charlie's stash."

AJ turned to Sasha. "Wouldn't the authorities check those facts before going through all this?"

Sasha thought of the room in the subterranean levels of Richter, of the time Linette showed her the many copies of her birth certificates. "We're not the only ones who can obtain a fake passport . . . or birth certificates."

AJ squeezed her hand, and that's when she realized he was holding it.

She slid her hand away, saw concern on his face. "This is all part of plan B. Make me the criminal. Connect me to my father, who made many enemies who may find taking a piece of me worth their while."

"I don't like this," AJ muttered.

"Claire, didn't you say you saw Pohl lingering in the gun range after I left?"

Neil tensed. Sasha knew his mind went where hers was stuck.

"Yeah. You'd turned his assassin job down, and he beelined to the range. Made me think he was picking out a replacement."

Neil turned to Sasha. "Did you use the range?"

Her skin crawled. "Yeah."

"Was anyone with you?" Neil asked.

The face of her friendly martial arts Instructor surfaced in her brain. "Brigitte. She challenged me after I beat her on the obstacle course." Sasha stood and moved to the window, where the protective fog started to lift. "How do you force someone to take a job they don't want?" She asked the rhetorical question to everyone in the room.

It was Claire who came to the conclusion first. "Pohl has your fingerprints on a gun. He's going to blackmail you . . . or worse, kill someone and say you did it."

Sasha turned first to Claire, who looked like she was going to get sick.

AJ appeared pissed.

And Neil. His head was already spinning to fix this before it happened.

"Who would he shoot?" Claire asked.

"Pohl won't shoot anyone. He'll give the gun to someone more skilled to assure a kill."

"But who?"

Sasha forced a smile onto her face. The last thing she wanted to do was scare Claire any more than she already was.

Neil straightened his shoulders and started barking orders. "You," he pointed at Sasha. "Assume protective custody until we are out of Europe. We can better control this situation with a larger detail."

"I don't take orders."

"You do now." And to make his point, he turned his attention to Claire. "You are inside, away from the windows, no contact with anyone that isn't in this house."

"You think he's gonna kill me?"

Sasha moved to Claire, glared at Neil.

AJ ran his hands through his hair.

"So far, AJ is the only one not mentioned. Either Pohl knows nothing about you, or you're a trump card."

Sasha thought of the night they'd met. "Brigitte was in the bar when we met. You spoke with her."

"Yeah, but she didn't know who I was."

"You told me you knew who she was . . . what makes you think she didn't know who you were the whole time? She called my attention to you before you sat down to flirt."

"That's a long shot."

"A long shot we're going to assume is right until proven otherwise," Neil told them. "Eat breakfast and ready your bags. We're pulling out as soon as I can arrange pilots."

Neil left the room without looking back.

"What armed service was he in?" AJ asked, deadpan.

Sasha sighed. "Marines."

Chapter Seventeen

Private jets, private pilots, and a small airport only the elite flew in and out of made for an easy exit when leaving the United Kingdom.

AJ walked behind Sasha and Claire as they had stepped into the airplane, and suddenly found himself lacking in his financial confidence.

The jet belonged to the same man who owned the manor house they'd just left. Like the home, the plane wasn't a budget model by any stretch of the imagination. Sasha had told him en route to the airfield that Mr. Harrison and his family traveled back and forth to the UK from California often. In order to avoid having to stop on the East Coast for fuel, they needed a larger plane.

So while AJ stood in the doorway of the aircraft with his mouth half-open at the pure opulence of the jet, Claire flopped into one of the many deluxe recliner chairs and said exactly what AJ was thinking. "This is the shit!"

"You're not kidding, kid."

Neil moved AJ aside and stepped into the cockpit to speak with the pilots.

Sasha spoke to the flight attendant while AJ walked through the jet, taking it all in. "I think I need to go back to school and step up my game," he said to no one in particular.

Claire caught his comment. "What do you do?"

"Nothing that can afford this," he told her. Not legally, anyway.

"Might I take your bag, sir?" The flight attendant reached for AJ's duffel.

He handed it over and she gathered Claire's before disappearing behind a galley wall.

Claire jumped up and moved to a closed door. "What's in here?" she asked Sasha.

"A bedroom."

"No way. That's awesome." The girl bounced in to check it out.

"You've obviously been on this plane before," AJ said to her.

"A couple of times."

"Back and forth to Europe?" he asked.

Sasha looked at him as if she wasn't going to answer.

He shook his head. "Just curious, Stick. You don't have to answer if you don't want to."

"Stick?"

AJ leaned in. "*Sex on a Stick* might make Claire uncomfortable."

He could see her pinching her lips together to keep from smiling.

AJ took advantage of the fact that Neil was busy talking with the pilots, the attendant was taking care of their luggage, and Claire had disappeared in the bedroom. His eyes traveled the length of her. Always the same look. Black leggings or spandex . . . or leather-looking pants with a tight cotton top and a black leather jacket to cover her arms in the cold. "I bet even your pajamas are black and clingy."

This time she whispered, "Who said I wore pajamas?"

Oh, yeah . . . his mind went there, and he once again looked her up and down. "That's just mean."

Now she was smiling.

"I never said I was nice."

His dick twitched in his pants.

Claire walked back into the main cabin. "When are we taking—"

Sasha and AJ took a step apart.

"I can go back in the bedroom if you two need to be alone," Claire said, grinning.

"We're good, right?" Sasha asked AJ, her eyes sparkling.

He didn't trust himself to speak.

Claire chuckled and seated herself in a recliner.

The flight attendant returned. "Would you like something to drink before we take off?"

"Oh, yeah. I want a beer," Claire said faster than AJ could open his mouth.

He and Sasha looked at the teenage girl.

"What?" Claire asked. "It's legal in Europe."

The flight attendant looked to Sasha for approval.

She did with a nod.

Neil walked back into the cabin, placed his bag under one of the seats. "We'll be in the air in ten minutes."

The flight attendant handed Claire the beer and replaced Neil's spot with the pilots.

Once the door to the plane was closed, the pilots put the aircraft in motion.

AJ sat in a rear-facing seat across from Sasha, who didn't appear to relax until they were in the air and leveling out.

Claire had found a pair of headphones and was watching a movie on the large television on one of the cabin walls.

Sasha unclenched her hands and pulled her stare away from the window. She glanced over at the distracted teen.

"You've taken on the role as her protector rather seriously," he said.

"Until we clear her name and runaway status, she's going to need it."

"And how do you plan to do that?"

Sasha turned to him. "Secure location. Have our lawyers find her original birth certificate. Get ahold of Linette and threaten the woman to pull her head out of her ass and stop playing pawn to Pohl."

"From what I could tell, Linette doesn't threaten easily."

"Depends on who she's scared of. Once I finish our conversation, it will be me."

Neil made his own observation. "You threaten the head of the school and Pohl pops one off in her head. Who do you think the authorities are going to blame?"

Sasha closed her lips together.

"Hard to frame Sasha for a murder in Europe when she's in the States," AJ pointed out.

"You mean if she has an alibi. An eyewitness that would keep her from the scene of whatever crime Pohl is planning on using to try and blackmail her."

"That, too," AJ said.

Neil and Sasha exchanged glances.

"You need a shadow, Sasha." His eyes slid to AJ.

Slowly, she started to shake her head. "No."

"Yes."

AJ wasn't completely sure what the yes and no were about.

"It's simple. Whatever you plan to do, take AJ with you."

He looked at Sasha. "What are you planning?"

"Nothing . . . yet."

Neil leaned forward, rested his arms on his knees. "Sasha won't sit idle. It's not in her DNA. As soon as we find anything on Pohl, she'll be right back out there, working on taking the man down."

"You're talking about me as if I'm not sitting right here," she said with a glare.

"Am I wrong?" Neil asked.

She kept silent.

"Keep AJ by your side or I put a detail on you."

"I'll lose your detail within an hour."

Neil released a rare smile. "If that detail is me?"

"You're too big to go unnoticed."

AJ smiled at Neil. "She has a point."

"You know I'm right on this one."

She unbuckled her seat belt and stood. "I'm going to get some sleep while I can." Without another word, she went into the bedroom and closed the door behind her.

"She's not going to sleep," AJ said.

"No. She's pissed. Knows I'm right. I'm not sure if you have any influence over her, but now would be the time to use it. She'd drop my detail in thirty minutes, and they're all damn good. We need more time to learn who this Pohl is. We need boots on the ground for every possible victim tied to Richter. She's going to want to be one of them."

"So we go to DC and investigate my sister."

Neil shook his head. "You're too close. I'll have someone else on your sister."

"That's ridiculous. I can be objective."

He laughed. "No. You can't. What if my man finds out your sister took a job with Pohl—"

"She would never have . . ."

Neil stopped him with a look.

"You admitted that you and your sister weren't close. She had a UN job that put her in contact with untold diplomats and lobbyists . . . people in power. No one would suspect your sister was anything but what she said she was. Did she travel for work?"

"Of course. She worked alongside other analysts in foreign countries who had poor water regulations."

"Did anyone of importance die in those countries when she was there?"

AJ's jaw clenched. "What the hell are you suggesting?"

Neil looked him dead in the eye. "That you're not objective." Neil sat back. "Now, go in there and convince Sasha to keep you by her side. That way I have one less person to worry about." He glanced at Claire, who was riveted in whatever movie she was watching.

"Sasha is much more qualified to keep herself safe than I am to protect her." Much as he hated to admit it.

"I'm aware of that. I need her to keep *you* safe. And if you're with her, I won't question if she's going off playing vigilante. She has no problem putting herself in danger, but I've yet to see her put anyone else in the crossfire. The bonus is if Pohl tries to put her in a place and a crime that you can say she wasn't in . . . even better."

AJ glanced toward the closed bedroom door. "Vigilante?"

Neil paused. "She's had a hard life. Now that she's trying to find her place, someone is trying to take that from her. She won't go down without a fight."

"How can you be so sure?"

His eyes glazed over, as if lost in thought. "Because she and I are a lot alike. Now, you take that one, I'll see this one is taken care of until this is over," he said, nodding toward the teenager.

AJ blew out a breath, stood. "What makes you think I have any influence over her?"

Was that a laugh? Yeah, Neil just laughed . . . something AJ had yet to see. "You're here, aren't you?"

⁓

She knew she should have locked the door.

Sasha had kicked her shoes off and lain out on the queen bed. She'd been watching the clouds when they allowed the ocean below them to peek through. Now that they had clustered together, she had closed her eyes to make good on her threat of resting.

Her eyes popped open the second the door opened and AJ snuck inside. Not bothering to move, she closed her eyes again. "What do you want?"

"Wow, this is really nice."

She peeked long enough to see him walking around the room. A sofa for two sat along the wall dividing the bedroom from the main cabin. And behind the bed was another bathroom, this one equipped with a shower.

"What does your friend Harrison do for a living?"

AJ was not in the room to talk about the plane or the man who owned it. She answered him anyway. "Shipping."

"What does he ship? Cocaine from Colombia?"

She cracked an eye, saw AJ looking out the window.

Fine, she could play possum. Sasha closed her eyes, took a deep breath, and willed her shoulders to relax.

He was staring. She felt his eyes and heard his breathing change.

Sasha counted her breaths, made it to five before she heard movement and felt a dip on the bed.

AJ had his back to her and he was toeing off his shoes.

"What do you think you're doing?"

Once the second shoe hit the floor, he spread out next to her, his back resting against the headboard. "Resting. I didn't think you'd mind."

"You thought wrong."

"I had no idea a queen-size bed fit in the back of a plane."

"Oh, for God's sake!" Sasha pushed herself upright and stared at him. Her outburst had him smiling.

That grin irritated the hell out of her. "What's so funny?"

"You're so damn adorable."

"Adorable?" She squeezed her eyes shut, opened them to find him still staring. "No one has ever called me adorable."

"Well, you are. Probably not very healthy of me to say this, but I like getting you riled up just to see all the adorbs oozing out."

"Oozing adorbs? Is that even a thing?"

His smile was all teeth. "It is with you."

The man was pleased with himself.

Sasha started to push herself off the bed. AJ captured her arm. "Okay, I'll stop teasing. Don't go."

"I'm not leaving because you're teasing, I'm leaving because you're sucking up all my air."

He stopped laughing. "Please." He released her arm and pulled the pillow she'd had her head on up farther on the bed and patted the space beside him. "Let's talk."

"If Neil sent you in here to change my mind . . ."

"Oh, he did."

Of course he did.

"But that's not what I came in here for."

Sasha crossed her legs on the bed and leaned against the wall of windows.

"Do you think there is a link between my sister and the people Pohl hires?"

Yes. She kept her answer to herself. "Define *link*."

"Maybe someone like Pohl approached her to work for them. Maybe she kept in contact with someone who did work for Pohl."

"The people Pohl hires are going to be loners. People who don't have family or friends as connections. Your sister doesn't fit the profile." Not at all. She and Claire, on the other hand, fit it perfectly.

"You clearly have friends," AJ said.

Could she say that about Neil and the rest of the crew? "He obviously didn't consider him a friend." It wasn't like she took Sunday dinners with the man and his family.

"His mistake."

She agreed. "Your sister didn't fit Pohl's agenda with her personal relationships or her physical attributes. She needed help on the obstacle courses and wasn't known for her hand-to-hand combat or marksmanship."

"I take it you looked up her grades."

"I didn't have to. I told you, I remember Amelia. She was smart, diplomatic, but not the top physical performer. Once the names are crunched, I'm sure we're going to find students in much better overall performance on Pohl's list of recruits."

"What if he didn't always recruit hired guns? What if he started out in areas of special agents for the various governments? Would she have been a recruit then?" Strain started to show on AJ's face.

"Why are you going down this road, AJ? Do you think your sister was part of something more than what she told you?"

He glanced at the door. "Neil suggested I wasn't objective enough to see what's right in front of me. You've known me a little longer, and I want to know your opinion."

The fact her opinion mattered to him was as foreign as her desire to put him at ease but not bullshit the man. "I think people are capable of doing just about anything to get what they want. Parents are capable of killing to keep their children safe. Men and women alike are willing to lie, cheat, and steal to put food on the table and a roof over their heads. Those examples are the easy ones. Things you and I can nod and agree with. Then there's the other kind of thieves or murderers. The kind that has no regard for life, their own or anyone else's. Add drugs to this person, take away anyone who cares about them, and they become desperate." She placed a hand on AJ's knee. "My point is, do I think your sister was capable of working for someone like Pohl? The answer is yes. Is it likely . . . no."

AJ stared absently across the room. She could tell by his expression he was contemplating that reality for the first time.

"AJ?"

He glanced at her.

"I'm seldom wrong about these things."

He shook his head, as if removing a thought from his brain. "We need to come up with a plan."

"We will."

153

"No, you and I. Neil seemed to think I had some kind of influence over you, so he sent me in here to convince you to keep me with you while you went after Pohl. Obviously he's mistaken. You're going to run off as soon as you get information, and I'm heading back to DC to dig into my sister's life more than I have. We convince Neil that we're taking off together, and he doesn't sic his men on you."

Sasha saw a flash inside her head in the form of an image of AJ rifling through his sister's home, maybe an office. What if he stumbled on a truth she didn't foresee? What if his trip to Germany led Amelia's killer back to him?

That thought didn't sit well in her gut. Outside of taking orders, she hadn't seen any evidence that AJ could identify a threat, let alone remove it. If he went off on his own, he could easily become a target if Pohl was connected. It was getting harder to see an endgame where Pohl wasn't connected.

"Don't tell me you're against the idea," AJ said.

Completely.

"I'm circling back to why Neil thinks you have some kind of pull with me."

AJ flashed his teeth again. "I know . . . crazy. I guess he sees the spark."

"The what?" Her thoughts shifted to AJ's words.

"Spark. That thing you feel when I walk in the room that you're refusing to acknowledge."

Her nipples—*little shits*—perked to attention. "That's ridiculous."

He chuckled.

"What?"

"It's okay. I get it. If you don't admit it, you can pretend it isn't there." AJ took that moment to look at his leg. The leg her hand was resting on.

She rolled her eyes and removed it. "I don't have to pretend any-thing. Does my body respond to yours? Yes. It's chemical. You undress me with your eyes and say things to purposely make me sexually aware you're here."

Amusement danced on his face.

"I never play where I eat," she told him.

He bent his leg, rested one of his arms on his knee. "What is that supposed to mean?"

"It means if you had picked me up in the bar in Germany, we would have fucked and I wouldn't have seen you again. Instead, you asked for my help and took sex off the table." Once the words left her lips, she took note of where they were both sitting, in a closed bedroom at thirty-some thousand feet.

Sasha wiggled to the edge of the bed and bent to retrieve her shoes.

"If I knew those were the rules, I would have changed my strategy."

She hoped he couldn't see her smile. She pushed her foot into one boot, zipped it up before turning to the next.

"You can't change what is," she said, her voice even.

Second boot zipped and she sat up, looked at AJ.

Poor guy looked like he'd just lost his puppy.

"Trust me, AJ. You don't want this."

She stood and took one step to the door.

AJ moved faster than she thought anyone could.

He blocked the door with his body and reached for her face with his hands. "Don't tell me what I don't want." And then to prove himself, he kissed her.

Stunned and silent. Two words Sasha never used to define herself when a man was taking what she didn't approve of first.

Yet there she stood, AJ's lips moving over hers, coaxing them open while her body tossed imaginary pom-poms in the air.

Push him away.

Yeah, her nipples were like beacons of *come and get me*. Pushing away wasn't going to happen.

Just a little friction. A small touch that wasn't her own.

She opened her mouth and kissed him back. The slide of his tongue along hers was like warm silk on cool skin.

Sasha reached for his waist.

Push him away.

She loved the feel of a man's waist as it narrowed to his hips. AJ wasn't a stranger to moving his muscles. Thick. Masculine.

She wanted to purr.

His arms wrapped around her, made her feel small in his embrace. And he kissed her. Assaulted her lips with a fever she was starting to catch.

Hot. So hot . . .

Sasha wanted her clothes off, and that single thought had her opening her mouth to catch her breath, her lips still pressed against his.

This road was dangerous.

Not something she was ready for.

She gripped his hips, hips she'd been fondling, and held him away.

AJ started to say something. She stopped him. "You made your point."

Their eyes met. His were soft and charged all at the same time.

What did hers look like?

His hands fell to her arms. "You're wrong."

She questioned him with a look.

"I do want this." Without saying anything else, he walked behind her to the private bathroom and closed the door.

Chapter Eighteen

By the time their flight landed on a private airstrip in Texas, it was past eight in the evening, but for those on the flight, their clocks told them it was well past two in the morning.

They stepped out of the jet and onto a nearly deserted tarmac. There were two cars, one for their party and the other for the flight crew.

Neil shuffled them to a waiting limousine and climbed in the front with the driver.

Sasha took a seat beside AJ and encouraged Claire to go back to sleep.

"We have a good hour before we'll get where we're going."

Claire didn't need to be told twice.

AJ ran his hand along the leather seat. "Let me guess, this is Mr. Harrison's, too."

"No. This is my sister-in-law's."

"Your late half brother's wife."

"You've been paying attention." She liked that in a man.

He looked out the window. "Following the bouncing ball." His voice was distant, like it had been the rest of the time they were on the plane after he'd kissed her.

"Well, keep your head up. Trina has remarried. Their home is the easiest to disappear in without the fear of being spotted."

"Remote?"

Sasha followed his gaze into the vastness of nothing that made up the long spans of space in Texas.

"Secure."

"Wouldn't Pohl think to look for you at her home?"

She'd considered that. Which was why she didn't plan on staying long. Make sure Claire was taken care of, find a direction, and move. Only now she needed to figure out how to do that with a 190-pound man at her side. "Maybe if there were some happy family photos of us. We're not that kind of a family."

AJ looked over his shoulder. "You and Trina don't get along?"

"No. We're just not . . ." Sasha couldn't even name what they weren't. She still felt the need to protect Trina, long after the threats of her father were gone. Trina's high-profile life kept Neil's security team on alert from time to time. Sasha was right there to lend a hand. "We're just not" was all Sasha could say.

AJ stretched his legs out in front of him and leaned his head back. "Aren't you tired?"

"I'll drop when we're inside." While they were moving, she needed to be alert. Even if she wasn't the one driving. Once she was at the ranch and had access to a gun, she'd feel better.

AJ closed his eyes. "You'll have to show me how you do it someday."

"Do what?"

"Hide the toothpicks holding your eyes open."

"It's adrenaline."

He smiled, even with his eyes closed. "Chemicals."

The memory of their conversation on the plane repeated in her head. "I aced chemistry."

AJ reached out, eyes still closed, and grabbed her hand. "So did I."

Sasha stiffened, not sure what to do.

"Relax, Stick. It's just a hand." He tucked her hand in his and sank deeper in the seat.

Pulling it away felt childish.

Leaving it there was awkward.

Claire was sound asleep, and from the way AJ was breathing, it wouldn't be long for him to nod off, too. She'd slip her hand away from his when he did.

$\sim\!\!\mathcal{D}$

For forty-five minutes, AJ held her hand. Not since junior high had he measured time while holding a girl's hand.

He let his mind rest, and every time he felt Sasha attempting to pull away, he moved a little and held it tighter.

It was comical just how uncomfortable she was with such a simple thing. For one brief moment he had wanted to make a joke and ask if she wasn't hugged as a child.

Thank God he'd been taught to think before he spoke. Because after hearing Sasha's story, he realized that no . . . she hadn't been hugged as a child. Affection was probably as foreign to her as hunger was to him. Yeah, his father could be a self-centered ass, but his mom had always been there to hug and kiss away the pain.

Who had done that for Sasha?

His heart hurt just thinking about it.

He felt the car slowing down and Sasha shifting in her seat.

AJ yawned away his pretend sleep and gave Sasha's hand one more squeeze before she slowly pulled it away.

"We're here."

AJ peered out the window, expecting to see a whole lot of nothing. That wasn't what he found.

They pulled up to a massive gate with someone in a guardhouse. It reminded him a little of Richter. Only on each side of the gate were eight- to ten-foot walls of stone and plants . . . up lights illuminated the walls and made the place feel like a fancy hotel.

Inside the walls, the views just kept coming, split rail fences with land beyond them. Tree-lined driveway that felt like it went on forever. They passed a house he thought was their destination. When they didn't stop, he kept quiet and waited.

Then he saw it.

"You sure this isn't a hotel?"

"Positive." Sasha leaned over and shook Claire's shoulder.

The girl woke with a jump.

"It's okay. We're here," Sasha coaxed.

Wide, sleepy eyes started to focus. "M'kay."

The car stopped and AJ reached for the door.

He stepped out and found himself awestruck by the size of the place. It stretched forever, a sprawling ranch that made the Harrison manor house appear way too prim and proper by comparison. "Wow."

Sasha accepted his hand as she got out of the car but let it go as quickly as she could.

I need to work on that.

"Whoa." Claire stood with her mouth gaping open. "Where are we going to stay next? Disneyland?"

"You made it." The voice belonged to a woman trotting down the steps of the house. Petite with long dark hair and honey skin, her smile spread from ear to ear.

AJ turned. "Trina?" he asked in a whisper.

Sasha nodded.

Trina stopped in front of Neil first. "I was starting to worry."

"Clean flight," Neil told her.

Trina opened her arms for a hug. "C'mon. It won't hurt."

Neil stepped into her hug reluctantly.

"Wade's coming. He was in the studio," Trina told him.

"My men?" Neil asked.

"In the kitchen. It's like old times in there."

Neil walked away and Trina turned her attention on the three of them. "I'm so glad you're here."

Trina was all smiles, and Sasha was even stiffer than when she held his hand. "I'm unsure what Neil has told you."

Trina laughed. "He says about half as much as you do. So next to nothing."

"This is AJ and Claire," Sasha introduced them.

Claire waved. "Thanks for having us."

Trina waved them inside. "You're welcome, darlin'. If you need anything, just ask. Please don't be shy."

"I don't think you have to worry about that," AJ said.

Claire glared over her shoulder toward him.

AJ winked.

He stood back with Sasha when Trina and Claire started up the stairs.

"No hugs and kiss hello?" he asked close to her ear.

Sasha looked at him as if he were crazy.

"Okay, got it."

They stepped into the foyer to find Neil shaking a man's hand. Jeans, button-down shirt, and cowboy boots. The man fit the ranch a million percent.

Up until that moment, the term *gobsmacked* had been more of a metaphor than reality.

Up until the exact moment when Mr. Cowboy turned to look at them.

"Hey, hon. Come here and meet Sasha's friends."

Trina's husband turned their way, all smiles. "Hello, Sasha. Lovely as always." The man didn't hesitate as he placed an arm around Sasha's shoulders for a hug.

She looked like she forgot to breathe. "Wade."

"AJ, this is my husband, Wade."

Wade put his hand out.

AJ grasped it and tried not to stutter. "Wade Thomas." Country singer superstar. No wonder they were riding in limos and flying on jets.

He grinned. "I take it Sasha didn't tell you."

"Neither did Neil."

Wade turned to Neil. "Really, man?"

"I forgot."

That made AJ laugh. "I'll try not to embarrass myself. Thank you for having us."

"Anything for family," Wade said.

Sasha shifted on the balls of her feet.

Claire stepped forward and waved. "I'm Claire and clueless. Should I know you?"

Wade and Trina laughed.

"Nope. Not at all," Wade said.

Trina started speaking in a language AJ didn't know. At first he thought it was German but then realized it sounded more Russian. Didn't matter, he didn't understand a word, but it appeared both Sasha and Claire caught what Trina was saying.

Claire started to laugh.

"You know I'm just going to make you tell me what you said later," Wade teased his wife.

"She said you're famous outside of the house," Claire told him.

Wade shifted his gaze. "And inside?"

Claire laughed.

Trina stepped around Wade. "Let's get out of the doorway. Are you guys hungry? I know it's a long flight, but—"

"I'm starving," Claire interrupted.

"I told you she wasn't shy," AJ said.

It was Claire's turn to say something he couldn't understand.

When Sasha laughed, he knew it had to be good.

"Ever feel like you're the butt of a joke, AJ?" Wade asked.

"Every day this week."

⌒◎

There had only been a handful of times that Sasha had been in Trina and Wade's home. Every time except one, Sasha had been part of the security detail policing the place. The other time was shortly after Lilliana was born. Even then, Sasha couldn't bring herself to stay longer than a couple of hours. Hours that she watched from the sideline while Trina and Wade accepted congratulations from family and friends.

Sasha and Trina were family by circumstance, not blood. A fact Sasha told herself often when she was face-to-face with the woman.

Yet here she was watching the sky change colors from a private balcony on Trina and Wade's ranch. It was hard to admit how well she'd rested the night before. They'd gone to bed long after midnight and here it was almost nine in the morning, and Sasha had just climbed out of the shower.

Unheard of.

She pulled out her stash of clothes and selected the cleanest pieces to wear. Laundry was in order . . . or a trip to a store. Not that there was time for that.

After tidying the room and piling up her clothes, Sasha tied her hair back and walked through the quiet house to find some coffee.

Noise from the kitchen told her she wasn't alone.

"Is that good?" Trina said in a high-pitched voice.

Poised in a high chair and shoving a fistful of what looked like Cheerios into her mouth was Lilliana.

At least that's what Sasha assumed. She hadn't seen the girl since she was a newborn. And that was nearly a year ago.

"She got big." And beautiful. But then that was a given considering Trina was a cross between the angelic girl next door and model beautiful. Her Latin American heritage gifted her curves in the right places and perfect skin. And Wade . . . the man may not have been Sasha's flavor, but he sure did fill out a pair of blue jeans.

"I know, right? I go to bed, and when I wake up, it's like she's a different person."

Lilliana giggled around her full mouth and waved a chubby fist in the air.

"Did you sleep well?"

"I did." *Really well.* Sasha crossed to the coffeepot and helped herself.

"Oh, let me help you—" Trina started to stand up.

"I've got it. Is everyone else still in bed?"

"Oh, no. Wade is out there somewhere with AJ. And Neil has already jumped on the computer and started barking orders to his guys."

That sounded about right. "And Claire?"

"Haven't seen her yet. She's a sweet girl."

Yeah, she was. And witty. The girl made her want to laugh. Except for some reason Sasha had spent her entire life trying not to. As if laughter was somehow a display of weakness.

She sat in Trina's kitchen, watching the joy on Lilliana's face, and wondered what it would feel like to laugh so freely.

Who had told her laughter was a weakness?

Sasha tried to smile . . . knew she sucked at it.

"Are you okay?" Trina asked.

"I'm fine." *Am I?*

Trina faked a smile to say she didn't believe her, and they both pretended all was good.

"Claire needs a safe place to stay while we clear up everything legal."

"Neil said the same thing. She's welcome here. You know that."

Sasha lowered her gaze. "Thank you."

Lilliana's laughter turned to a cry and Trina snapped into Mom mode. "What is it?"

As if the baby could tell her.

Trina fussed with the high chair and unfastened the belt around her waist. "C'mere." She patted her on the back once Lilliana was in her arms and started to shift from foot to foot.

Three steps in and the baby stopped fussing.

Trina was a natural.

"You make that look easy," Sasha found herself saying.

"It's not. Lord knows I wish it was." Trina repositioned her baby on her other shoulder and that's when all hell broke loose. As in Lilliana decided breakfast didn't agree with her stomach and she tossed all her cookies on Trina's chest.

Trina stopped moving. "Oh, boy." She looked at her daughter. "I bet you feel better." Trina grabbed a towel lying on the kitchen counter and wiped her baby's face.

Lilliana seemed oblivious of the mess she'd just created.

Trina, on the other hand, lifted Lilliana away from her chest and looked at Sasha. "Can you . . . while I clean this off?" she asked.

And without approval, Trina handed Sasha the baby, barely giving her enough time to put her coffee cup down. "I, ah . . ."

"I'll be right back. I'm sure she's done puking."

And Trina was gone.

Alone in the center of the kitchen, Sasha held a human who was less than a year old.

Lilliana regarded her with a similar expression to her own. One that said, *Who the hell is this and what am I supposed to do with them?*

Only Lilliana had a better grip on what to do. She reached out with her chubby, albeit sticky, hand and grabbed Sasha's nose.

And then laughed.

Giggled.

"What's so funny?"

Apparently, her question was amusing, since Lilliana giggled again.

A sticky baby hand was on her nose and all she could do was smile. "You defile your mother's shirt, and now you're making fun of my nose. I'm not sure I can trust you."

Lilliana thought the comment was worth another round of laughter.

Sasha moved her to her hip and walked toward the sink. There she ran the water and started to clean off the sticky. "You're kinda a mess, kid."

More giggles.

It was hard not to smile.

Lilliana wasn't as cooperative as Sasha had assumed she would be when it came to water and soap. She pushed her hands away and moved her face from side to side to avoid being cleaned. Still, Sasha managed. "I'm always going to win this . . . you might as well get used to it."

Now that the sponge bath was done, she grinned and went back to playing with Sasha's nose.

"Oh my God . . . that's a baby."

Claire stood in the doorway to the kitchen, her mouth open.

"Are you sure you've earned your diploma at Richter?" Sasha asked, teasing.

Claire walked closer, her eyes glued to Lilliana. "You know Richter. No one brings babies around."

How sad that Sasha knew exactly what Claire was going through. Babies were not a part of their lives as orphans. At least not once they moved to Richter. No nieces or nephews, brothers or sisters. No. They had no barometers for children unless they were in the primary education dorms at the school.

But holding a kid?

Had she ever held one?

Sasha found herself holding Lilliana tighter. As if she couldn't gauge if she held her hard enough to avoid dropping her.

"You're up . . . good." Trina walked back into the room, a new shirt and pair of jeans covered her legs. "What do you want for breakfast?"

Sasha turned to Trina to give her the baby, only to find her sister-in-law moving to the refrigerator.

"Eggs? Bacon. This is a working farm, we have plenty of breakfast food."

Claire moved to the kitchen window. "A real farm?"

"Cattle ranch. But Wade insisted on chickens and a garden. Not that I pretend to take care of any of that. But the eggs are good." Trina moved around the kitchen, pulling a pan from a cabinet and eggs from a basket.

"I thought you said Wade was a country singer," Claire said.

"He is. But the first part of that is *country*. And Wade is all that and more before he's a singer."

While Trina and Claire carried on, Sasha and Lilliana regarded each other in silence.

Something told Sasha that the silence wouldn't last for long.

"If he's so famous, why are you cooking?" Claire asked.

The question captured Sasha's attention.

Trina moved around the kitchen. "Well, when Neil called and said you were coming, we gave some of our help the week off. Probably better that they don't see who is here until we clear up any legal details." Trina glanced at Sasha, then back to Claire. Sasha had brought Claire up to speed on the investigation into AJ's sister's death on the flight over. The news didn't appear to impact her as much as seeing a baby. "Besides, I don't mind cooking. Once my mother-in-law finally moved out, I had an opportunity to cook a little more."

"Your mother-in-law lived here?"

"For a short time." Trina glanced at Sasha. Kept her answers short to Claire.

They both knew Trina's mother-in-law took a little work to move on after the marriage.

"I can't imagine living in a house with a mother-in-law."

Trina opened her mouth, only to have Claire cut her off. "Or even a mother."

"Oh." Trina stood dumbfounded. "I can't imagine."

Claire shrugged. "It's okay. Right, Sasha? We turned out okay."

"Yup."

Claire smiled at the baby to have that grin returned. "Can I hold her?"

"Sure," Trina said. "If she starts to squirm, just sit down on the floor with her. She's scooting around pretty well these days."

Claire reached her hands out to take her, and Sasha found herself reluctant to let go. "Don't drop her, even if she pukes on you."

Trina laughed.

"I won't. C'mere, cutie."

Once Sasha's arms were free, she picked up her coffee again. It'd been strangely satisfying to hold her, if even for a few minutes.

Trina cracked eggs into a bowl. "Did you want some, Sasha?"

"That would be nice."

Claire made faces and laughed when Lilliana tried to mimic her. It wasn't long before both of them were on the floor next to a pile of toys.

Bacon started to pop on the stove, dragging Sasha out of her baby trance. "Let me help you."

"I didn't know you cooked," Trina said.

"I don't. But I can manage bacon."

"My talents are limited, too." She lowered her voice. "Wade's cook is teaching me. And Wade is the master of a grill, so we won't starve."

Together they managed eggs, bacon, and biscuits. The biscuits were courtesy of the hired chef that wasn't there.

They ate and let Lilliana entertain them.

Claire asked questions about the ranch and kept Sasha from having to talk.

"I need to wash my clothes," she told Trina when they were finished eating.

"I can do that—"

She shook her head. "If you can direct me to the laundry room, I'll manage."

Trina smiled and motioned her to follow. "You have the baby, okay?" she asked Claire, who was content with the task of babysitting.

"It's just you and me, kid. Let's go pick up some guys," Claire said in a high-pitched voice.

They walked up the stairs and toward the bedrooms. "Grab your clothes. I'll show you the laundry room on this floor."

"You have two?"

"If you count the guesthouse and the staff quarters, we have four. Crazy, right? There is another laundry pair downstairs, but it's used mainly for cleaning towels and household stuff."

"It's a big place."

"Huge. And if Wade has his way, it will be even bigger in the next couple of years."

"Oh, why?"

"He wants his daughter to live here forever. He thinks that if he can buy neighboring ranches, she can have one and always be close by."

They stopped in her guest room and Sasha gathered an armful of clothes. "He's a good dad."

"He really is."

Sasha was happy they'd found each other.

"Is that all you have?" Trina asked.

Sasha glanced at her laundry pile. "We weren't shopping when we left Europe."

"I guess that's true. You know, you and Shannon are about the same size. She has several outfits here. I'm sure she won't mind you using them. Now that we're all having babies, it makes sense to leave clothes at each other's houses. Packing for kids is hard enough." Shannon was one of Trina's friends who lived in California.

"I'm not sure—"

"At least borrow something while you're doing laundry. She has great taste." Trina led her into a guest room, this one with a crib. She opened the closet and pushed through several hangers. "This is Shannon's stash."

Sasha looked down at what she was wearing, then back to the closet. The blue jeans were stylish enough. "You sure?"

"Of course. You change. I'll grab a laundry basket."

After sliding into jeans and an olive green short-waisted sweater, Sasha checked her appearance in a mirror. Not her normal outfit, but it worked. She turned to look at her back and grinned. Even her skinny butt looked good in denim.

In the laundry room, Trina stuck around and helped.

And by helping, Sasha meant did the work. "Wade and I hope you'll consider coming over for Christmas. We're going to California for Thanksgiving, since Lori will have the youngest babies. I know Reed and Lori would love to see you."

"Reed mentioned it."

"So you'll come?"

"We need to clear up all this before I can even speculate where I'll be."

Trina's face told Sasha that she knew the chances of her showing up were slim . . . even if everything going on in her life at that moment was in the past. As a polite woman, however, she didn't say a thing.

With the washer doing the work, they walked back downstairs, where Sasha planned on making a quick exit to find Neil. Talking about babies, cooking, and laundry was not in her skill set, and all the domestic stuff was weighing on her.

They found Claire sitting on the floor, her legs stretched out in front of her, and Lilliana curled up on her shoulder, fast asleep.

Both Sasha and Trina stopped in the doorway to stare.

Claire held the baby while quiet tears slid down her cheeks.

"What's wrong?" Trina asked softly.

Claire bit her lips and tried to talk. "I-I don't know how any mom can walk away."

While Sasha stared, Trina moved in and knelt down to her level. "Oh, honey."

Sasha realized then that Claire had been abandoned, not orphaned. The results were the same, but the trauma was completely different.

Claire started to cry with shuddered breaths.

A knot in Sasha's throat caught.

"Here, let me take her." Trina reached for her daughter.

Once Lilliana was on her mother's shoulder, Trina offered to help Claire up with a free hand.

Once on her feet, Claire walked straight to Sasha and placed her tear-streaked face on her chest. Claire's arms wrapped around her with a sob.

For a minute, Sasha just stood there, unsure what to do. No one had ever thrown themselves in her arms and cried before. One look at Trina and Sasha closed Claire into an embrace. One that sparked more tears.

It took a lot of effort to hold back emotion.

Sasha couldn't remember the last time she'd let that emotion happen, but it sure wanted to now. "Some people suck," she told Claire.

"Yeah."

The door leading from the kitchen to the outside opened and AJ walked in beside Wade.

Both men stopped when they saw the crying teenager.

AJ stepped forward. "What happened?"

Claire sucked in a breath and pulled away to collect herself. She looked up at Sasha with a brave face.

"Just a little female bonding," Trina announced.

Claire smiled through her pain.

"C'mon, Claire, help me put Lilly down for her nap."

Claire jumped at the opportunity to leave and Sasha was faced with the men alone.

"Is she okay?" AJ asked.

"She's fine." Sasha turned and wiped away a single tear that had managed to escape the jail she'd put it in.

Chapter Nineteen

AJ had never been in a war room before, but he was fairly certain the space Neil and his band of merry men congregated in resembled one. The night before, he'd met Cooper and Isaac, two of Neil's security guards. Jeb was Wade's personal bodyguard, who lived onsite and had joined them that morning. Two more men AJ hadn't been introduced to were brought in to relieve the man at the front entrance, as well as one on the far end of the property where deliveries were made for the working ranch portion of the estate. From AJ's count, there were eight armed guards onsite, not to mention the ranch hands, who had been told that there was a viable threat and they needed to report to Jeb or Neil if they saw or suspected anything.

They had taken over the guesthouse, moving living room furniture aside to make room for fold-up tables and laptop computers. The kitchen table was littered with pictures and information that eventually made it up onto the wall. In the center of the data sat an image of Amelia. Subject zero. Unlike anyone else on the wall who had died, the guys in the room hadn't put a black line through her image. AJ was pretty sure that was to save his feelings.

He watched from the side of the room while men buzzed around.

When the front door opened and Sasha walked in, three of the guys stopped what they were doing and stared.

"Sasha?" Cooper asked.

She narrowed her eyes. "You saw me last night," she said to him.

He looked her up and down. "Yeah, but I didn't know you owned anything that wasn't black." Cooper started to laugh and one of the other guys joined him.

"I don't. This is borrowed."

Cooper laughed harder. "Thank God. I was going to ask Wade if there was a doctor in the house to make sure you were feeling okay."

She walked by with a glare.

The man obviously knew her well. Personally, AJ liked the relaxed jeans and sweater look. The new clothes softened her hard edges. Or maybe that was Claire's doing.

She stood across from the wall of pictures and crossed her arms over her chest. "Where are we?" she asked.

Cooper stepped around her and waved a pen in the air. "Hold up, let's get Reed online."

Sasha nodded and stepped back.

AJ moved to her side. "Why Reed?"

"He's the private investigator. He sees things others don't."

One of the monitors picked up a live feed of a clean-cut man sitting behind a computer. "Hello."

"How's the picture?" Cooper asked.

"It's clear. Is Sasha there?"

Sasha moved in front of the camera. "Good morning. Are you a father yet?"

"Any day." Reed peered closer into his camera. "Are you wearing a sweater?"

Cooper chuckled.

"Yes." Sasha was irritated. "Are we doing this or talking fashion?"

"Get your panties out of your ass," Reed said, laughing. "Is AJ there?"

AJ stepped up. "Nice to see you in person," he said.

Reed nodded his approval. "Glad you filled out since your high school mug shot."

"That was a closed file."

"I have a can opener. Okay, let's get on with this. Turn the camera around and bring me up to date."

Cooper ran the meeting and used a yardstick to point at the wall. "Since Hofmann is our subject, we started there. Green dots signify covert intelligence. Information we were able to obtain from the liberated files off the dean's computer."

"Headmistress," Sasha corrected.

"The headmistress's computer. Hofmann did qualify for the green dot, as well as a yellow, signifying political ties and access." Cooper glanced at AJ. "Black dots are for honor marks in weapons and hand-to-hand combat. Again, not marks that Hofmann obtained."

"Do we have the school's definition of *covert intelligence*?" Reed asked.

"There are two. At least that's what was indicated in the files. Computer skills, which included writing code or hacking into the back doors of computers. And observed intelligence through pranks and mischief the students got into while attending the school."

"Sasha, did the school teach you how to hack into a computer?"

"Not in the general education classes."

"So that's a yes."

"More of a problem-solving course. That some of us might have used to learn how to obtain information not otherwise given to us freely."

"You should go into politics, Sasha," one of the men in the room said.

"AJ, did you know your sister could hack?" Neil asked.

"That's news to me. She could always fix our computers . . . but hacking?"

Sasha stepped forward. "If I remember Amelia, she was always following the rules. I doubt she was on the intelligence list for foul play."

"Okay, let's move on."

Cooper explained the lines drawn from Amelia to the two other deceased women, and the third that was missing. "Roommates at one time or another. Notice zero dots. Jocey and Keri graduated Richter, but they weren't going to be recruited for the CIA. Olivia, our missing student, however, has a stacked deck."

"Have we located her?" Reed asked.

"Nope. Just the location in Germany that AJ has reported as furnished but empty of anything personal."

The door opened and several heads turned to see Claire walk in the house.

"Who are all these other people on the board?" Reed asked.

Cooper glanced at the new addition to the room and continued. "Using this model, we've gone through and singled out those students with all the dots and then pulled their roommates during their senior year. If we found the potential recruits working, living with a family and seemingly normal jobs, we've indicated it with a bright orange dot. No explained or unexplained demise of anyone."

"It looks like you have a lot of orange dots."

Claire stepped forward and shook her head. "That's because you're not looking for the right people. Where is Sasha's picture?"

Cooper pointed to the top corner. Her roommates were all accounted for. No black line indicated any of them had died.

Claire reached up and pulled Sasha's picture down and pinned it next to Olivia and two other past students who were indicated as missing. "What do these four women have in common?"

"All the dots."

"No, they're all beautiful, yet nothing that stands out as so remarkable that they'll be remembered," Claire pointed out. "And you're missing a skill."

"Which one?" Neil asked.

Claire and Sasha looked at each other, and then Claire said something to Sasha in Russian.

"Right." Sasha walked to the wall, grabbed a marker, and put a blue dot by her image. "Everyone at Richter was mandated to speak German and English. A third language was required, but you didn't have to pass with fluency. I speak English, German, Russian, French, Italian, some Spanish, and enough Arabic to get me in trouble."

The room fell silent.

"And I speak English, German, Russian, some Italian, and Mandarin. I was going to add Arabic next year," Claire said.

"Holy shit. I need to go back to school," AJ said under his breath.

Some of the guys laughed.

"We know I was approached for a job, and Pohl had his eye on you," Sasha pointed out. "Which means we need to add another factor."

Claire must have been on the same page, because she started nodding. "We're both orphans. No families to tie us down or keep us from taking a dangerous job. And Pohl was my benefactor. I was given incentives to learn more languages than my roommates. Told that when I graduated, I'd have five thousand euros for every language I spoke fluently."

"Was there any data in the chip I gave you saying who else was Pohl's financial responsibility?"

Cooper shook his head. "No. But we do have who has families and who doesn't. We'll cross-reference that information and move forward."

AJ's head spun.

"What about Claire's original birth certificate?" Sasha asked.

"We have boots on the ground in New York and should have that by the end of the day," Neil said.

"Any closer to a real identity on Pohl or who he works for?" AJ asked.

"I'm working on that," Reed said from the computer screen. "It's an image search at this point."

"That's all for now, then," Neil reported. "We get back to work and return before the sun sets and see where we're at. First priority is clearing Claire's age. I'd rather deal solely with Pohl than our own police force. In the meantime, we need a rotation on the monitors here at the ranch. Fresh eyes on the screens every four hours."

"You got it, Boss," Cooper said. "You heard the man, let's get cracking."

Claire rubbed her hands together. "How can I help?"

"Oh, it's okay, kid . . ."

With hands on her hips, Claire asked, "How many languages do you speak?"

Cooper blinked. "One."

"Are you telling me there isn't anything in the headmistress's file that is in a language other than English?"

"Okay, fine."

Claire did a little victory dance and let Cooper lead her to a computer.

∞

"Did you want to get some fresh air?"

AJ's question had Sasha turning around in surprise. *No.* What she really wanted to do was dig into the files and look for links herself.

He leaned in. "That's my way of asking you to come outside with me so I can have a private word."

"Lead the way," she said.

Even during fall, Texas was warm. They walked out of the guesthouse and Sasha diverted him away from the main house. "Trina asked the cook to come back to prepare food for everyone. It's best she doesn't see me until we can clear my name."

They walked toward the stables and stopped at one of the fences that kept the horses penned in to graze. Sasha wasn't a big fan of country living, but it was hard to look over something as simple as a group of horses munching on grass and not feel her heart rate slow. "What's on your mind?"

"You really speak seven languages?"

"You brought me out here to clarify that?"

"There you go again, asking a question instead of answering me. No. I wanted to ask about the A-team in there. You said Neil was in security."

"He is."

"Those guys all look like they do more than watch monitors and eat donuts."

"I don't think I've ever seen Neil eat a donut." She found the thought strangely fascinating.

"Not my point."

"Neil recruits retired military service. That's why they all look like they can take care of themselves in a fight. I've seen a couple of them in action, so I can vouch for them. They're men who liked the adrenaline but not the drama of working under military orders. They want to work for what they believe in and not whatever political power is in office."

"You trust them."

"And they trust me. What are you getting at, AJ?"

He moved beside her, close enough for her to feel the warmth of his body, and leaned against the fence. "The last bit you and Claire were saying about being orphaned and the words *emotionally vulnerable*—words you said to Pohl: these things might have pertained to you at one point, but not now. I look around and I see family. I see an organized army working intelligence as if they're in a situation room looking for a mole in the Middle East. I do not see a profile of what Pohl needs. Yeah, you check off all the other boxes, but the one where you need him? No, not you."

Sasha leaned back. "When I went back to Richter, I told Linette I was searching for something. Direction. Maybe she thought that meant I was all that you mentioned."

"She's the one who invited him to come and see you."

"For a finder's fee." The thought still made her sick.

"Right. What does Linette do with her finder's fee? She lives on campus, right?"

"Yeah."

"Does she have family?"

Sasha shrugged. "I wouldn't know."

"Husband, kids?"

"Are you suggesting she works for Pohl?"

"I'm suggesting those guys in there look into her a little more. She runs the school, but who runs her? Board of directors for the school? Is there an advisory committee?"

Sasha thought of her parting conversation with Linette. Her defensiveness for inviting Pohl and the odd feeling inside of Sasha, hearing the woman act as if sacrificing a normal life for a few students was a small price to pay for all the other graduates that went on to do great things. "You're right. I think we do need to look harder at Linette."

AJ looked pleased with himself. "I may not be retired military, but I'm good for something."

She looked him up and down.

His grin brightened. "I'm good for that, too."

Sasha squeezed her eyes shut. "I'll keep that in mind."

He laughed.

"I have a question," she said as it surfaced in her head.

"Ask away."

"Your address in Florida is in a pretty nice part of town. Did you support that with criminal activity?"

He scooted closer until their shoulders touched. "I have a trust fund. Grandma Hofmann set Amelia and I up. Amelia didn't have to work, but it fulfilled her. Or that's what she said, anyway. I haven't found the kind of job, legal job, that keeps my interest for long. I skip around with a lot of blue-collar stuff to keep my other activities off the radar, but I don't depend on them to live."

"Hmmm."

"Does that worry you?"

"I'm no angel, Junior. I don't know very many people that don't have something to hide." The truth was, she probably wouldn't be attracted to the guy if he made an honest living as an accountant or some such mediocre job. The edge of danger always did something for her. It wasn't like she picked up the men in her past at the coffee shop while discussing the difference between the African roasted blends and those harvested in Mexico.

AJ twisted around until he was standing in front of her and his hands rested on the fence supporting her back.

She glanced to the side to see if anyone spotted them. "What are you doing?"

He pressed his body against hers, his intentions clear. "I'm going to kiss you and remind my senses how you taste."

There was a smile on her face at the sheer unexpectedness of his pursuit. "And if I don't want this kiss?" She wanted the kiss . . . shifted her legs in anticipation.

"You would have already removed my balls if you wanted me to stop."

She looked at his lips. "You've been paying close attention."

"And you like that."

He leaned closer but didn't touch her.

She pushed her chest into his. "Is this kiss going to happen sometime today, or do I have to wait?"

"The anticipation kills you, doesn't it?"

His lower lip brushed against hers.

Her body sparked and quickly simmered.

His laughing smile told her all she needed to know. He was taking control.

Something she wasn't used to.

"If you're going to kiss me, do it like you mean it."

AJ's laughing smile faded.

Oh, shit.

He closed her in.

Trapped was not a feeling of comfort.

And then . . . he kissed her. His body pressed against her from knees to lips. Like a boxer putting his whole body into the punch, AJ committed.

His lips were open on hers, she responded with complete possession of his mouth. Hands gripped the railing, unwilling to pull him in. Not that she needed to pull anything. His pelvis dug into hers, his excitement already evident. The feel of him, oh, man . . . all man.

One of his hands left the railing beside hers and slid along her waist and to her back. He pressed her closer, her nipples straining against the unfamiliar sweater.

She wanted his touch . . . needed it.

There was a weight to his kiss, one that told her this wasn't something that came around every day. This man knew her more than any she'd let touch her as intimately as he was now. The texture of his tongue along hers, the way his hand exposed a small portion of her back, and the heat of his bare skin on hers.

She wrapped one leg around his and let loose the railing she was gripping with all her energy.

The heat of him pressed against her stomach.

She moaned, wanted the contact lower. Her hips moved closer in response to her thoughts.

AJ's teeth grazed her lips.

Her nails bit into his back.

The sound of gravel kicking up a few yards away had Sasha opening her eyes.

Trina had stopped midstride, eyes glued to Sasha's.

AJ released her lips, looked down at her, and then over his shoulder. "I'm sorry. I, ah, was . . ."

AJ dropped his head onto Sasha's shoulder with a chuckle.

Trina shuffled her feet, turned one way and then another before taking a step back in the direction she'd appeared from. "I'll just leave you two . . ."

Sasha watched her disappear while her heartbeat returned to normal.

"Is she gone?"

She answered with a single nod and pulled back enough to see AJ's eyes.

AJ swiped his finger over her bottom lip and then licked it.

The action made her whole body clench.

"Probably best we didn't do this out here anyway," he said.

She felt a smile on her lips.

AJ's lips briefly met the side of her neck. "Do me a favor," he said.

The neck action distracted her. "Another one?"

The tip of his tongue met her skin. "Don't unman me if I sneak into your room at night."

She gripped his hips and moved him far enough away to keep his lips from her body.

Their eyes met.

"The risk of bodily harm makes it more exciting," she told him.

With that, she stepped around him and back toward the war room.

Chapter Twenty

Feeding time at the zoo was right up there with the table full of hungry men, a few good women, and a baby.

Back in her own comfortable, form-fitting black clothing, Sasha sat across from AJ and next to Claire. On the teenager's knee, Lilly giggled as her diapered butt kept bouncing with every move Claire made. Wade sat at one end of the table, and Trina at the other, her daughter's high chair to the side, not that it would be used, considering the fascination Claire had with the kid.

". . . Mandarin, encrypted at that." Cooper pointed a fork loaded with tri tip in Claire's direction. "Claire's a damn genius."

They were talking about some of the highlights of the day's findings. Apparently, Linette had what they'd dubbed The Mandarin File. Every highly skilled benefactor orphan who fit the portfolio that Pohl could possibly recruit from was cloaked in Mandarin.

"Gibberish Mandarin. Until Cooper broke the encryption," Claire explained.

Cooper shoved the meat in his mouth, talked around it. "We need her on our team, Neil."

All eyes went to the largest man at the table.

Neil glared at Cooper, glanced at Claire. "She's a child."

Sasha saw Claire's spine stiffen. "Bet *she* could outrun you," Claire said, looking Neil in the eye.

The murmurs at the table quieted.

Except for Sasha's voice. "I'll put money on that."

Claire smirked and rubbed noses with Lilly.

"I'd stay away from that mess if I were you, Neil," Wade said with a wink. "Women ganging up is never a good thing."

"Amen to that," AJ chimed in. "Try fleeing Europe with these two. Talk about fish out of water. Every time I turned around, Sasha was in a different disguise. Imagine a blonde housewife with that face."

All eyes turned to Sasha. Gazes narrowed and disbelief washed over everyone there.

Sasha locked eyes with AJ.

He smirked.

She clenched her jaw tight to keep from offering a single ounce of amusement.

"That's tough," Trina said, her head cocked to the side. "Maybe brunette with lots of highlights . . ."

"Barbie blonde. Valley accent. I wish I'd recorded it." AJ bit into a biscuit he'd smothered in butter.

Sasha lifted a small bite to her lips, hesitated. "I can blend in at a nursing home that only accepts men."

AJ pursed his lips together, shook his head. "That's taking the joy right out of fantasy, Stick."

Trina laughed. "I bet."

"That shoots all my fantasies to hell," Cooper added.

Sasha shot him a snarl. "Zip it."

He lifted his hands in front of his face, palms out. "I'm kidding. You're like a sister." He took a swig out of his glass of tea.

She brought her attention back to her dinner.

"A *hot* sister," Cooper said under his breath.

Neil, who almost never broke a smile, grinned.

Lilly started to fuss and reach for Trina.

Trina stood, lifted her daughter from Claire's arms. She looked across the table at AJ, then back to Sasha. "You're going to have to stand in line, Cooper."

"Ohhh . . ." Eyes fell between AJ and Sasha.

Heat simmered on her face.

"Someone needs to be changed," Trina said as she left the table to attend to her daughter's needs.

Claire sat a little taller and changed the subject. "I can teach you Mandarin, Cooper."

"And how long will that take?"

"Two years, if you're quick."

A wave of commentary erupted from the table.

"You'd be better off learning how to sing," Wade offered.

Sasha noticed Claire staring at Neil; disappointment hovered over her brow.

Neil was mopping up his food and disengaged with the conversation. He didn't seem to notice that a teenage girl was looking to the largest man at the table for approval.

Memories of Sasha's own childhood, and the need for positive affirmation, surfaced. "Claire has a point. Her language skills could prove valuable. At least while she's in college."

Neil lifted his eyes to Sasha, glanced at Claire.

"Too dangerous."

Claire leaned back, her chin lifted. "Who said anything about college? I can't afford that now." She reached over, grabbed Trina's wineglass, and took a drink. "Maybe the Service will have me. I'm a good shot."

Sasha lost her appetite, set her fork down. "They'd exploit everything you've learned."

Claire shrugged. "Don't all employers? Isn't that their job . . . find your strengths and use them for a fraction of what they're worth?"

The table had grown silent.

AJ sat forward. "We don't have to think about this tonight."

Claire waved the wineglass at him. "What's this *we* thing? I didn't know any of you a week ago. When this is all over, you'll all go back to your lives. I'll just . . ."

Sasha felt, more than saw, Claire trying to keep it together.

AJ leaned forward. "Teach me Mandarin."

Claire was onto him. "Why do you need to learn a new language, especially that one?"

AJ glanced at Sasha, then back to Claire. "Fine, teach me Russian. I have a feeling I'm going to need it."

Claire shook her head.

"No one is joining the military," Neil stated, his voice commanding everyone's attention. "Last I looked, we're in the States, and minors aren't allowed to drink alcohol. Put that down."

Hair on Sasha's neck stood up.

Claire slowly turned her head, met Neil's stare. "What's it to—"

"Now!" The walls shook.

She nearly dropped the wine.

"You want to work for me?" Neil looked directly at Claire.

She sat quietly.

"Your night is done once every dish on this table is clean. You report at oh five hundred. Showered, bed made. Is that clear?"

Claire blinked. "Uhm . . . h'okay."

Neil narrowed his already piercing gaze. "Excuse me."

She glanced at Sasha, then back. "Sir."

He nodded and turned his attention back to the last bite in his hand.

Trina walked back in the quiet and motionless room, stopped short of her husband. "What did I miss?"

Wade pulled his wife onto his lap. "Claire volunteered to wash the dishes."

Three people laughed . . .

Including Claire.

⌒

Sasha's shift on the cameras was scheduled to start at four in the morning. Instead of fighting sleep and the headache of jet lag, she made her excuses early to find the quiet in her own room.

She shed her clothing the moment the door to her room was closed and headed straight for the shower. With her hair balled in a knot on top of her head, she let the hot water ease some of the tension from her shoulders.

Things were moving along. They were on the tip of new information now that they had more names to run through their system.

Mandarin.

Sasha didn't realize Linette even spoke that language.

Then again, what did she really know about the woman? Almost nothing. It wasn't like the two of them had sat down for drinks at the pub the night she'd returned to Richter. Sasha smiled at the thought. Brigitte certainly turned out to be a lot more forthcoming than the headmistress.

Maybe looking into Linette's personal life would shed some light on things.

Sasha made a mental note to run Linette Lodovica's name through the paces.

She cut the water and grabbed the towel hanging off the shower door. The cool air of the room combined with her wet skin had her moving quickly to dry off.

A slight breeze coming from the bedroom along with a faint creak of a floorboard caused her skin to prickle.

Her heart rate sped up.

She dropped the towel and removed the needle-like hairpin from the top of her head. She palmed the would-be weapon and peeked out the door.

AJ stood in the open door of the balcony, his back to her.

Sasha considered retrieving the towel, then decided against it. She rested her shoulder on the threshold into the bathroom and adopted his relaxed stance.

"You're watching me, aren't you?" he asked without turning around.

Her answer was a long, deep breath.

He turned, slowly, and brought his gaze up last.

Shock registered on his face before he closed his eyes and turned his head. "Oh, damn. Sorry—"

How amusing. "You sneak into my room while I'm in the shower and you're sorry?"

AJ gave his head a firm shake and opened his eyes. She had to give the man credit, he was doing his best to keep his gaze on her face.

"No. I'm not . . ." His eyes drifted lower. He licked his bottom lip. The movement of his tongue brought her nipples to attention.

"Is there something I can do for you?" she asked, knowing damn well what he was there for. Even though she cautioned herself for provoking him, and going against her constant rule of not playing where she ate, Sasha also knew what pent up sexual tension did to her psyche. In order to concentrate, she really needed to purge the unknowns of this man from her head.

"I have you at an unfair advantage," AJ said.

She pushed off the doorway, revealed the pin in her hand, and quickly wound her hair back on the top of her head. "Even naked, I'm not without resources."

"Naked is your resource."

With a smile, she took several steps closer.

AJ stopped at the edge of the bed.

"Second thoughts?" she asked.

He shook his head.

Speechless. She liked that in a man.

He reached for her waist with both hands and pulled her closer.

She let her arms dangle, curious to see what he would do next without any prompts from her.

AJ traced her hip bone with his thumbs before sliding both palms up the sides of her body. He watched his own action, lips parted. When he reached her breasts, those thumbs teased the edges of them.

"I've wanted to taste these ever since I sat down across from you in the pub."

The thought of his lips on her had her chest rising and falling.

He kept his hands active, brushed just shy of her nipples and up to her collarbone, her neck. Both hands on her neck, thumbs brushing against her throat . . . yeah, anyone else and she'd have put a stop to that action. Instead she tried to control the shudder of her breathing as AJ circled the outsides of her ears and fanned his fingers into her hair. With one hand, he removed the pin and tossed it to the floor. "No weapons for you."

"I don't need—"

He stopped her from talking with a finger over her lips. He stepped closer and tugged gently on the hair in his hand before pressing his lips to the side of her throat.

Sasha closed her eyes, let the sensation of his tongue and teeth move up to the side of her ear. She tried to turn her head, meet his lips with hers, but he guided her head to the side with the control he had holding her hair. "Patience," he whispered.

Not one of her strong points.

Besides, she didn't want things slow. Hard and fast, that was the way she liked it.

Except there was something about the way he kissed the side of her jaw, skipped over her lips and moved to the other side. Something about the quiet things he whispered into her ear that she couldn't concentrate on because he had yet to really kiss her.

Sasha finally lifted her hands to his hips and waist, ran them down his ass and pulled him closer.

"Anxious?" he asked.

"Yes." She tugged at his shirt, pressed her hands onto the bare skin of his back.

AJ caught her hands, forced them off his back, and pinned them to her sides, all while his lips moved down the front of her chest.

"You're playing with danger," she warned him.

He teased her right nipple with his tongue.

"I know."

Her hands balled into small fists.

"You've already held off longer than I thought you would," he said as he moved his way to her left breast.

Her eyes rolled into the back of her head as he latched on before pulling away with a bite.

Her whole body shuddered as if a blast of cold air blew through the room.

The man had ten seconds . . . ten seconds before she turned this slow boat around. By the time she counted down to five, AJ took the back of her head in his hands, pulled her hair until she opened her eyes to look at him.

The darkness swirling in his eyes, the way his mouth hung open . . . she liked his hungry look.

He leaned down like he was going to kiss her.

She reached for his lips and he pulled away and grinned.

Unclenching her fists, she placed her palms against his chest.

Two seconds . . .

He must have seen her resolve to take charge and crushed his lips to hers. All fire, tongue, and passion.

While his hands controlled her head, hers pulled at his clothing. They broke apart only to clear his shirt over his head. His chest smashed against hers, she couldn't see it, but it felt glorious.

He pulled up for air, kissed her neck, ears, and jaw again, this time with more fire.

Sasha ran her hand down the length of him through his jeans. His hips surged into her palm.

"Do that again," he demanded.

This time she gripped him, and he had to stop kissing her to hold it together.

Oh, the control . . . how she loved the feel of him under her hand.

She placed one knee on the bed, then the other, all while working the buttons of his pants.

AJ stepped back and kicked off his shoes. Slightly out of reach, Sasha let her eyes travel down his chest and followed his hands when they worked to remove everything between them. He stared at her, and she took advantage of the position she was in.

Resting her butt on her heels, she ran a hand down her thigh and back up. She spread her knees farther apart and did it again.

AJ shook his pants free, briefs along with them, and stopped to stare.

His erection jutted out in front of him.

Sasha let her right hand dance up to the apex of her thighs, felt her own slickness as she brushed against the folds of her sex.

AJ placed his hands over hers, fingers locked together. Her neck strained, looking up at him. "You're so damn sexy, Sasha."

He kissed her again, dropped to his knees on the side of the bed, and moved his lips to her chest. Still holding her hands, he nudged her thighs farther apart.

Now this she could get used to, the cool air on her warm, wet skin. The top of AJ's head as he moved lower, spread her open farther. And like his gradual ease into kissing her, he hesitated over her, hot breath exciting her even more.

Sasha waited, knew it would be worth more if she didn't rush him.

The first brush of his tongue and she was lost. He latched on like he had with her breast, only this time he didn't let go. She brought her hips up to meet him, braced herself with one arm behind her, one on the back of AJ's head.

Everything inside of her wound tight.

"Harder, AJ," she choked out.

Thank God he took direction.

AJ filled his palms with her ass and made every tight part of her body shatter.

She choked on a cry, reminded herself that others might hear them if she released the scream that threatened, and rode her orgasm to the bitter end.

AJ met her eyes, his lips wet with the taste of her.

"You look pleased with yourself."

"Oh, I am."

She unfolded from her position, her knees and thighs now feeling the weight of exercise.

AJ reached for his jeans and returned with a condom in his hands.

Sasha scooted back up the bed, smiled as he crawled up beside her and pressed himself against her.

"Want more?" she asked.

He shook his head, pushed the hair from her face. "I haven't even started."

Chapter Twenty-One

Somewhere in the middle of the night, Sasha tried to kick him out of her bed. A move he knew without a doubt was her method of operation.

AJ didn't allow it.

He rolled her onto her side, pressed his naked body against hers, and tucked her into his embrace. Then he told her to stop fighting and go to sleep.

He wasn't sure what exactly happened that she didn't fight him, but after a few more minutes of fidgeting, her breathing had evened out and her body relaxed. The steady drum of a clock ticking somewhere in the room kept his brain company for the next thirty minutes before he joined her in slumber.

When he woke, she was gone. The sun had already crested the horizon and it was past seven. She'd had a four o'clock shift. He vaguely remembered her trying to slip away and him holding on. She uttered something about work and he rolled over and let go.

That was three hours ago.

He dragged her pillow close and buried his head in it. The scent of her filled his nose and reminded him of the look on her face when she climaxed. Abandon and bliss. He'd done that to her three times before he gave in to his own needs. Each time she grew louder, until he had to silence her with a hand over her lips or possibly wake up others in the house.

Not that AJ thought for a minute everyone on that floor didn't know exactly what was going on behind her bedroom door.

He stretched and pushed her pillow away. Ignoring his growing erection, he padded his way into her bathroom, used the toilet, and grabbed a towel. After gathering his clothes, he scurried across the hall before anyone rounded the corner and made his way to the shower.

A clean shave, clean clothes, and a smile that spoke volumes, he made his way downstairs and across the Thomas compound to where he knew Sasha was watching the monitors.

He moved through the kitchen, snagging a cup of black coffee on the way.

Isaac sat in front of a computer, a pair of earbuds zoning him out in the room.

Sasha sat, her back to him, eyes on the four monitors that had over a dozen camera angles of the ranch. She lifted a coffee cup high in the air. "I'll take a refill," she told him without turning around.

"How did you know it was me?"

She glanced over her shoulder, then back to the monitors. A wave of her hand at the surveillance had him shaking his head.

"Of course."

AJ leaned over, pressed his lips to her ear as he set his cup down and grabbed hers. "Good morning."

She backed away slightly. "None of that. I work with these guys."

"Isaac isn't paying attention."

"That's what he wants you to believe." Sasha brought AJ's coffee to her lips. He went back into the kitchen and refilled her mug and proceeded to use it.

"You've been staring at these for four hours?" he asked.

She looked at him over the rim of the coffee cup. "It's called surveillance."

He leaned back in the chair he sat in, pointed toward the monitors. "I can't imagine anyone attempting to get into this compound."

"Wade Thomas has a lot of rabid fans. Jeb has his hands full without the added stress of us here."

AJ looked around the war room and at the lone guy seeming to rock out under his earbuds while the glow of the computer monitor washed out the color on his face. On the main board there were several new pictures, colored dots, and lines spreading in all directions.

Amelia's image smiled down from the center of the wall.

His heart squeezed in his chest.

I'm going to find out who is responsible, he said in his head.

"You okay?" Sasha asked.

"Fine."

The front door opened, and Jeb and Cooper joined them. A printer sprang to life on Isaac's desk.

"Good morning," Jeb greeted them first. "Anything interesting going on?" He crossed to Sasha, who was already pushing her chair back and giving him space.

"Absolutely nothing," she told him.

"Excellent. Neil wants everyone back here in fifteen for a briefing." Jeb sat in the chair Sasha vacated.

"The missus made some fresh biscuits," Cooper told them.

AJ's stomach growled.

Sasha glanced at him, lowered her eyes to his abdomen. "You go ahead. I'm good with coffee."

He leaned close, watched as Sasha's whole body stiffened. He put his lips close to her ear and whispered, "You need your energy after last night." Then he walked past her without looking back.

In the main house, AJ found the kitchen and a whole lot more than just biscuits laid out.

Claire sat at the table, shoveling food in.

"This is nuts," he said, looking over the spread of three different types of breakfast meat, scrambled eggs in a warming dish, biscuits, fruit, and potatoes.

"Rose, the cook, said she loves it when the house is full of people so she has something to do. She already started on fresh bread to go with lunch." Claire pointed to the other side of the kitchen, where an extra large mixing bowl sat close to the stove and covered with a towel.

"As in homemade?"

"That's what *fresh* means."

AJ grabbed a plate and started to fill it. "Smart-ass."

"One of my *many* talents."

AJ set his plate aside, grabbed one for Sasha, filled it with fruit and a biscuit. He covered both plates with napkins and grabbed them with both hands. He watched Claire as she cleaned the last of the food off of her plate and moved to rinse it off.

"So what did Neil have you doing at five in the morning?"

"Scrubbing floors," she said without complaint. "I was given fifteen minutes to eat and have to be with the team at eight for the briefing." Adrenaline agreed with the girl.

He started to leave the room and hesitated. "Hey, Claire?"

She looked at him.

"When all this is said and done, you're not going to be alone."

Her motions stopped. Water ran down the drain and moisture gathered behind her eyes.

"We clear on that?" he asked. He wasn't sure how that looked, after, but he knew there was no way he could watch an eighteen-year-old orphan live on the streets.

A single tear slid down her cheek.

She nodded and bit her lip.

Back in the war room, AJ placed a plate of food in front of Sasha and ignored the roll of her eyes.

It didn't take long for her to start picking at the food.

AJ sat at a tall island in the back of the room while Neil gathered a stack of papers and started sifting through them.

Claire ran into the war room one minute before Neil's start time. "Am I late?"

"You're fine, kid." Cooper waved her over.

"I'm not a kid."

Neil pulled a piece of paper from his pile and handed it to Claire. "You're eighteen, but still a kid."

Claire took the paper, looked at it. "My birth certificate."

"Appears the administration at Richter is mistaken about your age. You're not seventeen like they told the authorities."

AJ met Sasha's eyes from across the room. Relief sat behind her stare.

"One less thing for us to worry about," AJ said.

"That won't stop any legal action on their end. So we're going to avoid that mountain of trouble by staying tucked away a little longer."

"No running out for pizza," Cooper teased Claire.

She nudged his shoulder with hers.

Neil nodded toward Cooper. "Bring everyone up on the new faces on the board."

AJ finished his food while Cooper pointed out six new pictures, four women and two men, whom he and Claire found from The Mandarin File. "There were two dozen names in the file from three years before Hofmann graduated until now. Of those twenty-four people, these are the faces of Pohl's recruits. The ones who took the job."

AJ was about to ask how he could be sure.

Cooper explained without being asked.

"These six people plugged into our algorithm . . . orphaned, or weak family relations. Five of them had an anonymous benefactor."

"Pohl?" Sasha asked.

"Possibly. We haven't cracked that file yet. We'll get there," Cooper told her. "All six of these people graduated from Richter, changed their names, and bought a flat somewhere in Europe. No records of employment, no air travel, no leases on vehicles . . ."

"All we found were bank accounts with minimal activity," Claire added. She looked at Neil, then Sasha.

Sasha offered a small smile.

Neil stared at the board.

"Do you recognize any of these people, Sasha?"

She unfolded from the sofa and crossed to the board.

AJ enjoyed her catlike walk and the way her legs went on forever until they reached her ass. He grinned, wondered if the bite he'd placed there the night before left a mark.

"This one. I didn't know him, but his roommate, Pierre Dufort. Pierre I could see in The Mandarin File. I don't recall anything remarkable about this guy."

"Maybe he excelled without letting on. Either way, he fit the profile. We are pulling pictures and files from as many sources as we can to match up roommates and determine if there are any missing links."

AJ stared at all the pictures, dots, and lines. "How is any of this getting us any closer to finding out who killed my sister?"

Sasha pivoted and gave him her full attention.

"It's all in the details and the patterns." Sasha placed her hand over Amelia's picture. "You started here, which led us to here." She pointed out Olivia. "I see Olivia as ground zero and all her roommates as victims. Is Olivia taking them out? Or is Olivia being flushed out? Is Olivia even alive? Does it stop here, or if we keep digging, will we find other cells of dead or missing Richter alumni who all have a Mandarin File operative in the mix? We won't know without the groundwork. Why is Pohl so invested that he singles me out as a kidnapper? Or maybe Pohl knows exactly who murdered your sister and these other women. We crack the benefactor code and find Pohl feeding that pond, and now we have a motive."

"A motive for him to kill innocent women?" AJ asked.

"Maybe Olivia went rogue. Maybe your sister and Olivia had a relationship after Richter? We have more questions than answers, so we keep digging. Now that we can prove Claire isn't a minor, and I'm not a kidnapper, I can get back to doing what I do best." She turned to stare at Neil.

The hair on AJ's nape prickled.

"No," Neil said clearly.

"Excuse me?"

"You're still a target."

Sasha placed both hands on her hips. "Not if I look like your grandmother."

"Don't fight me on this." Neil's words made her stand taller.

AJ's palms started to sweat. "Where would you go?"

"I'll find Olivia."

"How? Go back to Germany?" AJ asked. His pulse rose with his voice. The thought of her running off, even if she was more equipped to handle herself than anyone he'd ever met, made him ill.

"If I have to."

"We just escaped, and you want to go back?" Claire asked.

Isaac stood from his perch behind his computer while the printer buzzed to the side. "I don't think you have to go that far east," he said.

He grasped the picture, walked through the center of the room, past everyone, and tacked it up on the board. "Anyone in this picture look familiar?"

AJ narrowed his eyes, moved closer.

"Well, that's Creepazoid," Claire said from the side.

AJ swallowed . . . hard. There were four men, all standing together and posing for the picture. "That's my father."

Sasha moved closer to the picture, looked back at AJ.

"Where was this taken?" Neil asked Isaac.

"Board of directors meeting for Richter. Found this buried in a brochure for the school right before Alex Hofmann Senior took on the position as ambassador."

Acid started to roll in AJ's stomach. What the hell was his dad doing beside Pohl?

Neil crossed his arms over his chest. "You want out in the field, Sasha, looks like you have a target. You and AJ visit his dad and—"

"I work alone," Sasha said, her lips a thin line.

Neil turned his head slowly in AJ's direction.

"Not this time."

Chapter Twenty-Two

"You sure Shannon won't mind?" Sasha asked Trina as she rummaged through the closet of Trina's friend to fill a suitcase. Dressing like herself would not be a part of the plan for the next several days. Only one skintight black outfit had been tucked into the bottom of the case for if and when she needed to disappear at night. All she was missing was a wig or two. Not something Trina had on hand. Neil had a couple of different styles en route to the airplane that would take her and AJ to the East Coast.

"We've already gone over this. Shannon thinks the world of you."

Sasha wasn't used to hearing things like that. She was pretty sure her expression showed her doubt.

Trina turned away, reached on a high shelf, and removed two more sweaters. "We all do. If you gave us half a chance, you might realize that."

Sasha paused midstream, looked up from the suitcase. Her heart did a double beat and the feeling of blood rushing too quickly from her head had her sitting on the edge of the bed.

"I'm sorry . . . that wasn't called for," Trina said.

"No. It's not uncalled for." Sasha tossed a shirt into the suitcase and stared at her hands. Then, in Russian, she muttered, "I don't know how."

Trina set the sweaters down and sat on the bed next to her.

"I came to that conclusion a long time ago. I just thought that with time you'd realize that there are people here who care about you and that maybe you'd let us in."

She wanted to say she was trying but knew that would be a lie.

"I remember when you texted me after Wade proposed. In fact, I took a screenshot of the message because it meant so much that you reached out to congratulate me."

Sasha remembered that night. Wade had pulled his then girlfriend up onstage during a concert and then proceeded to propose to her in front of thousands of fans. Sasha had been in the wings, playing security without Trina even knowing she was there. Like everyone in the audience, she'd been stunned to see the open display of love and affection and more than a little moved by it.

"You deserve happiness," Sasha said.

"So do you. From where I'm sitting, you deserve more happiness than any of us. You've touched the lives of everyone here. You were a big part of helping Reed and Lori, keeping her away from your fath—Ruslan." Trina stuttered on the word *father*. Ruslan Petrov may have been the sperm donor, but he wasn't her father.

"You've gone into battle with Neil and his team. You stopped Ruslan from destroying all of our lives. You helped Avery find and chase away her demons, and you even flew all the way to Barcelona just to tell Shannon to stop being selfish and think of others before flying halfway around the world to escape her problems. Now you're helping that poor girl and AJ, a man you've only known a few weeks." Trina stopped long enough to stare.

Sasha took a deep breath.

"You help everyone. We trust that you'll be there. When will you trust that we will be here for you?"

"The moment you trust someone to be there is when they leave," Sasha muttered.

Trina squared her shoulders, placed her hands on her knees like she was going to stand. "You can't say that about anyone here. You trust us all, right now, just by being here. Now all you need to do is open the door a little wider and realize people love you."

She flinched.

Trina grinned and stood. "So, what is your disguise going to be? The Valley girl housewife or something completely different?"

The change of subject put Sasha at ease. "I haven't decided yet. Depends on what will throw AJ's father off the most."

Trina removed a long coat, tossed it on the bed. "I hope for AJ's sake his father isn't involved in any of this."

Not likely. "I agree."

"You know, I didn't quite see you with a guy like him."

Okay, now they were moving into completely uncharted territory. Sasha stood, took a defensive position over the suitcase, and continued to pack. "I'm not *with* him."

"That's not how it looked to me."

"He's an itch." Even saying it out loud felt like a violation.

Trina grinned. "Well, I haven't seen you scratch anyone. I kinda always pictured a guy with more tattoos than suits and riding beside you on a motorcycle."

She couldn't stop her amusement. "I've scratched that guy a time or two."

Laughing now, Trina nodded. "I knew it. AJ just seems so, I don't know . . . normal. Not a rebellious bone in his body."

Sasha thought of the night before, the way he held her down when he crawled on top of her. His occupation.

"Ohhh, I want to know what caused that expression," Trina teased.

Sasha wiped the smirk off her face. "He knows when to be defiant."

"I'll remember that."

The two of them finished packing a suitcase full of borrowed clothing and walked out of the room.

"And don't worry about Claire. Between hoop jumping for Neil and helping me out with Lilly, we'll keep her busy."

"I wasn't worried about Claire," Sasha lied.

"Sure you weren't. Just take care of you. No crazy risks."

"I'll try."

∽

AJ sat across from Sasha on yet another private plane, this time just the two of them and a plane that belonged to an oil company. Apparently there was no end to the wealth accumulated by her friends. They were an hour out from DC, where they had a rental car waiting.

Sasha was transforming. First the blue contacts went in, then the pale foundation that washed much of the color from her face. It was as if she were diluting her genes out of her system right before his eyes.

"Who is the one celebrity that you'd give it all up for to be with for one night?"

Her question caught up with his brain and he stuttered. "Ex-excuse me?"

"Celebrity crush. Who is it? Or artist. I'm not sure what blows your horn more."

She lined her lips with pink, filled it in with a nude lipstick.

Two Jennifers came to mind. "Is there a reason for this question?"

She smacked her lips together, peered over her nose while she put the cap on the lipstick and placed it back in her makeup bag. "I need a name. *Sasha* isn't going to work."

Ohhh . . . "Jennifer."

She held her breath, stared in disbelief. "Jennifer it is."

He was starting to like this fantasy.

"Do your parents know where you've been or what you've been doing?"

"They haven't known what I was doing since the seventh grade."

"When was the last time you spoke?"

"At Amelia's funeral. Wait, I did speak to my mom right before I flew to Germany."

"Not your dad?"

"No." He had made a routine of avoiding conversations with his father as much as humanly possible.

"Did you hint at flying overseas?"

AJ pinched the bridge of his nose. "I was angry he wasn't looking into Amelia's death harder. I was an ass . . . didn't realize that she was grieving and wasn't in a place to process anything other than the fact that my sister was gone." The weight of that sat in his chest.

"Have you processed that?"

AJ glanced up, had a hard time meeting her eyes. "Probably not. It's why I'm still functioning."

"Falling apart later is a good plan," she said softly.

He glanced over, found her studying her image in the mirror. "When was the last time you fell apart?"

AJ noticed her fists clench.

"Do you? Fall apart?"

He saw her go through a process . . . deep breath, relax her hands, ease her shoulders, close her eyes, and blow air out slowly. He'd seen this before . . . her reset button. He'd bet money she'd change the subject with her next words.

"You went to Vegas. Wanted to get lost in your grief. We met, spent the next several days consuming tequila and blowing money. You went back with me to LA. I rent a guesthouse in the Hollywood Hills. Not traceable. I wait tables. You've been footing the bill. My clothes, trip back home. You think I'm the one."

AJ ignored her change of subject, smiled at the way her resolve and control centered her. Apparently later hadn't come for her, and falling apart wasn't an option.

"The one?"

"Yeah. Jennifer Stone. Waitress and insecure. Never graduated from college, wanted to be an actress. I'll play it close enough to perfect to where they won't dismiss me on sight but want to know more about me. When your mother . . . or maybe your father opens up, that's when you start asking questions."

AJ sat back, rested his ankle on his knee at thirty thousand feet. "What kind of questions?"

"About raising children . . . boarding school? I'm the one, you're thinking about those things. How did your parents manage with your father working all the time? What was the goal? Did they regret anything? This is when you capture as much information as you can."

Could he do that?

"Stay focused. Don't fall down an emotional rabbit hole. Your sister's death has made you reconsider a lot of things. And that's what I want you to think about when we're there. Amelia. Can you do that?"

"Explain to me why we can't walk in there, show my father the picture, and ask what the hell is up?" Confront the question head-on. That was his way.

Sasha placed both hands on the table, stared with her lips in a thin line. "How well do you know your father? Do you know his friends, their friends? How about his time as the ambassador? How much were you aware of, living in the States while your sister was at Richter?"

Her questions were fired off so fast he couldn't begin to answer them.

"If your father is guilty of anything, he won't answer your questions with the truth." She paused. "But you already know that. We stay long enough to gather information, for me to get into your father's computer, see if there is any connection still lingering between him and Pohl."

"I can't fathom my father having anything to do with Amelia's death." He pictured his father's face at the funeral. He'd aged five years that week. He said next to nothing to anyone at the funeral or the reception after. It was his mother who thanked everyone for coming and played hostess.

"He may have no idea. Before we leave, we'll know one way or the other." Sasha turned back to the mirror, picked up the dirty blonde bob cut wig and pulled it over her head. Within a few minutes she'd managed to tuck and comb away any sign that the hair wasn't her own. She shook her head several times, fluffed the edges, and turned to smile at him. "What do you think?" Her question was said with her perfect American accent.

He walked over to her and touched the edges. Before she could protest, he leaned down and kissed her. "Not bad, *Jennifer*."

⁓

Sitting in the passenger seat of an economy rental car while AJ drove them from the airport to Amelia's condo offered Sasha the opportunity to watch his emotions. The closer they came to his sister's place, the harder he gripped the wheel.

"You certain your parents haven't gone in and cleared the place out?"

AJ shrugged. "I told them I'd do it. My mom wasn't in a place to do anything when I left."

"Your dad?"

"I never could read the man. Hopefully you'll have better luck." They'd picked up a dozen empty boxes that were in the trunk of the car. While they looked for any possible clue that Amelia may have left behind, they'd disguise their effort by packing some of her belongings.

He turned into a shared driveway and pulled into a parking space beside a compact car.

"Hers?" Sasha asked.

AJ nodded.

She placed her hand over his and squeezed.

He grasped ahold and held on.

"Ready?"

"Fall apart later, right?"

She could practically taste his pain. "That's right."

He faked a smile and pushed out of the car.

The second they were out, Sasha placed her hand in his and held on like a good girlfriend who was being supportive to her guy would.

They walked into the building and took the elevator up to Amelia's condo on the third floor.

Bits of the police tape hung from the entry. Evidence that the condo had been through a police investigation started at the door. Black powder used for dusting for prints peppered the frame.

AJ hesitated, then pushed past the door, and walked inside.

Once they were secure, she let loose his hand and dropped the smile.

The condo looked like it had been overturned and then someone attempted to put it back together. Mail overflowed the box sitting by the mail slot.

Sasha started doing her thing. "How long did she live here?"

"Since she took the position at the UN. Five years. She wanted a place she could lock up and leave when she was traveling." AJ picked up the mail that had fallen onto the floor and took it to the countertop separating the kitchen from the living room.

Clean lines, nothing fussy about the furniture. The monochromatic beige and shades of white reminded Sasha of the dorms at Richter. The only pops of color were two bright green pillows on the sofa and a framed picture hanging on the opposite wall. Sasha peered closer, recognized Amelia. "Do you know who is in this picture with your sister?"

AJ looked up from the mail. "No idea."

The phone rang, piercing the silence in the room.

AJ and Sasha both stared at it. When he moved to answer, she held up a hand, stopping him. The answering machine picked up in three rings, a woman's voice Sasha assumed was Amelia's greeted the caller. "You've reached me, you know what to do." A computer generated voice told Sasha that a solicitor, and not a person, was on the line. "This is the League of Disabled Veterans, we have you on file as a concerned patriot who has donated to our organization in the past. With the holidays fast approaching, we would like to reach out and—"

AJ moved to pick up the line. "Damn money sucking—"

Sasha stopped him before he could say more. "It's okay, honey. They don't know." She adopted her Jennifer voice and placed a finger over her lips to shush AJ before he asked any questions.

The answering machine finished the recording, and Sasha pressed the playback button. "You have two unheard messages." They listened to the first message, which was a series of tones, as if a fax machine had called in, and then the veterans call they'd just heard.

"What?" AJ asked.

Sasha picked up the phone, listened for the dial tone. Nothing.

"Does your sister have a radio? I think music will help us get through this, don't you?"

AJ moved through the room, ducked into the hall, and returned with a portable speaker and proceeded to connect his cell phone to the Bluetooth. Within two minutes music drowned out the silence.

She moved closer to AJ, lifted her lips to his ears. "Someone has been checking and erasing Amelia's messages remotely. We need to check for surveillance."

He nodded. "I'll go get the boxes."

The moment AJ left, Sasha turned her attention to the space. Where would she place cameras, bugs . . .

The minimalist furnishings didn't give her many options.

She removed her cell phone from her back pocket and moved through her built-in security and found the application she needed. Without being obvious, she turned on the scanner and walked around the room, pointing her camera at the walls, vents, and electronics. Sure enough . . . in the air return vent on the ceiling, a tiny red dot suggested a camera was watching. The question was who was on the other end, and if they were still watching. Turning her phone on mute, she started walking around as she pretended to be texting someone.

AJ walked back in, boxes overflowing his arms.

"We forgot tape," AJ said as he dumped the boxes in the center of the room.

"Maybe Amelia had some." Sasha knelt behind the counter and followed the glowing red lines on her phone, telling her there was some type of audio device close by.

"I don't think she was planning on moving."

"That doesn't mean she wouldn't have duct tape or some kind of thing like that. If not, we can just fold the boxes and tape them later." She opened and closed the cabinet under the sink and kept moving. The red lights pegged out a small basket filled with pens and highlighters.

"The dust in here is starting to affect my allergies." Sasha turned on the faucet and filled the kitchen sink.

AJ watched her from across the room, lifted a palm to the air, and questioned her with a silent lift of his eyebrows.

She pulled several sheets from the paper towels by the sink and proceeded to dunk them in the water and wipe off the countertop. She moved a wooden block filled with knives, cleaned up under them, shifted to the basket of pens, set it close to the edge of the sink, and dusted under it. "How about an outside storage? I bet there would be box tape—" Sasha moved quickly and the basket of pens, the one that held an audio bug, was dumped into the sink. "Oops."

AJ walked up behind her, looked in the sink while turning off the water. "We don't have to do this. It can wait."

Sasha removed the pens that were not bugged and took her time with the one in question.

"No, we should pack up a few things and take them with us." She picked up the pen, removed the cap, and knocked out the tiny microphone.

AJ stared into the sink, his lips pressed together.

Sasha turned into his arms, told him about the camera with a soft whisper in his ear. "Wash this down the sink, I'm going to check out the rest of the place."

He kissed the side of her neck and she left the kitchen in search of the bathroom. After searching the bedroom, small office space Amelia had made out of a nook, and the bathroom, Sasha determined the only device left was the camera that they couldn't disassemble without it being obvious that they had found it.

Not that it mattered, they couldn't linger.

"Honey?" Sasha called AJ from the bedroom.

He walked in with a box.

She closed the door behind him. "What the hell?" AJ asked, tension filling his shoulders.

"We have no way of knowing if the camera is still in use. Or who was watching. Pack up her computer, grab her files and photographs. I'll forward the calls from her phone to Neil, find out who is policing them."

"You can do that?"

She patted his chest. "Are you taking notes?"

"Wouldn't the police have found the camera and bugs?"

"The murder didn't happen here. Looks like they went through the place, but it's not completely trashed. And there is no way of knowing if these things were here when the cops came through."

He offered a slight grin. "I don't like this."

"Me either. We need to get out of here."

They doubled their efforts, filled three boxes, and then she pretended to start sneezing and they backed out of the house.

Chapter Twenty-Three

"This is not on me." Linette stared across her desk at Geoff. "You're the one who decided to make a media circus out of Claire and Sasha's departure."

"One more day was all I needed," he growled.

Linette played innocent. "For what? Sasha declined. Like the students before, she has the right to say no."

"Don't play coy with me, Linette. Claire and Sasha were mine. You know it, I know it. I want the girl back."

By *girl*, she knew he meant Claire. "You might have thought of that before calling a press conference. With Sasha, Claire won't need the life you offer."

He held her gaze. "You sound pleased with that."

Linette kept her emotions in check. "Recruitment is down and demand is high . . . isn't that right?"

"You don't know what you're talking about."

"You need us, Geoff. Blowing up the credibility of this school with false accusations against its students and alumni will only backfire on us all. An investigation will open up questions neither one of us wants to answer. I suggest you leave this one alone."

"Letting them walk is not an option."

"Going after Sasha is operational suicide."

"We'll see about that." Geoff turned on his heel and left.

Once her hands stopped shaking, Linette donned her robe and left her office. She crossed the campus and made her way to the lower classrooms.

Brigitte worked alongside her students without noticing her for several minutes. Once their eyes met, Linette nodded toward her office.

"Pohl just left. He's going after her," Linette told her when they were alone.

"Sasha . . ."

"Just like I said he would." Sasha showing up when she did had not been part of Linette's strategy, but she couldn't be happier for it.

Brigitte smiled. "Time to activate our contingency plan."

"I'm calling an emergency board meeting for a couple of days from now. By then we'll have the cleaners in and everything scrubbed."

"He isn't going to take it well."

"Pohl has ruled this school far too long," Linette told her. "We play into the fear of exposure and the board will fold."

"And Sasha?" Brigitte asked.

"You said it yourself, she's the best this school has ever produced. Pohl making her a target will only encourage her to expose him herself. We won't have to do anything."

"If only we could warn her."

"I already sent word."

"How?" Brigitte asked.

Linette smiled. "I can't tell you *all* my secrets."

Brigitte licked her lips. "I already know your biggest secret."

They holed up in a hotel that night just outside DC, combing over Amelia's computer. Sasha uploaded images to Neil to see if any of the faces in her many pictures could be traced back to Richter.

AJ found himself taking notes, watching the ways information moved in and out of Sasha's brain like a computer. Her hyperfocus when on task was impressive. There was a point when the glow of Amelia's laptop lit up her face and she muttered in Russian. She dug a little deeper in the files, smiled, nodded, and went at it again. Outside of a gun being cocked, AJ didn't think anything would take her off task.

By the time she looked up from the computer it was one in the morning. "Your sister was good," she'd told him.

AJ crawled up next to her on the king-size bed and looked down at the computer, which was in some kind of green screen mode. "Oh?"

"I finally cracked her security. I'm uploading all her files to Cooper, let him do the legwork on this while we're at your parents'."

"You think there's something to find?"

"She put up a lot of firewalls. I doubt she was just trying to hide her porn habit."

He cringed.

"Sorry."

"It's okay." *Not really.*

"Everyone has secrets, AJ. Even if it's just kink. Maybe she liked being able to keep her files hidden. Use a skill Richter taught her in her private life that she didn't use in her professional life."

"Or maybe my sister had a reason for someone to murder her."

Sasha kept silent, his words a shout in her ear.

"If you know something, you need to tell me."

"I'm not going to burden you with suspicion. That invites pain."

"There's something." He could see it in her eyes.

"Nothing concrete."

"Sasha?"

"There's a lot of firewalls. That's all. Maybe by this time tomorrow we'll know more. Right now, I'm curious as to why an analyst for the UN would need this much cloak-and-dagger. We have hidden surveillance in her home and someone catching her messages and keeping her answering machine from clogging up. It points to something."

"Not to mention she's dead. Why would someone need to clear her messages if she's dead?" AJ asked himself more than Sasha.

"Exactly. They're waiting for a message . . ."

"From someone who doesn't know she's gone."

"Perhaps. Or someone who wants to throw us off." Sasha ran a hand through her dark hair. Her wig had long since made its way to the side of the bed. "More questions than answers, but we're on the tip of something."

"Why isn't my father looking closer?" This was so obvious to him from day one, why not to his father?

"How do you know he isn't? He could have placed the taps."

AJ didn't see it.

"You have to consider every possibility. Everyone is a suspect."

"My father didn't kill my sister."

Sasha hesitated.

AJ's heart dropped hard.

"You both have trust funds, right? You and your sister? Grandmother's money, if I'm not mistaken."

"Yeah, so?"

"Did your sister have a will?"

He blinked.

"I'm guessing since she wasn't married and didn't have children, the answer to that is no. Which means the money reverted back to her parents. Your parents. Uncontested, your sister's accounts will be pushed through in six to eight months. The first place the authorities look when a murder has taken place is who has a motive. Money is a great motivator."

"It's not that much," AJ said.

"Four million dollars isn't chump change, AJ."

"How do you know how much we were given?"

"I know the name of the arresting officer when you were caught stealing a car."

He paused.

"Most people can live their entire lives without working a day on that kind of money. Amelia had a good paying job, invested her money. Her accounts had grown. Now all of that is in someone else's pocket."

"My parents didn't kill my sister for her money." His back stiffened.

"I didn't say they did. I'm saying you need to be open to all possibilities in order to see the evidence as it unfolds. If your sister had left the money to you, you'd be a suspect."

AJ felt instantly thankful Amelia hadn't felt the need to write up a will. He shook his head, leaned back against the headboard. "What an exhausting way to live."

"Thinking everyone is after you? Everyone has a motive to do harm? Yeah . . . it is."

He rolled his head to the side, took in Sasha's profile. In that moment he saw a sadness he hadn't seen in her before. "Tell me something about you that no one else knows."

Confusion marked her brow "What?"

"Anything."

"Why?"

"Because I want to know you better."

She cocked her head to the side as if contemplating whether or not to answer him.

Silence stretched out between them.

"It's okay, I'm being pushy—"

"Thunderstorms," she rushed out. "I love thunderstorms. I've walked into the middle of a field, or the courtyard at Richter, in the middle of a thunderstorm just to be a part of it."

"Sounds dangerous."

"Part of the appeal. I've never feared lightning or the sounds of gunshots or the screech of tires on pavement."

AJ reached for her, tugged a little when it became apparent she wasn't used to being held. "This won't hurt."

She shifted into his shoulder without relaxing.

"I love the smell of snow," he told her.

"You live in Florida."

"Yeah. Much harder to get laid living in the mountains alone than in a condo on the beach."

She chuckled, tucked in a little closer. "When was the last time you managed that?"

"Getting laid?"

"Yeah."

"Last night," he teased.

The comment was met with her elbow in his ribs. "Fine . . ." He thought back, answered honestly. "Three months ago. She was with her girlfriends for a beach vacation. What about you?"

Sasha ran her bare foot down his leg. "Rome, right before I went back to Germany."

He shouldn't feel jealous.

"Do you plan on seeing him again?" He regretted the question the moment it left his lips.

"That would require me knowing his name," she told him.

He wanted to ask if she was kidding but knew she wasn't.

"Does that bother you?" she asked.

"Should it?"

She unfolded from his embrace and swung a leg over his hips to straddle him. Looking down, it became apparent exactly where her thoughts were headed.

He lifted his hands, circled her waist.

His cock stirred.

"I know your name."

AJ dug his fingers into her hips, pulled her close. "And I know yours."

The Hofmann home sat in a Virginia suburb filled with pristine roads and manicured lawns. The houses were a mix of Georgian and Victorian, colonial, and somewhere in between. Sprawling landscapes with small clusters of dense trees framed the edges of properties.

The large brick home AJ pulled into wasn't modest by any means, but it didn't quite fit the description of a mansion or an estate like that of Trina and Wade.

Still, it wasn't without its charm. "Impressive," Sasha said, peering out the window.

"A regurgitated replication of every home my parents have ever lived in."

"You never lived here?"

AJ turned off the engine. "No. They bought this after returning from Germany. Dad wanted to be close enough to DC so he could work during the week and come home on the weekends."

Sounded like marriage trouble to Sasha's ears. "Does Daddy have affairs?" she asked without thinking.

"No . ." AJ paused. "Shit . . . I don't know."

Good, he was starting to think. "If you were happily married, would you want to stay away five nights a week?"

AJ looked through the windshield. "Next thing I know, you're going to tell me there isn't a Santa Claus."

She grinned, grasped the handle of the car door. "Remember, keep it simple and as close to the truth as possible. If you get stuck, punt to me."

"Got it . . . *Jennifer*."

"Let's do this," she said, pushing out of the car.

They walked to the front door, hand in hand.

"I'm glad you're here," he whispered right before he knocked on the door hard and followed it up with a ring of the doorbell.

They waited several seconds.

"Maybe we should have called," he said before pushing the doorbell a second time.

She heard the sound of footsteps rushing down stairs and a woman's voice saying she was coming.

The door swung open and AJ's mother's stunned expression turned quickly into a smile. "Oh, my . . . AJ, what are you doing here?" She opened her arms to him, glanced over his shoulder toward Sasha. "Did I know you were coming?"

AJ let go of Sasha's hand and pulled his mother into a hug. "Hey, Mom. We were in the neighborhood and thought we'd stop by."

"In the neighborhood my rear end." She hugged him tighter, kissed the side of his cheek.

He stepped away and turned to Sasha. "This is my girlfriend, Jennifer."

Sasha stuck her hand out. "I've heard a lot about you, Mrs. Hofmann."

Mrs. Hofmann looked between the two of them, eyes wide open. "It's Marjorie, please." They shook hands. "Please, come in."

AJ let Sasha walk in first, closed the door behind them. "Is Dad here?"

"No, he had an early tee time. If you'd called, we could have made sure he skipped his golf game."

They walked through a well-appointed hall filled with traditional furniture that matched the style of home. The walls had several large photographs of both AJ and Amelia in their earlier years. No Norman Rockwell family photographs. At least not in the hall.

AJ helped Sasha with her coat once they were in the family room.

"We were planning on staying in town for a couple of days. Thought I'd take you and Dad out for dinner or something."

Marjorie turned to see Sasha's coat in AJ's arms. "Let me help you with that."

AJ waved her off. "I got it, point out the closet."

"It's in the hall." She motioned back to where they'd just walked through. "I hope you'll stay here. We have room."

AJ walked away with the coats.

Sasha jumped in, all smiles. "We booked a hotel. I told AJ it was rude to show up unannounced, but he thought a surprise was a good idea."

AJ's mother had a genuinely kind smile. There was a strong family resemblance between Amelia and her mother. Similar height, same eyes . . . full-figured curves.

"Hopefully you can teach him a few manners that I somehow failed to," Marjorie said with a bashful grin.

"Oh, he's incredibly polite. You didn't fail, trust me." Sasha sat on the edge of the sofa, hands in her lap.

She seemed to like that.

AJ walked back into the room. "My ears were ringing."

Sasha patted the space beside her. "That's because we were talking about you."

"What's this about a hotel? We have plenty of room."

She jumped in before AJ could contradict her statement. "I told your mother that you suggested it but that I thought it was rude to show up expecting a bed."

Marjorie scowled. "It's never rude for my son to stay with us. But I appreciate your thought."

"Maybe next time." Sasha leaned her head on AJ's shoulder. "I hope we didn't interrupt anything."

"Nothing that can't be moved to next week. I can't believe you're here. I'd call Alex, but he doesn't have his cell phone on while he's on the golf course."

AJ leaned back on the couch, pulled Sasha with him. "It's okay. We don't have to run off."

"Have you had breakfast?"

Sasha nodded. "We ate."

"But I could use some coffee," AJ said.

She nudged his ribs with her elbow. "Honey, that's rude."

He smiled down at her. "It's my mom, it's not rude."

Marjorie turned to leave. "Not rude at all. I'll start a pot."

Chapter Twenty-Four

Claire was working on five hours of sleep. She'd stayed up while Cooper downloaded the last of Sasha's files. They had a full day planned, but it was starting with breakfast with Lilly. The girl was too stinkin' cute, even when she squeezed her eyes while dropping a stink bomb.

"Are you going to have more kids?" Claire asked Trina while she spooned another mouthful of mush into Lilly's face.

"I'd be pregnant right now if Wade had his way. I just lost the baby weight and want to give Lilly more time with just the two of us." Trina sat across the table, drinking coffee and watching.

"I want a big family." The conclusion had come to her the moment she fell in love with Lilly. "Lots of kids who all have each other to go to when things are hard."

Trina considered her over the brim of her cup. "I hope it happens for you. Just try and remember that sometimes family are the people you invite into your life, not just those born to you."

"You mean like you and Sasha?"

She nodded. "I'm blessed with people like Sasha. Several others that I know I can count on, day or night."

Claire spooned another scoop into Lilly's greedy mouth. She made open and closed lip motions and giggled around the food. "Growing up in a boarding school doesn't give you a lot of outside friendships."

"Weren't you close to anyone there?"

"Yeah. One of my roommates. But it isn't like I can reach out to her from here, even if I wasn't hiding." She'd thought about Jax more than once since leaving Richter. All she left was a note saying she'd contact her after graduation. Jax wasn't the kind of student Creepazoid recruited. Claire took comfort in that.

"You have a whole new set of friends now. You've spiked the protective bone in Neil, and I know AJ and Sasha aren't going to let you down."

Claire wiped slobber off of Lilly's face. "What about you, Lilly . . . are you gonna be around, too?"

"She's going to need an older cousin to teach her all about boys."

"I'm going to have to date before I can do that." Dating consisted of making out in dark corners of Richter with the intention of getting naked. For Claire, there weren't any naked worthy guys her age. The college age boys weren't interested in her.

"I didn't even consider that."

Claire hadn't either . . . until she sat next to Cooper and teased him about his lack of language skills. The man was waaay too hot for his own boots.

"Hmmm, I know that look," Trina hummed.

Heavy footfalls came from the hallway. Jeb walked in the room, a large box in his hands. "This was just delivered," he said, setting it on the table.

Trina looked over the box before attempting to pierce the tape holding it together with her fingernail.

Jeb remove a knife from his back pocket and helped her open the package.

In it was a bouquet of white lilies.

A confused look crossed Trina's face. "Wade?"

"Your husband sends you flowers instead of handing them to you?" Claire asked.

Trina shook her head, grabbed the card. "Not usually." She read the card, turned it over, and read it again. "I don't get it."

Jeb hesitated.

"Not from Wade?" Claire asked.

"No it's . . ." She handed the card to Jeb.

"'Miss Scarlet, Dining Room, Revolver. Yours Faithfully, Charles.'" Jeb looked up. "Who the hell is Charles?"

A deep chill ran down Claire's spine. "Let me see that." She read the note, looked at the flowers.

"Isn't that from the board game? Miss Scarlet in the dining room with the revolver?" Trina asked.

"Clue," Jeb said.

Claire remembered the game vaguely, or the reference to it.

"I get Scarlet . . . but who is Charles? Shouldn't it be Professor Plum or Colonel Mustard?" Trina asked.

"I don't like this," Jeb said, reaching for the box holding the flowers.

"This isn't a clue, it's a warning," Claire stated.

∞

"I'm really not much of a cook, I'm sorry to say," Sasha told Marjorie as they stood in the kitchen over what would become their dinner. Throughout the late morning and early afternoon, AJ had kept most of the conversation going. He'd played the part of doting boyfriend a little too well. They'd agreed to stay for dinner, and now Sasha was standing over the sink with a potato peeler in her hands.

AJ was gathering wood by a shed in the back of the yard and bringing it closer to the house. At least that was the excuse he used to give Sasha time alone with his mother. Alex Senior was due home anytime, a meeting Sasha was hoping would shed light on the Hofmann parents' dynamics.

"I wasn't either at your age. It wasn't until after AJ was born that I had to learn my way around the kitchen."

Sasha started the task of peeling the skin off the potato. "You didn't cook for Mr. Hofmann?" she asked.

"Not much in the beginning. We dined out a lot before the kids showed up." Marjorie's voice softened. "AJ would eat just about anything. Amelia was the picky one."

They hadn't talked much about her throughout the day. Only to say that they'd gone to her place and grabbed her mail and would return to do the rest at a later date.

"AJ's been pretty torn up about your daughter," Sasha told her.

"We all are."

"I'm so sorry," she said. "Have the police come up with anything?" Sasha watched Marjorie from the corner of her eye.

"No. I don't think we'll ever know who did this or why." She stopped spreading seasoning over the roast she was preparing long enough to look up at Sasha. "Losing a child is the worst possible pain. Maybe when I've processed the fact that she's gone I can spend my time trying to find out who did it. Right now I'm still numb."

Emotion welled behind Marjorie's eyes.

"I shouldn't have brought it up," Sasha told her.

"It's okay. I'm glad you're there for my son. I know he's been hard on himself since her death."

Sasha looked down at the sink, slowly worked the potato. "I don't really understand why. It's not like he could have stopped it from happening."

Marjorie started working on cutting an onion. "He wishes he'd had more time. They weren't close when Alex took the job in Germany. I think AJ wishes he'd gone to school with his sister. At least that's what he told us after her funeral."

Now they were getting somewhere. Sasha played dumb. "He told me something about a boarding school."

"A normal occurrence in Europe. People in the States don't understand the concept."

"Sounds strange to me."

She chopped the onion with a heavy hand. "If you ever visit Europe, you might understand."

Sasha finished one potato, picked up another. "AJ said he wanted to take me."

"Is that right?"

She shrugged, pushed some of the blonde wig out of her eyes with the back of her hand. "Yeah, I told him we were moving too fast, but he said that life was short and sometimes you just need to live it like tomorrow isn't going to happen." *Where had that come from?* The words left her lips and then registered in her head.

"He just lost his sister. I suppose his actions are normal."

Sasha felt herself going down that rabbit hole. "Rebound relationship."

The noise from the cutting board stopped and Sasha stood with water rushing down the sink stuck in the thought of AJ holding her tight. She'd felt his pain when he spoke of his sister. It wasn't until that moment that Sasha realized that he was reaching out to ease his loss.

"Oh, honey. I'm sure AJ sees you as more than a crutch after Amelia."

Sasha shook away her thoughts.

Marjorie had moved to her side, laid a hand on her shoulder. "I see the way my son looks at you. And maybe you don't know this, but he hasn't brought a girl home since he was in high school. The fact that you're here speaks volumes."

Sasha unclenched her hands, relaxed her shoulders, and took a deep breath. "I know," she lied. "For both our sakes, I'll stop him from dragging me to a chapel in Vegas."

AJ's mother blinked several times.

"I mean . . . not that he did that." Sasha went back to work, doubling her efforts with the potatoes. "He hinted. I said *no way*. Next thing I know we're on our way here to visit you."

"Isn't that interesting."

"I'm sorry. That was probably too much information. It isn't like he's asked me to marry him. There was a lot of tequila that night."

"Yet here you are."

Sasha offered the most innocent smile she could muster. "Crazy, right?"

The back door to the kitchen opened and AJ stood shaking out his coat. "I think I have enough firewood brought in for the night."

"Thank you, honey. Your father hates that chore."

The door from the front of the house closed as if AJ had timed it.

"Marjorie? Whose car is in the driveway?"

Sasha turned off the water and dried her hands on a kitchen towel. Time for round two.

"We're in the kitchen, Alex," AJ's mom called out.

Footfalls moved closer. "Who are *we*?"

AJ stiffened beside her, reached for her hand. When Alex Senior turned the corner, he stopped and tracked AJ with his eyes. There was a hesitation in his smile.

"Look who came to visit!"

Both men faced each other. AJ stood a good three inches taller than his father, broader in the shoulders.

Sasha felt the tension rising.

"AJ, aren't you going to introduce me?"

AJ released Sasha's hand and moved to his father with his hand out. "Hey, Dad."

They shook hands and then suffered an awkward half hug.

"Did we know you were coming?"

"No."

Marjorie moved beside her husband. "AJ wanted us to meet his girlfriend, Jennifer."

"I didn't know you had a girlfriend."

Adopting her Jennifer smile, Sasha lifted her hand. "He didn't until after he met me. Pleased to meet you, Mr. Hofmann. I've heard a lot about you."

Alex Hofmann grasped her hand to shake and let go as quickly as he could.

He looked down at himself and stepped back. "I'm going to go clean up. I take it you're staying for dinner."

"As long as you're okay with that," AJ said.

"Of course he's okay with that. Aren't you, Alex?" Marjorie asked.

Alex nodded. "Of course."

Sasha placed a hand on AJ's waist, gave a little nudge.

"After our last conversation, I wouldn't blame you if you wanted me to leave."

Alex hesitated and some of the harsh lines in his eyes softened. "We were all emotional that day. I've already put it behind me."

Chapter Twenty-Five

"It's a warning."

Claire stood in the middle of the war room while the card was passed around.

Jeb had taken the flowers outside and determined that they were in fact nothing but lilies. They'd arrived from a UPS truck and not a florist, so the team was working to figure out who had sent them.

"Miss Scarlet is Sasha. Right, everyone can see that."

Cooper nodded enthusiastically.

"In the dining room with the revolver. Richter's lower levels were reached through the dining hall. That's where the indoor range is, the martial arts gym . . . any of the stuff not written on the brochure of academia."

Trina sat beside Wade. "Who is Charles?"

"Checkpoint Charlie. He's the gatekeeper. The guy who is always there. The guy who isn't a teacher or any kind of administration, but who everyone knows."

"He mans the gates?" Neil asked.

"No. The front door. Kinda like a doorman, only more than that. He always knows what's going on. We could count on him to have our backs, so long as we weren't doing anything really stupid. On my birthday this year, he reminded me that the legal drinking age in Germany is eighteen, and that I might find something if I could pick the lock on his locker."

"I like this guy," Cooper said.

"Everyone loves Charlie."

"Like the maid or butler of the house. Knows everything that's going on," Wade offered.

"So he sends flowers to me?" Trina asked.

"Not just any flowers. Lilies. A flower associated with funerals." Claire was beaming now.

"Why does that make you smile?" Trina asked.

"At Richter, if lilies were placed in the vases in the dining hall, it meant all subterranean classes were canceled for the day. It's a code every student understood. It usually meant someone was visiting the school that had no idea about what we did down there. Any open house or graduation or promotion was littered with lilies."

"How does Charlie know where Sasha is?" Wade asked.

Claire shrugged. "I don't know. Maybe Sasha said something about Trina."

"Our relationship isn't a secret," Trina said. "Even though Sasha's pictures were kept out of the papers at the time of her father's death, I'm pretty sure her name was linked."

"Your late mother-in-law was Sasha's benefactor. The headmistress would have known that. Charlie might have overheard something." Claire sat on the edge of a sofa.

"Or the headmistress sent the flowers using Charlie's name because he can be trusted," Cooper suggested.

"Too dangerous for the head of the school to warn a past student." Neil took a few steps, turned, and took a few more. "I think you're right, Claire. The flowers are a warning to Sasha. If the program is being shut down, what do the players that lose the most want?"

"Revenge," Isaac said from the sidelines.

"Right. And punishment to those responsible."

"Sasha didn't do anything," Claire stated.

"They were grooming you. She helped you escape." Neil stared at her. "The warning is for both of you. They were sent here, which means someone knows where we are, or at least assumes going through Trina will get to Sasha."

"I don't like how that sounds, Neil," Wade said.

"I like it even less since Sasha's not here." Neil looked to Jeb. "No more deliveries. We stop them at the gate."

Trina moved to sit next to her husband. "I'm not going to be with Lori when she delivers the twins."

"I'm sure Lori will understand." Wade hugged his wife.

The room filled with silence as they all took in the weight of the threat.

Neil pointed at Claire. "You!"

She jumped.

"Anything to report on Amelia's computer files?"

"No . . . I was, uhm—"

He pointed to a vacant computer. "Cooper said they're in German. That puts them in your inbox."

She had an inbox? "Okay."

"Let's get to work, people. I want answers before the sun sets."

⤮

AJ sat beside Sasha, his arm draped over her shoulders while they finished a cup of coffee by the fireplace. Dinner had included wine and a surprisingly pleasant conversation with his father.

The longer they sat talking, the less he thought it was possible his dad had anything to do with Amelia's death. Maybe it was Sasha being there, or maybe it was the fact that Amelia no longer could stop in for dinner, but the chill off his dad seemed to have thawed.

Sasha had bugged his mother to pull out a few early photo albums and giggled like a lovesick girl when images of AJ's naked baby butt stared back at them. "How cute you were."

"Hey, I'm still cute."

Sasha did a little giggle squeak thing that he was associating with the Jennifer voice. She flipped to the back of the photo album and stuck out her lower lip. "That's all?"

His mother sighed. "I could bore you with pictures all day."

"I'm not bored. I love this kind of thing. My mom put all my baby pictures in storage and then didn't pay the fees. I don't have any pictures of me growing up."

"I'm sorry to hear that," his mom said.

"Why don't you show Jennifer some more? I'd like a word with AJ."

Sasha glanced over her shoulder, kissed AJ on the cheek.

His mom stood, glanced at his dad, then put on a well-practiced smile.

"C'mon, Jennifer. I keep them upstairs."

Sasha bounced a little too much. "I'd love to see pictures of AJ's grandparents," he heard Sasha say as they walked away. "I want to know what AJ's going to look like when he's old."

Once they left the room, his father stood and motioned toward his study. "I want something stronger than coffee," he announced.

AJ followed his father into his private space, closed the door behind him, and watched while Alex crossed to a shelf that housed books and a decanter filled with amber liquid. He poured two generous portions and handed one to AJ before taking a seat.

He sniffed the glass, took a sip. "I don't think I've ever shared a brandy with you before."

Alex lifted his glass into the air. "Past due." He took a generous swig, studied the contents of the glass as if they held the meaning of life. "She isn't what I expected," he finally said.

"Jennifer?"

He swirled the liquid, didn't look up. "I pictured tattoos and piercings. Purple hair, maybe."

"I don't deserve more credit than that?"

His dad glanced over his glass with a look that every parent perfected after the teenage years.

"Okay, fine. But I was never going to bring *that girl* home to meet my parents."

He smiled. "I like her. Even if she seems a little young."

AJ couldn't help but wonder what his dad would say about Sasha. The real Sasha.

"Is that why you brought me in here, to tell me your views on Jennifer?"

The smile on his father's face faded. He took another drink, tilted his head back as he swallowed.

"I've been a diplomat my entire life. Dealt with international crises without blinking an eye. I can ease tensions with a brandy and a smile when I need to, but damn if I didn't know what to do with you."

AJ sat back, let his father talk.

"Do you know where I was when I heard you'd stolen a car?"

AJ hesitated, wondered for a brief moment if his father knew more about him than AJ wanted.

"With the German chancellor. My secretary called. I took the call because he said it was an emergency from the States. I was sipping brandy with Von—" Alex shook his head. "He asked what had happened, and I told him. He poured another glass and told me what I already knew. You were looking for my attention and it was too damn late to give it to you. I needed to let you have your rebellion and be there when you fell."

AJ's jaw tightened. "Sound advice." Advice given years ago, after the one and only time he'd been caught with his hands under the hood of a stolen car.

Alex finished his brandy, stood to pour more. "You'd think. He also told me that if you crossed the line, I needed to walk away from you." He stopped midpour, looked out the dark window. "You stopped. Maybe you didn't care anymore, a giant middle finger to me. I was so thankful you ended your need to fall off the deep end. I don't think I ever told you that."

AJ felt a guilty knot in the back of his throat.

His dad turned to look at him. "I'm proud of you."

Oh, yeah, he didn't need to hear this. "Why? I've done nothing with my life." *Nothing you'd be proud of.*

Alex shook his head. "Your life has just begun. Decent girl, a head on your shoulders. You have a better sense of right and wrong than half the people out there."

AJ narrowed his eyes.

"I need to tell you something, but you have to promise me you'll keep this from your mother right now."

The hair on the backs of his arms stood up. "What?"

"I've hired a private firm to look into your sister's murder. I can't help but think the authorities aren't looking in the right places."

AJ's jaw slacked. "Why didn't you tell me?"

"You were angry when you left after the funeral. I'm going to do what I can to find out who did this, but if I fail . . . I don't want this to be yet another wedge between us." He lifted the brandy to his lips.

"We can't learn anything if we don't look," AJ told his father.

True pain sat behind his dad's expression. "I worried something like this would happen years ago when you kids were young and I was still working overseas. I never imagined I'd have to concern myself with it now."

"That's what you said when you tried to get me to attend the boarding school with Amelia."

"Your mother was so worried about moving to another country, you kids. She was convinced Germany was some third world place with political extremists everywhere. Boarding schools in Europe aren't uncommon. I agreed."

"Nothing crazy happened when you were in Germany," AJ prompted.

"No. If either of you had . . . if this had happened to Amelia when I was the ambassador, this would have been an international problem. Finding her killer would have only been a matter of time. Now the authorities spend time asking things like . . . Who were her friends, boyfriends? Did she have a drug problem? God, Amelia and drugs?" He shook his head. "Not Amelia."

"That wasn't who she was," AJ said.

"No, it wasn't. I may not have the kind of influence I once did, but I'm going to use what I have to find out who was behind this and bring them to justice."

Sasha's and his mother's voices carried from the hall.

AJ stood and set his empty glass down.

"Be careful, Alex," his dad told him. The use of his given name had him pause.

"I'm not Amelia."

"No. But I can't lose you. You're all I have left."

❦

"Talk to me," Sasha said the minute they pulled out of the Hofmann driveway.

"My dad told me that he was searching for Amelia's killer."

"That's why he wanted to talk to you alone." She'd seen by AJ's expression when she and Marjorie had joined them again that something important had happened. "Your thoughts on that?"

"There was a resolve about him . . . something different than I've ever seen before. He mentioned that he wasn't sure if we'd ever really know, but that he had to look." He glanced over at her before turning the corner. "That's something, isn't it?"

"Does your mother know?" The unspoken stress between the couple was apparent to her. They hardly looked at each other, let alone spoke to one another, the entire night. The conversation was all about AJ and her. Even Amelia's name wasn't brought up. Considering they were a little over a month out from her death, Sasha found that difficult to grasp, too.

"I don't know. Why?"

"Have your parents always slept in separate bedrooms?"

"Always. Dad worked long hours, Mom hated her routine being messed up."

"An unhappy marriage."

AJ shrugged. "They don't fight."

Sasha reached behind the seat to the small bag she'd left in the car while visiting AJ's parents. She found her phone and turned it on. "Couples fight when they are trying hard to resolve their issues. It's when they give up and silence becomes the norm that the happiness is gone."

"Huh . . . so you're a psychologist, too?"

A text from Reed had come in several hours earlier. Call Me.

"What else did you learn about my parents?" AJ asked.

Sasha dialed Reed's number, lifted the phone to her ear. "Hold up, I need to call Reed."

"Took long enough," Reed answered.

"Didn't need anyone backtracking my calls. What's up?"

"What do white lilies and Checkpoint Charlie have in common?"

Sasha chilled. "What happened?"

For the next few minutes, Reed explained what had been sent to Trina's home, the message, and the interpretation from Claire. All of which Sasha agreed were a warning and an announcement. Something was going south at Richter.

"You trust this Charlie guy?" Reed asked.

"I have no reason not to."

"Neil wants you back in Texas."

"Neil knows better than to order me around. Tell him to keep Claire safe. AJ and I will return when we have more answers."

Reed laughed. "I knew you were going to say that."

She hung up, told AJ about the call.

He gripped the wheel, signaled to get off the highway. "Things are going to get worse before they get better, aren't they?"

"Undoubtedly." Sasha noticed the street they were on. "Where are you going?"

"Back to the hotel."

"Pull over."

"What?"

"Pull over." She didn't have to say it again, AJ looked out the rear-view mirror and turned into a gas station.

Sasha turned in her seat to look at him. "All right." She took a deep breath. This was why she worked alone.

"What?"

"From this moment forward, we have no routine. We will not be going back to your sister's condo, your parents' home, the hotel we stayed in last night. The recon at your parents' is the longest we will sit still until we're back in Texas or we can safely say the killer is caught and there is no one sending lilies in warning." Her voice grew higher, her accent more curt as she spoke. "Always in motion. Never the same motion. Got it?"

He just stared.

"Amelia had a routine of running in the morning. Her killer knew exactly where she would be and when, waited until they could take her out without a witness, and then disappeared. We assume that same person is watching for us. Then there's whomever Pohl has hired to find me."

AJ's stare hardened. "Okay."

Sasha reached for the door.

"What are you doing?" he asked.

"I'm driving."

AJ put the car in drive. "I'm capable of driving the car, Sasha." He was pissed.

An argument sat on her lips.

Her phone rang, distracting her.

"What now?" Sasha answered after recognizing a secure line from the base in Texas.

"Wow, someone is tight. Everyone okay out there?" It was Cooper.

AJ took a hard left, putting them back on the street moving in the opposite direction of the hotel.

"Do you have information or is this a social call?"

"Fine, back to bitch mode . . ."

She would have flinched if Cooper wasn't right.

"We traced the camera feed in Amelia's condo."

"To where?"

"Up to a server, and right back down to her. It's motion linked so anytime someone was in the space, the camera picked up and recorded it."

"Why would she do that?"

"Still working on that. Claire is following a thread of deleted messages in German."

AJ returned to the highway, put his foot into the gas.

"Deleted, huh?"

"You know how that is. Maybe she wasn't as careful with them since they were encrypted to begin with, then written in a different language."

Sasha shook her head. "Only different if you don't speak it. Call me when you know more."

They hung up.

She waited to speak, felt the tension rolling off AJ.

"You going to tell me what that was about?"

He wasn't going to like it. "Your sister was either hiding something or paranoid. Since her computer was locked up like a chastity belt on a Disney princess, I'm guessing a little of both."

The princess comment had him easing up on the gas . . . slightly.

"Your sister was recording her own place. The camera I found was linked back to her."

"Why?"

"Not for security. Cameras that record thieves are obvious, deterrents for the actions because the dirtbags see them. Hidden cameras are to catch someone in the act without them knowing it. So either Amelia thought someone she trusted was ripping her off, or she suspected someone might come after her."

"If she thought she was in danger, wouldn't she have adopted the Richter way of life and avoided routine? Told someone? Something?"

"You would think." Only Amelia didn't.

"I don't believe she knew it was coming. We might not have been that close, but she would have said something to me."

Sasha couldn't help but wonder if that was AJ's way of wishful thinking.

"More questions than answers," AJ muttered. He ran a hand through his hair. "What the hell was going through your mind, Amelia?" he asked his sister as if she were right there to answer him.

Tension rolled off his shoulders.

Sasha placed a hand on his back and spoke calmly. "It will come together. It always does."

Chapter Twenty-Six

"I either need to run and jump over things or I need to shoot something. You pick," Claire said, standing toe-to-toe with Neil. She'd been staring at Amelia Hofmann's cryptic notes in German for hours and she was starting to go crazy. She had no issue with long hours, but the words were running together, and she knew that if she could just clear her brain, something would click.

"Wade has a home gym."

"Outside. Fresh air . . . get my brain cells working again."

"Fine. Cooper?" He waved the man over. "Take Claire out past the stables, set up some targets. Don't go any farther."

Cooper offered two thumbs up. "Some trigger time? Sounds good to me." He turned to Claire. "What do you want to shoot?"

"What do you have?"

Cooper smiled and motioned out the door. In the garage of the guesthouse they were using for a war room was a van that had rolled in the day after they arrived. She'd heard one of the guys yelling to another about getting something from the van, but she'd yet to see what was inside.

When Cooper opened up the back door, Claire was all smiles. She climbed in the back and ran her hand along the stocks of a small arsenal. "Sweet." She reached for the AR-15.

"Careful there, kid, they're all load—"

Claire didn't let him finish. She popped the magazine out, checked the chamber, left the round inside, and drove the magazine back where it belonged. She repeated the action with an M16 and a 9 mm pistol. With the safeties all in place, she turned back to Cooper. "Do we have any ear protection?"

A sexy smile sat on Cooper's face. "Okay, that was kinda hot."

She swallowed back the excitement his comment did for her insides and brushed past him. "Put it away, Cooper. You're too old for me."

Outside and past the stables had to be far enough away to not disturb the livestock or the people in the house. Because of the long-range distance the weapons could reach, they also needed to butt up against a hillside or risk bullets finding unwanted targets.

"We don't generally have paper targets," Cooper told her. "I could come up with something . . ."

Claire looked down range. "That's a fence post, isn't it?"

"The one about four hundred yards out?"

She nodded. "Think Wade will mind if we use it?" From where she was, the post seemed to have been abandoned next to a new fence some ten yards away. Or maybe it was a double barrier for some reason.

"I'm sure a few holes won't make that big of a difference."

Taking that as permission, Claire set the guns on the ground at her feet and lay down next to them. On her belly, she placed ear protection over her head.

She noticed Cooper put on his ears and focus a pair of binoculars at her target.

"You know, Cooper, I can't help but wonder if the flowers and message from Charlie were just a warning for Sasha . . . or if the school is on lockdown." She leaned over the gun, put the stock into her shoulder.

She dug the toes of her shoes into the loose dirt she was lying on to leverage herself against the kick.

"I doubt anyone would tell you if you called," Cooper said.

"Yeah, right. No one has a cell phone." She took a deep breath, stared down the barrel, and squeezed. The shot buzzed past the post on the right.

Cooper huffed and lowered the binoculars.

"Sites are off."

"All our guns are dialed in, kid. You're just—"

She fired off three more shots, one right after the other. The final one snapped a string of barbwire. Liking the sound of that, Claire burrowed down stronger and took three more shots.

"Off to the right. Not by much, though."

"Damn, girl."

She took that as praise. "What about a satellite image of the campus? Can we get that?"

"Overhead, yeah. I'm not sure how that will answer your questions."

It probably wouldn't. Not unless you could see into the eaves of the outside corridors, where the large containers would hold the lilies on shutdown days.

Claire unloaded the magazine and reached for the second rifle.

"Richter taught you how to shoot?" Cooper asked.

"Richter taught me everything." She took two test shots, hit the post but not the wire. "Jax would know what was going on. If anything."

"Who is Jax?"

"My roommate."

"You mean you had a friend? Did they allow that?"

Claire glanced up at Cooper. "Ha, ha, very funny." She leaned back over the gun, squeezed. Barbwire flapped in the sun. "Of course I have friends. Jax at the top of the list."

"Did she know you were going AWOL?"

"Oh, no. I couldn't tell her. If she'd known and the headmistress found out, she'd be the one in trouble."

"There's no way to get in touch with her?" Cooper asked.

She fired off the remainder of her ammunition. "Like I said, no cell phones."

"No computer access?"

"No . . . not . . . wait." Claire put the gun down. "Yes. The senior computer room."

"The what?"

She jumped from the dirt, swept most of it off her clothing. "Why didn't I think of that before? The senior computer room. Jax and I played an online game. It was our only access to conversation with others off campus. Not that we told anyone who or where we were. We thought it would be the perfect covert way to talk to each other once she was out of high school. I planned on staying through college." She looked at Cooper with a huge grin. "Of course. Unless Lodovica found the senior computer room, Jax will still have access and hello"—Claire hit Cooper midchest—"inside information."

Claire reached for the pistol, placed it in the back of her pants, and shouldered the rifles. "Gotta get online. It's almost midnight at Richter. Which is when Jax would be at the senior computer if she can."

On a mission, Claire doubled her pace back to the war room. Once inside, she went straight to her station, ignoring the looks from the others in the room. She set the rifles on the ground next to her desk and started searching for her game.

"She thinks she has a way to talk to a friend inside Richter via a video game," Cooper announced to everyone.

Claire saw Neil approach from the side.

"We set up profiles in a game, secret names, closed group. So when one of us left the school, we could still keep in touch. We played along with two of last year's seniors, but they bugged out six months ago."

Claire found the game and used her log-in information and waited for her profile to boot.

"Loki?" Cooper asked.

Claire nodded. "Jax is Yoda." She pointed to a chat room. Read Jax's last message and laughed. *Where the hell did you go?*

"What language is that?" Cooper asked.

"Our own." Claire constructed her reply in her head, had to type it out three times before pressing send. "It's like pig latin, only using German and Russian. Every other word is a different language and has the last vowel from the previous word. We thought it was clever."

Cooper nudged Neil. "Told you she was brilliant."

"Only if we get the spelling correct. Overkill if no one is looking."

"Magnificent if someone is," Cooper praised.

"I bet Sasha would crack the code in less than an hour."

"What did you say to her?"

Claire sat back and waited for a reply. Not that there was any guarantee there would be one right away. Jax didn't go into the senior computer room every day. None of them did. "I told her that the air on the outside was sweeter and asked if the flowers were in bloom."

"Code for lilies?" Neil asked.

She laughed. "We have codes for everything."

Cooper looked at the screen. "Now what?"

"We wait. If she responds without a code word, then we know she's been found out."

∞

AJ stretched out on the bed, a towel thrown over his lap. Noise from the bathroom told him Sasha was finished with her shower.

The evening played over in his head. His father's words, his mother's emotions or lack thereof.

Sasha.

He was itchy. Where did he fit in? He was way over his head with Sasha and her group of friends. They helped people, AJ stole from them. They were noble . . . he was a fraud.

"I'm proud of you." His father's words sounded in his head.

No matter how far AJ dug, he couldn't find one thing for his father to be proud of.

Amelia had been the one to leave the nest with a decent job, a noble one. Analyst for the UN. Just saying that out loud sounded like something. She traveled the world and, like her father, worked diplomatically to help countries get clean water to the people. So simple, so taken for granted. Amelia had taken on the job as if she knew people who were dying from a lack of clean water.

She'd been passionate about the position and never stopped yakking about it when they got together on the rare holiday that AJ bothered to visit.

What the hell was his father proud of him for? Not getting *caught* stealing cars? Because he didn't get taken out while jogging along a riverbank? Because AJ didn't listen to him and never stepped foot in Richter outside of the day his sister graduated, and again when he insisted on an audience with the grand headmistress and all her bitchiness?

AJ rubbed his face with the palms of both hands.

He dropped them to find Sasha standing in the doorway, one of his shirts thrown over her shoulders and covering only the essentials.

His cock stirred just looking at her. The action pissed him off.

"What crawled up your ass?" she asked.

"Nothing."

"Don't give me that. You clammed up the minute we left the interstate."

"I have a lot on my mind."

"Like what?"

He sat up. "Nothing. Okay. I'm not a goddamn woman. I don't want to talk about my feelings." With his outburst, he tossed the towel to the side and swung his legs over the edge of the bed. He tugged the jeans on that were lying on the floor, zipped them up.

He stared toward the door, needing to move.

Sasha jumped in front of him.

"Get out of my way, Sasha."

"Make me."

His breath came in short pants. "Move!"

"Fuck you."

He grasped her shoulders, lifted her to the side, and opened the door.

He made it three steps and she was there.

"Where're you going? Walking around Virginia without a shirt on in November is bound to capture attention."

"Do I look like I care?" he challenged.

"No, you don't." She moved right up next to him. Chest to chest. "You look like you're running from demons." She pushed him. "This is why I work alone." Another push "This."

AJ stumbled back, held his ground.

"I don't know what the hell is going on inside your head."

"Something you don't know. I didn't think that was possible." He was picking a fight with the wrong person, knew it as the words were coming out of his mouth but couldn't stop them.

Her nose flared. He swore if he looked hard enough, he could see steam blowing out the top of her head.

"You want to piss on me?" Her words were harsh, right in his face. "Pull it out and let it go, but you don't have the luxury of running off half-dressed in the middle of the night because you're having some kind of crisis. If you wanted to do that, it needed to happen before you followed me down a deserted road in the middle of Germany. We're in this together, whether you like this or not."

His chest heaved.

Her breath came in pants.

Tempers cooled and Sasha drew her arms over herself.

He realized then that she wore a T-shirt. Ass hanging out, bare legs.

What the hell was wrong with him?

He reached for her.

She flinched, backed up a step.

"Let's go inside," he said, his voice soothing.

She walked in front of him, looked over her shoulder.

Back inside the fifty-dollar-a-night motel room, he closed the door behind him and locked it. He moved to the thermostat and turned it up.

She stood between the bedroom and the bathroom, rested her hands on the door frame.

"Sasha . . ."

She held up a hand. "Save it."

An hour later, after they'd both crawled under the covers with a good foot of distance between them, AJ stared at the ceiling, completely aware that Sasha had yet to fall asleep. He found the words to say what he needed to. "The only redeemable thing I've ever done with my life is find you and chase down the truth behind my sister's death."

She rolled onto her back, joined him in studying the stains above them.

"I'm a politician's son with a trust fund. I don't have a respectable career or even a direction to follow to find one."

"You make it sound like you drive around in a Ferrari and treat people like crap."

"Not that extreme."

He heard Sasha exhale. "My biological father was a murderer, kidnapper, smuggler, I even found arms deals. He did drive around in the flashy car and eliminated anyone that got in his way, including my half brother. I, too, have a trust fund . . . of sorts. I don't have a career either."

He twisted his head to look at her. "You work with Neil."

"No. I help Reed out. Reed works with Neil."

"You say *tomato* . . ."

"We're not all that different, AJ. I just have a slightly different skill set than you."

He hissed out a laugh. "Yeah, right. Half a dozen languages, mad computer skills, master of disguises. I haven't seen you fight, but I heard you rival Catwoman."

That put a smile on her lips.

"I'm not sorry I have the training I do. Not that it's completely useful in the outside world unless I worked with someone like Pohl."

"Or Neil."

She sighed.

"But you don't like to stay in one place for long. Keep moving, avoid routine."

"Kept me alive so far."

"Keeps you alone," he said. "What happens when no one is after you, Sasha?"

She looked at him in the dark. "Apparently I return to my old school and run into trouble."

AJ rolled to his side, reached for her arm, and tucked her palm under his cheek. "I can't be sorry about that. You're the best thing that has happened to me in . . ." *Forever.*

"See, this is why I work alone, why I don't sleep with my lovers."

He kissed her fingers, tucked them away again. "What?"

"Pillow talk. That's what this is, right?"

"Yes, that is indeed what this is."

She squeezed her eyes shut, removed her hand from his, and rolled over on her side, offering her back. "We need an early start tomorrow."

He waited a good minute before rolling on his side, reaching around her waist, and pulling her up next to him.

She froze but didn't move away.

It took a half an hour for her to thaw and sleep to settle in. AJ finally closed his eyes and allowed himself to join her.

Chapter Twenty-Seven

Sasha walked out of the drugstore and dropped a package into the blue mailbox on the corner.

AJ sat on the hood of the rental car, sunglasses hiding his eyes.

She sat beside him and took the cup of coffee he offered. "Now what?" he asked.

Sasha looked at her watch. "We find out whatever intel the team managed overnight."

"And then what?"

"I've overlooked something. Can't help but think I need to get back into Richter."

"Impossible to break out of the place, how do you expect to break in?"

She sipped her coffee, liked the rich flavor. "Underestimating me is never a safe bet, AJ."

"Wouldn't that play right into their hands?"

"Friends close and enemies closer."

"I've heard that before."

She was already working out how to get back into Germany without the Neil roadblock.

Her phone buzzed in her back pocket. *Texas.*

"Good morning."

"Ohh, someone is in a much better mood today. Did you get some last night?"

Sasha rolled her eyes at Cooper's question. "One of these days I'm going to kick your ass," she warned him.

"Sounds like a promise."

That made her smile. She motioned for AJ to get back in the car. "What do you have for us?"

"Several things. I'm putting you on speaker."

She waited until they were inside the car with the doors closed and did the same with her phone so AJ could hear.

"Okay, so it's me, Neil, Claire . . . and Reed is dialed in."

"You a father yet?" Sasha asked once she heard Reed say hello.

"I think you're more anxious about it than I am," he told her.

"I doubt that," she said.

"AJ, you there?" Neil asked.

"I'm here."

"Okay, first off, who is MJ Hofmann?"

AJ stared at the phone. "My mother, why?"

"Your mother was on the board of directors at Richter while your sister attended. The picture of your father and Pohl was taken at a directors' gala and used as recruitment propaganda for other political figures to send their children to the school."

"How come I didn't know this?"

"Most of the names of the board members are initials and not easily traced. Several parents of attending students did come up in our research," Reed told them.

Sasha let the information sink in. "Did you find Alice Petrov's name?"

"We did, Sasha. But she used her maiden name."

"I'm not sure this is information that will help in any way, except to suggest that the Hofmanns knew some of the inner workings of Richter."

"Especially my mother," AJ said.

"Okay, Claire, you're up," Neil said.

Claire's voice was full of teenage cheer. "Hey, guys, you behaving out there?"

"Not if I can help it," Sasha teased her back.

"Awesome. Okay, so remember the senior computer room?"

"Of course."

"My friend Jax and I devised a way to talk inside a video game chat room so that when she left at the end of the year, I'd be able to keep in touch with her."

Sasha seemed to remember a few students during her time doing the same thing. "So you talked to Jax?"

"Yup. She left a message, all code you know . . . in case Lodovica caught wind. Anyway, long story short, Richter isn't just placing lilies in vases, they're planting those things. Everyone was kept out of the dining hall for the entire day, said something about a contamination. A crew came in, wrapped it up like they were going to fumigate. When it came down and the trucks left, the stairwell to the lower levels was sealed off, walls up. It's like it isn't even there."

The magnitude of what Claire was telling her took the wind out of her lungs. "Something big went down."

"I know, right? I have a few questions out to Jax and need to wait for her to sneak away to answer. They're on early curfew."

Sasha saw an even better reason to return to Germany.

"You still there?" Cooper asked.

"Yeah."

"Someone went into Amelia's condo last night. There was an obvious break in the feed the second the motion detector blipped on," Cooper told them.

"I take it you didn't see a face."

"Not even a shadow. Whoever went in knew the camera was there, but they didn't destroy it."

Sasha looked at AJ. "Guess that means we're going back to DC."

"Smells like someone is flushing you out, Sasha," Reed said.

"I smell that, too. Don't worry about me."

"Hey, AJ," Reed said.

"Yeah?"

"We need you to visit Amelia's coworkers while Sasha is at the condo."

"Why?"

Sasha already knew the answer to that.

"You're not going to like it, but we need you to cooperate."

"The suspense is riveting. Spit it out."

Sasha looked him in the eye. "To keep you safe. If you're inside a government building while I'm at the condo, then I don't have to worry about anyone's ass other than my own. If someone is watching and waiting to snag you to get to me . . ."

The look on his face told her he didn't like it.

"You could always go to the local police station and ask to talk with the detective on the case, that's an option, too," Cooper suggested with a laugh.

He hesitated.

"You being there can get you both killed," Neil said. "Your sister's office or the police station. Those are your options."

"Amelia was hiding something, AJ. I think talking with her coworkers with that in mind might offer some kind of explanation." Sasha wanted to give him a task.

AJ wrenched the car door open. "Fine. But I don't like it."

He stormed off and Sasha took the call off the speakerphone. "I have what I need. Neil, I need to talk to you privately."

Sasha stepped out of the car, waited for Neil to indicate he was the only one on the line.

"I'm listening."

"I sent you a package. I need DNA testing."

"Do I need to ask who?"

Sasha looked over her shoulder, saw AJ walking toward her. "I just need to know if they match."

"You got it."

She hung up the phone, tucked it away. "Ready?"

AJ opened the passenger door, waved his hand for her to get in. "I'm driving."

⚬

Walking into a police station was not an option. Not that AJ had any indication that his activities in Florida would follow him to DC, but there was no way of knowing.

A quick trip to a department store, and one thrown together suit later, AJ was exiting a taxi outside of the building where Amelia used to work. He'd called her boss, said he was only going to be in town for the day and really needed to talk.

He was a little surprised he wasn't met with some kind of excuse.

While Sasha ditched the blonde wig and slid into Catwoman, AJ channeled his father's diplomacy and walked into the office building and approached the security desk. After security made a phone call and handed him a temporary security badge to pin to his shirt, someone was walking him to the elevators and up to the floor where his sister spent her time when she wasn't abroad.

He walked through the office, past divided workstations and employees of all ages and nationalities. No one paid attention to him, which was the point in wearing a suit. If he'd walked in wearing jeans and a T-shirt, chances were people would notice.

Amelia's boss met AJ at the door. He lifted a hand. "Mr. Spedick, thank you for seeing me on such short notice."

"Absolutely. Come on in, Mr. Hofmann. I was expecting someone from the family to come by eventually." Spedick was in his early sixties, a slight peppering of gray in his dusty blond hair. His suit was unremarkable, his smile genuine. "We are all feeling the loss of your sister. I can't tell you how sorry we are." He took a seat behind his desk and encouraged AJ to sit.

"The funeral was a blur, but I do remember a large presence of her coworkers."

"Amelia was one of our more motivated younger employees. She had no problem influencing people. I don't think I knew one person who didn't say kind things about her."

AJ lifted both hands in the air. "Which is one of the reasons I'm here. If my sister was so well loved, why did someone murder her?"

"I'm sure the police can answer that better than we can."

"Except they aren't."

"What are you suggesting?" Spedick leaned forward on his desk.

"Nothing . . . I'm grasping at air. I need to exhaust everything I can find out on my own in order to move on, Mr. Spedick. So I'm here to see if maybe someone here says something that gives me a clue."

"If she was my sister . . . I would do the same thing."

"Then I can count on your help."

"Of course," he said, sitting back.

"I'm not entirely sure what Amelia did for your office, Mr. Spedick, or if anything was sensitive in nature."

"Amelia wasn't cleared for anything classified. If she had been, we would have started our own investigation."

"Is it possible that she came across something she wasn't supposed to see?"

"The local police asked the same thing at the time of her death. The answer is simple. There isn't anything to see. Our IT guys did a search of her computer, more to find out where she was on her research for our current work in South Africa than anything else. If they found anything, it would have been flagged. I can assure you nothing was there that shouldn't have been."

AJ considered telling the man that his sister had some serious hacking skills but thought better of revealing that.

"My sister didn't seem to have many friends outside work. It might help us find some closure if I could talk to some of them. Maybe she had a boyfriend or something that we didn't know anything about." AJ was stalling. He needed at least a half an hour in the building before Sasha finished at the condo and met him outside.

"She worked with Nina and Frank." He looked at his watch. "If we go now, we might catch them before they leave for lunch."

AJ followed Spedick down the hall and stopped at a grouping of desks. One had been stripped of any character, left only with a monitor and keyboard.

Spedick introduced AJ to the duo. "Please answer anything you can. I already told Mr. Hofmann we have no secrets in this department."

Nina pushed her chair back and stood while Frank shook his hand.

"If you stay through lunch, just let my secretary know. Feel free to take off early."

AJ thanked the man and shook his hand. "I appreciate your help."

"Anything we can do. Like I said, your sister was well loved. I'm very sorry for your loss." He walked back toward his office.

AJ pulled what he assumed was Amelia's old desk chair over and sat down.

"We really miss your sister. I look over and can't believe she's gone," Nina said, her eyes drifting to the empty desk.

"She was good people," Frank offered.

AJ had heard it all before. He cut straight to the chase. "Yeah, but someone wanted her dead and now she is. I'd really like to know if you guys have seen anything she was doing here that was worth dying for."

Frank actually laughed. "Not even the office birthday donuts."

Nina shook her head. "Most of our job is looking stuff up and working on reports. Yeah, Amelia had taken on the analyst role and was doing a decent amount of traveling, but that was a given since she spoke three languages."

"How much traveling?" AJ asked, even though he knew the answer.

"Every three weeks or so. Depended."

"What about when she was here. After work? Happy hour? Did she have a boyfriend?"

Frank laughed. "Not that I know of."

Nina and he shared a smile and then looked at AJ.

Nina's grin slowly faded. "She never talked about anyone."

"What about close friends? Anyone from the office?"

She shook her head. "Amelia tried hard to be an extrovert, but she spent a lot of time alone."

Frank leaned back. "I thought maybe there was someone she saw when she was traveling. But after a few shots on Cinco de Mayo she said she'd seen an old friend in Africa and started to remember the things that motivated her as a kid. That's when she started working out."

"Taking walks," Nina corrected.

He shrugged. "She was trying to lose weight."

AJ ran a hand over his chin. "Did she tell you who this friend was?"

They both shook their heads.

"Was it a man or a woman?"

"I think if it was a man, and there was anything romantic, I would have picked up on that," Nina said.

"We were always teasing her to go out on dates."

"Did she?"

"No." Nina exchanged glances with Frank. "I got the feeling her childhood wasn't all that great. Like maybe your parents fought or there was something that kept her from wanting that kind of life. When I asked her, she told me that keeping secrets was a Hofmann family trait."

He thought of his secrets, his mother's.

"Are you married?" Nina asked. "Have someone significant?"

AJ thought of Sasha but shook his head.

"If you ask yourself why that's the case for you, you might know why your sister didn't search out a boyfriend."

AJ paused. He'd never looked for more than temporary for fear of a woman learning his secrets.

What secrets was Amelia harboring?

He looked up to find both of them staring at him.

AJ shook off his thoughts, changed his expression. "Our parents do sleep in separate rooms."

Amelia's coworkers sighed as if that explained everything.

Chapter Twenty-Eight

Sasha scoped out Amelia's home. There was one floor-to-ceiling span of windows next to a sliding door leading onto a small balcony. The four floors of the complex gave one unit above her and two below. Hard to determine if anyone was in any adjacent units without knocking on doors. With binoculars, she scanned the rooftops of the buildings that could possibly house a shooter. If AJ weren't holding out for an all clear, Sasha would wait for whoever snuck into the condo before to show up again. There was no doubt in her eyes that they would return.

Time was not a luxury she had. There were secrets in the condo, or at least behind the camera's need, and someone wanted her to find out what they were.

And if she was wrong, and Pohl's people had found her . . .

Using one of the toys she'd brought with her, Sasha opened the electronic lock of the security door for the basement and went inside the building. She lit two Fourth of July favorites and rolled them to the corners of the room. The well-lit space funneled her out into a hallway on the first floor. Finding the space empty, she looked at her watch, started a timer, and then reached for the fire alarm.

As soon as the glass broke and the screeching bells shot at her from every direction, Sasha opened the door to the stairwell and started to climb.

Voices and footsteps swirled around as the stairs started to fill with people.

"I saw smoke," she told complete strangers who hurried past her.

Panic following the unknown gave her all the diversion she needed. Response time midday in DC was around nine minutes for fire to arrive. She'd be out in half that unless she found company.

At Amelia's door, Sasha stood to the side and slid the key into the lock. People were rushing past, purses and puppies, children and teddy bears in hand.

Sasha shoved open the door, let it slam against the wall, and ducked as she looked inside.

Nothing.

Before entering the room, she detonated another smoke bomb remotely; this one would crawl up the side of Amelia's building and cloak the windows to the outside.

Once she saw smoke, she moved into the condo, closed the door, and did a quick sweep.

Empty.

Avoiding the windows, she pushed the couch over to where the camera was hidden in the ceiling and exposed it. "I know you're watching," she said to whoever was on the other side. "I know who you work for."

"I doubt that," the voice came from the door.

She jumped from the couch, rolled onto the floor on her shoulder. When she came up on the balls of her feet, she caught a woman's leg as it flew at her face.

Sasha pivoted, avoided the blow, and moved in.

The woman was blonde, hair in a ponytail much like Sasha's. They both shopped at the same leotard boutique.

And she was fast.

Heart beating and feet moving, Sasha blocked as many punches as she sent.

"Who the hell are you?" Sasha said first in English, then in Russian.

The woman's eyes were green, or maybe they were contacts.

A foot to her chest and Sasha hit the wall behind her.

"The question is . . . ," the woman said as she managed another punch, splitting Sasha's lip before she recovered and slammed her attacker against the counter.

Sasha rolled away.

"Who do you work for?" Green Eyes moved in again, anger written all over her face.

"No one," Sasha managed.

The woman came at her again. "I don't believe you."

Sasha braced herself for the attack. "Fine," she said. "I could use the exercise."

Adrenaline pumped and fists flew.

Green Eyes got ahold of her arm and was met with an elbow upside her chin. She doubled back and linked an arm around Sasha's neck.

"I expected more from you, Budanov," the woman sparred.

Sasha caught the woman's instep, got the leverage she needed, and tossed her onto her back down on the floor. Foot to the woman's windpipe, Sasha paused. "How do you know me?"

Green Eyes stopped moving, opened her palms to her sides as if in surrender. "We had the same calculus class."

Sasha removed her foot and stared down, chest heaving. "You're Olivia."

Olivia used the distraction, caught Sasha's legs with her own, and they were both on the ground.

Glass shattered and above their heads, three rapid bullets ripped past them and burrowed into the sofa.

They both froze and rolled out of sight of the window.

"Start talking, Budanov."

Sasha pointed toward the balcony. "They with you?"

"I work alone."

"You work for Pohl," Sasha yelled above the shots that kept coming.

"Didn't like the benefit package," Olivia said, moving farther away from the window.

Sirens outside caught both their attention.

"Those bullets meant for you or me?" Sasha asked.

"Either guess works."

She wasn't sure if the shooter was changing positions or the authorities showing up moved them along. Didn't matter, it was time to move. "I'll kick your ass later, right now we need to move."

Green Eyes narrowed. "How do I know if I can trust you?"

"Go with your gut." And Sasha was out the door.

Behind her, Olivia followed.

She saw her car and started running toward it.

Olivia tackled her from behind right as the car shot into the air ten feet with a deafening explosion.

People came out of every door and every car.

Ears ringing, Olivia grabbed her hand, helped her to her feet, and directed them to a waiting motorcycle.

Now Sasha needed to trust.

She jumped on the back and Olivia kicked the bike to a start.

They raced away from the chaos and through the busy streets of DC.

Once they were certain no one followed, Olivia took the speed down a notch and found an empty alley. Sasha jumped off the bike and started firing questions.

"Who was shooting at us?"

Olivia wiped the blood from a cut on her face with the back of her hand. "Pohl's man? Whoever took out Amelia? Your guess is as good as mine."

"You worked with Pohl."

"Past tense. Didn't like the benefit package."

"Yeah, yeah, you said that. How do I know you're telling the truth?"

Olivia glared. "Trust your gut," she said slowly and deliberately.

"You knew about the camera."

Olivia pointed at her. "And it didn't take long to flush you out."

"Didn't take long for the happy shooter to flush both of us out."

Sasha ran a hand down her ponytail. "We gotta get out of DC." She looked at her watch. *AJ.*

She pulled her phone out of her back pocket, winced at the cracked screen, and dialed.

"Took you long enough."

"Meet me in the parking garage in ten minutes."

"You okay?"

"And do that thing you do so well. Have the car running."

"That's risky in a government building."

Yeah, she knew that. They'd deal with the consequences of grand theft another time. "How good are you at outrunning bullets on foot?"

Olivia turned over the motorcycle.

Sasha jumped on the back.

"Ten minutes."

૭

AJ hung up the phone and exited the main lobby of the building where he'd been hanging out in full view of security and the street. He walked up to the guard and smiled. "I'm sorry, but do you validate parking?"

The guy nodded. "You have your ticket?"

AJ patted his pockets, went through the motion of opening his wallet. "I must have dropped it."

The guard held up a hand, pulled a ticket from under the desk. "I got ya covered. Next time just bring it by when you check in."

AJ took the validation and walked through a back, unsecured hall and found the stairway leading to the underground garage. Employees were moving in and out, either leaving for a late lunch or returning from an early one.

AJ used the distraction of his cell phone and opened a text screen. He hesitated by a pillar and watched as cars entered the garage.

He followed one down another level and walked past it when a man parked. AJ put the phone to his ear. "Have to work late," he said to no one while the guy got out of his car, a sack of food in his hand.

He knelt down and untied his shoes, pulling the laces out. After the owner of the car turned the corner and he heard the sound of the door opening and closing, AJ moved in.

Within ten seconds he was in the car, thirty seconds later the engine was running.

He heard Sasha before he saw her.

She wasn't alone.

Sasha slid into the front seat, the other one jumped in the back.

"Don't ask, just drive."

The routine AJ understood. The blonde in the back ducked behind the seat, Sasha had already untied her hair, which was covering her face. AJ found a forgotten paper bag behind the seat the second he got in the car and now held it over his face as he pressed the validation ticket into the slot and exited the garage.

Once on the road, Sasha looked around the car. "You couldn't have found something with a little more speed?"

He looked over at her. "What happened to your face?"

The blonde in the back seat snorted. That's when AJ looked through the rearview mirror and saw bruises forming on the extra person in the car.

AJ took it slow through the streets of DC. The last thing he needed was to get pulled over in a stolen car.

Sasha kept looking around the outside of the car. "Pick it up, AJ, we need distance."

AJ took the corner fast enough to press her against the door, put the car in overdrive, and hit the freeway. Both hands on the wheel, he asked questions.

"Who is she?"

Sasha turned in her seat. "Olivia."

AJ did a double look in the mirror.

"You broke into my flat in Berlin," she told him.

"The missing roommate," AJ concluded.

She looked out the back window. "The only living roommate."

"Which made you a suspect," Sasha said.

"Why would I kill a PTA president and an insecure accountant from Wales?"

AJ turned in his seat. "You're leaving out one victim."

"Watch the road, Hofmann."

He turned back to swerve and avoid hitting a car on his left.

"I didn't take out any of them. Especially not Amelia." She leaned back in the seat.

Sasha reached over, placed a hand on AJ's leg. Support and understanding swam in her eyes.

"You worked for Pohl?"

"Not something I'm proud of. I didn't know what the hell I got myself into until I was in too deep to dig myself out. I thought I was the one going in and taking out the Osamas of the world."

"I can't imagine Pohl letting you leave."

"He isn't, is he? I'm sure he's behind all this. The first time I saw you in Amelia's condo, I thought you were working with him. The Sasha Budanov. You were slated for his kind of shit if there ever was one."

Sasha stared at her.

AJ watched from the corner of his eye.

"How do you know I'm not working for him now?"

"I don't. Except that having someone shoot at both of us is going a little extreme to gain my trust."

"Shooting?" AJ asked.

Sasha waved him off.

"Not that I give a flying fuck. I've wanted to put a bullet in my own brain more than once. If it wasn't for Amelia, I would have a long time ago. Now I just want to find out who took her out and make them pay."

That was a party AJ could go along with. Making someone pay, that was . . . Suicide, not so much.

"Seems sloppy of Pohl to kill all your Richter roommates to flush you out."

"Killing them is what he does. Or the people he hires us for, anyway. Bullets and execution, that's his style. Shooting out the wheels of a car is sloppy. Room for error. I didn't even catch on until Jocey ended up dead. I only found that out when I saw you in the flat in Germany. I recognized you and knew something wasn't adding up."

AJ glanced through the rearview mirror. "How did you know who I was?"

"You're Amelia's brother. The professional car thief that really should find a better way to use your talents."

Sasha squeezed his leg. "Professional, huh? And here you thought no one knew."

He switched lanes. "What I did twenty minutes ago was anything but . . . Amelia told you I was a thief?"

Olivia laughed. "I told her. She didn't want to believe it. But once I found out, I didn't keep it from her."

Damn.

"She loved you anyway."

"How do you know what my sister loved and didn't?" he asked.

Olivia stared out the window. "Because she was my only friend. I loved your sister and now she's dead."

Chapter Twenty-Nine

Claire sat on the sofa, hands on her knees while Sasha reported in on the speakerphone.

"I'm outside of Alamo rentals." She rattled off the address. "We need a car. There's three of us now. I don't have a lot of time and we need to put some miles behind us."

"Who's the extra wheel?" Neil asked.

"Olivia, our missing link. Amelia was her best friend. Olivia tried to leave Pohl's organization and people around her started dropping."

"Why the other roommates?"

"Olivia believes Pohl got word of a friendship from Richter and took them all out one at a time until he hit the right one."

"To make her come back," Neil said.

"Or teach her a lesson."

Claire watched as Neil paced the room. "Get back to Texas. We need to regroup."

"And bring a known assassin into Trina's home. Not in this lifetime. I have no way of knowing what she said is true. Only thing going for her is the fact that we were both dodging bullets."

Neil stopped moving. "Care to elaborate?"

"Are you okay?" Claire jumped in to ask.

"I don't have any extra holes. We need a car and time. Oh, and we may have liberated a vehicle from the parking garage of Amelia's office building."

Cooper started to laugh. "Let me guess, AJ."

"Yeah," she huffed. "Might need to run some interference with that one. When the smoke clears, Amelia Hofmann's condo is going to be found full of bullet holes and DNA. Won't take long for whoever is behind this to figure out that we're still alive and for the authorities to find us and make our jobs even harder."

"Police and questions."

"Right. Since we sent AJ to the office today . . . ," Sasha said.

"Someone is going to put this together."

"Alex Hofmann said he was hiring someone to look into his daughter's death. Might be a long shot to reach out to him to keep AJ's face and name out of anything that comes up. I'm buying twenty-four hours and then I'm headed back to Germany."

Claire cringed.

"Sasha!"

"I'm going, Neil. With or without a team. The answers are at Richter."

"And if that's Olivia's plan all along?" Neil asked.

Yeah, that's exactly what Claire was thinking.

"Then sending a team to be there will keep me alive."

Everyone in the room tensed.

"Twenty-four hours, Neil. Plenty of time to come up with a plan. Run away, or toward. You know my direction."

Tension rolled off of Neil in hot waves. He turned to Isaac. "Do we have a car?"

"Already called in," Isaac reported.

Neil put his head closer to the phone. "You have a car and twenty-four hours. I want a report every six."

"I'm capable—"

"We need to know you're alive."

For a minute Claire thought Sasha had already hung up. But her voice cracked when she came back on the line. "Copy that."

The phone disconnected and Neil snapped. "We need maps, aerial and surrounding areas of Richter. Claire, I need to know every last detail of that campus, cameras, security, lighting . . . everything. Someone get some coffee going. No one is getting any sleep tonight." He stormed from the room with a slam of the door.

Claire stood next to Cooper. "Is he okay?"

"Yeah, he's fine."

～۹

They holed up in a tiny town not far from Heritage Airfield, an airport large enough to land a private jet and small enough to avoid hassle.

"Can we trust her?" AJ asked. His eyes traveled over Sasha's shoulder to the woman standing in the small kitchenette of the motel room they rented.

Sasha wished she could answer that question without any skepticism. "Sixty forty," she told him.

"I don't like those odds."

"We don't have much of a choice right now. Friends close and enemies closer." Much as she hated to say it.

"I can hear you." Olivia jumped up to sit on the counter, her legs dangling. "Looks like you guys are all rock and a hard place."

Sasha crossed her arms over her chest, expression neutral. "You need to give me something or you'll be sleeping tied up." *Not a bad option.*

"I don't do kink."

"You do have a bad attitude," AJ growled.

Olivia glared. "You would, too, if your friend was killed just to make you submit. Amelia's death is on my shoulders. The only thing keeping me from putting a bullet in Pohl personally is needing to know who he hired to do the job. I want them, too."

AJ ran a hand through his hair.

"Who does Pohl work for?" Sasha asked.

"He's nothing but a pimp. He gathers assignments, farms them out. I never had contact with the actual client."

"Just so we're clear, you're an assassin." AJ's anger was measured by his words.

Olivia rolled her eyes. "Brilliant deduction, Watson. I'm sure your girlfriend here has already told you that."

"My sister would never associate herself with you."

"You'd like to believe that, wouldn't you? Makes it easier. Truth is, Amelia and I were close at Richter. I left the year before her. We stayed in contact using the senior computer." Olivia looked at Sasha. "Amelia was gifted in her ability to encrypt messages and use of computers. To the point that by the time she graduated, she'd devised an entire system that erased all correspondence within minutes."

"Why the camera at her home?" AJ asked.

"I disappeared from Pohl's radar six months ago. I insisted on the camera and recordings to track when she wasn't home. Just like I did on the flat in Germany. Just like I'm sure you do, Sasha."

Sasha nodded toward AJ. Her bare-bones studio flat she almost never slept in had more booby traps than Fort Knox.

"There isn't anything I'm going to be able to say to gain your trust. I wouldn't if I were you." She pushed off the counter and grabbed a glass before moving to the sink. "Pohl wants me dead. Rogue assassins get their heads patted with shovels. I knew that less than six months in. He recorded my first assignment. It was a test, he told me. Make sure I could take care of myself while gathering information for his client." Olivia turned on the water, her back to them. "He set me up. It was kill or be killed." She lifted the glass in the air after it was full. "I'm still here."

Sasha saw what would have been her had Alice not been there to direct her toward other places. "Who do you want dead?" Sasha asked her.

"Pohl . . . but that's too easy, isn't it? Lodovica farms for the man, cultivates and nurtures us. Who's to say Pohl is the only one she sends sacrificial lambs to? You take her out and then what? The board appoints another who does the same thing?"

AJ and Sasha exchanged looks. One that said they were both thinking of his mother, who once served on the board of directors of the school.

Sasha thought about her private conversations with the headmistress, the things she revealed. "The secrets are in the vault."

Olivia turned. "What vault?"

"Lower level. Below the range."

"I thought Claire said they'd sealed up the downstairs," AJ said.

"That doesn't mean they cleared everything out first. If they were smart, they did."

"Why not just destroy incriminating files?" AJ asked.

Olivia snorted. "Because it's impossible to keep all the players in line without all the dirt you have on them. A school as old and dirty as Richter would take a bomb to clean up."

AJ sat on the edge of one of the two beds. "I can see why you wouldn't go to the authorities and blow the whistle on Richter, but what about you, Sasha? Or Claire? Pohl went on television and called you out as a kidnapper and labeled Claire as a troubled teen in need of guidance."

"I have enemies. And if they have dirt, or created dirt on Claire as a troubled teen, who is going to listen to her?"

AJ tilted his head to the side. "What enemies?" AJ asked Sasha.

She opened her mouth to answer, her father's name on the tip of her tongue.

"Seems you have more powerful friends than you ever did enemies. Those same friends who are surrounding and protecting Claire right now. I may not have been involved with my father and all the diplomatic crap he did while serving as the ambassador, or even helped while he worked the Democratic campaign trail . . . but I did witness my fair share of organizations cutting their losses and distancing themselves from bad press. Who is to say that going to the embassy and filing formal complaints won't blow this whole thing up?"

Olivia set her glass down with a heavy hand. "The wheels of justice turn slowly. You put this Claire girl up or Sasha, and targets follow them. Dead within six hours. Guaranteed."

An itch started in the back of Sasha's brain. "Legitimate agencies recruit from Richter."

"It's not the legitimate ones we're concerned with," Olivia stated.

"No. But legitimate agencies will want to keep places like Richter going. Look at Claire," Sasha said to AJ. "Look how quickly she found a place on the team. She'd put any high school graduate in the States to shame. I didn't like the rules and restrictions, but I'm smarter for them."

"What are you suggesting?" he asked.

"If you bring the militaristic training aboveground, then what do you have?"

"A military boarding school."

"Right. You remove the secrets put in place after the Cold War and you have nothing more than a strict military school you can find all over the world."

AJ was staring at her. "I'm following you, Sasha, but I don't know where you're going."

"The school is on lockdown. Classrooms are boarded up, students are being diverted to PE and *self-defense* classes. Lodovica knows something is coming. If I were running Richter and thought an investigation was in the pipeline, I'd be building brick walls and calling them abandoned fallout shelters. I'd be preparing the students for changes and maybe even reassigning some students to other schools."

"Sounds like the headmistress is more aware of what's going on than a single AWOL student," AJ suggested.

"Lodovica knows me. She knows I was unhappy with Pohl's offer and thought less of her for it."

Olivia walked to the window, looked out the curtain. "Lodovica could care less. She allows Pohl to access anything he needs on his recruits to assure they work for him. I guarantee the man has your prints on a weapon that has already been used."

A memory sparked of Brigitte's anger that Pohl was following after her during her range time. "I'm sure that's true."

"The headmistress is nobody's friend," Olivia stated. "God, I could use a cigarette."

That itch in her head started to feel like nails on a chalkboard. "Pohl won't blackmail me now. He'll just try and kill me."

"Easy guess since there were bullets flying through Amelia's apartment a few hours ago." Olivia started to pace.

"He assumes I'll be dead. No longer a threat to him or the school." She scratched her head. "But the headmistress doesn't." She leaned her head back as that thought took root.

"Maybe she has more faith in your ability to outsmart Pohl," AJ said.

"Or maybe she stacked the deck."

Chapter Thirty

"Claire, your game is pinging." Isaac waved toward her computer.

She jumped up from her cross-legged position on the floor, shook out her right foot to stop the tingling, and limped to her desk. Cooper followed her and grabbed a rolling stool to sit by and watch.

Claire deciphered the first sentence, the cloaked code that told her Jax wasn't writing under duress. *What do Han and Denenberg have in common?*

Claire giggled as she responded. *They both wanna do Leia.*

"What is it?" Cooper asked.

"An inside joke. You'd have to know the staff to understand."

Claire waited for Jax to respond. She had to write a few words out and then put it together. "Wow."

"What is it?"

"She said that sometime last night over fifteen upperclassmen were removed from campus."

"Removed?"

Another message followed before Claire could respond. "The roommates said they were woken up after lights out, asked to move to another room, and when they returned, they were gone."

"Should we be worried?"

Claire typed in a reply asking if anyone had managed contact through the senior computers.

Her message popped up. "There are two that have made contact. Said their parents pulled them out."

"That's it? No more explanation than that?"

Claire shrugged. "Don't know what to tell ya, Coop. I never had parents. But I have heard that they say 'Cuz I said so' when they don't want an argument."

Jax kept typing.

"Looks like the martial arts studio has moved to a section of the primary school gym."

"Why would they do that?"

"No idea." Claire asked the question to Jax.

It's lame, Loki. Princess D is going over stuff we already know.

Claire looked up at Cooper. "Should I ask her anything else?"

"Not now. Just tell her to keep her conversations with you private. Don't tell any of your friends."

Claire started typing. "I already told her that, but I'll tell her again."

༜

"I'm starting to notice a theme in our relationship," AJ leaned over in his seat and whispered in Sasha's ear.

"We don't have a *relationship*," she said through stiff lips.

That struck him as funny although he didn't dare laugh. Sasha had been hyperfocused since they'd landed in Prague. Now they were on a train headed back into Germany.

"We travel really well together. I'm told that's a true test of compatibility. Small spaces and lots of uninterrupted time."

The redheaded version of Sasha lifted the magazine she was pretending to read. He could tell she was pretending because she'd keep it open on nothing but advertising for long periods of time before turning the page. "Don't read into us, Hofmann. Compatibility and relationships are for other people."

He looked across the small table in front of them. Olivia stared out the window, oftentimes letting her eyelids drop. None of them had slept much the night before and now jet lag was winning the battle, at least with him and the extra baggage. Sasha, on the other hand, was like the Energizer Bunny. Where she pulled her reserves from, he didn't know.

"I don't know about that. You're the Bonnie to my Clyde." He was teasing her, trying to get a smile, something out of her that had been missing since they'd visited his parents.

"He was an ex-con and she was a lovesick puppy who followed him around. We're hardly that." She dropped the magazine in her lap. It was late and the train was only half-full, with more people leaving than coming on at each stop.

"Yeah, maybe that isn't the right couple." He went through several couples in his head. Romeo . . . no, that didn't fit. Fred and Ethel. He shook the thought away. Scarlet . . . "I can't think of any."

"That's because we're not. Just drop it, Junior."

He placed a hand on her arm. "I get it. In my, ah . . . previous occupation, I didn't get close to anyone. For obvious reasons."

She lifted the magazine, covered her lips as she talked. "We have a few things to talk about when it comes to that."

He grinned. "If we don't have a *relationship*, what's there to discuss?"

The magazine went back to her lap, and she opened it to the same page of advertisements. "You're right. Forget I said that."

He laughed. "Yes, dear."

With a haughty finger, she flipped the page. "Don't even . . ."

He patted her arm, just because he knew it would get under her skin. "Whatever you say, sweetheart."

When her fist clenched, he thought he might need to dial it back a little.

They exited the train in Berlin and met the van Neil had waiting for them.

AJ didn't recognize the driver but Sasha did. She greeted him without using a name and kept silent on their short ride to where they were meeting the rest of the team.

They turned into what looked like an industrial park filled with warehouses off one of the freight lines that ran through the eastern part of the city. The kind of place AJ would use to exchange a stolen car for the purpose of having it stripped and sold for parts, or the slightly less popular repurposing through paint, VIN, and license plate decoys to be shipped to other states for sale. He told himself that insurance always paid out for the cars he jacked. At least that had been his target audience in the past few years. It wasn't like he stole the waitress's washed-up Ford from the diner parking lot. High-end and well loved. Heavily insured.

In the past.

How he'd managed to not get caught all this time, he wasn't sure. Probably because he didn't have to do it, there wasn't a drug habit to force it . . . it was more of an adrenaline thing.

He looked around the van and the faces inside. No shortage of adrenaline here.

They stopped and the back door flew open.

Cooper stood there wearing black from head to toe, a rifle of some sort slung over his shoulder, his lips smacking gum. "Hey ya."

AJ climbed out of the back, lifted a hand for Sasha. For a minute it looked like she was going to ignore it, so he leaned in, grabbed her waist, and lifted her out of the van.

She brushed his hands away. "Get. Off. Me."

Cooper chuckled.

Olivia placed a foot on the ground and Cooper stopped her. "Hold up, sugar." He removed a piece of cloth from his back pocket.

"Oh, please."

"I'm sure this isn't your first dance at the rodeo. Turn around."

She looked at him like he was kidding but gave him her back.

Once she was blindfolded, Cooper secured her handcuffs and led her beside them through the warehouse.

They walked with Cooper until he came to a room with one door and no windows. Inside he set Olivia on a bench. "For your safety, I've placed someone at the door. You need anything, just yell."

"This is overkill," she told him.

"Humor me then." He closed the door and waved over the guy who had been driving the van. They walked down a short hall and found the team.

Now *this* was a war room. Long boardroom table, chairs everywhere . . . laptops open, maps and photographs. And a half a dozen new faces.

Sasha walked up to Neil. "Trina and Wade?"

"Secure. Don't worry about them." He looked her up and down. "Good to see you're in one piece."

Claire came out of her chair and tossed her arms around AJ's waist. "So happy you're here."

He found himself hugging her back. "I see you raided Sasha's closet." She was dressed in a black leotard, hair in a ponytail. Only she skipped the high-heeled boots and went with a government issue combat style.

She chuckled and turned to Sasha. Watching them hug was almost as awkward as experiencing it himself. "This looks like it hurt." Claire pointed to Sasha's lip, which was slightly swollen from her fight with Olivia. Makeup did a good job of hiding it, but he could tell the difference.

"Bug bite," Sasha teased.

"Okay, let's bring you up to speed," Neil said.

"Before we start," Sasha stopped him, "can somebody go untie Lars and bring Olivia in?"

AJ looked at the door and then Cooper.

"She isn't a threat, Neil. She has intel we don't on Pohl."

While Sasha and Neil faced off, AJ followed Cooper down the hall.

The chair next to the room they'd locked Olivia in was empty, the door was wide open, and Olivia sat beside Lars, who was gagged, handcuffed, and lying on his side, staring at them.

"You're right," Olivia said the second they walked into the room. "This isn't my first rodeo. You don't want me in the loop, fine, I wouldn't trust me either. But a cot and a blanket would be just swell."

Sasha rounded the corner with a grin. "You don't disappoint."

Olivia stood, walked past AJ and Cooper, and winked.

"What the hell are they gonna do now, the Richter secret handshake?" Cooper asked.

AJ turned his head. "Wait, you don't have one of those, right?"

They both laughed.

⁓◯

"I can't protect you out there," Linette scolded Brigitte behind the closed door of her office. "These walls are secure, your cottage is a target."

"No one knows about us," Brigitte argued.

"Much as I would like to believe that, there are no guarantees. Sasha's taking too long. I'm reaching out to her tonight."

"What makes you think she's going to come? You drove her away, introducing her to Pohl."

Linette didn't appreciate her tone. "I did what I had to do. She fell into our lap, Brigitte. All we ever needed was one strong student to stand up to that man. When she walked back through that door, it was our way out. Our way of ending the decade-long harvest of our students. He has chosen an enemy he cannot win the war with. Not Sasha. Not her new friends and family." She crossed to her lover and grasped her hands. "The board is meeting tomorrow night. If I don't have something to hold over them, they will remove me from my position and put someone in my place that will continue the cycle."

"Most of the board has already removed their students."

"That doesn't mean they won't toss me out with them. I can't do it anymore."

"If Geoff learns what you've done . . ."

"Who is going to tell him, you? Come now. Everything is in motion. The time is now. Stay on campus, please. Give me a few more days."

Brigitte agreed and squeezed her hands.

Music blared in Claire's ears, compliments of a set of headphones Cooper had loaned her. Music. Who knew she'd want to hear it until her eardrums bled? It wasn't like Richter said they couldn't listen to it, but the stations they had access to were so politically correct she wanted to puke.

She reached for the packet of Oreos, her new favorite, and popped one in her mouth.

Cooper tapped her on the shoulder.

She pulled the headphones off. "What?"

"That's not how you eat them."

Wiping crumbs with the back of her hand, she talked with a mouthful of chocolaty goodness. "It's a cookie."

He took one from the bag and proceeded to remove the two halves and lick the cream from the center. "Middle stuff first." He put the two cookies back together and ate them both in one bite.

"No, no, no . . ." Isaac took one, opened it up, licked the cream, and then ate one cookie at a time.

The two men sat in debate over the art of eating an Oreo for the next few minutes.

When Claire turned her attention back to her computer, the video game app running on the side said she had a message. "Looks like Jax is at the computer."

Noise in the room settled.

Claire read the message, moved the words around in her head and put them together.

She started to respond and then stopped.

"What's wrong?" Sasha leaned over, looked at the screen.

"She asked if I was still with you," Claire told her.

Sasha peered closer. "What language is that?"

"She's probably just worried about you being alone," AJ suggested.

Claire shook her head. "She didn't start with our code."

"What code?" Sasha asked.

"A joke, snark . . . something we both know we know but no one else does. You know, like her first kiss was Fredrick in the stacks. Something like that." Claire read the message a second time. "'Is Sasha still with you,'" Claire read aloud.

Sasha read alongside her. "You're using German and Russian . . . only different."

Claire looked at Cooper. "Told you she'd crack it."

He put two thumbs up in the air.

"What does it mean if she isn't using her code?" Isaac asked.

"That she's not alone," Claire muttered.

"Someone found the computer room. How do we know this is even Jax talking?"

"We don't."

Neil placed both hands on the far end of the table. "Call them out. Tell them you know it's not your friend and ask them what they want."

"You sure?"

Neil narrowed his eyes.

"Okay, okay. Pull your knickers out of your ass."

Isaac cleared his throat, reached for his water.

She started typing. *This isn't Jax. Who are you and what do you want?* It took a minute, but the response was in English, no decoder ring needed.

Very clever encryption, Claire. But it's exhausting my brain. Is Sasha with you?

Cooper sat back. "Okay, even I can read that."

"Why are they asking?" Neil dictated.

Claire typed the question, waited for the response.

If she wants her freedom and yours, too, she might consider using some of her influence to alleviate the pressure from a certain benefactor. Otherwise business will continue as normal with the new administration.

Sasha grabbed the keyboard and started typing. *When is this new administration taking over?*

Neil moved around the desk to see what Sasha was typing.

Sasha looked at him, waited for his nod, and pressed send.

Twenty-one hours. It takes a large quorum for this kind of change. The meeting of the minds, past and present, need to approve.

"Tomorrow night," AJ said.

"How do we know this isn't a setup?" Cooper tossed his hands in the air.

"How do we know this isn't Pohl bringing the pigs in for slaughter?" Olivia asked.

AJ stood, started to pace. "Meeting of the minds, past and present. Schools are run by whom?"

"A school board," Cooper said.

Sasha lifted a hand, pointed at AJ. "Clever, Clyde."

"Got your back, Bonnie," he said with a wink.

"Someone want to tell me what the hell that meant?" Neil asked.

"AJ's mother was on the board. We need to make sure she is in attendance," Sasha suggested.

"And I will accompany her." AJ glanced around the room as if anticipating an argument.

No one denied him.

Twenty-one hours, Claire. Relay my message.

The chat room emptied.

Neil clapped his hands. "Okay, talk to me. What do you know about board meetings?"

"Meetings at night are parties," Olivia said. "Black-tie things disguised as fundraisers."

"During the day they take place in the auditorium," Sasha said. "Those were lily days."

"Still are," Claire added.

"So, some of the board knew about the normal operations of Richter and some didn't?" Cooper asked.

Olivia jumped out of the chair she was sitting in. "The board always knew. Why do you think Pohl is still around? The lilies were for their spouses. You need the perfect amount of balance in these situations. Those in the know and those who are clueless. Most of the teachers at Richter are oblivious of Pohl. They think they're providing the world with prodigies like Claire. They convince their spouse that arms training and martial arts is just 'smart.' Crazy world we live in and all that. They leave Richter with jobs in the CIA, British intelligence agencies, and the like, and no one blows the whistle."

"Are you telling me the board members all knew about Pohl and what he represented?" AJ asked. The anger in him didn't escape anyone in the room.

Olivia glared at him. "Are you that naive? People are not always what they seem, Car Klepto."

"My father could have been left in the dark," AJ mused out loud.

"High probability," Sasha said.

AJ ran both hands through his hair and rubbed them over his face. "Someone in that room knows who killed my sister."

"My money is on Pohl commissioning a hit," Olivia said.

"Then why the other roommates?" Claire asked. "I mean . . . Jax and I are close. Everyone at the school knows that. If Creepazoid hired me and five years later wanted to get to me, he wouldn't take out my other roommates."

"Unless it isn't Pohl and whoever made the hits wasn't going to risk asking around and raising any red flags," Sasha said.

"Amelia was friendly with everyone." Olivia paced the room.

"What about you?" Neil asked. "Were you friendly with everyone?"

Olivia's lips pressed together . . . she paused. "My roommates. But I cut it all off when I took the job with Pohl."

"Until you met back up with Amelia."

"Which was a total accident. I would never have sought her out and put her at risk." Olivia looked directly at AJ, remorse in her eyes. "I wasn't on a job when I reconnected with Amelia in South Africa. It had been three months since I'd been sent out. I'd had it. I wanted out and couldn't find a way. If I went to the authorities, it would be my neck in the noose, not the man who was blackmailing me. We were drinking one night and I told your sister enough to scare some sense into her. She wouldn't have it. She believed that we were smarter than the average person out there. Together we could find a way to break me out of the chains that I'd let myself get into. We met up a couple times after that, and when it seemed no one caught on to our friendship, I disappeared."

"Did you contact Amelia after that?" Neil asked.

"Once. Two months before she was murdered."

"You worked for Pohl. Only him, right?" Neil asked.

She nodded.

"You never had any contact with anyone, on any job, other than him?"

She shook her head. "Solo agent. I didn't have the luxury of a team." Olivia glanced around the room.

Neil leaned against a table, crossed his arms over his chest. "Then it's time for you to turn state's evidence."

Sasha felt her heart slam in her chest. There was no way of knowing how Olivia would respond to the suggestion.

"I'll be dead before I can testify."

"Not if we gather everything Richter is hiding and blow all the whistles," Sasha suggested. "Regardless of who falls." Her gaze met AJ's. "Even your mother."

"All guilty parties stand trial. Innocents go free," Claire said.

"That's not how things work in the real world," Olivia scoffed.

"As long as Pohl is a free man, you have no life. He will hunt you down and kill anyone you care for," Sasha reminded her.

Olivia lifted her chin.

Silence filled the room.

"I'll do it."

Sasha heard at least two of the men sigh.

"On one condition."

"Name it," Neil told her.

"I go out with you tonight. Part of the team."

"Out of the question."

Olivia faced off to Neil. The man towered over her, outweighed her by a hundred pounds of sheer muscle, but she didn't back down. "Then I won't be here when you get back."

"How do I know you won't escape while we're out?"

"You. Have. My. Word." Each word was its own sentence, all humor on Olivia's face gone.

Neil's jaw twitched.

Sasha wasn't sure she'd want the decision that was his to make. For what her opinion was worth, she believed Olivia would be there in the end. But trust needed time to be earned, and they hadn't known her long enough to grant her that.

"You team with me," Neil finally said.

Anxious looks moved around the room.

AJ took a giant step toward Olivia. "If you fuck this up."

"I owe your sister."

He tilted his head, clenched his fists. The tension in his frame called a warning in Sasha's head.

She jumped up, moved between them. "Let's take a walk."

Chapter Thirty-One

"Wait up." Sasha jogged after AJ as he stormed out of the room and down the hall.

He kept walking.

She doubled her steps to keep up. She got it. The need to move, the need to exercise emotion out of her system.

Her legs kept up with his. They marched through the warehouse, past the van that brought them there, and out the door. It was dark, a little after midnight in Berlin.

Cold air slapped her in the face.

She ignored it.

AJ turned, stopped. "My mother was on the board."

Sasha kept her lips tight. Let him vent.

"She knew . . . she had to know about Pohl. Why? What the hell does she have to hide?"

"I don't know, AJ. Maybe your mother didn't have a choice. Stuck in a loop like Olivia and unable to get out."

His nose flared. "My sister is dead. Nothing is worth that."

"You're making a lot of assumptions."

"Am I? If my mother is on a rat wheel she can't escape, then she has something to hide."

She stepped in front of him, reached for his arm. "What if your mother was protecting you? Maybe someone got wind of your occupation?"

"It wasn't an occupation when Amelia attended Richter."

"Are you sure about that?"

AJ looked toward the sky, his eyes moving back and forth as if searching his memory for the answer. "No. Yes . . . I'm sure. Amelia was out of Richter and in college."

"You mean to tell me you took a hiatus between the car you were caught stealing and the next?"

"Yes. I cased cars. Learned to open doors and hotwire them. Found blind buyers . . . I learned my trade long before I crossed the line. I wasn't going to get caught. I didn't get caught. I remember that first Christmas after Amelia was in college. I'd come off that first adrenaline high the Thanksgiving before. My sister was out of Richter. Dad was back in the States. My mother is guilty of something, protecting some-one . . . but it wasn't me."

"We get through the next twenty-four hours and you can ask your mother every question running through your head."

He shook his head. "None of her answers will matter."

Sasha followed him when he turned. "I know about betrayal, AJ. My mother had me to blackmail my father and he killed her for it. The bruises on my neck lasted for weeks when he tried to put me in the ground. I've met your parents, and while they may not tell you every-thing, they don't want to see you dead. Give this another day. We'll confront her together."

Their breath merged in the cold night. AJ reached for her, pulled her close.

The feel of his desperate arms around her was a life preserver.

For him.

For her.

She held on, leaned her cheek against his chest. Only when the brisk autumn air seeped into her soul did she say, "We have plans to make, Junior."

⤳

Twice in a week.

AJ nudged his tie into place, looked in the mirror. "If I'm going to wear suits, I really need to purchase ones that fit."

Sasha walked up behind him, smiled at their reflections in the mirror. She slid her arms around his waist. "I'm usually a leather and chains woman, but I like you in this."

He twisted around and held her face in his hands. He leaned over and kissed her. She pulled at his heart.

Her lips followed his as he ended their kiss.

"Another time, Stick. We have something to do tonight."

"You ready for this?"

"As much as I can be."

Sasha removed two cuff links from a small bag. "This one"—she waved the decorative metal in her hand before she attached it in place—"is a microphone. We can hear you, but you cannot hear us."

When she finished, she slid a tiny earpiece around her ear and secured it with an equally small clip into her hair. "It picks up voices within twelve inches."

"That's cool."

She grinned and picked up an empty glass with her right hand. She lifted it to her lips and started to talk. "You avoid detection with normal conversation. Like this. Headmistress . . ." Sasha said the word while the glass was close to her lips and then switched it to the other before extending her right hand toward AJ. "She shakes your hand, probably asks why you're there, we hear what she has to say. You talk with your hands, so the glass switches over, you point with it." Sasha demonstrated. "Before the glass becomes obvious, a scratch to the side of your neck, a pat on someone's shoulder. If you detect someone is watching you, say nothing. You're our eyes and ears. Richter's security detail will blend."

She reached up and secured a micro piece of metal just inside the lobe of his ear.

"So you can hear us," she told him.

He looked in the mirror when she was done, turned his head from side to side. "That's awesome. How many Olivias will be in the room?" he asked.

"I don't know. Assume there is at least one. And for God's sake, channel your inner girl and don't put your drink down, giving someone the opportunity to slip something into it."

He grinned. "I'll keep that in mind."

"Really, AJ. Someone in that room commissioned the hit on your sister. Chances are they're going to recognize you."

"My parents will recognize me." He'd called them shortly after they devised a plan. True disappointment swam in AJ's face when he learned they were planning on attending the Richter board alumni gathering.

Sasha sat beside AJ during the call, the conversation on speaker for everyone to hear. His dad answered the phone. "I got the strangest call today," AJ told him. "I think they thought they were calling you and Mom. Something about a school board emergency meeting. I didn't know Mom was on the school board at Richter . . ."

Alex admitted she had been while Amelia was in school and that they had been notified of the meeting and were en route to the airport now.

AJ's whole expression slid to the ground.

Sasha gripped his hand, kept him calm.

"Your mother insisted," Alex said.

"Are you going?"

"Of course. It was Amelia's school."

Neil waved his hands in the air to silence anything AJ might have said at that point. AJ said his goodbyes and hung up.

Sasha ran her hand up his arm, caught his eyes. "Play it easy. Tell them what we rehearsed and see what happens."

"When will I know it's time to leave?" he asked.

Sasha winked. "Oh, you'll know. Until then mingle, charm the ladies with that smile, and avoid corners where someone can escort you from the room without notice. Keep one eye on your parents."

"You got it, sweetheart."

Her eyes narrowed, this time with a playful smile. Apparently his endearments were growing on her.

"I'm stepping out of the room, let's test the microphone."

AJ watched her sleek ass exit with a slight sway of her hips. He waited a few seconds before lifting the cuff to his lips. "Can we get this over with so I can peel you out of those clothes and get you under my tongue?"

"Loud and clear," he heard her in his ear.

AJ licked his lips.

Sasha ducked her head back into the room and waved him out.

Unable to help himself, he slapped her butt.

She jumped, looked up at him as they walked into the war room. "By the way, everything you say is heard by everyone on the team." Inside the room, all eyes were on him.

"If you two are done with the slaps and giggles, we have work to do," Neil barked. "Skip the unnecessary chatter."

Claire laughed. "Somebody's in trouble," she said in a singsong voice.

Sasha had run more than one of these jobs, but never had it been this personal or had people she truly cared for been on the team. Okay, that wasn't true. But somehow AJ had moved to the top of that list.

Claire sat in the van with them, a stick of gum in her mouth, her smile was cheek to cheek.

Much as they wanted to leave her back at the warehouse, the firewalls inside Richter would make it impossible to relay intel to the outside.

The van stopped by a waiting town car.

Sasha's heartbeat sped up. Her eyes met AJ's.

"You're out first. Any sign of trouble, you know what to do."

He nodded and someone opened the back door. "Take care of her." AJ pointed to Cooper and Claire.

As he passed Sasha, she sucked in a deep breath. "Watch your back," she told him.

He reached for the back of her head, kissed her hard, and smiled. "Take care of you." Then he was out the door.

The van sped off the second the door was closed.

"Hello, Isaac. Nice hat," AJ's voice sounded in her ear.

She heard a car door close and then AJ's voice. "Can everyone hear me?"

"Team One," Sasha said.

"Team Two," Cooper replied.

"Team Three," Neil finished.

Ten minutes later, they'd found the first drop-off point. Neil, Olivia, and two more men exited the van and took off on foot.

Once they were back on the road, Neil did the same sound off.

AJ reported in. "There's a long line of cars."

"We need five minutes to get into position," Neil said, his breathing hard.

Sasha checked the time on her watch.

The van stopped and Claire lifted her fist up, tapped Cooper's. "Whoop, whoop."

"No side trips," Sasha warned her.

"Yes, Mom." And four more players were out of the van.

Sasha shouldered the duffel bag and barely let the van stop before slipping into the thick of trees outside the Richter walls.

Unlike everyone else, she worked alone. At least this early in the game.

"We're in," she heard Neil call out.

Sasha stopped at the edge of the wall surrounding the school and pulled out a frequency jammer and placed it between the two sensors. With the window open to cloak her entry, she tossed her bag over first, took three steps back, then ran, jumped, and scaled the wall. With her toys back in her bag, she headed straight for the dining hall.

∾

Breaking into Richter was a hell of a lot easier than breaking out . . . at least when Claire had her own personal ninja escort with lots of toys at their disposal.

Their party of four followed her as they moved closer to the administration building.

Lights filled the arches and pathways leading to the auditorium.

The dorms were relatively dark, with the exception of students peering out windows to get a glimpse of the event taking place below.

"In position," Neil announced.

Claire looked up to the roofline where Neil was supposed to be but saw nothing.

"East side of the administration building," Cooper told him.

"Copy. I see you."

Claire kept her back to the wall, pointed at the motion detector lights, and slid alongside it. Once at the door, she let Cooper pass.

Grabbing her key fob before leaving Richter the first time hadn't crossed her mind, so Cooper was up. He put some kind of magnetic gizmo on the door and within seconds the lock clicked open. Inside, she led them down the stairwell, light on her feet. Two security doors later and they emptied into the senior computer room.

She took one step and Cooper tossed out an arm to stop her.

Voices. Several of them cackled with a buzz of excitement.

Claire snuck a glance around the wall and pushed Cooper aside. "Busted!" she announced as she bounded around the corner.

Jax, Blane, Alina, and Stacey all jumped to their feet. One chair fell back and hit the floor with a crash.

Jax caught on first. "Oh my God. Look at you! What are you doing here?" She ran at her, arms wide.

Claire caught her BFF in a full hug and looked behind her. "I brought a few friends."

"What the hell is going on down there?" She heard Neil in her ear.

"Looks like we have four students that are not in their beds," Cooper told him.

"Damn it."

"Chill out, Neil. These guys are solid."

Jax looked at Claire like she was crazy. "Who are you talking to?"

Claire pointed to the tiny microphone positioned right in front of her lips. "Shh."

"Are you secure?" Neil asked.

Cooper responded an affirmative and brushed past Claire.

He dragged several devices from his bag and pushed his way in front of the main computer in the room.

"What's going on?" Blane asked.

Claire pushed her microphone aside and motioned for her friends to move back. "We just need to hijack the computer for a little while."

"No one leaves until we do," Cooper said loud enough for everyone to hear.

"These guys are awesome. I'll explain later."

"Claire, you're up."

Claire grabbed Jax's hand and led her away from their friends.

"Cooper, this is Yoda."

Jax pushed her arm. "You told him?"

"The question is, Did you tell anyone else?" Cooper asked.

Jax looked at him like he was crazy. "No."

Claire exchanged glances with Cooper. She stared down at the computer.

With her fingers intertwined, Claire cracked her knuckles and sat down. With one of their team at the door, Cooper, Claire, and Lars went to work.

Chapter Thirty-Two

Isaac opened the back door of the town car and AJ stepped out.

"See you on the inside," he said with a pat to Isaac's back.

AJ lifted his cuff to straighten his coat. "I'm going in."

"Copy," he heard Neil's voice.

His chest ached with the hard thump of his heart. He had to admit to liking the adrenaline swishing through his veins. Maybe he'd found something slightly more dangerous than stealing cars to make him happy. He stepped up to the man at the front door. Older gentleman, astute in his stance, gray hair and watchful eyes, exactly what Sasha had described.

In his hands he had a list of names. AJ stepped up when it was his turn.

"You must be Charlie," AJ said.

The man's eyes met his. "Sir?"

AJ glanced down at the list. "Hofmann." He waited a moment, saw Charlie find his family name. "I've heard a lot about you," AJ said.

"Is that so?"

"All good things." He hesitated. "My parents should be joining me shortly if they're not already here."

Charlie stepped back slightly and let AJ pass.

Good thing it was cold outside or he'd be sweating. AJ rubbed his cheek, spoke in the microphone. "I'm in."

"Copy," Neil said. "Team One, what's your position?"

There was some slight static in AJ's ear. "Almost there," he heard Sasha's voice. She was running.

AJ walked through the main building and back outside onto the lighted path toward the auditorium. He looked around the darkened perimeter of the grounds lit only by a few decorative lamps and the glow from the windows above. Clouds had started to move in, blocking out any help from the moon. He had a general idea of where everyone on the team was. He glanced at his watch and remembered the timeline. Once inside the auditorium, he grabbed a glass of wine from a passing waiter and moved to a more visible part of the room.

He smiled at a few people he passed, recognizing none of them. His parents weren't there. While English was the language most were speaking in the room, he heard bits of German and something more Slavic in nature. Dating Sasha, he really might consider learning another language. The bad words at minimum. AJ chuckled at the thought.

"Waiting on you, Team Two."

⌒୭

Cooper made the last strokes on the keyboard, and all the school's cameras fed to their monitors.

Claire and Cooper scanned them all.

Claire started recording.

Her friends behind them were muttering among themselves.

The camera above the Richter security guard watching the monitors showed two employees wearing faculty jackets and drinking coffee.

"Running a test," Cooper told the team. "Stand by."

"Main entrance," Claire said.

Cooper hit a command, the camera barely flickered, and the few seconds they'd been recording played back on a loop. On their portable monitor, they saw both the live and the recorded feeds. He clicked it off, and the live feed was back online.

Richter security didn't catch a thing.

"We're golden here," Cooper said.

"South dining hall," Sasha called out.

A button here, command there, and the live feed moved to the recorded loop of zero activity.

"Clear," Cooper said.

On his monitor, they saw Sasha move into the dining hall.

"There's activity in the kitchen," Claire warned.

They watched Sasha move past the doors leading into the kitchen and around to the side doors.

They followed her path, disrupting the live feeds with their recorded ones.

"Is she looking for the stairs to the sublevels?" Jax asked.

"You said they walled them in."

"They did."

"All the infrastructure is still there," Claire told them. "Ventilation, dumbwaiters."

Sasha disappeared from the camera's sight.

"Found what I need. Back in three minutes."

⁓

Sasha broke open the freshly painted locked cabinet to the dumbwaiter doors and looked inside. Out of her pack, she removed the cables she needed, secured them to the lift and then herself before crawling inside. She clicked on the light on her pack and closed the doors she'd just crawled through before lowering herself down.

Kicking off the walls, she rappelled down, knocking her foot along the way until it met with a hollow thud. Using as much leverage as she could, she pushed both heels into the door and broke it free.

Inside, she unhooked the cables and spun around in the dark space.

She was in the locker room of Denenberg's gym. She moved along the wall until she found a light switch.

Fluorescent lighting flickered to life and offered a stripped room. The showers were there, but all the benches and lockers had been removed. They'd even gone through the effort of blackening the tiles and dusting the floors. For a place that was in full operation less than a week before, it appeared to have been left to rot for several decades.

"First subfloor is empty," she reported as she made her way to the stairwell and down to the next floor.

～⑨～

"Mr. Hofmann?"

AJ turned with the sound of his name and found the stoic expression of the headmistress. She wore a long, formal evening gown, with a modest neckline and sleeves that went to her wrists. She looked less like the dictator of a boarding school and more like a woman in her maturity.

"Ms. Lodovica."

"Your presence here is surprising," she told him.

"I'm not sure it should be," he told her. "Board members past and present, isn't that right?"

"I don't recall you on the board."

"My mother asked me to join her," he lied.

"Keep her talking," Neil said in his ear.

AJ tilted his head to the voice. "When I came to you last month, I couldn't help but think Richter was hiding something."

Lodovica stood still, her practiced smile in place.

"And since I've become closer to my parents after Amelia's passing, I know a few things now that I didn't the last time I was here."

"We really were sorry to hear of her passing," she told him. "I assure you, I'd like to have your sister's killer behind bars as much as you do."

"I doubt as much, Headmistress."

"Truly, Mr. Hofmann. The students are family to me. I care greatly for them."

AJ bit his tongue. "Then you'll be happy to know we're getting closer to finding her killer and bringing them to justice."

Instead of the curt reply or brush-off he'd gotten the first time he'd stepped into the school, Lodovica placed a hand on his arm, gaze warm. "I truly hope you do. Now if you'll excuse me. I see someone I really must speak with."

He watched as she walked away and toward another beautifully dressed woman half her age.

Wiping imaginary lint from his lapel, he spoke into his sleeve. "Did you guys hear that?"

"Copy," Neil said.

"How did she sound to you, Team Two?" Sasha asked.

"Sincere," Claire replied.

"Me too. Okay, on the second subfloor. Range is toast. No stalls, nothing."

AJ moved around the room, listening to the team in his ear. Out of the corner of his eye, he noticed Isaac had joined him. The waiter uniform he wore matched perfectly . . . except his shoes.

Isaac nodded to his left.

Pohl.

The man stood talking with several people, drinks in hand. He looked up, saw a woman passing by, and scanned her briefly before turning his attention back to the men he was talking with.

Creepazoid.

Claire had it right. AJ lowered his gaze and listened to the chatter in his ear.

"Down on the lower level. Everyone still here?" Sasha asked.

AJ glanced over at Isaac. His voice came through. "Team Four."

The rest of the team sounded off.

"Fingers crossed, kids."

AJ held his breath.

"It's all here." Sasha's words were music to AJ's ears. Gathering the information in the school's locked room was the key to moving forward with their plan.

"Why would they clear out the top floors and leave the bottom?" Cooper asked.

"Because someone wants the information found. Like maybe whoever spoke to us last night?" Claire said.

AJ wanted to comment but decided to keep his ideas to himself.

"Okay. This is going to take some time."

Sasha opened the first filing cabinet and brought out a stack of papers. She removed a pair of clear glasses from her bag and turned them on. A digital display appeared before her eyes. "You getting this, Team Two?"

"Yup."

"Okay, here we go." Sasha opened the first file and flipped the pages as fast as she could before moving on to the next. None of it registered in her brain. She just kept flipping.

Claire leaned back in her chair, rested her legs up on the table, and turned to her friends. "So, any new gossip in the pipeline?"

As Sasha flipped pages, their computer recorded every document, every photo. Systematically all those images were filed and uploaded a second time to devices in Neil's and Isaac's tablets. If any one of them lost their packs, the others would have it.

"This is so completely badass," Jax squealed.

"No personal chatter!" Neil grunted.

Claire rolled her eyes, covered her microphone. "My boss makes Lodovica seem like an angel."

Jax and Stacey laughed. "You're not going to believe this, but Lodovica moved Princess D into the staff housing."

Claire's mouth gaped. "You mean she came out of the closet?"

"Stop the damn chatter, kid, or I'm cutting your mic!" Neil was pissed.

Claire put a hand in the air, stopped her friends from going on. "Yes, sir."

"That's better."

She smiled. As much as he tried to be such a hard-ass, there wasn't a lot of bite in his voice.

The only noise on the line was Sasha moving papers and the chatter of room noise where AJ was pretending to party.

"Did I hear that right? Lodovica is a lesbian?"

Sasha's question made Claire laugh with a snort.

"Jesus, this isn't a fucking chat line." Neil was pissed.

"Hold up. Princess D. That's Denenberg?" Sasha asked. The pages she was flipping hesitated briefly.

Claire waited to answer, nodded her head instead.

Cooper looked at her. "The yearling is nodding," he told the group.

"Bear with me, team. Thinking aloud here. Lodovica loses her place at Richter, a new headmistress comes in, everything is status quo. Remove Creepazoid, Lodovica has all this on the board members, she keeps her position. School removes the subfloors, loosens up the rules. Lodovica and Denenberg come out. Happily ever after and all that."

"Motive for flushing out an operative and putting the target on Pohl," Neil said.

"Only Pohl is still with us, isn't that right?"

Silence.

"How much longer, Team One?"

"Almost there," Sasha reported.

Chapter Thirty-Three

"AJ?"

The sound of his father's voice had him turning around.

Surprise washed over their faces.

His mother's shock faded quickly, replacing it were shifting eyes and hands that clasped in front of her like a shield.

"What on earth are you doing here?" his father asked while reaching out to shake his hand.

Before answering, he leaned down and kissed his mother's cheek. She had a hard time looking him in the eye.

"I received a tip," AJ said. The rehearsed lines easily fell from his lips.

"A what?"

AJ stopped a waiter and handed his mother a glass of wine.

He stepped closer to his parents, felt his own nerves settling. "I was told the person responsible for Amelia's murder was going to be here tonight."

His father's smile fell. The wineglass he'd brought to his lips paused midway, he shifted his feet and looked around the room.

"Are you sure?"

"Positive." AJ kept his eyes on his mother. "This school harbors a lot of secrets. Doesn't it, Mom?"

Marjorie set her wineglass down. "AJ, this is not the place."

"I think it's exactly the place."

"What are you talking about?" Alex Senior asked.

"Mom?" AJ directed the question to his mom.

Marjorie leaned close. "There are very powerful people in this room, AJ."

"You mean dangerous."

Her gaze shifted across the room. Linette stood watching them.

"What's going on, Marjorie?"

"I'll explain later. Please don't press me here."

On this, AJ had to agree. "She's right, Dad. We can all talk later."

"What is he talking about?" Alex asked his wife.

AJ paused and heard the chatter on his earpiece.

"I have everything we need. Moving on to phase two," Sasha told them.

One by one the teams reported in.

"AJ. What the hell?"

AJ turned to his dad. "I need you and Mom to stay in the center of the room. Do you have your phone on you?"

Alex tapped the breast pocket of his suit.

"Perfect. Now I need you both to trust me."

"You're scaring me, son."

"When I signal you, I need you to call in whatever distress code you know and have this place raining in police."

His mother reached out, grasped AJ's hand.

He grabbed her hand and removed it. "Mingle. Enjoy the party."

AJ lifted his sleeve to his lips, smiled, and said, "I'm ready on my end."

Chills danced down AJ's spine. He looked across the room and had to swallow. Sasha said she would be dressed for the party, but holy cow. Black dress, above the knee, formfitting with nothing demure about it whatsoever. The high heel stiletto boots made him want to purr.

"Is that . . . Jennifer?" his father asked.

"Her name is Sasha. I might have lied about her." He leaned forward, whispered in his father's ear. "I also still steal cars, but that's behind me now. Keep Mom by your side."

AJ left his stunned father and walked straight up to Sasha, lifted her lips to his for a soft kiss.

"Who is watching?"

"Everyone."

"Now what?" AJ asked.

Sasha tapped her earring. "Claire . . . you're up."

Neil's voice echoed. "Stay alert."

Pohl's eyes tracked her the moment she entered the room. Now that she was at AJ's side, Pohl's gaze drilled into her as if that alone could stop her beating heart.

Sasha watched as he moved to Linette's side and spoke in harsh whispers.

She brushed past him and headed their way.

"Sasha. You look well." Linette stopped short of them, her back to Pohl.

"How do you sleep at night?" AJ asked.

"Please, Sasha. The longer you stay, the more time he has to—"

"It's not me you need to worry about," Sasha told her. Leaning in, Sasha put a hand up to Linette's ear and slid a tiny transmitter into the woman's hair. "Whoever killed Amelia Hofmann is the one who should be afraid. They're getting exactly what they wanted."

Linette narrowed her eyes. "What are you suggesting?"

AJ lowered his voice. "Killing my sister to flush out Pohl's hit man worked."

The school intercom system sparked to life. The tone used to gather everyone's attention worked, and the room went silent.

Pohl's voice came through loud and clear. *"There are people in this world that government-like agencies would love to remove. But often their own bureaucratic red tape stops them from even finding these people. When you work for me and the people I recruit for, your job will be anything from obtaining information, analyzing, spying, engaging . . ."*

"Removing."

Guests looked back and forth, some gazes landed on Pohl.

He shifted in his shoes.

Olivia's encrypted voice followed the conversation Sasha had had with Pohl less than a week before.

"I thought I was taking on a legitimate job. What I ended up being was an assassin. Geoff Pohl blackmailed me, leaving me no choice but to be his hit man."

Pohl's voice followed. *"You could be part of a team responsible for making this world safer. Imagine being on the inside of stopping terrorists before they attack."*

"And you recruit children for this job?"

Olivia's voice followed. *"I was barely twenty-one. I had no idea what I was saying yes to. My innocent roommates from Richter are dead because of it. All those pompous board members think they're protecting their children. Geoff Pohl murders those children."*

Pohl started to move.

Sasha went into motion. "Stay here." She tracked him like radar on a submarine as he weaved in and out of stunned members of the board, family, and staff.

Olivia's encrypted voice kept talking. *"Lodovica recruits for him. Like lambs for slaughter. And the board supports her. They have to. Every dirty secret is tied up . . ."*

Behind Sasha, she heard a woman yell.

"Turn that off. It's lies. Linette didn't do this."

Sasha hesitated, turned.

Brigitte rushed to the center of the room, next to Linette. "This isn't your fault. None of it. I did."

Sasha's jaw dropped.

And someone grabbed her from behind.

∞

AJ lost track of Sasha when Brigitte pushed forward.

The PA continued to play the audiotape they'd spliced together. Much of the room was in motion.

"Now would be a good time to make that call," AJ told his dad.

"You did this?" Linette stood face-to-face with Brigitte.

"Keri was an accident. I mean, I didn't mean to kill her. Then it was done. I needed to move. All of my best students were being taken by him. You and I couldn't live our life. I'm tired of hiding."

"And Amelia?"

Brigitte shook her head. "I had no choice."

"How, Brig? Why? We just needed to be patient."

"You mean invisible? You mean live a life hidden behind walls? No, Linette. I couldn't wait. I did what I had to do. Pohl . . ."

The room watched as the drama unfolded. "What did Pohl say to you?"

"What do you think he said to me? If he goes, you go . . . and I won't be far behind."

"He knew it was you?" Linette asked.

"You'd like to think that no one knew about our affair, but that wasn't the case. He's been gloating to me for years, threatening to expose us and have both of us removed. Then how would we have stopped what he was doing?"

"Oh my God."

"I did it for you," she told her.

"You killed innocent people," Linette cried.

AJ stared at the woman who'd shot his sister.

He saw red.

Then he tuned into the com link in his ear.

"Move out, team," Neil's voice yelled.

AJ heard Sasha's rushed voice. "I need a . . ." He heard flesh hitting flesh. "Few minutes."

He scanned the room. Didn't see her and ran toward the door.

⁓

Sasha allowed whoever grabbed her to drag her a few feet, away from the people at the party and out into a dark corner of the courtyard.

"Pohl said you'd be hard to take down . . . nice and easy toward the car," the voice of the man coaxed her.

The second Sasha felt the butt of a gun on her back, she moved. Every instinctive lesson she'd been taught kicked in.

Her body twisted, her elbow came up to her assailant's temple, while her leg kicked his out from under him.

The gun skidded across the courtyard.

She retracted on the balls of her heeled feet, eyes alert.

Someone rushed her from the side while voices in her com link shouted orders.

"Retreat, Sasha. Authorities are on their way."

She took a blow to her side, kept to her feet, and spun the man rushing her toward the first one on the ground.

Scanning the area, she saw Pohl exiting the courtyard and took off running.

She reached the darkness of the arches, lost visual, and skidded to a halt.

The sound of someone breathing told her where he was before she saw him.

She turned in time to catch his blow to the side of her jaw instead of her temple.

It stunned her but didn't stop her movement. She twisted out of his range, hands up in a defensive position.

"It's over, Pohl."

Even in the dark she could see the heat in his eyes, the anger on his lips. "Even if you make it out of here alive, you'll be dead in twenty-four hours," he threatened her.

"Why wait? I'm here right now." She motioned with her hands for him to engage, kept to the shadows.

He didn't make a move.

She lowered her arms. "Too much of a coward to do any of the dirty work yourself."

"You've gone too far, Sasha. I'll have you and that adoptive family you've foolishly taken in before I'm done."

Her hair stood on end.

Thoughts of Trina, Lilly . . . AJ all surfaced.

"I don't think so." One step into the shadows and Pohl moved forward. Sasha leapt around a pillar and shot in from his side. It was like hitting a stone wall. With more agility than she thought the man possessed, Pohl slammed his fist into her gut and tossed her back. Wind rushed from her lungs while adrenaline fueled her reserves.

"Lucky punch," she mocked as she spun around with a kick to his knee followed by a jab to his face.

He lunged back and Sasha rushed forward and stopped short when she saw the muzzle of a gun gleam in the dim light from the corridor.

Before she could move out of range, she heard AJ shout her name.

Pohl hesitated.

A shot rang out and Pohl went down, holding a bloody hand as the gun skittered across the cobblestone path.

AJ ran toward her.

"The threat is neutralized. Fall out," Neil barked in her ear.

AJ fell on her, arms pulled her close.

"Are you okay?"

There were several parts that hurt but none that would stop her from moving.

Sirens filled the night air.

"We have to go," she told AJ.

"What about him?" he asked.

"I've got him."

They both turned to see Charlie, his foot resting on the forgotten gun. He reached down and picked up the weapon, aimed it at Pohl.

Sasha stepped out of AJ's arms. "He's dangerous, Charlie."

"I can handle it, young lady. Get out of here. You don't need a target on you."

"Thank you."

"You can thank me by staying alive. Now go."

Sasha didn't need to be told again. She grasped AJ's hand and headed back into the administration building and up the back stairs, where she slid one boot off after the other. In silence, she stepped into the black pants she'd worn earlier and pulled the skintight dress over her head. AJ helped her pull her shirt down and bent to secure the tie on her combat boots.

He shed his jacket and tie and followed her out a window and onto the roof.

Neil's voice came over her earpiece. "We've cleared the building."

"I'm out," Claire reported for her team.

Sasha hesitated on the edge of the building, AJ at her side. "Ladies first," he said with a wink and a grin.

She shimmied down the drainpipe and he followed right behind. They sprinted toward the walls of Richter and didn't look back.

Back in the van, everyone slowly took off their microphones, their earpieces, and shrugged out of their backpacks.

Claire offered Cooper a fist bump.

Neil looked at the empty expression on Olivia's face.

"What?"

Olivia scowled.

"I let you shoot him," Neil told her.

"In the hand. It doesn't count," Olivia argued.

AJ pulled Sasha back against his chest, and for the first time in days, she closed her eyes and let her mind rest.

Chapter Thirty-Four

AJ stood outside his parents' house, his hand in Sasha's, as soft rain fell over both of them.

"I can go in with you."

He shook his head. "No. I need to talk to them alone."

The last few days had been nearly as much of a tornado as the week before.

The team had done the legwork and now the legal wheels were turning. Murder, extortion, missing people, false imprisonment, falsifying records, false accusations . . . the list went on and on. Denenberg confessed to Amelia's murder and that of her other two roommates. She accused Pohl of blackmailing her into it. Lodovica was fighting child endangerment charges and placed on administrative leave until a full investigation could be made.

An entirely new executive staff swept into the school to keep the doors open, although nearly half the students had been relocated to other schools scattered throughout Germany.

And Olivia had disappeared. At least that's what Neil had told them once she went into protective custody.

If he knew where she was, he didn't tell Sasha, AJ, or anyone else on the team.

And when Pohl allegedly committed suicide while in police custody, no one was surprised. It was hard to say if Pohl did take himself out or if one of his disgruntled employees did the deed . . . or, more likely, whomever he actually worked for.

AJ took one last look over his shoulder at Sasha. Wearing her Sasha normal, she huddled under a long black coat covering her shoulders and offered a reassuring smile.

AJ lifted his hand to the door, knocked three times.

His father answered. One look at AJ's face and his smile faded. "Come in."

He followed him inside and waited in the hall.

"Let me take your coat."

"I'm not staying long."

"Are you sure, I can make—"

"Is Mom here?"

"No, she's, ah . . . visiting your grandmother."

AJ looked around the hallway. Saw the pictures of Amelia and him as children. "How long did it take you to get out of Germany?" he asked, hoping the small talk would make the conversation easier.

"Three days and a lot of contacts to clear our names of any wrongdoing."

AJ shook his head, huffed out a laugh. "When people don't pay for their crimes, they tend to continue making them." He thought of his own path to stealing cars. A career he put behind him.

His father blew out a long breath. "AJ, can we please sit down?"

"Did she tell you?"

He made eye contact with his father.

Alex blinked his gaze away.

A knot formed in AJ's throat. "Did you know?"

"I wondered. I didn't want to know."

"Mom had an affair."

His father didn't deny him.

"You're not my father."

Alex looked at him now. "I will always be your father. I raised you." His voice cracked.

"What about Amelia?"

He shook his head. "Amelia was mine. Or so your mother said. I suppose we will never really know now."

"Why?"

"I don't know, AJ. Your mother and I haven't been happy for a long time. She went through so many changes over the years. When your mother realized I was taking the position in Germany, she found Richter. She joined the board, and within a month someone had discovered the truth about you. Fearing the scandal at the time, your mother chose to keep her secret and everything Richter was about."

AJ glanced around the walls of his parents' home. "Stuck on the rat wheel of lies."

"I wasn't a good husband. I put my career first and didn't leave time for her or you kids."

AJ thought about his own life, the one he left behind in Florida. "We all make mistakes. Learning from them and moving on . . . isn't that what you've always said?"

"Sometimes that's easy to say and hard to do." His dad motioned to his den. "Sit down for a while. Let's talk about this."

He tugged his coat tighter. "I need time to process this. Sasha is waiting for me."

"Have her come in," his dad said.

"No. Maybe next time. I wanted to stop by before I left town. Get this out in the open."

His dad stepped forward, placed a hand on his arm. "Your mother's not a bad person. She loves you very much."

He wasn't sure what to think about that. AJ reached for the door.

"I love you, son."

AJ turned to the man he'd always called his father.

"I love you, too, Dad. I'll be in touch."

When his father pulled him in for a hug, it took a long time for him to let go.

Sasha opened the car door and stepped out into the rain. "How did it go?"

"As good as can be expected, I guess."

"And you?"

He squeezed his eyes shut. "I could really use a shot of tequila."

She laughed. "Okay, Clyde, let's see what we can do about that."

⌒⑤

Sasha stretched her toes out toward the fireplace and curled closer to her heat source under the blanket.

AJ pulled her closer, their bodies still humming from the sex they were coming down from. Outside, the snow had started to fall in big flakes, ensuring that they wouldn't be leaving the cabin anytime soon.

Once they left AJ's parents' place, they tossed a dart on a map and flew to Utah. They'd found an Airbnb cabin just outside of Park City and rented it for the week.

"I need you to know, I've never stayed in one place for an entire week willingly." She drew invisible circles on his chest with her fingernails.

"I'll just tie you up, then."

"Seriously, AJ. I get jumpy."

He linked his fingers with hers. "Every time you twitch, I'll bring you in here, strip you naked, and make love to you until you're too tired to move."

That was a pleasant thought.

"And if that doesn't work, I'll take you outside, strip you naked, and make love to you in the snow."

She ran her foot up his leg. "That might prove difficult."

"I'm willing to try."

They both watched the fire for a while.

"Are you going to go back to Florida when we leave here?" Much as she hated to ask, she really wanted to know. They hadn't talked about their future or feelings, just running and jumping from one thing to another. Until now. And in a week's time, if AJ wanted to return to his old life, she'd just as soon know so she could prepare her heart for the goodbye.

Just thinking about it made her shiver.

"Do you want to go to Florida?" he asked.

"I can't say it's ever held any appeal."

He kissed the tips of her fingers. "I think it might be counterintuitive to return to the state of my crimes while I'm trying to turn a new leaf."

She looked up at him. "No more *liberating* vehicles?"

"Not unless we need a getaway car from someone chasing us." There had been some fancy footwork to make that go away in DC. Not to mention the big check given to the guy AJ jacked the car from.

"I'd like to avoid that for a while."

"I somehow doubt it will be for long. You like the adrenaline rush as much as I do."

She sighed. "Okay, so no Florida."

"What about you? I don't even know where you live."

"Doesn't matter. I rent a new place every few months."

"You're kidding."

She closed her eyes. "Always in motion."

AJ let loose her hand and brought his to the side of her face. "You don't have to live that way anymore, Sasha. No one is hunting you down."

"It's more than being hunted. It's also about needing a reason to stay." She'd hovered in Texas for a while, then realized that Trina really didn't need her, and that's when she'd started to move again.

"I want to give you a reason to stay," he told her.

"What do you mean?"

He leaned up on an elbow, and she had no choice but to move her head off his shoulder. "I want me to be the reason you want to stay. I don't really care where, or for how long. I mean, until we can both agree on a place. I want there to be an *us*, Sasha."

Okay . . . so this was what looking at tomorrow was like.

She swallowed and felt equal parts fear and excitement. "I don't know how to do that," she told him, honestly.

"There's nothing you have to do, you just don't leave. Another guy realizes how hot you are, you tell him to buzz off and I break his arm. You know, what couples do."

"I don't think breaking arms is part of that."

"It can be. We can set a new trend."

Now she was smiling.

AJ swallowed hard and sat up. The blanket slid to his waist.

She followed his motion and his eyes landed on her chest. He leaned over, kissed one of her breasts, and lifted the blanket up to cover her. "Too distracting for what I have to say."

Sasha held the cover in place and crossed her legs under her.

"I know this is new. We've been through some pretty serious stuff. But I've never felt for anyone the way I feel for you."

"I like you, too, AJ."

"Nope. This isn't *like*. This isn't ultra liking . . . max liking. This is that other *L* word I'm afraid to say because I think you might run in the opposite direction if I say it. And I don't want to risk that."

Her eyes felt heavy and she needed to blink several times to keep them from watering. "I don't know what to do with that."

"I know. But that's okay, because I'm not going anywhere. We're going to make love in front of the fireplace. Forage in the forest for firewood. Have a few snowball fights. Fight over who cooks the worst. And when we get tired of here, we'll go somewhere else. We! Us."

She wrapped her arms around her chest. Could she do that? Roots . . . even shallow ones were foreign.

"Try for me," AJ said.

Her nod started slowly and grew. "Okay. Let's do this *us* thing."

AJ reached for the blanket, pulled it away. "Glad you see it my way."

Laughter reached the snow outside before he pulled her under him and kissed away her fears.

Epilogue

Reed and Lori's condo in a high building in downtown Los Angeles had been decorated with white lights and green garland. A beautiful flocked Christmas tree stood proud beside the floor to ceiling window. There were presents overflowing underneath, and holiday music filled the room.

AJ stood beside her, a cocktail in his hand. He wore a turtleneck sweater and slacks, while Sasha went with a festive red Oscar de la Renta. The home was filled with people. Every one of them Sasha knew.

And babies.

So many babies.

"Scary, isn't it?" Claire looked around the room, waving a chocolate martini in the air. "Better not drink the water around here."

AJ scowled. "I'm not ready for that."

"Oh, thank God. Neither am I," Sasha muttered.

He leaned over, kissed the side of her head.

Lori walked toward them, one of her baby girls in her arms. Once she moved closer, Sasha recognized which one. "Would you mind holding her? I need to get a few things in the kitchen."

"Of course."

Sasha took the infant in her arms and smiled at the cherub cheeks and bright blue eyes.

Claire chuckled and followed Lori as she walked away. "I'll help."

Holding a baby might have been foreign, but she was getting used to it. Much like the *us* and *we* thing she had going with AJ.

"You're very adorable," she said in Russian. "But I'm not ready."

"Which one is that?" AJ asked.

"You can't tell?"

"They're twins. I'm not supposed to tell."

"It's Samantha. Sasha has a little attitude in her upper lip." She didn't think she'd ever get used to the fact that Reed and Lori had named one of their daughters after her. They'd heard the news two days after they arrived in Utah. Sasha had cried. Supersobbing ugly cry, and AJ held her while she did.

"How you doin' over there?" Reed asked from several feet away, Sasha in his arms.

"You take care of that one, I have this one."

The doorbell rang and Shannon and her husband, Victor, came into the room, a car seat in his hands.

"Another one?" AJ asked.

"I warned you."

Sasha moved to the edge of the sofa and looked down. Samantha had closed her eyes, little pouty lips slightly open as she slept. It was one of the most adorable things she'd ever seen. "Still not ready," she whispered.

Lori walked back over. "Here, let me put her to bed."

Sasha handed over the eight-pound bundle and jumped up to find a drink.

"It's really not contagious," Trina said from across the room.

"It is with this group," Avery said. She and her husband, Liam, were tag teaming their son during the party.

"So, Claire, how are you liking the new place?" Wade asked her once she came back into the room.

"It's perfect. I already talked to Jax, and she's coming as soon as she graduates in June." Neil had set her up in a house in Encino that his sister-in-law had owned for years. It was ideal for Claire. Close enough to commute to work, which was with the security team, and UCLA, where she was taking classes to get her degree. "The two of us single and living in Southern California, I can't believe this is my life."

"Enjoy it," Shannon told her. "Don't let some guy come in and mess that up for a while."

"Hey." Victor, Shannon's husband, nudged her arm.

"She's only eighteen."

Victor narrowed his eyes. "Then why are you drinking?"

Claire laughed. "There's a rule, if you speak more than four languages, you get to consume alcohol."

"That's not a rule," Wade said.

She scanned the room. "Everyone here who didn't have a drink before they were twenty-one, please raise their hands."

Crickets . . .

She lifted her glass. "Cheers."

AJ sat on the arm of the sofa, placed his hand on Sasha's shoulder. "I'm taking Claire home. She isn't driving," he told everyone.

"How long are you guys staying in town?" Reed asked.

Sasha glanced at AJ. "We're going to stay through the twenty-sixth. Neil's wife invited us over for . . . what do they call it?" AJ asked.

"Boxing Day," Sasha reminded him.

"Yeah, I guess it's a thing."

"I'm so happy you decided to join us. I hope we can expect to see you more often," Trina said.

Sasha felt AJ squeeze her shoulder. "As long as no one gives me the pregnant pills, I'll be . . ." She paused. "*We'll* be around."

Trina stood and grabbed a package from behind the chair. "I know we said no adult gifts, but I thought you might like this."

Trina handed her the present. The gold metallic wrapping paper and silver ribbon sparkled in the white lights of the room. "Trina . . ."

"I know."

Sasha ran her hand over the package and felt tears in her eyes.

"You're not supposed to cry until after you open it," Reed teased.

Sasha glanced at the eager faces around the room, her eyes landing on Claire.

"Gifts mean a lot more when you never get them," Claire told everyone in the room.

Avery moaned. "Okay, now I'm going to cry."

"Never get presents?" AJ asked.

"By-product of being an orphan." She wiped the tears and opened the gift. Two framed photographs. Sasha ran her hand down the picture of Alice and Fedor. The woman who saved her and her half brother she never had the chance to meet. Her throat knotted. The second picture was of Trina, Wade, and Lilly.

She was crying again.

"I know you move around a lot. I thought you might like to bring your family with you."

Sasha set the photographs down and choked back her emotions. She stood and crossed the room to her onetime sister-in-law. She opened her arms and hugged her for the first time.

When she let go, she realized that nothing had shattered, and nothing had hurt, that maybe hugging wasn't such a bad thing.

"Looks like it's time to open stuff up." Liam took his son's hand and led him to the Christmas tree.

For the next half hour, the toddlers opened presents and the parents of sleeping babies opened things for their children. And Claire. Watching her open several gifts from people she hardly knew was a gift in itself.

Trina waved Sasha over into the kitchen, where she was talking with Lori, Avery, and Shannon. "All right, ladies. I thought since we've been a little too busy to have our club meeting, maybe it's time for something different."

"What meeting?" Sasha asked.

"We called it the First Wives Club," Avery said.

"And since we're all married . . ." Trina stopped, glanced at Sasha. "Okay, you're not, but from the looks of things, that isn't going to be long."

"That's assuming a lot," Sasha said.

Trina paused. "Sure, okay." She reached into a bag and pulled out four copies of the same book. "I was thinking *book club*. You know, give us something to talk about other than baby clothes and diaper rash."

"'*The Ten Million Dollar Bride*'?" Lori read the title out loud.

Trina started to laugh. "Yeah, it's about a woman who marries a man for a ten-million-dollar payout."

"You're kidding me?" Avery asked, laughing.

"Cathartic, right?"

"It's a romance novel." Lori was still looking at the cover.

"Great deduction, Einstein. It has great reviews and it made the *New York Times*."

Sasha waved the book in the air. "You want me to be a part of a book club?"

Trina looked at her like she was crazy. "Well, yeah. We meet every three months. How hard can it be to read a book every three months?"

Avery tapped her copy of the book on Sasha's arm. "If I have to read a romance novel, you have to read a romance novel."

"I really don't," Sasha teased.

"I'm in," Shannon said.

Lori set her copy aside. "Would it convince you if I told you we try and have our meetings . . . or book clubs, in different locations every time?"

"What kind of locations?"

"Any place we can shop. Paris, Barcelona, New York, San Diego."

She looked at the book again. How painful could it be? "Okay, I'm in."

୧

Later that night, in the guest room of Claire's new place, AJ was toeing off his shoes while she slipped out of her dress.

"Are you going to tell me what's up with this book?"

"What do you mean, what's up? It's a book."

"With a woman in a wedding dress on the cover."

"Trina gave it to me." Sasha stepped into the bathroom, grabbed her toothbrush.

"You sure this isn't her way of dropping a hint?"

She shoved the brush in her mouth, talked around it. "If it is, she dropped it to the wrong person." Swish, rinse, spit.

Back in the bedroom, Sasha removed the rest of her clothes and got under the covers.

AJ smiled at her. "A woman that sleeps naked. I'm a lucky man."

He took her place in the bathroom, came back a couple of minutes later just as naked as she was.

With the lights off and AJ lying beside her, she snuggled next to him and noticed the time. "It's Christmas Day."

"This is the best Christmas ever."

"I think so, too."

"I have something for you, but I didn't wrap it," he told her.

She spread her hand over his hip, squeezed.

"Not that, although I'm happy to oblige."

"I'm always happy when you oblige."

He stopped her hand and turned to his side to look at her. He pressed his lips against hers and took his time as he kissed her. Everything softened, mind, body, and soul. When he moved away, he whispered, "I love you, Sasha."

She closed her eyes, rested her forehead against his lips. "Say it again."

"I love you with everything I am. If I could wrap my heart up in a box and give it to you, I would."

Again with the tears.

She met his gaze and kissed him hard. When she moved back, her lips moved without sound.

"Say that again," he said, smiling.

Sasha opened her mouth and tried again. "I love you, too."

He traced her bottom lip with his thumb. "All right. Now we're getting somewhere."

She laughed. "I'm not ready to have your babies."

"Oh, no, no . . . we have a couple more steps before we go there." AJ tucked her under him, pinned her legs with one of his. "But make no mistake, the babies you have . . . will be mine."

He sealed his promise with a kiss.

Acknowledgments

As always, thanks to my team at Montlake for all your hard work to make a manuscript a novel. Thanks to my executive editor, Maria Gomez, for believing in my work and not questioning the stories I want to tell. To my new developmental editor, Holly Ingraham, thank you for helping me shape Sasha's story into a fitting conclusion to the First Wives series.

For my agent, Jane . . . this one was hard to write on the heels of my father's stroke, but you were there every step of the way, pom-poms in hand, reminding me that *I can* when all I could think was *I can't*.

Thank you to my readers who wanted to hear Sasha's story almost as much as I wanted to write it. I hope you enjoy it.

Now back to Jocey Hogan. Lady, when you told me that you ditched the CIA to follow the guy and become the PTA guru of our kids' elementary school, I knew I had to write that story. You speak three languages? Or is it four? I forgot. You're smart and beautiful, inside and out, and I'm glad to call you my friend. Thank you for your unwavering support of my career and life choices. Here is to all the bottles of wine we have shared in the past and will in the future.

I love you, my friend. Cheers.

Catherine

About the Author

Photo © 2015 Julianne Gentry

New York Times, #1 *Wall Street Journal*, and *USA Today* bestselling author Catherine Bybee has written thirty books that collectively have sold more than five million copies and been translated into more than eighteen languages. Raised in Washington State, Bybee moved to Southern California in the hope of becoming a movie star. After growing bored with waiting tables, she returned to school and became a registered nurse, spending most of her career in urban emergency rooms. She now writes full-time and has penned the Not Quite Series, the Weekday Brides Series, the Most Likely To Series, and the First Wives Series. For more information, visit www.catherinebybee.com.